William Shakespeare, Samuel Johnson

Complete Works with Life, Compendium and Concordance

Volume 5

William Shakespeare, Samuel Johnson

Complete Works with Life, Compendium and Concordance
Volume 5

ISBN/EAN: 9783337400989

Printed in Europe, USA, Canada, Australia, Japan

Cover: Foto ©Andreas Hilbeck / pixelio.de

More available books at **www.hansebooks.com**

THE DR. JOHNSON EDITION.

THE

COMPLETE WORKS

OF

SHAKESPEARE

WITH LIFE, COMPENDIUM, AND
CONCORDANCE.

Illustrated with Fifty Photogravures.

VOL. V.

PHILADELPHIA:
THE GEBBIE PUBLISHING CO., Limited.
1896.

CONTENTS.

List of Illustrations.

VOLUME V.

(vi)

TIMON OF ATHENS.

PERSONS REPRESENTED.

TIMON, *a noble Athenian.*

LUCIUS,
LUCULLUS, } *Lords, and Flatterers of* TIMON.
SEMPRONIUS,

VENTIDIUS, *one of* TIMON'S *false Friends.*

ALCIBIADES, *an Athenian General.*

APEMANTUS, *a churlish Philosopher.*

FLAVIUS, *Steward to* TIMON.

FLAMINIUS,
LUCILIUS, } TIMON'S *Servants.*
SERVILIUS,

CAPHIS,
PHILOTUS,
TITUS, } *Servants to* TIMON'S *Creditors.*
LUCIUS,
HORTENSIUS,

Two Servants *of* VARRO.

The Servant *of* ISIDORE.

Two of TIMON'S Creditors.

CUPID *and* Maskers.

Three Strangers.

Poet.

Painter.

Jeweller.

Merchant.

An Old Athenian.

A Page.

A Fool.

PHRYNIA,
TIMANDRA, } *Mistresses to* ALCIBIADES.

Other Lords, Senators, Officers, Soldiers, Thieves,
and Attendants.

SCENE,—ATHENS, *and the Woods adjoining.*

TIMON OF ATHENS.

---◆---

ACT I.

SCENE I.—ATHENS. *A Hall in* TIMON'S *House.*

Enter Poet, Painter, Jeweller, Merchant, *and others, at*
several doors.

Poet. Good-day, sir.
Pain.　　　　　　I am glad you are well.
Poet. I have not seen you long: how goes the world?
Pain. It wears, sir, as it grows.
Poet.　　　　　　　　Ay, that's well known:
But what particular rarity? what strange,
Which manifold record not matches? See,
Magic of bounty! all these spirits thy power
Hath conjur'd to attend. I know the merchant.
　Pain. I know them both; th' other's a jeweller.
　Mer. O, 'tis a worthy lord!
　Jew.　　　　　　Nay, that's most fix'd.
　Mer. A most incomparable man; breath'd, as it were,
To an untirable and continuate goodness:
He passes.
　Jew. I have a jewel here.
　Mer. O, pray, let's see't: for the Lord Timon, sir?
　Jew. If he will touch the estimate: but, for that—
　Poet. [reciting to himself.] *When we for recompense have*
　　prais'd the vile
It stains the glory in that happy verse
Which aptly sings the good.
　Mer.　　　　　　'Tis a good form.
　　　　　　　　　　[*Looking at the jewel.*
　Jew. And rich: here is a water, look ye.
　Pain. You are rapt, sir, in some work, some dedication
To the great lord.
　Poet.　　　　A thing slipp'd idly from me.
Our poesy is as a gum, which oozes
From whence 'tis nourish'd: the fire i' the flint

Shows not till it be struck; our gentle flame
Provokes itself, and, like the current, flies
Each bound it chafes.   What have you there?

     Pain. A picture, sir.—And when comes your book forth?

     Poet. Upon the heels of my presentment, sir,—
Let's see your piece.

     Pain.   'Tis a good piece.

     Poet. So 'tis: this comes off well and excellent.

     Pain. Indifferent.

     Poet.   Admirable: how this grace
Speaks his own standing! what a mental power
This eye shoots forth! how big imagination
Moves in this lip! to the dumbness of the gesture
One might interpret.

     Pain. It is a pretty mocking of the life.
Here is a touch; is't good?

     Poet.   I will say of it
It tutors nature: artificial strife
Lives in these touches, livelier than life.

Enter certain Senators, *and pass over.*

     Pain. How this lord is follow'd!

     Poet. The senators of Athens:—happy man!

     Pain. Look, more!

     Poet. You see this confluence, this great flood of visitors.
I have, in this rough work, shap'd out a man,
Whom this beneath world doth embrace and hug
With amplest entertainment: my free drift
Halts not particularly, but moves itself
In a wide sea of wax: no levell'd malice
Infects one comma in the course I hold;
But flies an eagle flight, bold, and forth on,
Leaving no track behind.

     Pain. How shall I understand you?

     Poet.   I will unbolt to you.
You see how all conditions, how all minds,—
As well of glib and slippery creatures as
Of grave and austere quality,—tender down
Their services to Lord Timon: his large fortune,
Upon his good and gracious nature hanging,
Subdues and properties to his love and tendance
All sorts of hearts; yea, from the glass-fac'd flatterer
To Apemantus, that few things loves better
Than to abhor himself: even he drops down
The knee before him, and returns in peace
Most rich in Timon's nod.

Pain.   I saw them speak together.
Poet. Sir, I have upon a high and pleasant hill
Feign'd Fortune to be thron'd: the base o' the mount
Is rank'd with all deserts, all kind of natures,
That labour on the bosom of this sphere
To propagate their states: amongst them all,
Whose eyes are on this sovereign lady fix'd,
One do I personate of Lord Timon's frame,
Whom Fortune with her ivory hand wafts to her;
Whose present grace to present slaves and servants
Translates his rivals.
    Pain.   'Tis conceiv'd to scope.
This throne, this Fortune, and this hill, methinks,
With one man beckon'd from the rest below,
Bowing his head against the steepy mount
To climb his happiness, would be well express'd
In our condition.
    Poet.   Nay, sir, but hear me on.
All those which were his fellows but of late,—
Some better than his value,—on the moment
Follow his strides, his lobbies fill with tendance,
Rain sacrificial whisperings in his ear,
Make sacred even his stirrup, and through him
Drink the free air.
    Pain.   Ay, marry, what of these?
Poet. When Fortune, in her shift and change of mood,
Spurns down her late belov'd, all his dependents,
Which labour'd after him to the mountain's top,
Even on their knees and hands, let him slip down,
Not one accompanying his declining foot.
    Pain. 'Tis common:
A thousand moral paintings I can show
That shall demonstrate these quick blows of Fortune's
More pregnantly than words.   Yet you do well
To show Lord Timon that mean eyes have seen
The foot above the head.

   Trumpets sound.   Enter TIMON, *attended; the* Servant *of*
          VENTIDIUS *talking with him.*

   Tim.   Imprison'd is he, say you?
Ven. Serv. Ay, my good lord: five talents is his debt;
His means most short, his creditors most strait:
Your honourable letter he desires
To those have shut him up; which failing him,
Periods his comfort.
    Tim.   Noble Ventidius!   Well;

I am not of that feather to shake off
My friend when he most needs me.   I do know him
A gentleman that well deserves a help,—
Which he shall have: I'll pay the debt, and free him.
   Ven. Serv. Your lordship ever binds him.
   Tim. Commend me to him: I will send his ransom;
And, being enfranchis'd, bid him come to me:—
'Tis not enough to help the feeble up,
But to support him after.—Fare you well.
   Ven. Serv. All happiness to your honour!   [*Exit.*

Enter an Old Athenian.

   Old Ath. Lord Timon, hear me speak.
   Tim.   Freely, good father.
   Old Ath. Thou hast a servant nam'd Lucilius.
   Tim. I have so: what of him?
   Old Ath. Most noble Timon, call the man before thee.
   Tim. Attends he here, or no?—Lucilius!

Lucilius *comes forward from among the* Attendants.

   Luc. Here, at your lordship's service.
   Old Ath. This fellow here, Lord Timon, this thy creature
By night frequents my house.   I am a man
That from my first have been inclin'd to thrift;
And my estate deserves an heir more rais'd
Than one which holds a trencher.
   Tim.   Well; what further?
   Old Ath. One only daughter have I, no kin else,
On whom I may confer what I have got:
The maid is fair, o' the youngest for a bride,
And I have bred her at my dearest cost
In qualities of the best.   This man of thine
Attempts her love: I pr'ythee, noble lord,
Join with me to forbid him her resort;
Myself have spoke in vain.
   Tim.   The man is honest.
   Old Ath. Therefore he will be, Timon:
His honesty rewards him in itself;
It must not bear my daughter.
   Tim.   Does she love him?
   Old Ath. She is young and apt:
Our own precedent passions do instruct us
What levity's in youth.
   Tim. [*to* Lucilius.] Love you the maid?
   Luc. Ay, my good lord; and she accepts of it.
   Old Ath. If in her marriage my consent be missing,

I call the gods to witness, I will choose
Mine heir from forth the beggars of the world,
And dispossess her all.
    Tim.　　　　　　　How shall she be endow'd,
If she be mated with an equal husband?
    Old Ath. Three talents on the present; in future, all.
    Tim. This gentleman of mine hath serv'd me long:
To build his fortune I will strain a little,
For 'tis a bond in men. Give him thy daughter:
What you bestow, in him I'll counterpoise,
And make him weigh with her.
    Old Ath.　　　　　　Most noble lord,
Pawn me to this your honour, she is his.
    Tim. My hand to thee; mine honour on my promise.
    Luc. Humbly I thank your lordship: never may
That state or fortune fall into my keeping
Which is not ow'd to you!
               [*Exeunt* LUCILIUS *and* Old Athenian.
    Poet. Vouchsafe my labour, and long live your lordship!
    Tim. I thank you; you shall hear from me anon:
Go not away.—What have you there, my friend?
    Pain. A piece of painting, which I do beseech
Your lordship to accept.
    Tim.　　　　　　Painting is welcome.
The painting is almost the natural man;
For since dishonour traffics with man's nature,
He is but outside: these pencill'd figures are
Even such as they give out. I like your work;
And you shall find I like it: wait attendance
Till you hear further from me
    Pain.　　　　　　The gods preserve you!
    Tim. Well fare you, gentleman: give me your hand:
We must needs dine together.—Sir, your jewel
Hath suffer'd under praise.
    Jew.　　　　　　What, my lord! dispraise?
    Tim. A mere satiety of commendations,
If I should pay you for't as 'tis extoll'd
It would unclew me quite.
    Jew.　　　　　　My lord, 'tis rated
As those which sell would give. But you well know,
Things of light value, differing in the owners.
Are prized by their masters: believe't, dear lord.
You mend the jewel by the wearing it.
    Tim. Well mock'd.
    Mer. No, my good lord; he speaks the common tongue,
Which all men speak with him.

Tim. Look, who comes here: will you be chid?

Enter APEMANTUS.

Jew. We'll bear, with your lordship.

Mer.   He'll spare none.

Tim. Good-morrow to thee, gentle Apemantus!

Apem. Till I be gentle, stay thou for thy good-morrow;
When thou art Timon's dog, and these knaves honest.

Tim. Why dost thou call them knaves? thou know'st

Apem. Are they not Athenians?   [them not.

Tim. Yes.

Apem. Then I repent not.

Jew. You know me, Apemantus?

Apem. Thou knowest I do; I call'd thee by thy name.

Tim. Thou art proud, Apemantus.

Apem. Of nothing so much as that I am not like Timon.

Tim. Whither art going?

Apem. To knock out an honest Athenian's brains.

Tim. That's a deed thou'lt die for.

Apem. Right, if doing nothing be death by the law.

Tim. How likest thou this picture, Apemantus?

Apem. The best, for the innocence.

Tim. Wrought he not well that painted it?

Apem. He wrought better that made the painter; and
yet he's but a filthy piece of work.

Pain. You are a dog.

Apem. Thy mother's of my generation: what's she, if I
be a dog?

Tim. Wilt dine with me, Apemantus?

Apem. No; I eat not lords.

Tim. An thou shouldst, thou'dst anger ladies.

Apem. O, they eat lords; so they come by great bellies.

Tim. That's a lascivious apprehension.

Apem. So thou apprehendest it: take it for thy labour.

Tim. How dost thou like this jewel, Apemantus?

Apem. Not so well as plain-dealing, which will not cost
a man a doit.

Tim. What dost thou think 'tis worth?

Apem. Not worth my thinking.—How now, poet!

Poet. How now, philosopher!

Apem. Thou liest.

Poet. Art not one?

Apem. Yes.

Poet. Then I lie not.

Apem. Art not a poet?

Poet. Yes.

Apem. Then thou liest: look in thy last work, where thou hast feign'd him a worthy fellow.

Poet. That's not feign'd,—he is so.

Apem. Yes, he is worthy of thee, and to pay thee for thy labour: he that loves to be flattered is worthy o' the flatterer. Heavens, that I were a lord!

Tim. What wouldst do then, Apemantus?

Apem. Even as Apemantus does now, hate a lord with my heart.

Tim. What, thyself?

Apem. Ay.

Tim. Wherefore?

Apem. That I had no angry wit to be a lord.—Art not thou a merchant?

Mer. Ay, Apemantus.

Apem. Traffic confound thee, if the gods will not!

Mer. If traffic do it, the gods do it.

Apem. Traffic's thy god, and thy god confound thee!

Trumpet sounds. Enter a Servant.

Tim. What trumpet's that?

Serv. 'Tis Alcibiades, and some twenty horse, All of companionship.

Tim. Pray, entertain them; give them guide to us.—

                                          [Exeunt some Attendants.

You must needs dine with me:—go not you hence Till I have thank'd you:—when dinner's done Show me this piece.—I am joyful of your sights.

Enter ALCIBIADES, *with his company.*

Most welcome, sir!   *[They salute.*

   Apem.   So, so, there!—

Aches contract and starve your supple joints!—

That there should be small love 'mongst these sweet knaves,

And all this court'sy! The strain of man's bred out

Into baboon and monkey.

   Alcib. Sir, you have sav'd my longing, and I feed

Most hungerly on your sight

   Tim.   Right welcome, sir!

Ere we depart we'll share a bounteous time

In different pleasures. Pray you, let us in.

                                [Exeunt all but APEMANTUS.

Enter two Lords.

1 *Lord.* What time o' day is't, Apemantus?

Apem. Time to be honest.

1 *Lord.* That time serves still.

Apem. The more accursed thou, that still omitt'st it.

2 *Lord.* Thou art going to Lord Timon's feast.

Apem. Ay; to see meat fill knaves, and wine heat fools.

2 *Lord.* Fare thee well, fare thee well.

Apem. Thou art a fool to bid me farewell twice.

2 *Lord.* Why, Apemantus?

Apem. Shouldst have kept one to thyself, for I mean to give thee none.

1 *Lord.* Hang thyself.

Apem. No, I will do nothing at thy bidding : make thy requests to thy friend.

2 *Lord.* Away, unpeaceable dog, or I'll spurn thee hence.

Apem. I will fly, like a dog, the heels o' the ass.   [*Exit.*

1 *Lord.* He's opposite to humanity. Come, shall we in
And taste Lord Timon's bounty? he outgoes
The very heart of kindness.

2 *Lord.* He pours it out; Plutus, the god of gold,
Is but his steward: no meed but he repays
Sevenfold above itself; no gift to him
But breeds the giver a return exceeding
All use of quittance.

1 *Lord.*   The noblest mind he carries
That ever govern'd man.

2 *Lord.* Long may he live in fortunes! Shall we in?

1 *Lord.* I'll keep you company.   [*Exeunt*

SCENE II.—ATHENS.   *Room of State in* TIMON'S *House.*

*Hautboys playing loud music. A great banquet served
in;* FLAVIUS *and others attending; then enter* TIMON,
ALCIBIADES, LUCIUS, LUCULLUS, SEMPRONIUS, *and other
Athenian Senators, with* VENTIDIUS, *and* Attendants. *Then
comes, dropping after all,* APEMANTUS, *discontentedly.*

Ven. Most honour'd Timon,
It hath pleas'd the gods to remember my father's age,
And call him to long peace.
He is gone happy, and has left me rich:
Then, as in grateful virtue I am bound
To your free heart, I do return those talents,
Doubled with thanks and service, from whose help
I deriv'd liberty.

Tim.   O, by no means,
Honest Ventidius ; you mistake my love:
I gave it freely ever; and there's none

Can truly say he gives if he receives:
If our betters play at that game, we must not dare
To imitate them; faults that are rich are fair.

Ven. A noble spirit!

        [*They all stand ceremoniously looking on* TIMON.

Tim. Nay, my lords, ceremony was but devis'd at first
To set a gloss on faint deeds, hollow welcomes,
Recanting goodness, sorry ere 'tis shown;
But where there is true friendship there needs none.
I'ray, sit; more welcome are ye to my fortunes
Than my fortunes to me.   [*They sit.*

  1 *Lord.* My lord, we always have confess'd it.

  Apem. Ho, ho, confess'd it! hang'd it, have you not?

  Tim. O, Apemantus!—you are welcome.

  Apem.   No;
You shall not make me welcome.
I come to have thee thrust me out of doors.

  Tim. Fie, thou art a churl; you have got a humour there
Does not become a man; 'tis much to blame.—
They say, my lords, *ira furor brevis est;*
But yond man is ever angry.
Go, let him have a table by himself;
For he does neither affect company
Nor is he fit for't, indeed.

  Apem. Let me stay at thine apparel, Timon:
I come to observe; I give thee warning on't.

  Tim. I take no heed of thee; thou art an Athenian, therefore welcome: I myself would have no power; pr'ythee, let
my meat make thee silent.

  Apem. I scorn thy meat; 'twould choke me, for I should
ne'er flatter thee.—O you gods, what a number of men eat
Timon, and he sees 'em not! it grieves me to see
So many dip their meat in one man's blood;
And all the madness is, he cheers them up too.
I wonder men dare trust themselves with men:
Methinks they should invite them without knives;
Good for their meat and safer for their lives.
There's much example for't; the fellow that sits next him
now, parts bread with him, pledges the breath of him in a
divided draught, is the readiest man to kill him: 't has
been prov'd. If I were a huge man I should fear to drink
at meals,
Lest they should spy my windpipe's dangerous notes:
Great men should drink with harness on their throats.

  Tim. My lord, in heart; and let the health go round.

  2 *Lord.* Let it flow this way, my good lord.

Apem. Flow this way! A brave fellow! he keeps his
tides well.—Those healths will make thee and thy state
look ill, Timon.
Here's that which is too weak to be a sinner,
Honest water, which ne'er left man i' the mire:
This and my food are equals; there's no odds:
Feasts are too proud to give thanks to the gods.

APEMANTUS'S GRACE.

Immortal gods, I crave no pelf;
I pray for no man but myself;
Grant I may never prove so fond,
To trust man on his oath or bond;
Or a harlot for her weeping;
Or a dog that seems a-sleeping;
Or a keeper with my freedom;
Or my friends, if I should need 'em.
Amen. So fall to't:
Rich men sin, and I eat root.   [*Eats and drinks.*

Much good dich thy good heart, Apemantus!

Tim. Captain Alcibiades, your heart's in the field now.

A'cib. My heart is ever at your service, my lord.

Tim. You had rather be at a breakfast of enemies than a
dinner of friends.

Alcib. So they were bleeding-new, my lord, there's no
meat like 'em; I could wish my best friend at such a
feast.

Apem. Would all those flatterers were thine enemies,
then, that then thou might'st kill 'em, and bid me to 'em.

I *Lord.* Might we but have that happiness, my lord,
that you would once use our hearts, whereby we might
express some part of our zeals, we should think ourselves
for ever perfect.

Tim. O, no doubt, my good friends, but the gods themselves have provided that I shall have much help from
you: how had you been my friends else? why you have
that charitable title from thousands, did not you chiefly
belong to my heart? I have told more of you to myself
than you can with modesty speak in your own behalf; and
thus far I confirm you. O you gods, think I, what need
we have any friends if we should ne'er have need of 'em?
they were the most needless creatures living, should we
ne'er have use for 'em; and would most resemble sweet
instruments hung up in cases, that keep their sounds to
themselves. Why, I have often wished myself poorer,
that I might come nearer to you. We are born to do
benefits: and what better or properer can we call our own
than the riches of our friends? O, what a precious com-

fort 'tis to have so many, like brothers, commanding one
another's fortunes! O joy, e'en made away ere it can be
born! Mine eyes cannot hold out water, methinks: 'to
forget their faults I drink to you.

Apem. Thou weepest to make them drink, Timon.

2 Lord. Joy had the like conception in our eyes,
And at that instant like a babe sprung up.

Apem. Ho, ho! I laugh to think that babe a bastard.

3 Lord. I promise you, my lord, you mov'd me much.

Apem. Much!   [*Tucket sounded.*

Tim. What means that trump?

Enter a Servant.

How now!

Serv. Please you, my lord, there are certain ladies most
desirous of admittance.

Tim. Ladies! what are their wills?

Serv. There comes with them a forerunner, my lord,
which bears that office, to signify their pleasures.

Tim. I pray, let them be admitted.

Enter CUPID.

Cup. Hail to thee, worthy Timon;—and to all
That of his bounties taste!—The five best senses
Acknowledge thee their patron; and come freely
To gratulate thy plenteous bosom:
The ear, taste, touch, smell, pleas'd from thy table rise;
They only now come but to feast thine eyes.

Tim. They are welcome all; let 'em have kind admittance.
Music, make their welcome!   [*Exit* CUPID.

1 Lord. You see, my lord, how ample you're belov'd.

Music. Re-enter CUPID, *with a mask of* Ladies *as Amazons,
with lutes in their hands, dancing and playing.*

Apem. Hoy-day, what a sweep of vanity comes this way
They dance! they are mad women.
Like madness is the glory of this life,
As this pomp shows to a little oil and root.
We make ourselves fools to disport ourselves,
And spend our flatteries to drink those men
Upon whose age we void it up again,
With poisonous spite and envy.
Who lives that's not depraved or depraves?
Who dies that bears not one spurn to their graves
Of their friends' gift?
I should fear those that dance before me now

Would one day stamp upon me: 't has been done;
Men shut their doors against a setting sun.

The Lords *rise from table, with much adoring of* Timon;
*and, to show their loves, each singles out an Amazon, and
all dance, men with women, a lofty strain or two to the
hautboys, and cease.*

Tim. You have done our pleasures much grace, fair
    ladies,
Set a fair fashion on our entertainment,
Which was not half so beautiful and kind;
You have added worth unto't and lustre,
And entertain'd me with mine own device;
I am to thank you for't.

1 Lady. My lord, you take us even at the best.

Apem. Faith, for the worst is filthy; and would not cold
taking, I doubt me.

Tim. Ladies, there is an idle banquet attends you:
Please you to dispose yourselves.

All Ladies. Most thankfully, my lord.
                        [*Exeunt* Cupid *and* Ladies.

Tim. Flavius,—

Flav. My lord?

Tim.   The little casket bring me hither.

Fav. Yes, my lord.—[*Aside.*] More jewels yet!
There is no crossing him in his humour,
Else I should tell him,—well, i' faith, I should,
When all's spent, he'd be cross'd then, an he could.
'Tis pity bounty had not eyes behind,
That man might ne'er be wretched for his mind.
                   [*Exit, and returns with the casket.*

1 Lord. Where be our men?

Serv. Here, my lord, in readiness.

2 Lord. Our horses!

Tim.   O my friends,
I have one word to say to you. Look you, my good lord,
I must entreat you, honour me so much
As to advance this jewel; accept it, and wear it.
Kind my lord.

1 Lord. I am so far already in your gifts,—

All. So are we all.

Enter a Servant.

Serv. My lord, there are certain nobles of the senate
Newly alighted, and come to visit you.

Tim. They are fairly welcome.

Flav.　　　　　　　　　　I beseech your honour,
Vouchsafe me a word; it does concern you near

Tim. Near; why, then, another time i'll near thee:
I pr'ythee, let's be provided to show 'em entertainment.

Flav. I scarce know how.　　　　　　　　[*Aside.*

Enter a second Servant.

2 *Serv.* May it please your honour, Lord Lucius,
Out of his free love, hath presented to you
Four milk-white horses, trapp'd in silver.

Tim. I shall accept them fairly: let the presents
Be worthily entertained.

Enter a third Servant.

　　　　　　　　　　How now! what news?

3 *Serv.* Please you, my lord, that honourable gentleman, Lord Lucullus, entreats your company to-morrow to
hunt with him; and has sent your honour two brace of
greyhounds.

Tim. I'll hunt with him; and let them be receiv'd,
Not without fair reward.

Flav. [*aside.*]　　　　What will this come to?
He commands us to provide, and give great gifts,
And all out of an empty coffer:
Nor will he know his purse; or yield me this,
To show him what a beggar his heart is,
Being of no power to make his wishes good:
His promises fly so beyond his state
That what he speaks is all in debt, he owes
For every word: he is so kind that he now
Pays interest for't; his land's put to their books.
Well, would I were gently put out of office
Before I were forc'd out!
Happier is he that has no friend to feed
Than such that do e'en enemies exceed.
I bleed inwardly for my lord.　　　　　　[*Exit.*

Tim.　　　　　　　　You do yourselves
Much wrong, you bate too much of your own merits:
Here, my lord, a trifle of our love.

2 *Lord.* With more than common thanks I will receive it.

3 *Lord.* O, he is the very soul of bounty!

Tim. And now I remember, my lord, you gave
Good words the other day of a bay courser
I rode on: it is yours because you lik'd it.

3 *Lord.* O, I beseech you, pardon me, my lord, in that.

Tim. You may take my word, my lord; I know no man
Can justly praise but what he does affect:
I weigh my friend's affection with mine own;
I'll tell you true. I'll call to you.
    All Lords.   O, none so welcome.
    Tim. I take all and your several visitations
So kind to heart, 'tis not enough to give;
Methinks I could deal kingdoms to my friends
And ne'er be weary.—Alcibiades,
Thou art a soldier, therefore seldom rich;
It comes in charity to thee: for all thy living
Is 'mongst the dead; and all the lands thou hast
Lie in a pitch'd field.
    Alcib.   Ay, defil'd land, my lord.
    1 *Lord.* We are so virtuously bound,—
    Tim.   And so
Am I to you.
    2 *Lord.*   So infinitely endear'd,—
    Tim. All to you.—Lights, more lights!
    1 *Lord.*   The best of happiness,
Honour, and fortunes keep with you, Lord Timon!
    Tim. Ready for his friends.
             [*Exeunt* ALCIBIADES, Lords, &c.
    Apem.   What a coil 's here!
Serving of becks and jutting-out of bums!
I doubt whether their legs be worth the sums
That are given for 'em. Friendship 's full of dregs:
Methinks false hearts should never have sound legs.
Thus honest fools lay out their wealth on court'sies.
    Tim. Now, Apemantus, if thou wert not sullen I would
be good to thee.
    Apem. No, I'll nothing: for if I should be bribed too,
there would be none left to rail upon thee; and then thou
wouldst sin the faster. Thou givest so long, Timon, I fear
me thou wilt give away thyself in paper shortly: what
need these feasts, pomps, and vain-glories?
    Tim. Nay, an you begin to rail on society once, I am
sworn not to give regard to you. Farewell; and come with
better music.   [*Exit.*
    Apem. So;—thou'lt not hear me now,—thou shalt not
then, I'll lock thy heaven from thee.
O, that men's ears should be
To counsel deaf, but not to flattery!   [*Exit.*

ACT II.

SCENE I.—ATHENS. *A Room in a* Senator's *House.*

Enter a Senator, *with papers in his hand.*

Sen. And late, five thousand;—to Varro and to Isidore
He owes nine thousand; besides my former sum,
Which makes it five-and-twenty.—Still in motion
Of raging waste? It cannot hold; it will not.
If I want gold, steal but a beggar's dog
And give it Timon, why, the dog coins gold:
If I would sell my horse and buy twenty more
Better than he, why, give my horse to Timon,
Ask nothing, give it him, it foals me, straight,
And able horses: no porter at his gate;
But rather one that smiles, and still invites
All that pass by.   It cannot hold; no reason
Can found his state in safety.   Caphis, ho!
Caphis, I say!

Enter CAPHIS.

Caph.   Here, sir; what is your pleasure?
Sen. Get on your cloak and haste you to Lord Timon;
Importune him for my moneys; be not ceas'd
With slight denial; nor then silenc'd, when—
Commend me to your master—and the cap
Plays in the right hand, thus:—but tell him
My uses cry to me, I must serve my turn
Out of mine own; his days and times are past,
And my reliances on his fracted dates
Have smit my credit: I love and honour him;
But must not break my back to heal his finger:
Immediate are my needs; and my relief
Must not be toss'd and turn'd to me in words,
But find supply immediate.   Get you gone:
Put on a most importunate aspéct,
A visage of demand; for, I do fear,
When every feather sticks in his own wing
Lord Timon will be left a naked gull,
Which flashes now a phœnix.   Get you gone.
Caph. I go, sir.
Sen. Take the bonds along with you,
And have the dates in compt.
Caph.   I will, sir.
Sen.   Go.   [*Exeunt*

SCENE II.—ATHENS. *A Hall in* TIMON's *House.*

Enter FLAVIUS, *with many bills in his hand.*

Flav No care, no stop! so senseless of expense
That he will neither know how to maintain it
Nor cease his flow of riot: takes no account
How things go from him: nor resumes no care
Of what is to continue: never mind
Was to be so unwise to be so kind.
What shall be done? he will not hear, till feel:
I must be round with him now he comes from hunting.
Fie, fie, fie, fie!

Enter CAPHIS, *and the* Servants *of* ISIDORE *and* VARRO.

Caph.   Good-even, Varro: what,
You come for money?
  Var. Serv.   Is't not your business too?
  Caph. It is:—and yours too, Isidore?
  Isid. Serv.   It is so.
  Caph. Would we were all discharg'd!
  Var. Serv.   I fear it.
  Caph. Here comes the lord.

Enter TIMON, ALCIBIADES, *and* Lords, *&c.*

Tim. So soon as dinner's done we'll forth again,
My Alcibiades.—With me? what is your will?
  Caph. My lord, here is a note of certain dues.
  Tim. Dues! whence are you?
  Caph.   Of Athens here, my lord.
  Tim. Go to my steward.
  Caph. Please it your lordship, he hath put me off
To the succession of new days this month:
My master is awak'd by great occasion
To call upon his own; and humbly prays you
That, with your other noble parts, you'll suit
In giving him his right.
  Tim.   Mine honest friend,
I pr'ythee but repair to me next morning.
  Caph. Nay, good my lord,—
  Tim.   Contain thyself, good friend.
  Var. Serv. One Varro's servant, my good lord,—
  Isid. Serv.   From Isidore;
He humbly prays your speedy payment,—
  Caph. If you did know, my lord, my master's wants,—

Var. Serv. 'Twas due on forfeiture, my lord, six weeks
And past,—
Isid. Serv. Your steward puts me off, my lord;
And I am sent expressly to your lordship.
Tim. Give me breath.—
I do beseech you, good my lords, keep on;
I'll wait upon you instantly.—   [*Exeunt* ALCI. *and* Lords.
Come hither: pray you,   [*To* FLAVIUS.
How goes the world, that I am thus encounter'd
With clamorous demands of date-broke bonds,
And the detention of long-since-due debts,
Against my honour?
Flav.   Please you, gentlemen,
The time is unagreeable to this business:
Your importunacy cease till after dinner;
That I may make his lordship understand
Wherefore you are not paid.
Tim.   Do so, my friends.—
See them well entertained.   [*Exit.*
Flav.   Pray, draw near.   [*Exit.*

Enter APEMANTUS *and* Fool.

Caph. Stay, stay, here comes the fool with Apemantus:
let 's ha' some sport with 'em.
Var. Serv. Hang him, he'll abuse us.
Isid. Serv. A plague upon him, dog!
Var. Serv. How dost, fool?
Apem. Dost dialogue with thy shadow?
Var. Serv. I speak not to thee.
Apem. No, 'tis to thyself.—Come away.   [*To the* Fool.
Isid. Serv. [*to* VAR. Serv.] There 's the fool hangs on
your back already.
Apem. No, thou stand'st single, thou art not on him yet.
Caph. Where 's the fool now?
Apem. He last asked the question.—Poor rogues and
usurers' men! bawds between gold and want!
All Serv. What are we, Apemantus?
Apem. Asses.
All Serv. Why?
Apem. That you ask me what you are, and do not know
yourselves.—Speak to 'em, fool.
Fool. How do you, gentlemen?
All Serv. Gramercies, good fool: how does your mistress?
Fool. She 's e'en setting on water to scald such chickens
as you are. Would we could see you at Corinth.
Apem. Good! gramercy.

Fool. Look you, here comes my mistress' page.

Enter Page.

Page. [*to the* Fool.] Why, how now, captain? what do you in this wise company? How dost thou, Apemantus?

Apem. Would I had a rod in my mouth, that I might answer thee profitably.

Page. Pr'ythee, Apemantus, read me the superscription of these letters: I know not which is which.

Apem. Canst not read?

Page. No.

Apem. There will little learning die, then, that day thou art hanged. This is to Lord Timon; this to Alcibiades. Go; thou wast born a bastard, and thou'lt die a bawd.

Page. Thou wast whelped a dog, and thou shalt famish a dog's death. Answer not, I am gone.

Apem. E'en so thou outrun'st grace. [*Exit* Page.] Fool, I will go with you to Lord Timon's.

Fool. Will you leave me there?

Apem. If Timon stay at home.—You three serve three usurers?

All Serv. Ay; would they served us!

Apem. So would I,—as good a trick as ever hangman served thief.

Fool. Are you three usurers' men?

All Serv. Ay, fool.

Fool. I think no usurer but has a fool to his servant; my mistress is one, and I am her fool. When men come to borrow of your masters they approach sadly and go away merry; but they enter my mistress' house merrily and go away sadly: the reason of this?

Var. Serv. I could render one.

Apem. Do it, then, that we may account thee a whore-master and a knave; which, notwithstanding, thou shalt be no less esteemed.

Var. Serv. What is a whoremaster, fool?

Fool. A fool in good clothes, and something like thee. 'Tis a spirit: sometime it appears like a lord; sometimes like a lawyer; sometime like a philosopher, with two stones more than 's artificial one. He is very often like a knight; and, generally, in all shapes that man goes up and down in from fourscore to thirteen this spirit walks in.

Var. Serv. Thou art not altogether a fool.

Fool. Nor thou altogether a wise man: as much foolery as I have, so much wit thou lackest.

Apem. That answer might have become Apemantus.

All Serv. Aside, aside; here comes Lord Timon.

Re-enter TIMON and FLAVIUS.

Apem. Come with me, fool, come.

Fool. I do not always follow lover, elder brother, and woman; sometime the philosopher.

[*Exeunt* APEMANTUS *and* Fool.

Flav. Pray you, walk near; I'll speak with you anon.

[*Exeunt* Servants.

Tim. You make me marvel: wherefore, ere this time,
Had you not fully laid my state before me;
That I might so have rated my expense
As I had leave of means?

Flav. You would not hear me
At many leisures I propos'd.

Tim. Go to:
Perchance some single vantages you took
When my indisposition put you back;
And that unaptness made your minister
Thus to excuse yourself.

Flav. O my good lord,
At many times I brought in my accounts,
Laid them before you; you would throw them off,
And say you found them in mine honesty.
When, for some trifling present, you have bid me
Return so much, I have shook my head and wept;
Yea, 'gainst the authority of manners, pray'd you
To hold your hand more close: I did endure
Not seldom, nor no slight checks, when I have
Prompted you, in the ebb of your estate,
And your great flow of debts. My loved lord,
Though you hear now,—too late!—yet now's a time,
The greatest of your having lacks a half
To pay your present debts.

Tim. Let all my land be sold.

Flav. 'Tis all engag'd, some forfeited and gone;
And what remains will hardly stop the mouth
Of present dues: the future comes apace:
What shall defend the interim? and at length
How goes our reckoning?

Tim. To Lacedæmon did my land extend.

Flav. O my good lord, the world is but a word:
Were it all yours to give it in a breath,
How quickly were it gone!

Tim. You tell me true.

Flav. If you suspect my husbandry or falsehood,

Call me before the exactest auditors
And set me on the proof. So the gods bless me,
When all our offices have been oppress'd
With riotous feeders; when our vaults have wept
With drunken spilth of wine; when every room
Hath blaz'd with lights and bray'd with minstrelsy;
I have retir'd me to a wasteful cock,
And set mine eyes at flow.
  Tim.   Pr'ythee, no more.
  Flav. Heavens, have I said, the bounty of this lord!
How many prodigal bits have slaves and peasants
This night englutted! Who is not Timon's?
What heart, head, sword, force, means, but is Lord Timon's
Great Timon, noble, worthy, royal Timon!
Ah! when the means are gone that buy this praise
The breath is gone whereof this praise is made:
Feast-won, fast-lost; one cloud of winter showers,
These flies are couch'd.
  Tim.   Come, sermon me no further:
No villanous bounty yet hath pass'd my heart;
Unwisely, not ignobly, have I given.
Why dost thou weep? Canst thou the conscience lack
To think I shall lack friends? Secure thy heart;
If I would broach the vessels of my love,
And try the argument of hearts by borrowing,
Men and men's fortunes could I frankly use
As I can bid thee speak.
  Flav.   Assurance bless your thoughts!
  Tim. And, in some sort, these wants of mine are crown'd
That I account them blessings; for by these
Shall I try friends: you shall perceive how you
Mistake my fortunes; I am wealthy in my friends.
Within there! Flaminius! Servilius!

  Enter FLAMINIUS, SERVILIUS, *and other* Servants.

  Serv. My lord? my lord?—
  Tim. I will despatch you severally:—you to Lord Lucius;
—to Lord Lucullus you; I hunted with his honour to-day;
—you to Sempronius: commend me to their loves; and I
am proud, say, that my occasions have found time to use
'em toward a supply of money: let the request be fifty
talents.
  Flam. As you have said, my lord.
  Flav. Lord Lucius and Lucullus? hum!   [*Aside.*
  Tim. Go you, sir [*to another* Serv.], to the senators,—
Of whom, even to the state's best health, I have

Deserv'd this hearing,—bid 'em send o' the instant
A thousand talents to me.

Flav.   I have been bold,—
For that I knew it the most general way,—
To them to use your signet and your name;
But they do shake their heads, and I am here
No richer in return.

Tim.   Is't true? can't be?

Flav. They answer, in a joint and corporate voice,
That now they are at fall, want treasure, cannot
Do what they would; are sorry—you are honourable,—
But yet they could have wish'd—they know not—
Something hath been amiss—a noble nature
May catch a wrench—would all were well—'tis pity;—
And so, intending other serious matters,
After distasteful looks, and these hard fractions,
With certain half-caps and cold-moving nods,
They froze me into silence.

Tim.   You gods, reward them!
Pr'ythee, man, look cheerly. These old fellows
Have their ingratitude in them hereditary:
Their blood is cak'd, 'tis cold, it seldom flows;
'Tis lack of kindly warmth they are not kind;
And nature, as it grows again toward earth,
Is fashion'd for the journey dull and heavy.—
Go to Ventidius [*to a* Serv.]; pr'ythee, [*to* FLAVIUS,] be
        not sad,
Thou art true and honest; ingeniously I speak,
No blame belongs to thee:—[*to* Serv.] Ventidius lately
Buried his father; by whose death he's stepp'd
Into a great estate: when he was poor,
Imprison'd, and in scarcity of friends,
I clear'd him with five talents: greet him from me;
Bid him suppose some good necessity
Touches his friend, which craves to be remember'd
With those five talents:—[*to* FLAV.]—That had,—give't
        these fellows
To whom 'tis instant due. Ne'er speak or think
That Timon's fortunes 'mong his friends can sink.

Flav. I would I could not think it: that thought is
        bounty's foe;
Being free itself it thinks all others so.   [*Exeunt.*

ACT III.

SCENE I.—ATHENS. *A Room in* LUCULLUS' *House.*

FLAMINIUS waiting. Enter a Servant to him.

Serv. I have told my lord of you; he is coming down to you.

Flam. I thank you, sir.

Enter LUCULLUS.

Serv. Here's my lord.

Lucul. [*aside.*] One of Lord Timon's men? a gift, I warrant. Why, this hits right; I dreamt of a silver basin and ewer to-night.—Flaminius, honest Flaminius; you are very respectively welcome, sir.—Fill me some wine. [*Exit* Servant.]—And how does that honourable, complete, free-hearted gentleman of Athens, thy very bountiful good lord and master?

Flam. His health is well, sir.

Lucul. I am right glad that his health is well, sir: and what hast thou there under thy cloak, pretty Flaminius?

Flam. Faith, nothing but an empty box, sir; which, in my lord's behalf, I come to entreat your honour to supply; who, having great and instant occasion to use fifty talents, hath sent to your lordship to furnish him, nothing doubting your present assistance therein.

Lucul. La, la, la, la,—nothing doubting, says he? Alas, good lord! a noble gentleman 'tis, if he would not keep so good a house. Many a time and often I ha'e dined with him and told him on't; and come again to supper to him of purpose to have him spend less; and yet he would embrace no counsel, take no warning by my coming. Every man has his fault, and honesty is his: I ha'e told him on't, but I could ne'er get him from't.

Re-enter Servant, *with wine.*

Serv. Please your lordship, here is the wine.

Lucul. Flaminius, I have noted thee always wise. Here's to thee.

Flam. Your lordship speaks your pleasure.

Lucul. I have observed thee always for a towardly prompt spirit,—give thee thy due,—and one that knows what belongs to reason; and canst use the time well, if the time use thee well: good parts in thee.—Get you gone, sirrah [*to the* Servant, *who goes out.*]—Draw nearer, honest Flaminius. Thy lord's a bountiful gentleman : but thou art wise; and thou knowest well enough, although thou comest to me, that this is no time to lend money; especially upon bare friendship, without security. Here's three solidares for thee : good boy, wink at me, and say thou saw'st me not. Fare thee well.

Flam. Is't possible the world should so much differ :
And we alive that liv'd! Fly, damned baseness,
To him that worships thee.   [*Throwing the money back.*

Lucul. Ha! now I see thou art a fool, and fit for thy master.   [*Exit.*

Flam. May these add to the number that may scald thee!
Let molten coin be thy damnation,
Thou disease of a friend and not himself!
Has friendship such a faint and milky heart,
It turns in less than two nights? O you gods.
I feel my master's passion! This slave
Unto his honour has my lord's meat in him :
Why should it thrive and turn to nutriment
When he is turn'd to poison?
O, may diseases only work upon't!
And when he's sick to death, let not that part of nature
Which my lord paid for, be of any power
To expel sickness, but prolong his hour!   [*Exit.*

SCENE II.—ATHENS.   *A public Place.*

Enter LUCIUS, *with three* Strangers.

Luc. Who, the Lord Timon? he is my very good friend, and an honourable gentleman.

1 *Stran.* We know him for no less, though we are but strangers to him. But I can tell you one thing, my lord, and which I hear from common rumours,—now Lord Timon's happy hours are done and past, and his estate shrinks from him.

Luc. Fie, no, do not believe it; he cannot want for money.

2 *Stran.* But believe you this, my lord, that, not long ago, one of his men was with the Lord Lucullus to borrow so many talents; nay, urged extremely for't, and showed what necessity belonged to't, and yet was denied.

Luc. How?

2 *Stran.* I tell you, denied, my lord.

Luc. What a strange case was that! now, before the gods, I am ashamed on't. Denied that honourable man! there

was very little honour showed in't. For my own part, I
must needs confess I have received some small kindnesses
from him, as money, plate, jewels, and such like trifles,
nothing comparing to his; yet, had he mistook him and
sent to me, I should ne'er have denied his occasion so
many talents.

Enter SERVILIUS.

Ser. See, by good hap, yonder's my lord; I have sweat to
see his honour.—My honoured lord,—   [*To* LUCIUS.

Luc. Servilius! you are kindly met, sir. Fare thee well:
commend me to thy honourable-virtuous lord, my very
exquisite friend.

Ser. May it please your honour, my lord hath sent,—

Luc. Ha! what has he sent? I am so much endeared to
that lord; he's ever sending: how shall I thank him,
thinkest thou? And what has he sent now?

Ser. Has only sent his present occasion now, my lord;
requesting your lordship to supply his instant use with so
many talents.

Luc. I know his lordship is but merry with me;
He cannot want fifty-five hundred talents.

Ser. But in the meantime he wants less, my lord.
If his occasion were not virtuous
I should not urge it half so faithfully.

Luc. Dost thou speak seriously, Servilius?

Ser. Upon my soul, 'tis true, sir.

Luc. What a wicked beast was I to disfurnish myself
against such a good time, when I might ha' shown
myself honourable! how unluckily it happened that I
should purchase the day before for a little part, and undo
a great deal of honour!—Servilius, now, before the gods, I
am not able to do't,—the more beast, I say. I was sending
to use Lord Timon myself, these gentlemen can witness;
but I would not for the wealth of Athens I had done't
now. Commend me bountifully to his good lordship; and
I hope his honour will conceive the fairest of me, because
I have no power to be kind: and tell him this from me, I
count it one of my greatest afflictions, say, that I cannot
pleasure such an honourable gentleman. Good Servilius,
will you befriend me so far as to use mine own words
to him?

Ser. Yes, sir, I shall.

Luc. I'll look you out a good turn, Servilius. [*Exit* SER.
True, as you said, Timon is shrunk indeed;
And he that's once denied will hardly speed.   [*Exit.*

1 *Stran.* Do you observe this, Hostilius?
2 *Stran.*   Ay, too well.
1 *Stran.* Why, this is the world's soul; and just of the
     same piece
Is every flatterer's spirit.   Who can call him
His friend that dips in the same dish? for, in
My knowing, Timon has been this lord's father,
And kept his credit with his purse;
Supported his estate; nay, Timon's money
Has paid his men their wages: he ne'er drinks
But Timon's silver treads upon his lip;
And yet,—O see the monstrousness of man
When he looks out in an ungrateful shape!—
He does deny him, in respect of his,
What charitable men afford to beggars.
     3 *Stran.* Religion groans at it.
     1 *Stran.*   For mine own part,
I never tasted Timon in my life,
Nor came any of his bounties over me
To mark me for his friend; yet I protest,
For his right noble mind, illustrious virtue,
And honourable carriage,
Had his necessity made use of me,
I would have put my wealth into donation,
And the best half should have return'd to him,
So much I love his heart: but, I perceive,
Men must learn now with pity to dispense:
For policy sits above conscience.   [*Exeunt.*

SCENE III.—ATHENS.   *A Room in* SEMPRONIUS' *House.*

Enter SEMPRONIUS *and a* Servant *of* TIMON'S.

Sem. Must he needs trouble me in't,—hum!—'bove all
     others?
He might have tried Lord Lucius or Lucullus;
And now Ventidius is wealthy too,
Whom he redeem'd from prison: all these
Owe their estates unto him.
     Serv.   My lord,
They have all been touch'd and found base metal; for
They have all denied him.
     Sem.   How! have they denied him?
Has Ventidius and Lucullus denied him?
And does he send to me?   Three? hum!—
It shows but little love or judgment in him:

Must I be his last refuge? His friends, like physicians,
Thrive, give him over: must I take the cure upon me?
Has much disgrac'd me in't; I am angry at him,
That might have known my place: I see no sense for't,
But his occasions might have woo'd me first;
For, in my conscience, I was the first man
That e'er received gift from him:
And does he think so backwardly of me now
That I'll requite it last? No:
So it may prove an argument of laughter
To the rest, and 'mongst lords I be thought a fool.
I had rather than the worth of thrice the sum
Had sent to me first, but for my mind's sake;
I had such a courage to do him good. But now return,
And with their faint reply this answer join;
Who bates mine honour shall not know my coin.   [*Exit.*

    Serv. Excellent! Your lordship's a goodly villain. The
devil knew not what he did when he made man politic,—
he cross'd himself by't: and I cannot think but, in the end,
the villanies of man will set him clear. How fairly this
lord strives to appear foul! takes virtuous copies to be
wicked; like those that under hot ardent zeal would set
whole realms on fire:
Of such a nature is his politic love.
This was my lord's best hope; now all are fled,
Save only the gods: now his friends are dead,
Doors, that were ne'er acquainted with their wards
Many a bounteous year, must be employ'd
Now to guard sure their master.
And this is all a liberal course allows;
Who cannot keep his wealth must keep his house.   [*Exit.*

SCENE IV.—ATHENS.   *A Hall in* TIMON'S *House.*

Enter two Servants *of* VARRO *and the* Servant *of* LUCIUS,
  meeting TITUS, HORTENSIUS, *and other* Servants *of*
  TIMON'S *creditors, waiting his coming out.*

    1 *Var. Serv.* Well met; good-morrow, Titus and Horten-
Tit. The like to you, kind Varro.   [sius.
Hor.   Lucius!
What, do we meet together?
    Luc. Serv.   Ay, and I think
One business does command us all; for mine
Is money.
    Tit. So is theirs and ours.

Enter PHILOTUS.

Luc. Serv.   And Sir Philotus too?
Phi. Good-day at once.
Luc. Serv.   Welcome, good brother.
What do you think the hour?
Phi.   Labouring for nine.
Luc. Serv. So much?
Phi.   Is not my lord seen yet?
Luc. Serv.   Not yet.
Phi. I wonder on't; he was wont to shine at seven.
Luc. Serv. Ay, but the days are waxed shorter with him:
You must consider that a prodigal course
Is like the sun's; but not, like his, recoverable.
I fear
'Tis deepest winter in Lord Timon's purse;
That is, one may reach deep enough and yet
Find little.
Phi.   I am of your fear for that.
Tit. I'll show you how to observe a strange event.
Your lord sends now for money.
Hor.   Most true, he does.
Tit. And he wears jewels now of Timon's gift,
For which I wait for money.
Hor. It is against my heart.
Luc. Serv.   Mark how strange it shows,
Timon in this should pay more than he owes:
And e'en as if your lord should wear rich jewels
And send for money for 'em.
Hor. I am weary of this charge, the gods can witness:
I know my lord hath spent of Timon's wealth,
And now ingratitude makes it worse than stealth.
  1 *Var. Serv.* Yes, mine's three thousand crowns: what's
          yours?
Luc. Serv. Five thousand mine.
  1 *Var. Serv.* 'Tis much deep: and it should seem by the
          sum
Your master's confidence was above mine;
Else, surely, his had equall'd.

Enter FLAMINIUS.

Tit. One of Lord Timon's men.
Luc. Serv. Flaminius! sir, a word: pray is my lord ready
to come forth?
Flam. No, indeed, he is not.
Tit. We attend his lordship; pray, signify so much.

Flam. I need not tell him that; he knows you are too diligent.   [*Exit.*

Enter FLAVIUS, *in a cloak, muffled.*

Luc. Serv. Ha! is not that his steward muffled so? He goes away in a cloud: call him, call him.

Tit. Do you hear, sir?

Both Var. Serv. By your leave, sir,—

Flav. What do you ask of me, my friends?

Tit. We wait for certain money here, sir.

Flav.   **Ay,**
If money were as certain as your waiting
'Twere sure enough.
Why then preferr'd you not your sums and bills
When your false masters eat of my lord's meat?
Then they could smile, and fawn upon his debts,
And take down th' interest into their gluttonous maws.
You do yourselves but wrong to stir me up;
Let me pass quietly:
Believ't my lord and I have made an end;
I have no more to reckon, he to spend.

Luc. Serv. Ay, but this answer will not serve.

Flav. If 'twill not serve 'tis not so base as you;
For you serve knaves.   [*Exit.*

1 Var. Serv. How! what does his cashier'd worship mutter?

2 Var. Serv. No matter what; he's poor, and that's revenge enough. Who can speak broader than he that has no house to put his head in? such may rail against great buildings.

Enter SERVILIUS.

Tit. O, here's Servilius; now we shall know some answer.

Ser. If I might beseech you, gentlemen, to repair some other hour, I should derive much from't; for, take't of my soul, my lord leans wondrously to discontent: his comfortable temper has forsook him; he is much out of health, and keeps his chamber.

Luc. Serv. Many do keep their chambers are not sick:
And, if it be so far beyond his health,
Methinks he should the sooner pay his debts,
And make a clear way to the gods.

Ser.   Good gods!

Tit. We cannot take this for answer, sir.

Flam. [*Within.*] Servilius, help!—my lord! my lord!

Enter TIMON, *in a rage;* FLAMINIUS *following.*

Tim. What, are my doors oppos'd against my passage?
Have I been ever free, and must my house
Be my retentive enemy, my gaol?
The place which I have feasted, does it now,
Like all mankind, show me an iron heart?
 Luc. Serv. Put in now, Titus.
 Tit. My lord, here is my bill.
 Luc. Serv. Here's mine.
 Hor. Serv. And mine, my lord.
 Both Var. Serv. And ours, my lord.
 Phi. All our bills.
 Tim. Knock me down with 'em: cleave me to the girdle.
 Luc. Serv. Alas, my lord,—
 Tim. Cut my heart in sums.
 Tit. Mine, fifty talents.
 Tim. Tell out my blood.
 Luc. Serv. Five thousand crowns, my lord.
 Tim. Five thousand drops pays that.—
What yours?—and yours?
 1 Var. Ser. My lord,—
 2 Var. Ser. My lord,—
 Tim. Tear me, take me, and the gods fall upon you! [*Exit.*
 Hor. Faith, I perceive our masters may throw their caps
at their money: these debts may well be called desperate
ones, for a madman owes 'em.   [*Exeunt.*

Re-enter TIMON *and* FLAVIUS.

 Tim. They have e'en put my breath from me, the slaves.
Creditors!—devils.
 Flav. My dear lord,—
 Tim. What if it should be so?
 Flam. My lord,—
 Tim. I'll have it so.—My steward!
 Flav. Here, my lord.
 Tim. So fitly? Go, bid all my friends again,
Lucius, Lucullus, and Sempronius; all:
I'll once more feast the rascals.
 Flav.   O my lord,
You only speak from your distracted soul;
There is not so much left to furnish out
A moderate table.
 Tim.   Be't not in thy care; go,
I charge thee, invite them all: let in the tide
Of knaves once more; my cook and I'll provide. [*Exeunt.*

SCENE V.—ATHENS. *The Senate House.*

The Senate *sitting.*

1 *Sen.* My lords, you have my voice to it; the fault's
Bloody; 'tis necessary he should die:
Nothing emboldens sin so much as mercy.
   2 *Sen.* Most true; the law shall bruise him.

Enter ALCIBIADES, *attended.*

  Alcib. Honour, health, and compassion to the senate!
  1 *Sen.* Now, captain?
  Alcib. I am an humble suitor to your virtues;
For pity is the virtue of the law,
And none but tyrants use it cruelly.
It pleases time and fortune to lie heavy
Upon a friend of mine, who, in hot blood,
Hath stepp'd into the law, which is past depth
To those that without heed do plunge into't.
He is a man, setting his fate aside,
Of comely virtues:
Nor did he soil the fact with cowardice,—
An honour in him which buys out his fault,—
But with a noble fury and fair spirit,
Seeing his reputation touch'd to death,
He did oppose his foe:
And with such sober and unnoted passion
He did behove his anger ere 'twas spent,
As if he had but prov'd an argument.
  1 *Sen.* You undergo too strict a paradox,
Striving to make an ugly deed look fair:
Your words have took such pains, as if they labour'd
To bring manslaughter into form, and set quarrelling
Upon the head of valour; which, indeed,
Is valour misbegot, and came into the world
When sects and factions were newly born:
He's truly valiant that can wisely suffer
The worst that man can breathe; and make his wrongs
His outsides,—to wear them like his raiment, carelessly;
And ne'er prefer his injuries to his heart,
To bring it into danger.
If wrongs be evils, and enforce us kill,
What folly 'tis to hazard life for ill?
  Alcib. My lord,—
  1 *Sen.* You cannot make gross sins look clear:
To revenge is no valour, but to bear.

Alcib. My lords, then, under favour, pardon me,
If I speak like a captain :—
Why do fond men expose themselves to battle,
And not endure all threats? sleep upon't,
And let the foes quietly cut their throats,
Without repugnancy ? but if there be
Such valour in the bearing, what make we
Abroad? why, then, women are more valiant,
That stay at home, if bearing carry it ;
And th' ass more captain than the lion ; the fellow
Loaden with irons wiser than the judge,
If wisdom be in suffering. O my lords,
As you are great, be pitifully good :
Who cannot condemn rashness in cold blood ?
To kill, I grant, is sin's extremest gust ;
But, in defence, by mercy, 'tis most just.
To be in anger is impiety ;
But who is man that is not angry ?
Weigh but the crime with this.
   2 Sen. You breathe in vain.
   Alcib.   In vain ! his service done
At Lacedæmon and Byzantium
Were a sufficient briber for his life.
   1 Sen. What's that ?
   Alcib. Why, I say, my lords, h'as done fair service,
And slain in fight many of your enemies :
How full of valour did he bear himself
In the last conflict, and made plenteous wounds !
   2 Sen. He has made too much plenty with 'em, he
Is a sworn rioter : he has a sin that often
Drowns him, and takes his valour prisoner :
If there were no foes, that were enough
To overcome him : in that beastly fury
He has been known to commit outrages
And cherish factions : 'tis inferr'd to us,
His days are foul and his drink dangerous.
   1 Sen. He dies.
   Alcib. Hard fate! he might have died in war.
My lords, if not for any parts in him,—
Though his right arm might purchase his own time,
And be in debt to none,—yet, more to move you,
Take my deserts to his, and join them both :
And, for I know your reverend ages love
Security, I'll pawn my victories, all
My honours to you, upon his good returns.
If by this crime he owes the law his life,

Why, let the war receiv't in valiant gore;
For law is strict, and war is nothing more.

1 Sen. We are for law,—he dies; urge it no more,
On height of our displeasure: friend or brother,
He forfeits his own blood that spills another.

Alcib. Must it be so? it must not be. My lords,
I do beseech you, know me.

2 Sen. How!

Alcib. Call me to your remembrances.

3 Sen.   What!

Alcib. I cannot think but your age has forgot me;
It could not else be I should prove so base
To sue, and be denied such common grace:
My wounds ache at you.

1 Sen.   Do you dare our anger?
'Tis in few words, but spacious in effect;
We banish thee for ever.

Alcib.   Banish me!
Banish your dotage; banish usury,
That makes the senate ugly.

1 Sen. If, after two days' shine, Athens contain thee,
Attend our weightier judgment.   And, not to swell our
                              spirit,
He shall be executed presently.   [*Exeunt* Senators.

Alcib. Now the gods keep you old enough; that you may
Only in bone, that none may look on you!   [live
I am worse than mad : I have kept back their foes,
While they have told their money, and let out
Their coin upon large interest; I myself
Rich only in large hurts;—all those for this?
Is this the balsam that the usuring senate
Pours into captains' wounds? Ha! banishment?
It comes not ill; I hate not to be banish d;
It is a cause worthy my spleen and fury,
That I may strike at Athens.   I'll cheer up
My discontented troops, and lay for hearts.
'Tis honour with most lands to be at odds;
Soldiers should brook as little wrongs as gods.   [*Exit.*

SCENE VI.—ATHENS.   *A magnificent Room in*
TIMON'S *House.*

Music.   Tables set out: Servants *attending.   Enter divers*
Lords, *at several doors.*

1 Lord. The good time of day to you, sir.

2 *Lord.* I also wish it to you. I think this honourable lord did but try us this other day.

1 *Lord.* Upon that were my thoughts tiring when we encountered: I hope it is not so low with him as he made it seem in the trial of his several friends.

2 *Lord.* It should not be by the persuasion of his new feasting.

1 *Lord.* I should think so: he hath sent me an earnest inviting, which many my near occasions did urge me to put off; but he hath conjured me beyond them, and I must needs appear.

2 *Lord.* In like manner was I in debt to my importunate business, but he would not hear my excuse. I am sorry when he sent to borrow of me, that my provision was out.

1 *Lord.* I am sick of that grief too, as I understand how all things go.

2 *Lord.* Every man here's so. What would he have borrowed of you?

1 *Lord.* A thousand pieces.

2 *Lord.* A thousand pieces!

1 *Lord.* What of you?

2 *Lord.* He sent to me, sir,—Here he comes.

Enter TIMON *and* Attendants.

Tim. With all my heart, gentlemen both.—And how fare you?

1 *Lord.* Ever at the best, hearing well of your lordship.

2 *Lord.* The swallow follows not summer more willing than we your lordship.

Tim. Nor more willingly leaves winter; such summer-birds are men. [*Aside.*]—Gentlemen, our dinner will not recompense this long stay: feast your ears with the music awhile, if they will fare so harshly o' the trumpet's sound; we shall to't presently.

1 *Lord.* I hope it remains not unkindly with your lordship that I returned you an empty messenger.

Tim. O, sir, let it not trouble you.

2 *Lord.* My noble lord,—

Tim. Ah, my good friend! what cheer?

2 *Lord.* My most honourable lord, I am e'en sick of shame that, when your lordship this other day sent to me, I was so unfortunate a beggar.

Tim. Think not on't, sir.

2 *Lord.* If you had sent but two hours before,—

Tim. Let it not cumber your better remembrance.—Come, bring in all together. [*The banquet brought in.*

2 *Lord.* All covered dishes!

1 *Lord.* Royal cheer, 1 warrant you.

3 *Lord.* Doubt not that, if money and the season can yield it.

1 *Lord.* How do you? What's the news?

3 *Lord.* Alcibiades is banished: hear you of it

.1 & 2 *Lord.* Alcibiades banished!

3 *Lord.* 'Tis so, be sure of it.

1 *Lord.* How! how!

2 *Lord.* I pray you, upon what?

Tim. My worthy friends, will you draw near?

3 *Lord.* I'll tell you more anon. Here's a noble feast toward.

2 *Lord.* This is the old man still.

3 *Lord.* Will't hold? will t hold?

2 *Lord.* It does: but time will—and so,—

3 *Lord.* I do conceive.

Tim. Each man to his stool with that spur as he would to the lip of his mistress: your diet shall be in all places alike. Make not a city feast of it, to let the meat cool ere we can agree upon the first place: sit, sit. The gods require our thanks.—

You great benefactors, sprinkle our society with thankfulness. For your own gifts make yourselves praised: but reserve still to give, lest your deities be despised. Lend to each man enough, that one need not lend to another: for, were your godheads to borrow of men, men would forsake the gods. Make the meat be beloved more than the man that gives it. Let no assembly of twenty be without a score of villains: if there sit twelve women at the table, let a dozen of them be—as they are. The rest of your fees, O gods,—the senators of Athens, together with the common tag of people,—what is amiss in them, you gods, make suitable for destruction. For these my present friends,—as they are to me nothing, so in nothing bless them and to nothing are they welcome.

Uncover, dogs, and lap.

           [*The dishes, when uncovered, are seen to be full of warm water.*

Some speak. What does his lordship mean?

Some other. I know not.

Tim. May you a better feast never behold,

You knot of mouth-friends! smoke and lukewarm water

Is your perfection. This is Timon's last;

Who, stuck and spangled with your flatteries,

Washes it off, and sprinkles in your faces

           [*Throwing the water in their faces.*

Your reeking villany. Live loath'd and long,

Most smiling, smooth, detested parasites,

Courteous destroyers, affable wolves, meek bears,

You fools of fortune, trencher-friends, time's flies,
Cap and knee slaves, vapours, and minute-jacks!
Of man and beast the infinite malady
Crust you quite o'er!—What, dost thou go?
Soft, take thy physic first,—thou too,—and thou;—
Stay, I will lend thee money, borrow none.—

        [*Throws the dishes at them, and drives them out.*

What, all in motion?   Henceforth be no feast
Whereat a villain's not a welcome guest.
Burn, house! sink, Athens! henceforth hated be
Of Timon, man, and all humanity!   [*Exit.*

Re-enter the Lords.

1 *Lord.* How now, my lords!
2 *Lord.* Know you the quality of Lord Timon's fury?
3 *Lord.* Pish! did you see my cap?
4 *Lord.* I have lost my gown.
1 *Lord.* He's but a mad lord, and naught but humour
sways him.   He gave me a jewel the other day, and now
he has beat it out of my hat:—did you see my jewel?
3 *Lord.* Did you see my cap?
2 *Lord.* Here 'tis.
4 *Lord.* Here lies my gown.
1 *Lord.* Let's make no stay.
2 *Lord.* Lord Timon's mad.
3 *Lord.*   I feel't upon my bones.
4 *Lord.* One day he gives us diamonds, next day stones.
        [*Exeunt.*

ACT IV.

SCENE I.— *Without the Walls of Athens.*

Enter TIMON.

  Tim. Let me look back upon thee, O thou wall
That girdlest in those wolves, dive in the earth
And fence not Athens! Matrons, turn incontinent!
Obedience fail in children! slaves and fools,
Pluck the grave wrinkled senate from the bench
And minister in their steads! to general filths
Convert, o' the instant, green virginity,—
Do't in your parent's eyes! bankrupts, hold fast;
Rather than render back, out with your knives
And cut your trusters' throats! bound servants, steal!
Large-handed robbers your grave masters are,

And pill by law! maid, to thy master's bed,—
Thy mistress is o' the brothel! son of sixteen,
Pluck the lin'd crutch from thy old limping sire, •
With it beat out his brains! piety and fear,
Religion to the gods, peace, justice, truth,
Domestic awe, night-rest, and neighbourhood,
Instruction, manners. mysteries, and trades,
Degrees, observances, customs, and laws,
Decline to your confounding contraries,
And let confusion live!—Plagues incident to men,
Your potent and infectious fevers heap
On Athens, ripe for stroke! thou cold sciatica,
Cripple our senators, that their limbs may halt
As lamely as their manners! lust and liberty
Creep in the minds and marrows of our youth,
That 'gainst the stream of virtue they may strive
And drown themselves in riot! itches, blains,
Sow all the Athenian bosoms; and their crop
Be general leprosy! breath infect breath;
That their society, as their friendship, may
Be merely poison! Nothing I'll bear from thee
But nakedness, thou detestable town!
Take thou that too, with multiplying banns!
Timon will to the woods; where he shall find
The unkindest beast more kinder than mankind.
The gods confound,—hear me. ye good gods all,—
The Athenians both within and out that wall!
And grant, as Timon grows, his hate may grow
To the whole race of mankind, high and low!
Amen.   [*Exit.*

SCENE II.—ATHENS.   *A Room in* TIMON'S *House.*

Enter FLAVIUS, *with two or three* Servants.

1 *Serv.* Hear you, master steward, where's our master?
Are we undone? cast off? nothing remaining?

Flav. Alack, my fellows, what should I say to you?
Let me be recorded by the righteous gods,
I am as poor as you.

1 *Serv.*   Such a house broke!
So noble a master fall'n! All gone! and not
One friend to take his fortune by the arm
And go along with him!

2 *Serv.*   As we do turn our backs
To our companion thrown into his grave,

So his familiars from his buried fortunes
Slink all away; leave their false vows with him,
Like empty purses pick'd; and his poor self,
A dedicated beggar to the air,
With his disease of all-shunn'd poverty,
Walks, like contempt, alone.—More of our fellows.

Enter other Servants.

Flav. All broken implements of a ruin'd house.
3 *Serv.* Yet do our hearts wear Timon's livery,
That see I by our faces; we are fellows still,
Serving alike in sorrow: leak'd is our bark;
And we, poor mates, stand on the dying deck
Hearing the surges threat: we must all part
Into this sea of air.
    Flav.   Good fellows all,
The latest of my wealth I'll share amongst you.
Wherever we shall meet, for Timon's sake,
Let's yet be fellows; let's shake our heads, and say,
As 'twere a knell unto our master's fortune,
We have seen better days. Let each take some.
                    [*Giving them money.*
Nay, put out all your hands. Not one word more:
Thus part we rich in sorrow, parting poor.
             [*Servants embrace, and part several ways.*
O, the fierce wretchedness that glory brings us!
Who would not wish to be from wealth exempt
Since riches point to misery and contempt?
Who would be so mock'd with glory? or to live
But in a dream of friendship?
To have his pomp, and all what state compounds,
But only painted, like his varnish'd friends?
Poor honest lord, brought low by his own heart,
Undone by goodness! Strange, unusual blood,
When man's worst sin is, he does too much good!
Who then dares to be half so kind again?
For bounty, that makes gods, does still mar men.
My dearest lord,—bless'd to be most accurs'd,
Rich only to be wretched,—thy great fortunes
Are made thy chief afflictions. Alas, kind lord!
He's flung in rage from this ingrateful seat
Of monstrous friends; nor has he with him to
Supply his life, or that which can command it.
I'll follow and enquire him out:
I'll ever serve his mind with my best will;
Whilst I have gold, I'll be his steward still.   [*Exit.*

SCENE III.—THE WOODS. *Before* TIMON'S *Cave.*

Enter TIMON.

Tim. O blessed breeding sun, draw from the earth
Rotten humidity; below thy sister's orb
Infect the air! Twinn'd brothers of one womb,—
Whose procreation, residence, and birth
Scarce is dividant,—touch them with several fortunes;
The greater scorns the lesser: not nature,
To whom all sores lay siege, can bear great fortune
But by contempt of nature.
Raise me this beggar and deny't that lord;
The senator shall bear contempt hereditary,
The beggar native honour.
It is the pasture lards the rother's sides,
The want that makes him lean. Who dares, who dares,
In purity of manhood stand upright,
And say, *This man 's a flatterer?* if one be,
So are they all; for every grise of fortune
Is smooth'd by that below: the learned pate
Ducks to the golden fool: all is oblique;
There 's nothing level in our cursed natures
But direct villany. Therefore, be abhorr'd
All feasts, societies, and throngs of men!
His semblable, yea, himself Timon disdains:
Destruction fang mankind!—Earth, yield me roots!
                                        [*Digging.*

Who seeks for better of thee, sauce his palate
With thy most operant poison! What is here?
Gold? yellow, glittering, precious gold? No, gods,
I am no idle votarist. Roots, you clear heavens!
Thus much of this will make black, white; foul, fair;
Wrong, right; base, noble; old, young; coward, valiant.
Ha, you gods! why this? what this, you gods? why, this
Will lug your priests and servants from your sides;
Pluck stout men's pillows from below their heads:
This yellow slave
Will knit and break religions; bless the accurs'd;
Make the hoar leprosy ador'd; place thieves,
And give them title, knee, and approbation,
With senators on the bench: this is it
That makes the wappen'd widow wed again;
She whom the spital-house and ulcerous sores
Would cast the gorge at, this embalms and spices
To the April day again. Come, damned earth,

Thou common whore of mankind, that putt'st odds
Among the rout of nations, I will make thee
Do thy right nature.—[*March afar off.*] Ha! a drum:—
    Thou'rt quick,
But yet I'll bury thee: thou'lt go, strong thief,
When gouty keepers of thee cannot stand:—
Nay, stay thou out for earnest.   [*Keeping some gold.*

   Enter ALCIBIADES, *with drum and fife, in warlike*
     manner; PHRYNIA *and* TIMANDRA.

  Alcib.   What art thou there? speak.
  Tim. A beast, as thou art. The canker gnaw thy heart
For showing me again the eyes of man!
  Alcib. What is thy name? Is man so hateful to thee,
That art thyself a man?
  Tim. I am *misanthropos*, and hate mankind.
For thy part, I do wish thou wert a dog,
That I might love thee something.
  Alcib.   I know thee well;
But in thy fortunes am unlearn'd and strange.
  Tim. I know thee too; and more than that I know thee
I not desire to know. Follow thy drum;
With man's blood paint the ground, gules, gules:
Religious canons, civil laws are cruel;
Then what should war be? This fell whore of thine
Hath in her more destruction than thy sword,
For all her cherubin look.
  Phr.   Thy lips rot off!
  Tim. I will not kiss thee; then the rot returns
To thine own lips again.
  Alcib. How came the noble Timon to this change?
  Tim. As the moon does, by wanting light to give:
But then renew I could not, like the moon;
There were no suns to borrow of.
  Alcib.   Noble Timon,
What friendship may I do thee?
  Tim.   .   None, but to
Maintain my opinion.
  Alcib.   What is it, Timon?
  Tim. Promise me friendship, but perform none: if thou
wilt not promise, the gods plague thee, for thou art a man!
if thou dost perform, confound thee, for thou art a man!
  Alcib. I have heard in some sort of thy miseries.
  Tim. Thou saw'st them when I had prosperity.
  Alcib. I see them now; then was a blessed time.
  Tim. As thine is now, held with a brace of harlots.

Timan. Is this the Athenian minion whom the world
Voic'd so regardfully?

Tim. Art thou Timandra?

Timan. Yes.

Tim. Be a whore still! they love thee not that use thee;
Give them diseases, leaving with thee their lust.
Make use of thy salt hours: season the slaves
For tubs and baths; bring down rose-check'd youth to
The tub-fast and the diet.

Timan. Hang thee, monster!

Alcib. Pardon him, sweet Timandra; for his wits
Are drown'd and lost in his calamities.—
I have but little gold of late, brave Timon,
The want whereof doth daily make revolt
In my penurious band: I have heard and griev'd,
How cursed Athens, mindless of thy worth,
Forgetting thy great deeds, when neighbour states,
But for thy sword and fortune, trod upon them,—

Tim. I pr'ythee, beat thy drum, and get thee gone.

Alcib. I am thy friend, and pity thee, dear Timon.

Tim. How dost thou pity him whom thou dost trouble?
I had rather be alone.

Alcib. Why, fare thee well:
Here is some gold for thee.

Tim. Keep it, I cannot eat it.

Alcib. When I have laid proud Athens on a heap,—

Tim. Warr'st thou 'gainst Athens?

Alcib. Ay, Timon, and have cause.

Tim. The gods confound them all in thy conquest;
And thee after, when thou hast conquer'd!

Alcib. Why me, Timon?

Tim. That, by killing of villains,
Thou wast born to conquer my country.
Put up thy gold: go on,—here's gold,—go on;
Be as a planetary plague, when Jove
Will o'er some high-vic'd city hang his poison
In the sick air: let not thy sword skip one:
Pity not honour'd age for his white beard,
He is an usurer: strike me the counterfeit matron:
It is her habit only that is honest,
Herself's a bawd: let not the virgin's cheek
Make soft thy trenchant sword; for those milk paps,
That through the window-bars bore at men's eyes,
Are not within the leaf of pity writ,
But set them down horrible traitors: spare not the babe,
Whose dimpled smiles from fools exhaust their mercy;

Think it a bastard, whom the oracle
Hath doubtfully pronounc'd thy throat shall cut,
And mince it sans remorse: swear against objects;
Put armour on thine ears and on thine eyes;
Whose proof nor yells of mothers, maids, nor babes,
Nor sight of priests in holy vestments bleeding,
Shall pierce a jot. There's gold to pay thy soldiers:
Make large confusion; and, thy fury spent,
Confounded be thyself! Speak not, be gone.

    Alcib. Hast thou gold yet? I'll take the gold thou giv'st
      me,
Not all thy counsel.

    Tim. Dost thou, or dost thou not, heaven's curse upon
      thee!

    Phr. and Timan. Give us some gold, good Timon: hast
      thou more?

    Tim. Enough to make a whore forswear her trade,
And to make whores, a bawd. Hold up, you sluts,
Your aprons mountant: you are not oathable,—
Although I know you'll swear, terribly swear,
Into strong shudders and to heavenly agues,
The immortal gods that hear you,—spare your oaths,
I'll trust to your conditions: be whores still;
And he whose pious breath seeks to convert you,
Be strong in whore, allure him, burn him up;
Let your close fire predominate his smoke,
And be no turncoats: yet may your pains six months
Be quite contrary: and thatch your poor thin roofs
With burdens of the dead;—some that were hang'd,
No matter:—wear them, betray with them: whore still;
Paint till a horse may mire upon your face:
A pox of wrinkles!

    Phr. and Timan. Well, more gold.—What then?—
Believ't, that we'll do anything for gold.

    Tim. Consumptions sow
In hollow bones of man; strike their sharp shins,
And mar men's spurring. Crack the lawyer's voice,
That he may never more false title plead,
Nor sound his quillets shrilly: hoar the flamen,
That scolds against the quality of flesh
And not believes himself: down with the nose,
Down with it flat; take the bridge quite away
Of him that, his particular to foresee,
Smells from the general weal: make curl'd-pate ruffians
      bald;
And let the unscarr'd braggarts of the war

Derive some pain from you: plague all;
That your activity may defeat and quell
The source of all erection.—There's more gold:—
Do you damn others and let this damn you,
And ditches grave you all!

    Phr. and Timan. More counsel with more money, bounte-
        ous Timon.

    Tim. More whore, more mischief first; I have given you
        earnest.

    Alcib. Strike up the drum towards Athens! Farewell
        Timon:

If I thrive well I'll visit thee again.

    Tim. If I hope well I'll never see thee more.

    Alcib. I never did thee harm.

    Tim. Yes, thou spok'st well of me.

    Alcib.   Call'st thou that harm?

    Tim. Men daily find it. Get thee away, and take

Thy beagles with thee.

    Alcib.   We but offend him.—Strike!

        [*Drum beats. Exeunt* ALCIB., PHR., *and* TIM.

    Tim. That nature, being sick of man's unkindness,

Should yet be hungry!—Common mother, thou,   [*Digging.*
Whose womb unmeasurable and infinite breast
Teems and feeds all; whose self-same mettle,
Whereof thy proud child, arrogant man, is puff'd,
Engenders the black toad and adder blue,
The gilded newt and eyeless venom'd worm,
With all the abhorred births below crisp heaven
Whereon Hyperion's quickening fire doth shine;
Yield him, who all thy human sons doth hate,
From forth thy plenteous bosom, one poor root!
Ensear thy fertile and conceptious womb,
Let it no more bring out ingrateful man!
Go great with tigers, dragons, wolves, and bears;
Teem with new monsters, whom thy upward face
Hath to the marbled mansion all above
Never presented!—O, a root,—dear thanks!
Dry up thy marrows, vines, and plough-torn leas;
Whereof ingrateful man, with liquorish draughts
And morsels unctuous, greases his pure mind,
That from it all consideration slips!

Enter APEMANTUS.

More man? plague, plague!

    Apem. I was directed hither: men report
Thou dost affect my manners, and dost use them.

Tim. 'Tis, then, because thou dost not keep a dog
Whom I would imitate: consumption catch thee!
Apem. This is in thee a nature but affected;
A poor unmanly melancholy sprung
From change of fortune. Why this spade? this place?
This slave-like habit? and these looks of care?
Thy flatterers yet wear silk, drink wine, lie soft;
Hug their diseas'd perfumes, and have forgot
That ever Timon was. Shame not these woods
By putting on the cunning of a carper.
Be thou a flatterer now, and seek to thrive
By that which has undone thee: hinge thy knee,
And let his very breath whom thou'lt observe
Blow off thy cap: praise his most vicious strain,
And call it excellent: thou wast told thus;
Thou gav'st thine ears, like tapsters that bid welcome,
To knaves and all approachers: 'tis most just
That thou turn rascal; hadst thou wealth again
Rascals should have't. Do not assume my likeness.
　Tim. Were I like thee, I'd throw away myself.
　Apem. Thou hast cast away thyself, being like thyself;
A madman so long, now a fool. What, think'st
That the bleak air, thy boisterous chamberlain,
Will put thy shirt on warm? Will these moss'd trees,
That have outliv'd the eagle, page thy heels,
And skip when thou point'st out? Will the cold brook,
Candied with ice, caudle thy morning taste
To cure thy o'ernight's surfeit? call the creatures,—
Whose naked natures live in all the spite
Of wreakful heaven; whose bare unhoused trunks,
To the conflicting elements expos'd,
Answer mere nature,—bid them flatter thee;
O, thou shalt find,—
　　Tim.　　　　　　A fool of thee: depart.
　Apem. I love thee better now than e'er I did.
　Tim. I hate thee worse.
　Apem.　　　　　Why?
　Tim.　　　　　　　Thou flatter'st misery.
　Apem. I flatter not; but say thou art a caitiff.
　Tim. Why dost thou seek me out?
　Apem.　　　　　　　　To vex thee.
　Tim. Always a villain's office or a fool's.
Dost please thyself in't?
　Apem.　　　　Ay.
　Tim.　　　　　　What! a knave too?
　Apem. If thou didst put this sour-cold habit on

To castigate thy pride, 'twere well: but thou
Dost it enforcedly; thou'dst courtier be again
Wert thou not beggar. Willing misery
Outlives incertain pomp, is crown'd before
The one is filling still, never complete;
The other, at high wish: best state, contentless,
Hath a distracted and most wretched being,
Worse than the worst, content.
Thou should'st desire to die, being miserable.
    Tim. Not by his breath that is more miserable.
Thou art a slave, whom Fortune's tender arm
With favour never clasp'd; but bred a dog.
Hadst thou, like us from our first swath, proceeded
The sweet degrees that this brief world affords
To such as may the passive drugs of it
Freely command, thou wouldst have plung'd thyself
In general riot; melted down thy youth
In different beds of lust; and never learn'd
The icy precepts of respect, but follow'd
The sugar'd game before thee. But myself,
Who had the world as my confectionary;
The mouths, the tongues, the eyes, and hearts of men
At duty, more than I could frame employment;
That numberless upon me stuck, as leaves
Do on the oak, have with one winter's brush
Fell from their boughs, and left me open, bare
For every storm that blows;—I, to bear this,
That never knew but better, is some burden:
Thy nature did commence in sufferance, time
Hath made thee hard in't. Why shouldst thou hate men?
They never flatter'd thee: what hast thou given?
If thou wilt curse, thy father, that poor rag,
Must be thy subject; who, in spite, put stuff
To some she beggar, and compounded thee
Poor rogue hereditary. Hence! be gone!—
If thou hadst not been born the worst of men,
Thou hadst been a knave and flatterer.
    Apem.   Art thou proud yet?
    Tim. Ay, that I am not thee.
    Apem.   I, that I was
No prodigal.
    Tim.   I, that I am one now:
Were all the wealth I have shut up in thee,
I'd give thee leave to hang it. Get thee gone.—
That the whole life of Athens were in this!
Thus would I eat it.   [*Eating a root.*

Apem.　　　　　Here; I will mend thy feast.

　　　　　　　　　[*Offering him something.*

Tim. First mend my company, take away thyself.

Apem. So I shall mend mine own by the lack of thine.

Tim. 'Tis not well mended so, it is but botch'd;
If not, I would it were.

Apem. What wouldst thou have to Athens?

Tim. Thee thither in a whirlwind. If thou wilt,
Tell them there I have gold; look, so I have.

Apem. Here is no use for gold.

Tim.　　　　　The best and truest:
For here it sleeps, and does no hired harm.

Apem. Where ly'st o' nights, Timon?

Tim.　　　　　Under that's above me.
Where feed'st thou o' days, Apemantus?

Apem. Where my stomach finds meat; or, rather, where
I eat it.

Tim. Would poison were obedient, and knew my mind!

Apem. Where wouldst thou send it!

Tim. To sauce thy dishes.

Apem. The middle of humanity thou never knewest,
but the extremity of both ends: when thou wast in thy
gilt and thy perfume they mocked thee for too much
curiosity; in thy rags thou knowest none, but art despised
for the contrary. There's a medlar for thee, eat it.

Tim. On what I hate I feed not.

Apem. Dost hate a medlar?

Tim. Ay, though it look like thee.

Apem. An thou hadst hated medlars sooner, thou shouldst
have loved thyself better now. What man didst thou ever
know unthrift that was beloved after his means?

Tim. Who without those means thou talkest of didst
thou ever know beloved?

Apem. Myself.

Tim. I understand thee; thou hadst some means to keep
a dog.

Apem. What things in the world canst thou nearest
compare to thy flatterers?

Tim. Women nearest; but men, men are the things
themselves. What wouldst thou do with the world, Apemantus, if it lay in thy power?

Avem. Give it the beasts, to be rid of the men.

Tim. Wouldst thou have thyself fall in the confusion
of men, and remain a beast with the beasts?

Apem. Ay, Timon.

Tim. A beastly ambition, which the gods grant thee t'

attain to! If thou wert the lion, the fox would beguile thee: if thou wert the lamb, the fox would eat thee: if thou wert the fox, the lion would suspect thee, when, peradventure, thou wert accused by the ass: if thou wert the ass, thy dullness would torment thee; and still thou livedst but as a breakfast to the wolf: if thou wert the wolf, thy greediness would afflict thee, and oft thou shouldst hazard thy life for thy dinner: wert thou the unicorn, pride and wrath would confound thee, and make thine own self the conquest of thy fury: wert thou a bear, thou wouldst be killed by the horse; wert thou a horse, thou wouldst be seized by the leopard; wert thou a leopard, thou wert german to the lion, and the spots of thy kindred were jurors on thy life: all thy safety were remotion; and thy defence absence. What beast couldst thou be, that were not subject to a beast? and what a beast art thou already, that seest not thy loss in transformation!

Apem. If thou couldst please me with speaking to me, thou might'st have hit upon it here: the commonwealth of Athens is become a forest of beasts.

Tim. How has the ass broke the wall, that thou art out of the city?

Apem. Yonder comes a poet and a painter: the plague of company light upon thee! I will fear to catch it, and give way: when I know not what else to do, I'll see thee again.

Tim. When there is nothing living but thee, thou shalt be welcome. I had rather be a beggar's dog than Apemantus.

Apem. Thou art the cap of all the fools alive.

Tim. Would thou wert clean enough to spit upon!

Apem. A plague on thee, thou art too bad to curse!

Tim. All villains that do stand by thee are pure.

Apem. There is no leprosy but what thou speak'st.

Tim. If I name thee.—
I'll beat thee, but I should infect my hands.

Apem. I would my tongue could rot them off!

Tim. Away, thou issue of a mangy dog!
Choler does kill me that thou art alive;
I swoon to see thee.

Apem.   Would thou wouldst burst!

Tim.   Away,
Thou tedious rogue! I am sorry I shall lose
A stone by thee.   [*Throws a stone at him.*

Apem.   Beast!

Tim.   Slave!

Apem.   Toad!

Tim.   Rogue, rogue, rogue!
                    [APEM. *retreats backward, as going.*
I am sick of this false world; and will love naught
But even the mere necessities upon't.
Then, Timon, presently prepare thy grave;
Lie where the light foam of the sea may beat
Thy grave-stone daily: make thine epitaph,
That death in me at others' lives may laugh.
O thou sweet king-killer and dear divorce
                    [*Looking on the gold.*
'Twixt natural son and sire! thou bright defiler
Of Hymen's purest bed! thou valiant Mars!
Thou ever young, fresh, lov'd, and delicate wooer,
Whose blush doth thaw the consecrated snow
That lies on Dian's lap! thou visible god,
That solder'st close impossibilities,
And mak'st them kiss! that speak'st with every tongue
To every purpose! O thou touch of hearts!
Think, thy slave, man, rebels: and by thy virtue
Set them into confounding odds, that beasts
May have the world in empire!
    Apem.   Would 'twere so!—
But not till I am dead.—I'll say thou'st gold:
Thou wilt be throng'd to shortly.
    Tim.   Throng'd to?
    Apem.   Ay.
    Tim. Thy back, I pr'ythee.
    Apem.   Live, and love thy misery!
    Tim. Long live so, and so die! [*Exit* APEMANTUS.] I am
        quit.
More things like men?—Eat, Timon, and abhor them.

Enter Thieves.

1 *Thief.* Where should he have this gold? It is some poor
fragment, some slender ort of his remainder: the mere
want of gold and the falling-from of his friends drove him
into this melancholy.

2 *Thief.* It is noised he hath a mass of treasure.

3 *Thief.* Let us make the assay upon him: if he care not
for't, he will supply us easily; if he covetously reserve it,
how shall 's get it?

2 *Thief.* True; for he bears it not about **him**, 'tis hid.

1 *Thief.* Is not this he?

Thieves. Where?

2 *Thief.* 'Tis his description.

3 *Thief.* He; I know him.

Thieves. Save thee, Timon.

Tim. Now, thieves?

Thieves. Soldiers, not thieves.

Tim. Both too; and women's sons.

Thieves. We are not thieves, but men that much do want.

Tim. Your greatest want is, you want much of meat.
Why should you want? Behold, the earth hath roots;
Within this mile break forth a hundred springs:
The oaks bear mast, the briers scarlet hips;
The bounteous housewife, nature, on each bush
Lays her full mess before you. Want! why want?

1 *Thief.* We cannot live on grass, on berries, water,
As beasts and birds and fishes.

Tim. Nor on the beasts themselves, the birds, and fishes;
You must eat men. Yet thanks I must you con,
That you are thieves profess'd; that you work not
In holier shapes: for there is boundless theft
In limited professions. Rascal thieves,
Here's gold. Go, suck the subtle blood o' the grape
Till the high fever seethe your blood to froth,
And so 'scape hanging: trust not the physician;
His antidotes are poison, and he slays
More than you rob: take wealth and lives together;
Do villany, do, since you protest to do't,
Like workmen. I'll example you with thievery:
The sun 's a thief, and with his great attraction
Robs the vast sea: the moon 's an arrant thief,
And her pale fire she snatches from the sun:
The sea 's a thief, whose liquid surge resolves
The moon into salt tears: the earth 's a thief,
That feeds and breeds by a composture stolen
From general excrement: each thing 's a thief:
The laws, your curb and whip, in their rough power
Have uncheck'd theft. Love not yourselves; away,
Rob one another;—there's more gold;—cut throats;
All that you meet are thieves. To Athens go,
Break open shops; nothing can you steal
But thieves do lose it: steal not less for this
I give you; and gold confound you howsoe'er!
Amen.   [TIMON *retires to his cave.*

3 *Thief.* Has almost charmed me from my profession by
persuading me to it.

1 *Thief.* 'Tis in the malice of mankind that he thus advises
us; not to have us thrive in our mystery.

2 *Thief.* I'll believe him as an enemy, and give over my
trade.

1 *Thief.* Let us first see peace in Athens: there is no
time so miserable but a man may be true. [*Exeunt* Thieves.

Enter FLAVIUS.

Flav. O you gods!
Is yond despis'd and ruinous man my lord?
Full of decay and failing? O monument
And wonder of good deeds evilly bestow'd!
What an alteration of honour
Has desperate want made!
What viler thing upon the earth than friends
Who can bring noblest minds to basest ends!
How rarely does it meet with this time's guise,
When man was wish'd to love his enemies!
Grant I may ever love, and rather woo
Those that would mischief me than those that do!—
Has caught me in his eye: I will present
My honest grief unto him; and, as my lord,
Still serve him with my life.—My dearest master!

TIMON *comes forward from his cave.*

Tim. Away! what art thou?
Flav.   Have you forgot me, sir?
Tim. Why dost ask that? I have forgot all men;
Then, if thou grant'st thou'rt a man, I have forgot thee.
Flav. An honest poor servant of yours.
Tim. Then I know thee not:
I ne'er had honest man about me, I; all
I kept were knaves, to serve in meat to villains.
Flav. The gods are witness,
Ne'er did poor steward wear a truer grief
For his undone lord than mine eyes for you.
Tim. What, dost thou weep?—Come nearer;—then I love
          thee
Because thou art a woman, and disclaim'st
Flinty mankind; whose eyes do never give
But thorough lust and laughter. Pity's sleeping:
Strange times, that weep with laughing, not with weeping!
Flav. I beg of you to know me, good my lord,
To accept my grief, and, whilst this poor wealth lasts,
To entertain me as your steward still.
Tim. Had I a steward
So true, so just, and now so comfortable?
It almost turns my dangerous nature mild.
Let me behold thy face. Surely, this man
Was born of woman.—

Forgive my general and exceptless rashness,
You perpetual-sober gods! I do proclaim
One honest man,—mistake me not,—but one;
No more, I pray,—and he's a steward.—
How fain would I have hated all mankind!
And thou redeem'st thyself: but all, save thee,
I fell with curses.
Methinks thou art more honest now than wise;
For by oppressing and betraying me
Thou might'st have sooner got another service:
For many so arrive at second masters
Upon their first lord's neck   But tell me true,—
For I must ever doubt, though ne'er so sure,—
Is not thy kindness subtle, covetous,
If not a usuring kindness, and, as rich men deal gifts,
Expecting in return twenty for one?
      Flav. No, my most worthy master; in whose breast
Doubt and suspect, alas, are plac'd to late:
You should have fear'd false times when you did feast:
Suspect still comes where an estate is least.
That which I show, heaven knows, is merely love,
Duty, and zeal to your unmatched mind,
Care of your food and living; and, believe it,
My most honour'd lord,
For any benefit that points to me,
Either in hope or present, I'd exchange
For this one wish,—that you had power and wealth
To requite me, by making rich yourself.
      Tim. Look thee, 'tis so!—Thou singly honest man,
Here, take:—the gods, out of my misery,
Have sent thee treasure. Go, live rich and happy;
But thus condition'd:—thou shalt build from men;
Hate all, curse all; show charity to none;
But let the famish'd flesh slide from the bone
Ere thou relieve the beggar: give to dogs
What thou deny'st to men; let prisons swallow 'em,
Debts wither 'em to nothing: be men like blasted woods,
And may diseases lick up their false bloods!
And so, farewell and thrive.
      Flav.   O, let me stay,
And comfort you, my master.
      Tim.   If thou hat'st curses,
Stay not; but fly whilst thou'rt bless'd and free:
Ne'er see thou man, and let me ne'er see thee.
                              [*Exeunt severally.*

ACT V.

Enter Poet *and* Painter; Timon *watching them from his cave.*

Pain. As I took note of the place, it cannot be far where he abides.

Poet. What's to be thought of him? Does the rumour hold for true that he's so full of gold?

Pain. Certain: Alcibiades reports it; Phrynia and Timandra had gold of him: he likewise enriched poor straggling soldiers with great quantity: 'tis said he gave unto his steward a mighty sum.

Poet. Then this breaking of his has been but a try for his friends.

Pain. Nothing else: you shall see him a palm in Athens again, and flourish with the highest Therefore 'tis not amiss we tender our loves to him, in this supposed distress of his: it will show honestly in us; and is very likely to load our purposes with what they travail for, if it be a just and true report that goes of his having.

Poet. What have you now to present unto him?

Pain. Nothing at this time but my visitation: only I will promise him an excellent piece.

Poet. I must serve him so too,—tell him of an intent that's coming toward him.

Pain. Good as the best. Promising is the very air o' the time: it opens the eyes of expectation: performance is ever the duller for his act; and but in the plainer and simpler kind of people the deed of saying is quite out of use. To promise is most courtly and fashionable: performance is a kind of will or testament which argues a great sickness in his judgment that makes it.

Tim. Excellent workman! thou canst not paint a man so bad as is thyself.

Poet. I am thinking what I shall say I have provided for him: it must be a personating of himself: a satire against the softness of prosperity, with a discovery of the infinite flatteries that follow youth and opulency.

Tim. Must thou needs stand for a villain in thine own work? wilt thou whip thine own faults in other men? Do so, I have gold for thee.

Poet. Nay, let's seek him:

Then do we sin against our own estate
When we may profit meet and come too late.
 Pain. True;
When the day serves, before black-corner'd night,
Find what thou want'st by free and offer'd light.
Come.
 Tim. I'll meet you at the turn. What **a god's gold**,
That he is worshipp'd in a baser temple
Than where swine feed!
'Tis thou that rigg'st the bark, and plough'st the foam:
Settlest admired reverence in a slave:
To thee be worship! and thy saints for aye
Be crown'd with plagues, that thee alone obe
Fit I meet them.   *[Advancing from his cave.*
 Poet. Hail, worthy Timon!
 Pain.   Our late noble master!
 Tim. Have I once liv'd to see two honest men?
 Poet. Sir,
Having often of your open bounty tasted,
Hearing you were retir'd, your friends fall'n off,
Whose thankless natures,—O abhorred spirits!—
Not all the whips of heaven are large enough:
What! to you,
Whose star-like nobleness gave life and influence
To their whole being! I'm rapt, and cannot cover
The monstrous bulk of this ingratitude
With any size of words.
 Tim. Let it go naked, men may see't the better:
You that are honest, by being what you are,
Make them best seen and known.
 Pain.   He and myself
Have travail'd in the great shower of your gifts,
And sweetly felt it.
 Tim.   Ay, you are honest men.
 Pain. We are hither come to offer you our service.
 Tim. Most honest men! Why, how shall I requite you?
Can you eat roots, and drink cold water? no.
 Both. What we can do, we'll do, to do you service.
 Tim. Ye're honest men: ye've heard that I have gold;
I am sure you have: speak truth; ye're honest men.
 Pain. So it is said, my noble lord: but therefore
Came not my friend nor I.
 Tim. Good honest men!—Thou draw'st a counterfeit
Best in all Athens: thou'rt indeed the best;
Thou counterfeit'st most lively.
 Pain.   So, so, my lord.

Tim. E'en so, sir, as I say.—And, for thy fiction,
                              [*To the* Poet.
Why, thy verse swells with stuff so fine and smooth
That thou art even natural in thine art.—
But for all this, my honest-natur'd friends,
I must needs say you have a little fault:
Marry, 'tis not monstrous in you; neither wish I
You take much pains to mend.

    Both.   Beseech your honour
To make it known to us.

    Tim.   You'll take it ill.

    Both. Most thankfully, my lord.

    Tim.   Will you indeed?

    Both. Doubt it not, worthy lord.

    Tim. There's never a one of you but trusts a knave
That mightily deceives you.

    Both.   Do we, my lord?

    Tim. Ay, and you hear him cog, see him dissemble,
Know his gross patchery, love him, feed him,
Keep in your bosom: yet remain assur'd
That he's a made-up villain.

    Pain. I know none such, my lord.

    Poet.   Nor I.

    Tim. Look you, I love you well; I'll give you gold
Rid me these villains from your companies:
Hang them or stab them, drown them in a draught,
Confound them by some course, and come to me,
I'll give you gold enough.

    Both. Name them, my lord; let's know them.

    Tim. You that way, and you this,—but two in company:
Each man apart, all single and alone,
Yet an arch-villain keeps him company.
If where thou art two villains shall not be, [*To the* Painter.
Come not near him.—If thou wouldst not reside
                              [*To the* Poet.
But where one villain is, then him abandon.—
Hence! pack! there's gold,—ye came for gold, ye slaves:
You have done work for me, there's payment: hence!—
You are an alchemist, make gold of that:—
Out, rascal dogs!   [*Exit, beating and driving them out.*

      Enter FLAVIUS *and two* Senators.

    Flav. It is in vain that you would speak with Timon;
For he is set so only to himself
That nothing but himself, which looks like man,
Is friendly with him.

1 *Sen.*   Bring us to his cave:
It is our part and promise to the Athenians
To speak with Timon.
    2 *Sen.*   At all times alike
Men are not still the same: 'twas time and griefs
That fram'd him thus: time, with his fairer hand,
Offering the fortunes of his former days,
The former man may make him.   Bring us to him,
And chance it as it may.
    Flav.   Here is his cave.—
Peace and content be here! Lord Timon! Timon!
Look out, and speak to friends; the Athenians,
By two of their most reverend senate, greet thee:
Speak to them, noble Timon.

        TIMON *comes from his Cave.*

    Tim. Thou sun, that comfort'st, burn!—Speak, and be
        hang'd:
For each true word a blister! and each false
Be as a cauterizing to the root o' the tongue,
Consuming it with speaking!
    1 *Sen.*   Worthy Timon.—
    Tim. Of none but such as you, and you of Timon.
    1 *Sen.* The senators of Athens greet thee, Timon.
    Tim. I thank them; and would send them back the
        plague,
Could I but catch it for them.
    1 *Sen.*   O, forget
What we are sorry for ourselves in thee.
The senators with one consent of love
Entreat thee back to Athens; who have thought
On special dignities, which vacant lie
For thy best use and wearing.
    2 *Sen.*   They confess
Toward thee forgetfulness too general, gross:
Which now the public body,—which doth seldom
Play the recanter,—feeling in itself
A lack of Timon's aid, hath sense withal
Of its own fail, restraining aid to Timon;
And send forth us to make their sorrow'd render,
Together with a recompense more fruitful
Than their offence can weigh down by the dram;
Ay, even such heaps and sums of love and wealth
As shall to thee blot out what wrongs were theirs,
And write in thee the figures of their love,
Ever to read them thine.

Tim.   You witch me in it;
Surprise me to the very brink of tears:
Lend me a fool's heart and a woman s eyes,
And I'll beweep these comforts, worthy senators.

1 *Sen.* Therefore so please thee to return with us,
And of our Athens,—thine and ours,—to take
The captainship, thou shalt be met with thanks,
Allow'd with absolute power, and thy good name
Live with authority:—so soon we shall drive back
Of Alcibiades the approaches wild;
Who, like a boar too savage, doth root up
His country's peace.

2 *Sen.*   And shakes his threat'ning sword
Against the walls of Athens.

1 *Sen.*   Therefore, Timon,—

Tim. Well, sir, I will; therefore, I will, sir; thus,—
If Alcibiades kill my countrymen,
Let Alcibiades know this of Timon,
That Timon cares not. But if he sack fair Athens,
And take our goodly aged men by the beards,
Giving our holy virgins to the stain
Of contumelious, beastly, mad-brain'd war;
Then let him know,—and tell him Timon speaks it,
In pity of our aged and our youth,—
I cannot choose but tell him that I care not,
And let him tak't at worst; for their knives care not,
While you have throats to answer; for myself,
There's not a whittle in the unruly camp
But I do prize it at my love, before
The reverend'st throat in Athens. So I leave you
To the protection of the prosperous gods,
As thieves to keepers.

Flav.   Stay not, all's in vain.

Tim. Why, I was writing of my epitaph;
It will be seen to-morrow: my long sickness
Of health and living now begins to mend,
And nothing brings me all things. Go, live still;
Be Alcibiades your plague, you his,
And last so long enough!

1 *Sen.*   We speak in vain.

Tim. But yet I love my country; and am not
One that rejoices in the common wreck,
As common bruit doth put it.

1 *Sen.*   That's well spoke.

Tim. Commend me to my loving countrymen,—   [them.

1 *Sen.* These words become your lips as they pass thorough

2 *Sen.* And enter in our ears like great triumphers
In their applauding gates.
 Tim.   Commend me to them;
And tell them that, to ease them of their griefs,
Their fears of hostile strokes, their aches, losses,
Their pangs of love, with other incident throes
That nature's fragile vessel doth sustain
In life's uncertain voyage, I will some kindness do them,—
I'll teach them to prevent wild Alcibiades' wrath.
 1 *Sen.* I like this well; he will return again.
 Tim. I have a tree, which grows here in my close,
That mine own use invites me to cut down,
And shortly must I fell it: tell my friends,
Tell Athens, in the sequence of degree,
From high to low throughout, that whoso please
To stop affliction, let him take his halter,
Come hither, ere my tree hath felt the axe,
And hang himself.—I pray you, do my greeting. [him.
 Fav. Trouble him no further; thus you still shall find
 Tim. Come not to me again: but say to Athens,
Timon hath made his everlasting mansion
Upon the beached verge of the salt flood;
Who once a day with his embossed froth
The turbulent surge shall cover: thither come,
And let my grave-stone be your oracle.—
Lips, let sour words go by and language end:
What is amiss, plague and infection mend!
Graves only be men's works and death their gain!
Sun, hide thy beams! Timon hath done his reign.
        [*Retires to his cave.*
 1 *Sen.* His discontents are unremovably
Coupled to nature.
 2 *Sen.* Our hope in him is dead: let us return,
And strain what other means is left unto us
In our dear peril.
 1 *Sen.*   It requires swift foot. [*Exeunt.*

———

SCENE II.—*The Walls of Athens.*

Enter two Senators *and a* Messenger.

 1 *Sen.* Thou hast painfully discover'd: are his files
As full as thy report?
 Mess.   I have spoke the least:
Besides, his expedition promises
Present approach.

2 Sen. We stand much hazard if they bring not Timon.

Mess. I met a courier, one mine ancient friend;
Whom, though in general part we were oppos'd,
Yet our old love had a particular force,
And made us speak like friends:—this man was riding
From Alcibiades to Timon's cave
With letters of entreaty, which imported
His fellowship i' the cause against your city,
In part for his sake mov'd.

1 Sen.   Here come our brothers.

Enter Senators *from* TIMON

3 Sen. No talk of Timon, nothing of him expect.—
The enemies' drum is heard, and fearful scouring
Doth choke the air with dust: in, and prepare:
Ours is the fall, I fear; our foes the snare.   *[Exeunt*

SCENE III.—THE WOODS. TIMON'S *Cave, and a
rude Tomb scen.*

Enter a Soldier *seeking* TIMON.

Sold. By all description this should be the place.
Who 's here? speak, ho!—No answer?—What is this?
Timon is dead, who hath outstretch'd his span:
Some beast rear'd this; there does not live a man.
Dead, sure; and this his grave,—what 's on this tomb
I cannot read; the character I'll take with wax:
Our captain hath in every figure skill,
An ag'd interpreter, though young in days:
Before proud Athens he 's set down by this,
Whose fall the mark of his ambition is.   *[Exit.*

SCENE IV.—*Before the Walls of Athens.*

Trumpets sound. Enter ALCIBIADES *and* Forces.

Alcib. Sound to this coward and lascivious town
Our terrible approach.   *[A parley sounded.*

Enter Senators *on the Walls.*

Till now you have gone on, and fill'd the time
With all licentious measure, making your wills
The scope of justice; till now, myself, and such
As slept within the shadow of your power,
Have wander'd with our travers'd arms, and breath'd

Our sufferance vainly.   Now the time is flush,
When crouching marrow, in the bearer strong,
Cries, of itself. *No more:* now breathless wrong
Shall sit and pant in your great chairs of ease;
And pursy insolence shall break his wind
With fear and horrid flight.
    1 *Sen.*   Noble and young,
When thy first griefs were but a mere conceit,
Ere thou hadst power or we had cause of fear,
We sent to thee, to give thy rages balm,
To wipe out our ingratitude with loves
Above their quantity.
    2 *Sen.*   So did **we woo**
Transformed Timon to our city's love,
By humble message and by promis'd means;
We were not all unkind, nor all deserve
The common stroke of war.
    1 *Sen.*   These walls of ours
Were not erected by their hands from whom
You have receiv'd your griefs: nor are they such
That these great towers, trophies, and schools should **fall**
For private faults in them.
    2 *Sen.*   Nor are they living
Who were the motives that you first went out;
Shame, that they wanted cunning, in excess,
Hath broke their hearts.   March, noble lord,
Into our city with thy banners spread:
By decimation and a tithed death,—
If thy revenges hunger for that food
Which nature loathes,—take thou the destin'd **tenth;**
And by the hazard of the spotted die
Let die the spotted.
    1 *Sen.*   All have not offended;
For those that were, it is not square to take,
On those that are, revenges: crimes, like lands,
Are not inherited.   Then, dear countryman,
Bring in thy ranks, but leave without thy rage:
Spare thy Athenian cradle, and those kin
Which, in the bluster of thy wrath, must fall
With those that have offended: like a shepherd
Approach the fold and cull the infected forth,
But kill not all together
    2 *Sen.*   What thou wilt,
Thou rather shalt enforce it with thy smile
Than hew to't with thy sword.
    1 *Sen.*   Set but thy **foot**

Against our rampir'd gates and they shall ope;
So thou wilt send thy gentle heart before
To say thou'lt enter friendly.
    2 Sen.   Throw thy glove,
Or any token of thine honour else,
That thou wilt use the wars as thy redress,
And not as our confusion, all thy powers
Shall make their harbour in our town till we
Have seal'd thy full desire.
    Alcib.   Then there 's my glove;
Descend, and open your uncharged ports;
Those enemies of Timon's and mine own,
Whom you yourselves shall set out for reproof,
Fall, and no more: and,—to atone your fears
With my more noble meaning,—not a man
Shall pass his quarter or offend the stream
Of regular justice in your city's bounds,
But shall be render'd to your public laws
At heaviest answer.
    Both.   'Tis most nobly spoken.
    Alcib. Descend, and keep your words.
           [*The* Senators *descend and open the gates.*

Enter a Soldier.

    Sol. My noble general, Timon is dead;
Entomb'd upon the very hem o' the sea;
And on his grave-stone this insculpture, which
With wax I brought away, whose soft impression
Interprets for my poor ignorance.
    Alcib. [reads.] *Here lies a wretched corse, of wretched*
        soul bereft:
Seek not my name: a plague consume you wicked caitiffs left!
Here lie I, Timon; who, alive, all living men did hate:
Pass by, and curse thy fill; but pass, and stay not here thy
These well express in thee thy latter spirits: [*gait.*
Though thou abhorr'dst in us our human griefs,
Scorn'dst our brain's flow, and those our droplets which
From niggard nature fall, yet rich conceit
Taught thee to make vast Neptune weep for aye
On thy low grave, on faults forgiven.   Dead
Is noble Timon : of whose memory
Hereafter more.—Bring me into your city,
And I will use the olive with my sword :
Make war breed peace; make peace stint war; make each
Prescribe to other, as each other's leech.
Let our drums strike.   [*Exeunt.*

CORIOLANUS.

PERSONS REPRESENTED.

CAIUS MARCIUS CORIOLANUS, *a noble Roman.*
TITUS LARTIUS, }
COMINIUS,   } *Generals against the Volscians.*
MENENIUS AGRIPPA, *Friend to* CORIOLANUS.
SICINIUS VELUTUS, }
JUNIUS BRUTUS,   } *Tribunes of the People.*
YOUNG MARCIUS, *Son to* CORIOLANUS.
A Roman Herald.
TULLUS AUFIDIUS, *General of the Volscians.*
Lieutenant *to* AUFIDIUS.
Conspirators *with* AUFIDIUS.
A Citizen of Antium.
Two Volscian Guards.

VOLUMNIA, *Mother to* CORIOLANUS.
VIRGILIA, *Wife to* CORIOLANUS.
VALERIA, *Friend to* VIRGILIA.
Gentlewoman *attending on* VIRGILIA.

Roman *and* Volscian Senators, Patricians, Ædiles, Lictors,
    Soldiers, Citizens, Messengers, Servants *to* AUFIDIUS,
    and other Attendants.

SCENE,—*Partly in* ROME, *and partly in the Territories of
    the Volscians and Antiates.*

CORIOLANUS.

---◆---

ACT I.

SCENE I.—ROME. *A Street.*

Enter a company of mutinous Citizens, *with staves, clubs, and other weapons.*

1 *Cit.* Before we proceed any further, hear me speak.

Citizens. Speak, speak.

1 *Cit.* You are all resolved rather to die than to famish?

Citizens. Resolved, resolved.

1 *Cit.* First, you know Caius Marcius is chief enemy to the people.

Citizens. We know't, we know't.

1 *Cit.* Let us kill him, and we'll have corn at our own price. Is't a verdict?

Citizens. No more talking on't; let it be done: away, away!

2 *Cit.* One word, good citizens.

1 *Cit.* We are accounted poor citizens; the patricians good. What authority surfeits on would relieve us: if they would yield us but the superfluity, while it were wholesome, we might guess they relieved us humanely; but they think we are too dear: the leanness that afflicts us, the object of our misery, is an inventory to particularize their abundance; our sufferance is a gain to them.—Let us revenge this with our pikes ere we become rakes: for the gods know I speak this in hunger for bread, not in thirst for revenge.

2 *Cit.* Would you proceed especially against Caius Marcius?   ′

1 *Cit.* Against him first: he's a very dog to the commonalty.

2 *Cit.* Consider you what services he has done for his country?

1 *Cit.* Very well; and could be content to give him good report for't, but that he pays himself with being proud.

2 Cit. Nay, but speak not maliciously.

1 Cit. I say unto you, what he hath done famously he did it to that end : though soft-conscienced men can be content to say it was for his country, he did it to please his mother, and to be partly proud ; which he is, even to the altitude of his virtue.

2 Cit. What he cannot help in his nature you account a vice in him. You must in no way say he is covetous.

1 Cit. If I must not, I need not be barren of accusations ; he hath faults, with surplus, to tire in repetition. [*Shouts within.*] What shouts are these? The other side o'the city is risen : why stay we prating here? to the Capitol!

Citizens. Come, come.

1 Cit. Soft! who comes here?

2 Cit. Worthy Menenius Agrippa; one that hath always loved the people.

1 Cit. He's one honest enough ; would all the rest were so!

Enter Menenius Agrippa.

Men. What work's, my countrymen, in hand? where go
    you
With bats and clubs? the matter? speak, I pray you.

1 Cit. Our business is not unknown to the senate; they have had inkling this fortnight what we intend to do, which now we'll show 'em in deeds. They say poor suitors have strong breaths; they shall know we have strong arms too.

Men. Why, masters, my good friends, mine honest neigh-
    bours,
Will you undo yourselves?

1 Cit. We cannot, sir, we are undone already.

Men. I tell you, friends, most charitable care
Have the patricians of you. For your wants,
Your suffering in this dearth, you may as well
Strike at the heaven with your staves as lift them
Against the Roman state ; whose course will on
The way it takes, cracking ten thousand curbs
Of more strong link asunder than can ever
Appear in your impeachment: for the dearth,
The gods, not the patricians, make it; and
Your knees to them, not arms, must help. Alack,
You are transported by calamity
Thither where more attends you; and you slander
The helms o'the state, who care for you like fathers,
When you curse them as enemies.

1 Cit. Care for us! True, indeed! They ne'er cared for

us yet. Suffer us to famish, and their storehouses crammed
with grain; make edicts for usury, to support usurers;
repeal daily any wholesome act established against the
rich; and provide more piercing statutes daily, to chain up
and restrain the poor. If the wars eat us not up, they
will; and there's all the love they bear us.

Men. Either you must
Confess yourselves wondrous malicious,
Or be accus'd of folly. I shall tell you
A pretty tale : it may be you have heard it;
But, since it serves my purpose, I will venture
To stale't a little more.

1 *Cit.* Well, I'll hear it, sir: yet you must not think to
fob-off our disgrace with a tale : but, an't please you, deliver.

Men. There was a time when all the body's members
Rebell'd against the belly; thus accus'd it :—
That only like a gulf it did remain
I' the midst o' the body, idle and unactive,
Still cupboarding the viand, never bearing
Like labour with the rest; where the other instruments
Did see and hear, devise, instruct, walk, feel,
And, mutually participate, did minister
Unto the appetite and affection common
Of the whole body. The belly answered,—

1 *Cit.* Well, sir, what answer made the belly?

Men. Sir, I shall tell you.—With a kind of smile,
Which ne'er came from the lungs, but even thus,—
For, look you, I may make the belly smile
As well as speak,—it tauntingly replied
To the discontented members, the mutinous parts
That envied his receipt ; even so most fitly
As you malign our senators for that
They are not such as you.

1 *Cit.*   Your belly's answer? What!
The kingly-crowned head, the vigilant eye,
The counsellor heart, the arm our soldier,
Our steed the leg, the tongue our trumpeter,
With other muniments and petty helps
In this our fabric, if that they,—

Men.   What then?—
'Fore me, this fellow speaks!—what then? what then?

1 *Cit.* Should by the cormorant belly be restrain'd,
Who is the sink o' the body,—

Men.   Well, what then?

1 *Cit.* The former agents, if they did complain,
What could the belly answer ?

Men.   I will tell you;
If you'll bestow a small,—of what you have little,—
Patience awhile, you'll hear the belly's answer.
    1 *Cit.* You are long about it.
    Men.   Note me this, good friend;
Your most grave belly was deliberate,
Not rash like his accusers, and thus answer'd:
True is it, my incorporate friends, quoth he,
That I receive the general food at first
Which you do live upon: and fit it is,
Because I am the storehouse and the shop
Of the whole body: but, if you do remember,
I send it through the rivers of your blood,
Even to the court, the heart,—to the seat o' the brain;
And, through the cranks and offices of man,
The strongest nerves and small inferior veins
From me receive that natural competency
Whereby they live: and though that all at once
You, my good friends,—this says the belly,—mark me,—
    1 *Cit.* Ay, sir; well, well.
    Men.   *Though all at once cannot*
See what I do deliver out to each,
Yet I can make my audit up, that all
From me do back receive the flour of all,
And leave me but the bran.   What say you to't?
    1 *Cit.* It was an answer: how apply you this?
    Men. The senators of Rome are this good belly,
And you the mutinous members: for, examine
Their counsels and their cares; digest things rightly
Touching the weal o' the common; you shall find,
No public benefit which you receive
But it proceeds or comes from them to you,
And no way from yourselves.—What do you think,—
You, the great toe of this assembly?
    1 *Cit.* I the great toe? why the great toe?
    Men. For that, being one o' the lowest, basest, poorest,
Of this most wise rebellion, thou go'st foremost:
Thou rascal, that art worst in blood to run,
Lead'st first to win some vantage.—
But make you ready your stiff bats and clubs:
Rome and her rats are at the point of battle;
The one side must have bale.—

                Enter CAIUS MARCIUS.

                        Hail, noble Marcius!
    Mar. Thanks.—What's the matter, you dissentious rogues,

That, rubbing the poor itch of your opinion,
Make yourselves scabs?
  1 Cit.   We have ever your good word.
  Mar. He that will give good words to ye will flatter
Beneath abhorring.—What would you have, you curs,
That like nor peace nor war? the one affrights you,
The other makes you proud. He that trusts to you,
Where he should find you lions finds you hares;
Where foxes, geese: you are no surer, no,
Than is the coal of fire upon the ice,
Or hailstone in the sun. Your virtue is
To make him worthy whose offence subdues him,
And curse that justice did it. Who deserves greatness
Deserves your hate; and your affections are
A sick man's appetite, who desires most that
Which would increase his evil. He that depends
Upon your favours swims with fins of lead,
And hews down oaks with rushes. Hang ye! Trust ye!
With every minute you do change a mind;
And call him noble that was now your hate,
Him vile that was your garland. What's the matter,
That in these several places of the city
You cry against the noble senate, who,
Under the gods, keep you in awe, which else
Would feed on one another?—What's their seeking?
  Men. For corn at their own rates; whereof, they say,
The city is well stor'd.
  Mar.   Hang 'em! They say!
They'll sit by the fire and presume to know
What's done i' the Capitol; who's like to rise,
Who thrives and who declines; side factions, and give out
Conjectural marriages; making parties strong,
And feebling such as stand not in their liking
Below their cobbled shoes. They say there's grain enough!
Would the nobility lay aside their ruth
And let me use my sword, I'd make a quarry
With thousands of these quarter'd slaves, as high
As I could pick my lance.
  Men. Nay, these are almost thoroughly persuaded;
For though abundantly they lack discretion,
Yet are they passing cowardly. But, I beseech you,
What says the other troop?
  Mar.   They are dissolved: hang 'em!
They said they were an-hungry; sigh'd forth proverbs,—
That hunger broke stone walls, that dogs must eat,
That meat was made for mouths, that the gods sent not

Corn for the rich men only:—with these shreds
They vented their complainings; which being answer'd,
And a petition granted them,—a strange one,
To break the heart of generosity,
And make bold power look pale,—they threw their caps
As they would hang them on the horns o' the moon,
Shouting their emulation.

Men.   What is granted them?

Mar. Five tribunes, to defend their vulgar wisdoms,
Of their own choice: one 's Junius Brutus,
Sicinius Velutus, and I know not.—'Sdeath!
The rabble should have first unroof'd the city
Ere so prevail'd with me: it will in time
Win upon power, and throw forth greater themes
For insurrection's arguing.

Men.   This is strange.

Mar. Go, get you home, you fragments!

Enter a Messenger, *hastily.*

Mess. Where 's Caius Marcius?

Mar.   Here: what 's the matter?

Mess. The news is, sir, the Volsces are in arms.

Mar. I am glad on't: then we shall ha' means to vent
Our musty superfluity.—See, our best elders.

Enter COMINIUS, TITUS LARTIUS, *and other* Senators;
JUNIUS BRUTUS *and* SICINIUS VELUTUS.

1 Sen. Marcius, 'tis true that you have lately told us,—
The Volsces are in arms.

Mar.   They have a leader,
Tullus Aufidius, that will put you to't.
I sin in envying his nobility;
And were I anything but what I am,
I would wish me only he.

Com.   You have fought together.

Mar. Were half to half the world by the ears, and he
Upon my party, I'd revolt, to make
Only my wars with him: he is a lion
That I am proud to hunt.

1 Sen.   Then, worthy Marcius,
Attend upon Cominius to these wars.

Com. It is your former promise.

Mar.   Sir, it is;
And I am constant.—Titus Lartius, thou
Shalt see me once more strike at Tullus' face.
What, art thou still? stand'st out?

Tit.　　　　　　　　　　No, Caius Marcius;
I'll lean upon one crutch and fight with the other
Ere stay behind this business.
　　Men.　　　　　　　　　O, true bred!
　　1 *Sen.* Your company to the Capitol; where, I know,
Our greatest friends attend us.
　　Tit.　　　　　　　　　Lead you on:
Follow, Cominius; we must follow you;
Right worthy your priority.
　　Com.　　　　　　　　Noble Marcius!
　　1 *Sen.* Hence to your homes; be gone! [*To the* Citizens.
　　Mar.　　　　　　　　Nay, let them follow:
The Volsces have much corn; take these rats thither
To gnaw their garners.—Worshipful mutineers,
Your valour puts well forth: pray, follow.
　　　　　　[*Exeunt* Senators, COM., MAR., TIT., *and* MEN.
　　　　　　　Citizens *steal away.*
　　Sic. Was ever man so proud as is this Marcius?
　　Bru. He has no equal.
　　Sic. When we were chosen tribunes for the people,—
　　Bru. Mark'd you his lip and eyes?
　　Sic.　　　　　　　　Nay, but his taunts.
　　Bru. Being mov'd, he will not spare to gird the
　　　　　gods.
　　Sic. Be-mock the modest moon.
　　Bru. The present wars devour him: he is grown
Too proud to be so valiant.
　　Sic.　　　　　　　　Such a nature,
Tickled with good success, disdains the shadow
Which he treads on at noon: but I do wonder
His insolence can brook to be commanded
Under Cominius.
　　Bru.　　　　　　Fame, at the which he aims,—
In whom already he is well grac'd,—cannot
Better be held, nor more attain'd, than by
A place below the first: for what miscarries
Shall be the general's fault, though he perform
To the utmost of a man; and giddy censure
Will then cry out of Marcius, *O, if he*
Had borne the business!
　　Sic.　　　　　　　Besides, if things go well,
Opinion, that so sticks on Marcius, shall
Of his demerits rob Cominius.
　　Bru. Come:
Half all Cominius' honours are to Marcius,
Though Marcius earn'd them not; and all his faults

To Marcius shall be honours, though, indeed,
In aught he merit not.
Sic.   Let's hence, and hear
How the despatch is made; and in what fashion,
More than in singularity, he goes
Upon this present action.
Bru.   Let's along.   [*Exeunt.*

SCENE II.—CORIOLI.   *The Senate House.*

Enter TULLUS AUFIDIUS *and certain* Senators.

1 Sen. So, your opinion is, Aufidius,
That they of Rome are enter'd in our counsels,
And know how we proceed.
Auf.   Is it not yours?
What ever hath been thought on in this state,
That could be brought to bodily act ere Rome
Had circumvention! 'Tis not four days gone
Since I heard thence; these are the words: I think
I have the letter here; yes, here it is: [*Reads.*
They have press'd a power, but it is not known
Whether for east or west: the dearth is great;
The people mutinous: and it is rumour'd,
Cominius, Marcius your old enemy,—
Who is of Rome worse hated than of you,—
And Titus Lartius, a most valiant Roman,
These three lead on this preparation
Whither 'tis bent: most likely 'tis for you·
Consider of it.
1 Sen.   Our army's in the field:
We never yet made doubt but Rome was ready
To answer us.
Auf.   Nor did you think it folly
To keep your great pretences vail'd till when
They needs must show themselves; which in the hatching,
It seem'd, appear'd to Rome. By the discovery
We shall be shorten'd in our aim; which was,
To take in many towns ere, almost, Rome
Should know we were afoot.
2 Sen.   Noble Aufidius,
Take your commission; hie you to your bands:
Let us alone to guard Corioli:
If they set down before 's, for the remove
Bring up your army; but I think you'll find
They've not prepar'd for us.

Auf.   O, doubt not that;
I speak from certainties.   Nay, more,
Some parcels of their power are forth already,
And only hitherward.   I leave your honours.
If we and Caius Marcius chance to meet,
'Tis sworn between us we shall ever strike
Till one can do no more.
    All.   The gods assist you!
    Auf. And keep your honours safe!
    1 *Sen.*   Farewell.
    2 *Sen.*   Farewell.
    All. Farewell.   [*Exeunt.*

SCENE III.—ROME.   *An Apartment in* MARCIUS'S *House.*

Enter VOLUMNIA *and* VIRGILIA: *they sit down on two low
stools and sew.*

    Vol. I pray you, daughter, sing, or express yourself in a
more comfortable sort: if my son were my husband, I should
freelier rejoice in that absence wherein he won honour
than in the embracements of his bed where he would show
most love.   When yet he was but tender-bodied, and the
only son of my womb; when youth with comeliness plucked
all gaze his way; when, for a day of king's entreaties, a
mother should not sell him an hour from her beholding; I,
—considering how honour would become such a person;
that it was no better than picture-like to hang by the wall
if renown made it not stir,—was pleased to let him seek
danger where he was like to find fame.   To a cruel war I
sent him; from whence he returned, his brows bound with
oak.   I tell thee, daughter, I sprang not more in joy at first
hearing he was a man-child than now in first seeing he had
proved himself a man.
    Vir. But had he died in the business, madam? how then?
    Vol. Then his good report should have been my son; I
therein would have found issue.   Hear me profess sincerely,
—had I a dozen sons, each in my love alike, and none less
dear than thine and my good Marcius, I had rather had
eleven die nobly for their country than one voluptuously
surfeit out of action.

               Enter a Gentlewoman.
    Gent. Madam, the Lady Valeria is come to visit you.
    Vir. Beseech you, give me leave to retire myself.
    Vol. Indeed you shall not.

Methinks I hear hither your husband's drum ;
See him pluck Aufidius down by the hair ;
As children from a bear, the Volsces shunning him :
Methinks I see him stamp thus, and call thus, —
Come on, you cowards! you were got in fear
Though you were born in Rome: his bloody brow
With his mail'd hand then wiping, forth he goes,
Like to a harvest-man that 's task'd to mow
Or all, or lose his hire.

Vir. His bloody brow! O Jupiter, no blood!

Vol. Away, you fool! it more becomes a man
Than gilt his trophy : the breasts of Hecuba,
When she did suckle Hector, look'd not lovelier
Than Hector's forehead when it spit forth blood
At Grecian swords contending.—Tell Valeria
We are fit to bid her welcome.   [*Exit* Gentlewoman.

Vir. Heavens bless my lord from fell Aufidius !

Vol. He'll beat Aufidius' head below his knee,
And tread upon his neck.

Re-enter Gentlewoman, *with* VALERIA *and her* Usher.

Val. My ladies both, good-day to you.

Vol. Sweet madam.

Vir. I am glad to see your ladyship.

Val. How do you both? you are manifest housekeepers.
What are you sewing here? A fine spot, in good faith.—
How does your little son?

Vir. I thank your ladyship ; well, good madam.

Vol. He had rather see the swords and hear a drum than
look upon his schoolmaster.

Val. O' my word, the father's son : I'll swear 'tis a very
pretty boy. O' my troth, I looked upon him o' Wednesday
half an hour together : has such a confirmed countenance.
I saw him run after a gilded butterfly ; and when he caught
it he let it go again ; and after it again ; and over and over
he comes, and up again ; catched it again : or whether his
fall enraged him, or how 'twas, he did so set his teeth and
tear it ; O, I warrant, how he mammocked it !

Vol. One on 's father's moods.

Val. Indeed, la, 'tis a noble child.

Vir. A crack, madam.

Val. Come, lay aside your stitchery ; I must have you
play the idle huswife with me this afternoon.

Vir. No, good madam ; I will not out of doors.

Val. Not out of doors !

Vol. She shall, she shall.

Vir. Indeed, no, by your patience; I'll not over the threshold till my lord return from the wars.

Val. Fie, you confine yourself most unreasonably: come, you must go visit the good lady that lies in.

Vir. I will wish her speedy strength, and visit her with my prayers; but I cannot go thither.

Vol. Why, I pray you?

Vir. 'Tis not to save labour, nor that I want love.

Val. You would be another Penelope: yet they say all the yarn she spun in Ulysses' absence did but fill Ithaca full of moths. Come; I would your cambric were sensible as your finger, that you might leave pricking it for pity. Come, you shall go with us.

Vir. No, good madam, pardon me; indeed I will not forth.

Val. In truth, la, go with me; and I'll tell you excellent news of your husband.

Vir. O, good madam, there can be none yet.

Val. Verily, I do not jest with you; there came news from him last night.

Vir. Indeed, madam?

Val. In earnest, it 's true; I heard a senator speak it. Thus it is:—The Volsces have an army forth; against whom Cominius the general is gone, with one part of our Roman power: your lord and Titus Lartius are set down before their city Corioli; they nothing doubt prevailing, and to make it brief wars. This is true, on mine honour; and so, I pray, go with us.

Vir. Give me excuse, good madam; I will obey you in everything hereafter.

Vol. Let her alone, lady; as she is now, she will but disease our better mirth.

Val. In troth, I think she would.—Fare you well then. —Come, good sweet lady.—Pr'ythee, Virgilia, turn thy solemness out o' door, and go along with us.

Vir. No, at a word, madam; indeed I must not. I wish you much mirth.

Val. Well, then, farewell.   [*Exeunt.*

SCENE IV.—*Before Corioli.*

Enter, with drums and colours, MARCIUS, TITUS LARTIUS, Officers, *and* Soldiers.

Mar. Yonder comes news:—a wager they have met.

Lart. My horse to yours, no.

Mar.　　　　　　　　　　　　'Tis done.
Lart.　　　　　　　　　　　　　　　Agreed.

Enter a Messenger.

Mar. Say, has our general met the enemy?
Mess. They lie in view; but have not spoke as yet.
Lart. So, the good horse is mine.
Mar.　　　　　　　　　　　　　I'll buy him of you.
Lart. No, I'll nor sell nor give him: lend you him I will
For half a hundred years.—Summon the town.
Mar. How far off lie these armies?
Mess.　　　　　　　　　　　Within this mile and half.
Mar. Then shall we hear their 'larum, and they ours.—
Now, Mars, I pr'ythee, make us quick in work,
That we with smoking swords may march from hence
To help our fielded friends!—Come, blow thy blast.

They sound a parley.　Enter, on the Walls, some Senators
and others.

Tullus Aufidius, is he within your walls?
1 *Sen.* No, nor a man that fears you less than he,
That's lesser than a little.　Hark, our drums
　　　　　　　　　　　　　　　[*Drums afar off.*
Are bringing forth our youth! we'll break our walls,
Rather than they shall pound us up: our gates,
Which yet seem shut, we have but pinn'd with rushes;
They'll open of themselves.　Hark you far off!
　　　　　　　　　　　　　　　[*Alarum afar off.*
There is Aufidius; list what work he makes
Amongst your cloven army.
Mar.　　　　　　　　　O, they are at it!
Lart. Their noise be our instruction.—Ladders, ho!

The Volsces *enter and pass over.*

Mar. They fear us not, but issue forth their city.
Now put your shields before your hearts, and fight　[*Titus*:
With hearts more proof than shields. — Advance, brave
They do disdain us much beyond our thoughts,
Which makes me sweat with wrath.—Come on, my fellows:
He that retires I'll take him for a Volsce,
And he shall feel mine edge.

Alarums, and exeunt Romans *and* Volsces *fighting.　The*
Romans *are beaten back to their trenches.　Re-enter*
MARCIUS.

Mar. All the contagion of the south light on you,

You shames of Rome!—you herd of—Boils and plagues
Plaster you o'er, that you may be abhorr'd
Further than seen, and one infect another
Against the wind a mile! You souls of geese,
That bear the shapes of men, how have you run
From slaves that apes would beat! Pluto and hell!
All hurt behind; backs red, and faces pale
With flight and agued fear! Mend, and charge home,
Or, by the fires of heaven, I'll leave the foe
And make my wars on you: look to't: come on;
If you'll stand fast we'll beat them to their wives,
As they us to our trenches followed.

Another alarum. The Volsces *and* Romans *re-enter, and
the fight is renewed. The* Volsces *retire into Corioli, and*
Marcius *follows them to the gates.*

So, now the gates are ope:—now prove good seconds:
'Tis for the followers fortune widens them,
Not for the fliers: mark me, and do the like.

                                [He enters the gates.

  1 *Sol.* Fool-hardiness: not I.
  2 *Sol.*   Nor I. [Marcius *is shut in.*
  1 *Sol.* See, they have shut him in.
  All.   To the pot, I warrant him.

                                [Alarum continues.

Re-enter Titus Lartius.

  Lart. What is become of Marcius?
  All.   Slain, sir, doubtless.
  1 *Sol.* Following the fliers at the very heels,
With them he enters; who, upon the sudden,
Clapp'd-to their gates: he is himself alone,
To answer all the city.
  Lart.   O noble fellow!
Who, sensible, outdares his senseless sword,
And when it bows stands up! Thou art left, Marcius:
A carbuncle entire, as big as thou art,
Were not so rich a jewel. Thou wast a soldier
Even to Cato's wish, not fierce and terrible
Only in strokes; but with thy grim looks and
The thunder-like percussion of thy sounds
Thou mad'st thine enemies shake, as if the world
Were feverous and did tremble.

  Re-enter Marcius, *bleeding, assaulted by the enemy.*

  1 *Sol.*   Look, 'sir.

Lart.   O, 'tis Marcius!
Let's fetch him off, or make remain alike.

> [*They fight, and all enter the city.*

SCENE V.— *Within* CORIOLI. *A Street.*

Enter certain Romans, *with spoils.*

1 *Rom.* This will I carry to Rome.
2 *Rom.* And I this.
3 *Rom.* A murrain on't! I took this for silver.

> [*Alarum continues still afar off.*

Enter MARCIUS *and* TITUS LARTIUS *with a trumpet.*

Mar. See here these movers that do prize their hours
At a crack'd drachm! Cushions, leaden spoons,
Irons of a doit, doublets that hangmen would
Bury with those that wore them, these base slaves,
Ere yet the fight be done, pack up:—down with them!—
And hark, what noise the general makes!—To him! –
There is the man of my soul's hate, Aufidius,
Piercing our Romans: then, valiant Titus, take
Convenient numbers to make good the city;
Whilst I, with those that have the spirit, will haste
To help Cominius.
Lart.   Worthy sir, thou bleed'st;
Thy exercise hath been too violent for
A second course of fight.
Mar.   Sir, praise me not;
My work hath yet not warm'd me: fare you well:
The blood I drop is rather physical
Than dangerous to me: to Aufidius thus
I will appear, and fight.
Lart.   Now the fair goddess, Fortune,
Fall deep in love with thee; and her great charms
Misguide thy opposers' swords! Bold gentleman,
Prosperity be thy page!
Mar.   Thy friend no less
Than those she placeth highest!—So, farewell.
Lar. Thou worthiest Marcius!—   [*Exit* MARCIUS.
Go, sound thy trumpet in the market-place;
Call thither all the officers o' the town,
Where they shall know our mind: away!   [*Exeunt.*

SCENE VI.—*Near the Camp of* COMINIUS.

Enter COMINIUS *and* Forces, *retreating.*

Com. Breathe you, my friends: well fought; we are come off
Like Romans, neither foolish in our stands
Nor cowardly in retire: believe me, sirs,
We shall be charg'd again. Whiles we have struck,   ·
By interims and conveying gusts we have heard
The charges of our friends. Ye Roman gods,
Lead their successes as we wish our own,
That both our powers, with smiling fronts encountering,
May give you thankful sacrifice!—

Enter a Messenger.

                            Thy news
Mess. The citizens of Corioli have issued,
And given to Lartius and to Marcius battle:
I saw our party to their trenches driven,
And then I came away.
    Com.   Though thou speak'st truth,
Methinks thou speak'st not well. How long is't since?
    Mess. Above an hour, my lord.
    Com. 'Tis not a mile; briefly we heard their drums:
How couldst thou in a mile confound an hour,
And bring thy news so late?
    Mess.   Spies of the Volsces
Held me in chase, that I was forc'd to wheel
Three or four miles about: else had I, sir,
Half an hour since brought my report.
    Com.   Who 's yonder,
That does appear as he were flay'd? O gods!
He has the stamp of Marcius; and I have
Before-time seen him thus.
    Mar. [*within.*]   Come I too late?
    Com. The shepherd knows not thunder from a tabor
More than I know the sound of Marcius' tongue
From every meaner man.

Enter MARCIUS.

    Mar.   Come I too late?
    Com. Ay, if you come not in the blood of others,
But mantled in your own.
    Mar.   O! let me clip you
In arms as sound as when I woo'd; in heart

As merry as when our nuptial day was done,
And tapers burn'd to bedward!

Com.   Flower of warriors,
How is't with Titus Lartius?

Mar. As with a man busied about decrees:
Condemning some to death and some to exile;
Ransoming him or pitying, threat'ning the other;
Holding Corioli in the name of Rome,
Even like a fawning greyhound in the leash,
To let him slip at will.

Com.   Where is that slave
Which told me they had beat you to your trenches?
Where's he? call him hither.

Mar.   Let him alone;
He did inform the truth: but for our gentlemen,
The common file,—a plague!—tribunes for them!—
The mouse ne'er shunn'd the cat as they did budge
From rascals worse than they.

Com.   But how prevail'd you?

Mar. Will the time serve to tell? I do not think.
Where is the enemy? are you lords o' the field?
If not, why cease you till you are so?

Com.   Marcius,
We have at disadvantage fought, and did
Retire, to win our purpose.

Mar. How lies their battle? know you on which side
They have placed their men of trust?

Com.   As I guess, Marcius,
Their bands in the vaward are the Antiates,
Of their best trust; o'er them Aufidius,
Their very heart of hope.

Mar.   I do beseech you,
By all the battles wherein we have fought,
By the blood we have shed together, by the vows
We have made to endure friends, that you directly
Set me against Aufidius and his Antiates;
And that you not delay the present, but,
Filling the air with swords advanc'd and darts,
We prove this very hour.

Com.   Though I could wish
You were conducted to a gentle bath,
And balms applied to you, yet dare I never
Deny your asking: take your choice of those
That best can aid your action.

Mar.   Those are they
That most are willing.—If any such be here,—

As it were sin to doubt,—that love this painting
Wherein you see me smear'd; if any fear
Lesser his person than an ill report;
If any think brave death outweighs bad life,
And that his country's dearer than himself;
Let him alone, or so many so minded,
Wave thus [*waving his hand*], to express his disposition,
And follow Marcius.

> [*They all shout, and wave their swords; take him up
> in their arms, and cast up their caps.*

O, me alone! make you a sword of me?
If these shows be not outward, which of you
But is four Volsces? none of you but is
Able to bear against the great Aufidius
A shield as hard as his.   A certain number,
Though thanks to all, must I select from all: the rest
Shall bear the business in some other fight,
As cause will be obey'd.   Please you to march;
And four shall quickly draw out my command,
Which men are best inclin'd.
    Com.   March on, my fellows:
Make good this ostentation, and you shall
Divide in all with us.   [*Exeunt.*

SCENE VII.—*The Gates of Corioli.*

TITUS LARTIUS, *having set a guard upon* Corioli, *going with
drum and trumpet toward* COMINIUS *and* CAIUS MARCIUS,
enters with a Lieutenant, *a party of* Soldiers, *and a* Scout.

    Lart. So, let the ports be guarded: keep your duties
As I have set them down.   If I do send, despatch
Those centuries to our aid; the rest will serve
For a short holding: if we lose the field
We cannot keep the town.
    Lieut.   Fear not our care, sir.
    Lart. Hence, and shut your gates upon 's.—
Our guider, come; to the Roman camp conduct us. [*Exeunt.*

SCENE VIII.—*A* Field *of Battle between the Roman and
the Volscian Camps.*

Alarum   Enter, *from opposite sides,* MARCIUS *and* AUFIDIUS.

    Mar. I'll fight with none but thee; for I do hate thee
Worse than a promise-breaker.

Auf.   We hate alike:
Not Afric owns a serpent I abhor
More than thy fame and envy.   Fix thy foot.
   Mar. Let the first budger die the other's slave,
And the gods doom him after!
   Auf.   If I fly, Marcius,
Halloo me like a hare.
   Mar.   Within these three hours, Tullus,
Alone I fought in your Corioli walls,
And made what work I pleas'd: 'tis not my blood
Wherein thou seest me mask'd; for thy revenge
Wrench up thy power to the highest.
   Auf.   Wert thou the Hector
That was the whip of your bragg'd progeny,
Thou shouldst not scape me here.—
          [*They fight, and certain* Volsces *come to*
                    the aid of Aufidius.
Officious, and not valiant,—you have sham'd me
In your condemned seconds.
          [*Exeunt fighting, driven in by* Mar.

———

SCENE IX.—*The Roman Camp.*

*Alarum.   A retreat is sounded.   Flourish.   Enter, at one
   side,* Cominius *and* Romans; *at the other side,* Marcius,
   with his arm in a scarf, and other Romans.

   Com. If I should tell thee o'er this thy day's work,
Thou'lt not believe thy deeds: but I'll report it
Where senators shall mingle tears with smiles;
Where great patricians shall attend, and shrug,
I' the end admire; where ladies shall be frighted,
And, gladly quak'd, hear more; where the dull tribunes,
That, with the fusty plebeians, hate thine honours, ˙
Shall say, against their hearts, *We thank the gods
Our Rome hath such a soldier!*
Yet cam'st thou to a morsel of this feast,
Having fully dined before.

   Enter Titus Lartius, *with his power, from the pursuit.*
   Lart.   O general,
Here is the steed, we the caparison:
Hadst thou beheld,—
   Mar.   Pray now, no more; my mother
Who has a charter to extol her blood,
When she does praise me grieves me.   I have done

As you have done,—that's what I can; induc'd
As you have been,—that's for my country:
He that has but effected his good will
Hath overta'en mine act.

Com.   You shall not be
The grave of your deserving; Rome must know
The value of her own: 'twere a concealment
Worse than a theft, no less than a traducement,
To hide your doings; and to silence that
Which, to the spire and top of praises vouch'd,
Would seem but modest: therefore, I beseech you,—
In sign of what you are, not to reward
What you have done,—before our army hear me.

Mar. I have some wounds upon me, and they smart
To hear themselves remember'd.

Com.   Should they not,
Well might they fester 'gainst ingratitude,
And tent themselves with death. Of all the horses, —
Whereof we have ta'en good, and good store,—of all
The treasure in this field achiev'd and city,
We render you the tenth; to be ta'en forth
Before the common distribution at
Your only choice.

Mar.   I thank you, general;
But cannot make my heart consent to take
A bribe to pay my sword: I do refuse it;
And stand upon my common part with those
That have beheld the doing.

[*A long flourish. They all cry,* "Marcius! Marcius!"
cast up their caps and lances: COMINIUS *and*
LARTIUS *stand bare.*

Mar. May these same instruments which you profane
Never sound more! When drums and trumpets shall
I' the field prove flatterers, let courts and cities be
Made all of false-fac'd soothing!
When steel grows soft as the parasite's silk,
Let him be made a coverture for the wars!
No more, I say! for that I have not wash'd
My nose that bled, or foil'd some debile wretch,—
Which, without note, here's many else have done,—
You shout me forth in acclamations hyperbolical;
As if I loved my little should be dieted
In praises sauc'd with lies.

Com.   Too modest are you;
More cruel to your good report than grateful
To us that give you truly: by your patience,

If 'gainst yourself you be incens'd, we'll put you,—
Like one that means his proper harm,—in manacles,
Then reason safely with you.—Therefore be it known,
As to us, to all the world, that Caius Marcius
Wears this war's garland: in token of the which,
My noble steed, known to the camp, I give him,
With all his trim belonging; and from this time,
For what he did before Corioli, call him,
With all the applause and clamour of the host,
CAIUS MARCIUS CORIOLANUS.—
Bear the addition nobly ever!

       [*Flourish.   Trumpets sound, and drums.*

 All. Caius Marcius Coriolanus!

 Cor. I will go wash;
And when my face is fair you shall perceive
Whether I blush or no: howbeit, I thank you.—
I mean to stride your steed; and at all times
To undercrest your good addition
To the fairness of my power.

 Com.   So, to our tent;
Where, ere we do repose us, we will write
To Rome of our success.—You, Titus Lartius,
Must to Corioli back: send us to Rome
The best, with whom we may articulate,
For their own good and ours.

 Lart.   I shall, my lord.

 Cor. The gods begin to mock me. I, that now
Refus'd most princely gifts, am bound to beg
Of my lord general.

 Com.   Take't: 'tis yours.—What is't?

 Cor. I sometime lay here in Corioli
At a poor man's house; he us'd me kindly:
He cried to me; I saw him prisoner;
But then Aufidius was within my view,
And wrath o'erwhelm'd my pity: I request you
To give my poor host freedom.

 Cor.   O, well begg'd!
Were he the butcher of my son he should
Be free as is the wind. Deliver him, Titus.

 Lart. Marcius, his name?

 Cor.   By Jupiter, forgot:—
I am weary; yea, my memory is tir'd.—
Have we no wine here?

 Com.   Go we to our tent:
The blood upon your visage dries; 'tis time
It should be look'd to: come.   [*Exeunt.*

SCENE X.—*The Camp of the* Volsces.

A flourish.   Cornets.   Enter TULLUS AUFIDIUS, *bloody,
with two or three* Soldiers.

Auf. The town is ta'en!
1 *Sol.* 'Twill be deliver'd back on good condition.
Auf. Condition!—
I would I were a Roman; for I cannot,
Being a Volsce, be that I am.—Condition!
What good condition can a treaty find
I' the part that is at mercy?—Five times, Marcius,
I have fought with thee; so often hast thou beat me;
And wouldst do so, I think, should we encounter
As often as we eat.—By the elements,
If e'er again I meet him beard to beard,
He's mine or I am his: mine emulation
Hath not that honour in't it had; for where
I thought to crush him in an equal force,—
True sword to sword,—I'll potch at him some way
Or wrath or craft may get him.
  1 *Sol.*   He's the devil.
  Auf. Bolder, though not so subtle. My valour's poison'd
With only suffering stain by him; for him
Shall fly out of itself: nor sleep nor sanctuary,
Being naked, sick; nor fane nor Capitol,
The prayers of priests nor times of sacrifice,
Embarquements all of fury, shall lift up
Their rotten privilege and custom 'gainst
My hate to Marcius: where I find him, were it
At home, upon my brother's guard, even there,
Against the hospitable canon, would I
Wash my fierce hand in's heart. Go you to the city;
Learn how 'tis held; and what they are that must
Be hostages for Rome.
  1 *Sol.*   Will not you go?
  Auf. I am attended at the cypress grove:
I pray you,—
'Tis south the city mills,—bring me word thither
How the world goes, that to the pace of it
I may spur on my journey.
  1 *Sol.*   I shall, sir.   [*Exeunt.*

ACT II.

SCENE I.—ROME. *A public Place.*

Enter MENENIUS, SICINIUS, *and* BRUTUS.

Men. The augurer tells me we shall have news to-night.

Bru. Good or bad?

Men. Not according to the prayer of the people, for they love not Marcius.

Sic. Nature teaches beasts to know their friends.

Men. Pray you, who does the wolf love?

Sic. The lamb.

Men. Ay, to devour him; as the hungry plebeians would the noble Marcius.

Bru. He's a lamb indeed, that baas like a bear.

Men. He's a bear indeed, that lives like a lamb. You two are old men: tell me one thing that I shall ask you.

Both Trib. Well, sir.

Men. In what enormity is Marcius poor in, that you two have not in abundance?

Bru. He's poor in no one fault, but stored with all.

Sic. Especially in pride.

Bru. And topping all others in boasting.

Men. This is strange now: do you two know how you are censured here in the city, I mean of us o' the right-hand file? Do you?

Both Trib. Why, how are we censured?

Men. Because you talk of pride now,—will you not be angry?

Both Trib. Well, well, sir, well.

Men. Why, 'tis no great matter; for a very little thief of occasion will rob you of a great deal of patience: give your dispositions the reins, and be angry at your pleasures; at the least, if you take it as a pleasure to you in being so. You blame Marcius for being proud?

Bru. We do it not alone, sir.

Men. I know you can do very little alone; for your helps are many, or else your actions would grow wondrous single: your abilities are too infant-like for doing much alone. You talk of pride: O that you could turn your eyes toward the napes of your necks, and make but an interior survey of your good selves! O that you could!

Bru. What then, sir?

Men. Why, then you should discover a brace of unmeriting, proud, violent, testy magistrates,—alias, fools,—as any in Rome.

Sic. Menenius, you are known well enough too.

Men. I am known to be a humorous patrician, and one that loves a cup of hot wine with not a drop of allaying Tiber in't: said to be something imperfect in favouring the first complaint, hasty and tinder-like upon too trivial motion; one that converses more with the buttock of the night than with the forehead of the morning. What I think I utter, and spend my malice in my breath. Meeting two such wealsmen as you are,—I cannot call you Lycurguses,—if the drink you give me touch my palate adversely, I make a crooked face at it. I cannot say your worships have delivered the matter well when I find the ass in compound with the major part of your syllables: and though I must be content to bear with those that say you are reverend grave men, yet they lie deadly that tell you have good faces. If you see this in the map of my microcosm, follows it that I am known well enough too? What harm can your bisson conspectuities glean out of this character, if I be known well enough too?

Bru. Come, sir, come, we know you well enough.

Men. You know neither me, yourselves, nor anything. You are ambitious for poor knaves' caps and legs: you wear out a good wholesome forenoon in hearing a cause between an orange-wife and a fosset-seller; and then rejourn the controversy of threepence to a second day of audience.— When you are hearing a matter between party and party, if you chanced to be pinched with the colic, you make faces like mummers; set up the bloody flag against all patience; and, in roaring for a chamber-pot, dismiss the controversy bleeding, the more entangled by your hearing : all the peace you make in their cause is calling both the parties knaves. You are a pair of strange ones.

Bru. Come, come, you are well understood to be a prefecter giber for the table than a necessary bencher in the Capitol.

Men. Our very priests must become mockers if they shall encounter such ridiculous subjects as you are. When you speak best unto the purpose it is not worth the wagging of your beards; and your beards deserve not so honourable a grave as to stuff a botcher's cushion or to be entombed in an ass's pack-saddle. Yet you must be saying, Marcius is proud; who, in a cheap estimation, is worth all your predecessors since Deucalion; though peradventure some of the best of them were hereditary hangmen. God-den to

your worships : more of your conversation would infect my
brain, being the herdsmen of the beastly plebeians : I will
be bold to take my leave of you.

[BRUTUS *and* SICINIUS *retire.*

Enter VOLUMNIA, VIRGILIA, VALERIA, *&c.*

How now, my as fair as noble ladies,—and the moon,
were she earthly, no nobler,—whither do you follow your
eyes so fast?

Vol. Honourable Menenius, my boy Marcius approaches;
for the love of Juno, let 's go.

Men. Ha! Marcius coming home!

Vol. Ay, worthy Menenius; and with most prosperous
approbation.

Men. Take my cap, Jupiter, and I thank thee.—Hoo!
Marcius coming home!

Vol. Vir. Nay, 'tis true.

Vol. Look, here 's a letter from him : the state hath another, his wife another; and I think there's one at home for
you.

Men. I will make my very house reel to-night.—A letter
for me?

Vir. Yes, certain, there 's a letter for you ; I saw it.

Men. A letter for me! It gives me an estate of seven
years' health ; in which time I will make a lip at the physician: the most sovereign prescription in Galen is but em-
piricutic, and, to this preservative, of no better report than
a horse-drench. Is he not wounded? he was wont to come
home wounded.

Vir. O, no, no, no.

Vol. O, he is wounded, I thank the gods for't.

Men. So do I too, if it be not too much.—Brings a
victory in his pocket?—The wounds become him.

Vol. On 's brows: Menenius, he comes the third time
home with the oaken garland.

Men. Has he disciplined Aufidius soundly?

Vol. Titus Lartius writes,—they fought together, but Aufidius got off.

Men. And 'twas time for him too, I'll warrant him that:
an he had stayed by him, I would not have been so fidiused
for all the chests in Corioli, and the gold that 's in them.
Is the senate possessed of this?

Vol. Good ladies, let 's go.—Yes, yes, yes ; the senate has
letters from the general, wherein he gives my son the whole
name of the war: he hath in this action outdone his former
deeds doubly.

Val. In troth, there's wondrous things spoke of him.

Men. Wondrous! ay, I warrant you, and not without his true purchasing.

Vir. The gods grant them true!

Vol. True, pow, wow.

Men. True! I'll be sworn they are true.—Where is he wounded?—[*To the* Tribunes, *who come forward.*] God save your good worships! Marcius is coming home: he has more cause to be proud.—Where is he wounded?

Vol. I' the shoulder and i' the left arm: there will be large cicatrices to show the people when he shall stand for his place. He received in the repulse of Tarquin seven hurts i' the body.

Men. One i' the neck and two i' the thigh,—there's nine that I know.

Vol. He had, before this last expedition, twenty-five wounds upon him.

Men. Now it's twenty-seven : every gash was an enemy's grave. [*A shout and flourish.*] Hark! the trumpets.

Vol. These are the ushers of Marcius: before him
He carries noise, and behind him he leaves tears;
Death, that dark spirit, in 's nervy arm doth lie;
Which, being advanc'd, declines, and then men die.

A sennet. Trumpets sound. Enter COMINIUS *and* TITUS LARTIUS ; *between them,* CORIOLANUS, *crowned with an oaken garland; with* Captains, Soldiers, *and a* Herald.

Her. Know, Rome, that all alone Marcius did fight
Within Corioli gates: where he hath won,
With fame, a name to Caius Marcius; these
In honour follows Coriolanus :—
Welcome to Rome, renowned Coriolanus!   [*Flourish.*

All. Welcome to Rome, renowned Coriolanus!

Cor. No more of this, it does offend my heart;
Pray now, no more.

Com.   Look, sir, your mother!

Cor.   O,
You have, I know, petition'd all the gods
For my prosperity!   [*Kneels.*

Vol.   Nay, my good soldier, up;
My gentle Marcius, worthy Caius, and
By deed-achieving honour newly nam'd,—
What is it?—Coriolanus must I call thee?
But, O, thy wife!

Cor.   My gracious silence, hail!
Wouldst thou have laugh'd had I come coffin'd home,
That weep'st to see me triumph? Ah, my dear,
Such eyes the widows in Corioli wear,
And mothers that lack sons.
  Men.   Now the gods crown thee!
  Cor. And live you yet?—O my sweet lady, pardon.
           [*To* VALERIA.
  Vol. I know not where to turn.—O, welcome home;—
And welcome, general;—and you are welcome all.
  Men. A hundred thousand welcomes.—I could weep
And I could laugh; I am light and heavy.—Welcome:
A curse begin at very root on 's heart
That is not glad to see thee!—You are three
That Rome should dote on: yet, by the faith of men,
We have some old crab trees here at home that will not
Be grafted to your relish. Yet welcome, warriors:
We call a nettle but a nettle; and
The faults of fools but folly.
  Com.   Ever right.
  Cor. Menenius ever, ever.
  Her. Give way there, and go on!
  Cor.   Your hand, and yours:
       [*To his wife and mother.*
Ere in our own house I do shade my head,
The good patricians must be visited;
From whom I have receiv'd not only greetings,
But with them change of honours.
  Vol.   I have lived
To see inherited my very wishes,
And the buildings of my fancy: only
There's one thing wanting, which I doubt not but
Our Rome will cast upon thee.
  Cor.   Know, good mother,
I had rather be their servant in my way
Than sway with them in theirs.
  Com.   On, to the Capitol.
     [*Flourish. Cornets. Exeunt in state,
      as before. The* Tribunes *remain.*
  Bru. All tongues speak of him, and the bleared sights
Are spectacled to see him: your prattling nurse
Into a rapture lets her baby cry
While she chats him: the kitchen malkin pins
Her richest lockram 'bout her reechy neck,
Clambering the walls to eye him: stalls, bulks, windows,
Are smother'd up, leads fill'd, and ridges hors'd

With variable complexions; all agreeing
In earnestness to see him: seld-shown flamens
Do press among the popular throngs, and puff
To win a vulgar station: our veil'd dames
Commit the war of white and damask, in
Their nicely gawded cheeks, to the wanton spoil
Of Phœbus' burning kisses: such a pother,
As if that whatsoever god who leads him
Were slily crept into his human powers,
And gave him graceful posture.
  Sic.   On the sudden,
I warrant him consul.
  Bru.   Then our office may,
During his power, go sleep.
  Sic. He cannot temperately transport his honours
From where he should begin and end; but will
Lose those that he hath won.
  Bru.   In that there's comfort.
  Sic. Doubt not the commoners, for whom we stand,
But they, upon their ancient malice, will forget,
With the least cause, these his new honours; which
That he'll give them make I as little question
As he is proud to do't.
  Bru.   I heard him swear,
Were he to stand for consul, never would he
Appear i' the market-place, nor on him put
The napless vesture of humility;
Nor, showing, as the manner is, his wounds
To the people, beg their stinking breaths.
  Sic.   'Tis right.
  Bru. It was his word: O, he would miss it rather
Than carry it but by the suit of the gentry to him,
And the desire of the nobles.
  Sic.   I wish no better
Than have him hold that purpose, and to put it
In execution.
  Bru. 'Tis most like he will.
  Sic. It shall be to him then, as our good wills,
A sure destruction.
  Bru.   So it must fall out
To him or our authorities. For an end,
We must suggest the people in what hatred
He still hath held them; that to's power he would
Have made them mules, silenc'd their pleaders, and
Dispropertied their freedoms: holding them,
In human action and capacity,

Of no more soul nor fitness for the world
Than camels in their war; who have their provand
Only for bearing burdens, and sore blows
For sinking under them.
   Sic.   This, as you say, suggested
At some time when his soaring insolence
Shall touch the people,—which time shall not want,
If it be put upon't; and that's as easy
As to set dogs on sheep,—will be his fire
To kindle their dry stubble; and their blaze
Shall darken him for ever.

Enter a Messenger.

   Bru.   What's the matter?
   Mess. You are sent for to the Capitol. 'Tis thought
That Marcius shall be consul:
I have seen the dumb men throng to see him, and
The blind to hear him speak: matrons flung gloves,
Ladies and maids their scarfs and handkerchers,
Upon him as he pass'd: the nobles bended
As to Jove's statue; and the commons made
A shower and thunder with their caps and shouts:
I never saw the like.
   Bru.   Let's to the Capitol;
And carry with us ears and eyes for the time,
But hearts for the event.
   Sic.   Have with you. [*Exeunt.*

SCENE II.—ROME. *The Capitol.*

Enter two Officers, *to lay cushions.*

   1 *Off.* Come, come; they are almost here. How many stand for consulships?

   2 *Off.* Three, they say: but 'tis thought of every one Coriolanus will carry it.

   1 *Off.* That's a brave fellow; but he's vengeance proud, and loves not the common people.

   2 *Off.* Faith, there have been many great men that have flattered the people, who ne'er loved them; and there be many that they have loved, they know not wherefore: so that, if they love they know not why, they hate upon no better a ground: therefore, for Coriolanus neither to care whether they love or hate him manifests the true knowledge he has in their disposition; and, out of his noble carelessness, lets them plainly see't.

1 *Off.* If he did not care whether he had their love or
no, he waved indifferently 'twixt doing them neither good
nor harm; but he seeks their hate with greater devotion
than they can render it him; and leaves nothing undone
that may fully discover him their opposite. Now, to seem
to affect the malice and displeasure of the people is as
bad as that which he dislikes,—to flatter them for their
love.

2 *Off.* He hath deserved worthily of his country: and his
ascent is not by such easy degrees as those who, having
been supple and courteous to the people, bonnetted, without any further deed to have them at all into their estimation and report: but he hath so planted his honours in
their eyes, and his actions in their hearts, that for their
tongues to be silent, and not confess so much, were a
kind of ingrateful injury; to report otherwise were a malice
that, giving itself the lie, would pluck reproof and rebuke
from every ear that heard it.

1 *Off.* No more of him; he is a worthy man: make way,
they are coming.

A Sennet. Enter, with Lictors *before them,* COMINIUS *the
Consul,* MENENIUS, CORIOLANUS, Senators, SICINIUS,
and BRUTUS. *The Senators take their places; the Tribunes take theirs also by themselves.*

Men. Having determin'd of the Volsces, and
To send for Titus Lartius, it remains,
As the main point of this our after-meeting,
To gratify his noble service that
Hath thus stood for his country: therefore please you,
Most reverend and grave elders, to desire
The present consul, and last general
In our well-found successes, to report
A little of that worthy work perform'd
By Caius Marcius Coriolanus; whom
We meet here, both to thank and to remember
With honours like himself.

1 *Sen.*   Speak, good Cominius:
Leave nothing out for length, and make us think
Rather our state's defective for requital
Than we to stretch it out.—Masters o' the people,
We do request your kindest ears; and, after,
Your loving motion toward the common body,
To yield what passes here.

Sic.   We are convented
Upon a pleasing treaty; and have hearts

Inclinable to honour and advance
The theme of our assembly.
   Bru.   Which the rather
We shall be bless'd to do, if he remember
A kinder value of the people than
He hath hereto priz'd them at.
   Men.   That's off, that's off;
I would you rather had been silent.   Please you
To hear Cominius speak?
   Bru.   Most willingly:
But yet my caution was more pertinent
Than the rebuke you give it.
   Men.   He loves your people;
But tie him not to be their bedfellow.—
Worthy Cominius, speak.
             [CORIOLANUS *rises, and offers to go away.*
             Nay, keep your place.
   1 *Sen.* Sit, Coriolanus; never shame to hear
What you have nobly done.
   Cor.   Your honours' pardon:
I had rather have my wounds to heal again
Than hear say how I got them.
   Bru.   Sir, I hope
My words disbench'd you not.
   Cor.   No, sir; yet oft,
When blows have made me stay, I fled from words.
You sooth'd not, therefore hurt not: but your people,
I love them as they weigh.
   Men.   Pray now, sit down.
   Cor. I had rather have one scratch my head i' the
       sun
When the alarum were struck, than idly sit
To hear my nothings monster'd.   [*Exit.*
   Men.   Masters o' the people,
Your multiplying spawn how can he flatter,—
That's thousand to one good one,—when you now see
He had rather venture all his limbs for honour
Than one on's ears to hear it?—Proceed, Cominius.
   Com. I shall lack voice: the deeds of Coriolanus
Should not be utter'd feebly.—It is held
That valour is the chiefest virtue, and
Most dignifies the haver: if it be,
The man I speak of cannot in the world
Be singly counterpois'd.   At sixteen years,
When Tarquin made a head for Rome, he fought
Beyond the mark of others: our then dictator,

Whom with all praise I point at, saw him fight,
When with his Amazonian chin he drove
The bristled lips before him: he bestrid
An o'erpress'd Roman, and i' the consul's view
Slew three opposers: Tarquin's self he met,
And struck him on his knee: in that day's feats,
When he might act the woman in the scene,
He prov'd best man i' the field, and for his meed
Was brow-bound with the oak.   His pupil age
Man-enter'd thus, he waxed like a sea;
And in the brunt of seventeen battles since
He lurch'd all swords of the garland.   For this last,
Before and in Corioli, let me say,
I cannot speak him home: he stopp'd the fliers;
And by his rare example made the coward
Turn terror into sport: as weeds before
A vessel under sail, so men obey'd,
And fell below his stem: his sword,—death's stamp,—
Where it did mark, it took; from face to foot
He was a thing of blood, whose every motion
Was timed with dying cries: alone he enter'd
The mortal gate of the city, which he painted
With shunless destiny; aidless came off,
And with a sudden re-enforcement struck
Corioli like a planet.   Now all 's his:
When, by and by, the din of war 'gan pierce
His ready sense; then straight his doubled spirit
Re-quicken'd what in flesh was fatigate,
And to the battle came he; where he did
Run reeking o'er the lives of men as if
'Twere a perpetual spoil: and till we call'd
Both field and city ours he never stood
To ease his breast with panting.

   Men.   Worthy man!
   1 *Sen.* He cannot but with measure fit the honours
Which we devise him.
   Com.   Our spoils he kick'd at;
And look'd upon things precious as they were
The common muck of the world: he covets less
Than misery itself would give; rewards
His deeds with doing them; and is content
To spend the time to end it.
   Men.   He 's right noble:
Let him be call'd for.
   1 *Sen.*   Call Coriolanus.
   Off. He doth appear.

Re-enter CORIOLANUS.

Men. The senate, Coriolanus, are well pleas'd
To make thee consul.

Cor.   I do owe them still
My life and services.

Men. ·   It then remains
That you do speak to the people.

Cor.   I do beseech you
Let me o'erleap that custom; for I cannot
Put on the gown, stand naked, and entreat them,
For my wounds' sake, to give their suffrage: please you
That I may pass this doing.

Sic.   Sir, the people
Must have their voices; neither will they bate
One jot of ceremony.

Men.   Put them not to't:—
Pray you, go fit you to the custom; and
Take to you, as your predecessors have,
Your honour with your form.

Cor.   It is a part
That I shall blush in acting, and might well
Be taken from the people.

Bru.   Mark you that?

Cor. To brag unto them,—thus I did, and thus ;—
Show them the unaching scars which I should hide,
As if I had receiv'd them for the hire
Of their breath only!—

Men.   Do not stand upon't.—
We recommend to you, tribunes of the people,
Our purpose to them ;—and to our noble consul
Wish we all joy and honour.

Sen. To Coriolanus come all joy and honour!

                [*Flourish.   Exeunt all but* SIC. *and* BRU.

Bru. You see how he intends to use the people.

Sic. May they perceive 's intent!   He will requite
        them
As if he did contemn what he requested
Should be in them to give.

Bru.   Come, we'll inform them
Of our proceedings here: on the market-place
I know they do attend us   [*Exeunt.*

SCENE III.—ROME.   *The Forum.*

Enter several Citizens.

1 *Cit.* Once, if he do require our voices, we ought not to deny him.

2 *Cit.* We may, sir, if we will.

3 *Cit.* We have power in ourselves to do it, but it is a power that we have no power to do: for if he show us his wounds and tell us his deeds, we are to put our tongues into those wounds, and speak for them; so, if he tell us his noble deeds, we must also tell him our noble acceptance of them. Ingratitude is monstrous: and for the multitude to be ingrateful, were to make a monster of the multitude; of the which we, being members, should bring ourselves to be monstrous members.

1 *Cit.* And to make us no better thought of, a little help will serve; for once we stood up about the corn, he himself stuck not to call us the many headed multitude.

3 *Cit.* We have been called so of many; not that our heads are some brown, some black, some auburn, some bald, but that our wits are so diversely coloured; and truly I think, if all our wits were to issue out of one skull, they would fly east, west, north, south; and their consent of one direct way should be at once to all the points o' the compass.

2 *Cit.* Think you so? Which way do you judge my wit would fly?

3 *Cit.* Nay, your wit will not so soon out as another man's will,—'tis strongly wedged up in a block-head; but if it were at liberty, 'twould, sure, southward.

2 *Cit.* Why that way?

3 *Cit.* To lose itself in a fog; where being three parts melted away with rotten dews, the fourth would return, for conscience' sake, to help to get thee a wife.

2 *Cit.* You are never without your tricks:—you may, you may.

3 *Cit.* Are you all resolved to give your voices? But that's no matter, the greater part carries it. I say, if he would incline to the people, there was never a worthier man. Here he comes, and in the gown of humility: mark his behaviour. We are not to stay altogether, but to come by him where he stands, by ones, by twos, and by threes. He's to make his requests by particulars; wherein every one of us has a single honour, in giving him our own voices with our own tongues: therefore follow me, and I'll direct you how you shall go by him.

All. Content, content.   [*Exeunt*

Enter CORIOLANUS *and* MENENIUS.

Men. O sir, you are not right : have you not known
The worthiest men have done't!
Cor.   What must I say?—
I pray, sir,—Plague upon't! I cannot bring
My tongue to such a pace.—*Look, sir;—my wounds;—*
I got them in my country's service, when
Some certain of your brethren roar'd, and ran
From the noise of our own drums.
Men.   O me, the gods!
You must not speak of that: you must desire them
To think upon you.
Cor.   Think upon me! hang 'em!
I would they would forget me, like the virtues
Which our divines lose by 'em.
Men.   You'll mar all :
I ll leave you. Pray you, speak to 'em, I pray you,
In wholesome manner.
Cor.   Bid them wash their faces
And keep their teeth clean.   [*Exit* MENENIUS.
So, here comes a brace :

Re-enter two Citizens.

You know the cause, sirs, of my standing here.
  1 *Cit.* We do, sir; tell us what hath brought you to't.
  Cor. Mine own desert.
  2 *Cit.* Your own desert!
  Cor. Ay, not mine own desire.
  1 *Cit.* How! not your own desire!
  Cor. No, sir, 'twas never my desire yet to trouble the
poor with begging.
  1 *Cit.* You must think, if we give you anything, we hope
to gain by you.
  Cor. Well then, I pray, your price o' the consulship?
  1 *Cit.* The price is to ask it kindly.
  Cor. Kindly! sir, I pray, let me ha'it: I have wounds
to show you, which shall be yours in private.—Your good
voice, sir; what say you?
  2 *Cit.* You shall ha' it, worthy sir.
  Cor. A match, sir.—There is in all two worthy voices
begg'd —I have your alms: adieu.
  1 *Cit.* But this is something odd.
  2 *Cit.* An 'twere to give again,—but 'tis no matter.
                        [*Exeunt two* Citizens.

Coriolanus, Act II, Scene III.

Re-enter other two Citizens.

Cor. Pray you now, if it may stand with the tune of your voices that I may be consul, I have here the cus-tomary gown.

3 Cit. You have deserved nobly of your country, and you have not deserved nobly.

Cor. Your enigma?

3 Cit. You have been a scourge to her enemies, you have been a rod to her friends; you have not, indeed, loved the common people.

Cor. You should account me the more virtuous, that I have not been common in my love. I will, sir, flatter my sworn brother, the people, to earn a dearer estimation of them; 'tis a condition they account gentle: and since the wisdom of their choice is rather to have my hat than my heart, I will practise the insinuating nod, and be off to them most counterfeitly; that is, sir, I will counterfeit the bewitchment of some popular man, and give it bountifully to the desirers. Therefore, beseech you, I may be consul.

4 Cit. We hope to find you our friend; and therefore give you our voices heartily.

3 Cit. You have received many wounds for your country.

Cor. I will not seal your knowledge with showing them. I will make much of your voices, and so trouble you no further.

Both Cit. The gods give you joy, sir, heartily! [*Exeunt.*

Cor. Most sweet voices!—
Better it is to die, better to starve,
Than crave the hire which first we do deserve.
Why in this wolfish toge should I stand here,
To beg of Hob and Dick, that do appear,
Their needless vouches? Custom calls me to't:—
What custom wills, in all things should we do't,
The dust on antique time would lie unswept,
And mountainous error be too highly heap'd
For truth to o'erpeer. Rather than fool it so,
Let the high office and the honour go
To one that would do thus.—I am half through;
The one part suffer'd, the other will I do.
Here come more voices.

Re-enter other three Citizens.

Your voices: for your voices I have fought;
Watch'd for your voices; for your voices bear
Of wounds two dozen odd; battles thrice six

I have seen and heard of; for your voices have
Done many things, some less, some more: your voices:
Indeed, I would be consul.

  5 *Cit.* He has done nobly, and cannot go without any
honest man's voice.

  6 *Cit.* Therefore let him be consul: the gods give him
joy, and make him good friend to the people!

  All 3 Citizens. Amen, amen.—God save thee, noble
consul!   [*Exeunt.*

  Cor. Worthy voices!

Re-enter MENENIUS, *with* BRUTUS *and* SICINIUS.

  Men. You have stood your limitation; and the tribunes
Endue you with the people's voice:—remains
That, in the official marks invested, you
Anon do meet the senate.

  Cor.   Is this done?
  Sic. The custom of request you have discharg'd:
The people do admit you; and are summon'd
To meet anon, upon your approbation.

  Cor. Where? at the senate-house?
  Sic.   There, Coriolanus.
  Cor. May I change these garments?
  Sic.   You may, sir.
  Cor. That I'll straight do; and, knowing myself again,
Repair to the senate-house.

  Men. I'll keep you company.—Will you along?
  Bru. We stay here for the people.
  Sic.   Fare you well.
                    [*Exeunt* COR. *and* MEN
He has it now; and by his looks methinks
'Tis warm at his heart.

  Bru. With a proud heart he wore his humble weeds.
Will you dismiss the people?

Re-enter Citizens.

  Sic. How now, my masters! have you chose this man?
  1 *Cit.* He has our voices, sir.
  Bru. We pray the gods he may deserve your loves.
  2 *Cit.* Amen, sir:—to my poor unworthy notice,
He mocked us when he begg'd our voices.
  3 *Cit.*   Certainly,
He flouted us downright.
  1 *Cit.* No, 'tis his kind of speech,—he did not mock us
  2 *Cit.* Not one amongst us, save yourself, but says

He us'd us scornfully: he should have show'd us
His marks of merit, wounds receiv'd for 's country.
  Sic. Why, so he did, I am sure.
  Citizens.   No, no; no man saw 'em.
  3 Cit. He said he had wounds, which he could show if
      private;
And with his hat, thus waving it in scorn,
I would be consul, says he; *aged custom,*
But by your voices, will not so permit me;
Your voices therefore: when we granted that,
Here was, *I thank you for your voices,—thank you,—*
Your most sweet voices:—now you have left your voices
I have no further with you:—was not this mockery?
  Sic. Why, either were you ignorant to see 't?
Or, seeing it, of such childish friendliness
To yield your voices?
  Bru.   Could you not have told him,
As you were lesson'd,—when he had no power,
But was a petty servant to the state,
He was your enemy; ever spake against
Your liberties, and the charters that you bear
I' the body of the weal: and now, arriving
A place of potency and sway o' the state,
If he should still malignantly remain
Fast foe to the plebeii, your voices might
Be curses to yourselves? You should have said,
That as his worthy deeds did claim no less
Than what he stood for, so his gracious nature
Would think upon you for your voices, and
Translate his malice towards you into love,
Standing your friendly lord.
  Sic.   Thus to have said,
As you were fore-advis'd, had touch'd his spirit
And tried his inclination; from him pluck'd
Either his gracious promise, which you might,
As cause had call'd you up, have held him to;
Or else it would have gall'd his surly nature,
Which easily endures not article
Tying him to aught; so, putting him to rage,
You should have ta'en the advantage of his choler,
And pass'd him unelected.
  Bru.   Did you perceive
He did solicit you in free contempt
When he did need your loves; and do you think
That his contempt shall not be bruising to you
When he hath power to crush? Why, had your bodies

No heart among you? Or had you tongues to cry
Against the rectorship of judgment?
   Sic.   Have you
Ere now denied the asker? and now again,
On him that did not ask but mock, bestow
Your su'd-for tongues?
   3 *Cit.* He's not confirm'd; we may deny him yet.
   2 *Cit.* And will deny him:
I'll have five hundred voices of that sound.   ['em.
   1 *Cit.* I twice five hundred, and their friends to piece
   Bru. Get you hence instantly; and tell those friends
They have chose a consul that will from them take
Their liberties; make them of no more voice
Than dogs, that are as often beat for barking
As therefore kept to do so.
   Sic.   Let them assemble;
And, on a safer judgment, all revoke
Your ignorant election: enforce his pride
And his old hate unto you: besides, forget not
With what contempt he wore the humble weed;
How in his suit he scorn'd you: but your loves,
Thinking upon his services, took from you
The apprehension of his present portance,
Which, most gibingly, ungravely, he did fashion
After the inveterate hate he bears you.
   Bru.   Lay
A fault on us, your tribunes; that we labour'd,—
No impediment between,—but that you must
Cast your election on him.
   Sic.   Say you chose him
More after our commandment than as guided
By your own true affections; and that your minds,
Pre-occupied with what you rather must do
Than what you should, made you against the grain
To voice him consul. Lay the fault on us.
   Bru. Ay, spare us not. Say we read lectures to you,
How youngly he began to serve his country,
How long continued: and what stock he springs of—
The noble house o' the Marcians; from whence came
That Ancus Marcius, Numa's daughter's son,
Who, after great Hostilius, here was king;
Of the same house Publius and Quintus were,
That our best water brought by conduits hither;
And Censorinus, darling of the people,
And nobly nam'd so, twice being censor,
Was his great ancestor.

Sic.   One thus descended,
That hath beside well in his person wrought
To be set high in place, we did commend
To your remembrances: but you have found,
Scaling his present bearing with his past,
That he's your fixed enemy, and revoke
Your sudden approbation.
    Bru.   Say you ne'er had done't,—
Harp on that still,—but by our putting on:
And presently, when you have drawn your number,
Repair to the Capitol.
    Citizens.   We will so; almost all
Repent in their election.   [*Exeunt.*
    Bru.   Let them go on;
This mutiny were better put in hazard
Than stay, past doubt, for greater:
If, as his nature is, he fall in rage
With their refusal, both observe and answer
The vantage of his anger.
    Sic.   To the Capitol,
Come: we will be there before the stream o' the people;
And this shall seem, as partly 'tis, their own,
Which we have goaded onward.   [*Exeunt.*

ACT III

SCENE I.—ROME.   *A Street.*

Cornets.   Enter CORIOLANUS, MENENIUS, COMINUS, TITUS
LARTIUS, Senators, *and* Patricians.

    Cor. Tullus Aufidius, then, had made new head?
    Lart. He had, my lord; and that it was which caus'd
Our swifter composition.
    Cor. So then the Volsces stand but as at first;
Ready, when time shall prompt them, to make road
Upon 's again.
    Com.   They are worn, lord consul, so
That we shall hardly in our ages see
Their banners wave again.
    Cor.   Saw you Aufidius?
    Lart. On safeguard he came to me; and did curse
Against the Volsces, for they had so vilely
Yielded the town: he is retir'd to Antium.
    Cor. Spoke he of me?

Lart.   He did, my lord.

Cor.   How? what?

Lart. How often he had met you, sword to sword;
That of all things upon the earth he hated
Your person most; that he would pawn his fortunes
To hopeless restitution, so he might
Be call'd your vanquisher.

Cor.   At Antium lives he?

Lart. At Antium.

Cor. I wish I had a cause to seek him there,
To oppose his hatred fully.—Welcome home. [*To* LARTIUS.

Enter SICINIUS *and* BRUTUS.

Behold! these are the tribunes of the people,
The tongues o' the common mouth. I do despise them;
For they do prank them in authority,
Against all noble sufferance.

Sic.   Pass no further.

Cor. Ha! what is that?

Bru. It will be dangerous to go on: no further.

Cor. What makes this change?

Men. The matter?

Com. Hath he not pass'd the nobles and the commons?

Bru. Cominius, no.

Cor.   Have I had children's voices?

1 *Sen.* Tribunes, give way; he shall to the market-place.

Bru. The people are incens'd against him.

Sic.   Stop,
Or all will fall in broil.

Cor.   Are these your herd?—
Must these have voices, that can yield them now,
And straight disclaim their tongues?—What are your
          offices?
You being their mouths, why rule you not their teeth?
Have you not set them on?

Men.   Be calm, be calm.

Cor. It is a purpos'd thing, and grows by plot,
To curb the will of the nobility:
Suffer't, and live with such as cannot rule,
Nor ever will be rul'd.

Bru.   Call't not a plot:
The people cry you mock'd them; and of late,
When corn was given them gratis, you repin'd;
Scandal'd the suppliants for the people,—call'd them
Time-pleasers, flatterers, foes to nobleness.

Cor. Why, this was known before.

Bru.   Not to them all.

Cor. Have you inform'd them sithence?

Bru.   How! I inform them!

Cor. You are like to do such business.

Bru.   Not unlike,
Each way, to better yours.

Cor. Why, then, should I be consul? By yon clouds,
Let me deserve so ill as you, and make me
Your fellow tribune.

Sic.   You show too much of that
For which the people stir: if you will pass
To where you are bound, you must inquire your way,
Which you are out of, with a gentler spirit;
Or never be so noble as a consul,
Nor yoke with him for tribune.

Men.   Let's be calm.

Com. The people are abus'd; set on. This palt'ring
Becomes not Rome; nor has Coriolanus
Deserv'd this so dishonour'd rub, laid falsely
I' the plain way of his merit.

Cor.   Tell me of corn!
This was my speech, and I will speak 't again,—

Men. Not now, not now.

1 *Sen.*   Not in this heat, sir, now

Cor. Now, as I live, I will.—My nobler friends,
I crave their pardons:
For the mutable, rank-scented many, let them
Regard me as I do not flatter, and
Therein behold themselves: I say again,
In soothing them we nourish 'gainst our senate
The cockle of rebellion, insolence, sedition,
Which we ourselves have plough'd for, sow'd, and scatter'd,
By mingling them with us, the honour'd number;
Who lack not virtue, no, nor power, but that
Which they have given to beggars.

Men.   Well, no more.

1 *Sen.* No more words, we beseech you.

Cor.   How! no more!
As for my country I have shed my blood,
Not fearing outward force, so shall my lungs
Coin words till their decay against those measles
Which we disdain should tetter us, yet sought
The very way to catch them.

Bru.   You speak o' the people
As if you were a god to punish, not
A man of their infirmity.

Sic.   'Twere well
We let the people know 't.
    Men.   What, what? his choler?
    Cor. Choler!
Were I as patient as the midnight sleep,
By Jove, 'twould be my mind!
    Sic.   It is a mind
That shall remain a poison where it is,
Not poison any further.
    Cor.   Shall remain!—
Hear you this Triton of the minnows? mark you
His absolute *shall?*
    Com.   'Twas from the canon.
    Cor.   *Shall!*
O good, but most unwise patricians! why,
You grave, but reckless senators, have you thus
Given Hydra leave to choose an officer,
That with his peremptory *shall*, being but
The horn and noise o' the monster, wants not spirit
To say he'll turn your current in a ditch,
And make your channel his? If he have power,
Then vail your ignorance: if none, awake
Your dangerous lenity. If you are learn'd,
Be not as common fools; if you are not,
Let them have cushions by you. You are plebeians
If they be senators: and they are no less
When, both your voices blended, the great'st taste
Most palates theirs. They choose their magistrate;
And such a one as he, who puts his *shall*,
His popular *shall*, against a graver bench
Than ever frown'd in Greece. By Jove himself,
It makes the consuls base: and my soul aches
To know, when two authorities are up,
Neither supreme, how soon confusion
May enter 'twixt the gap of both, and take
The one by the other.
    Com.   Well, on to the market-place.
    Cor. Whoever gave that counsel, to give forth
The corn o' the storehouse gratis, as 'twas us'd
Sometime in Greece,—
    Men.   Well, well, no more of that.
    Cor. Though there the people had more absolute power,—
I say, they nourish'd disobedience, fed
The ruin of the state.
    Bru.   Why, shall the people give
One that speaks thus their voice?

Cor.   I'll give my reasons,
More worthier than their voices.   They know the corn
Was not our recompense, resting well assur'd
They ne'er did service for't : being press'd to the war,
Even when the navel of the state was touch'd,
They would not thread the gates,—this kind of service
Did not deserve corn gratis : being i' the war,
Their mutinies and revolts, wherein they show'd
Most valour, spoke not for them.   The accusation
Which they have often made against the senate,
All cause unborn, could never be the motive
Of our so frank donation.   Well, what then?
How shall this bisson multitude digest
The senate's courtesy?   Let deeds express
What 's like to be their words :—*We did request it·*
We are the greater poll, and in true fear
They gave us our demands:—thus we debase
The nature of our seats, and make the rabble
Call our cares fears : which will in time
Break ope the locks o' the senate, and bring in
The crows to peck the eagles.
Men.   Come, enough.
Bru. Enough, with over-measure.
Cor.   No, take more :
What may be sworn by, both divine and human,
Seal what I end withal!—This double worship,—
Where one part does disdain with cause, the other
Insult without all reason ; where gentry, title, wisdom,
Cannot conclude but by the yea and no
Of general ignorance,—it must omit
Real necessities, and give way the while
To unstable slightness : purpose so barr'd, it follows,
Nothing is done to purpose.   Therefore, beseech you,—
You that will be less fearful than discreet ;
That love the fundamental part of state
More than you doubt the change on't ; that prefer
A noble life before a long, and wish
To vamp a body with a dangerous physic
That 's sure of death without it,—at once pluck out
The multitudinous tongue ; let them not lick
The sweet which is their poison : your dishonour
Mangles true judgment, and bereaves the state
Of that integrity which should become 't ;
Not having the power to do the good it would,
For the ill which doth control 't.
Bru.   Has said enough.

Sic. Has spoken like a traitor, and shall answer
As traitors do.

Cor. Thou wretch, despite o'erwhelm thee!—
What should the people do with these bald tribunes?
On whom depending, their obedience fails
To the greater bench: in a rebellion,
When what 's not meet, but what must be, was law,
Then were they chosen; in a better hour
Let what is meet be said it must be meet,
And throw their power i' the dust.

Bru. Manifest treason.

Sic. This a consul? no.

Bru. The ædiles, ho!—Let him be apprehended.

Sic. Go, call the people [*exit* BRUTUS];—in whose name
    myself
Attach thee as a traitorous innovator,
A foe to the public weal. Obey, I charge thee,
And follow to thine answer.

Cor. Hence, old goat!

Sen. and Pat. We'll surety him.

Com. Aged sir, hands off.

Cor. Hence, rotten thing! or I shall shake thy bones
Out of thy garments.

Sic. Help, ye citizens!

Re-enter BRUTUS, *with the Æ*diles *and a rabble of* Citizens.

Men. On both sides more respect.

Sic. Here 's he that would take from you all your power.

Bru. Seize him, ædiles.

Citizens. Down with him! down with him!

2 Sen. Weapons, weapons, weapons!
    [*They all bustle about* CORIOLANUS.
Tribunes, patricians, citizens!—what, ho!—
Sicinius, Brutus, Coriolanus, citizens!

Citizens. Peace, peace, peace; stay, hold, peace!

Men. What is about to be?—I am out of breath;
Confusion 's near; I cannot speak.—You, tribunes
To the people,—Coriolanus, patience:—
Speak, good Sicinius.

Sic. Hear me, people; peace!

Citizens. Let 's hear our tribune: peace!—Speak, speak.

Sic. You are at point to lose your liberties: [speak.
Marcius would have all from you; Marcius,
Whom late you have nam'd for consul.

Men. Fie, fie, fie!
This is the way to kindle, not to quench.

1 *Sen.* To unbuild the city, and to lay all flat.

Sic. What is the city but the people?

Citizens.   True,

The people are the city.

Bru. By the consent of all, we were establish'd
The people's magistrates.

Mit.   You so remain.

Men. And so are like to do.

Cor. That is the way to lay the city flat;
To bring the roof to the foundation,
And bury all which yet distinctly ranges,
In heaps and piles of ruin.

Sic.   This deserves death.

Bru. Or let us stand to our authority,
Or let us lose it.—We do here pronounce,
Upon the part o' the people, in whose power
We were elected theirs, Marcius is worthy
Of present death.

Sic.   Therefore lay hold of him;
Bear him to the rock Tarpeian, and from thence
Into destruction cast him.

Bru.   Ædiles, seize him!

Citizens. Yield, Marcius, yield!

Men.   Hear me one word;
Beseech you, tribunes, hear me but a word.

Æd. Peace, peace!

Men. Be that you seem, truly your country's friends,
And temperately proceed to what you would
Thus violently redress.

Bru.   Sir, these cold ways,
That seem like prudent helps, are very poisonous
Where the disease is violent.—Lay hands upon him,
And bear him to the rock.

Cor.   No; I'll die here. [*Draws his sword.*
There's some among you have beheld me fighting:
Come, try upon yourselves what you have seen me.

Men. Down with that sword!—Tribunes, withdraw
        awhile.

Bru. Lay hands upon him.

Men.   Help Marcius, help,
You that be noble; help him, young and old!

Citizens. Down with him, down with him!

        [*In this mutiny the* Tribunes, *the* Ædiles, *and the*
          People *are beat in.*

Men. Go, get you to your house; be gone, away!
All will be naught else.

2 *Sen.* Get you gone.

Cor. Stand fast;
We have as many friends as enemies.

Men. Shall it be put to that?

1 *Sen.* The gods forbid!
I pr'ythee, noble friend, home to thy house;
Leave us to cure this cause.

Men. For 'tis a sore upon us,
You cannot tent yourself: be gone, beseech you.

Com. Come, sir, along with us.

Cor. I would they were barbarians,—as they are,
Though in Rome litter'd,—not Romans,—as they are not,
Though calv'd i' the porch o' the Capitol,—

Men. Be gone;
Put not your worthy rage into your tongue;
One time will owe another.

Cor. On fair ground
I could beat forty of them.

Men. I could myself
Take up a brace o' the best of them; yea, the two tribunes.

Com. But now 'tis odds beyond arithmetic;
And manhood is call'd foolery when it stands
Against a falling fabric.—Will you hence,
Before the tag return? whose rage doth rend
Like interrupted waters, and o'erbear
What they are used to bear.

Men. Pray you, be gone:
I'll try whether my old wit be in request
With those that have but little: this must be patch'd
With cloth of any colour.

Com. Nay, come away.
[*Exeunt* COR., COM., *and others.*

1 *Pat.* This man has marr'd his fortune.

Men. His nature is too noble for the world:
He would not flatter Neptune for his trident,
Or Jove for 's power to thunder. His heart's his mouth:
What his breast forges, that his tongue must vent;
And, being angry, does forget that ever
He heard the name of death. [*A noise within.*
Here's goodly work!

2 *Pat.* I would they were a-bed!

Men. I would they were in Tiber! What, the vengeance,
Could he not speak 'em fair?

Re-enter BRUTUS *and* SICINIUS, *with the rabble.*

Sic. Where is this viper

That would depopulate the city and
Be every man himself?
    Men.   You worthy tribunes, —
    Sic. He shall be thrown down the Tarpeian rock
With rigorous hands: he hath resisted law,
And therefore law shall scorn him further trial
Than the severity of the public power,
Which he so sets at naught.
    1 *Cit.*   He shall well know
The noble tribunes are the people's mouths,
And we their hands.
    Citizens. He shall, sure on't.
    Men.   Sir, sir,—
    Sic.   Peace!
    Men. Do not cry havoc, where you should but hunt
With modest warrant.
    Sic.   Sir, how comes't that you
Have holp to make this rescue?
    Men.   Hear me speak :—
As I do know the consul's worthiness,
So can I name his faults,—
    Sic.   Consul!—what consul?——
    Men. The consul Coriolanus.
    Bru.   He consul!
    Citizens. No, no, no, no, no.
    Men. If, by the tribunes' leave, and yours, good people,
I may be heard, I would crave a word or two;
The which shall turn you to no further harm
Than so much loss of time.
    Sic.   Speak briefly, then;
For we are peremptory to despatch
This viperous traitor: to eject him hence
Were but one danger; and to keep him here
Our certain death: therefore it is decreed
He dies to-night.
    Men.   Now the good gods forbid
That our renowned Rome, whose gratitude
Towards her deserved children is enroll'd
In Jove's own book, like an unnatural dam
Should now eat up her own!
    Sic. He's a disease that must be cut away.
    Men. O, he's a limb that has but a disease;
Mortal, to cut it off; to cure it, easy.
What has he done to Rome that's worthy death?
Killing our enemies, the blood he hath lost,—
Which I dare vouch is more than that he **hath**

By many an ounce,—he dropt it for his country;
And what is left, to lose it by his country
Were to us all, that do't and suffer it,
A brand to the end o' the world.
    Sic.   This is clean kam.
    Bru. Merely awry: when he did love his country,
It honour'd him.
    Men.   The service of the foot,
Being once gangren'd, is not then respected
For what before it was.
    Bru.   We'll hear no more.—
Pursue him to his house and pluck him thence;
Lest his infection, being of catching nature,
Spread further.
    Men.   One word more, one word.
This tiger-footed rage, when it shall find
The harm of unscann'd swiftness, will, too late,
Tie leaden pounds to 's heels. Proceed by process;
Lest parties,—as he is belov'd,—break out,
And sack great Rome with Romans.
    Bru.   If it were so,—
    Sic. What do ye talk?
Have we not had a taste of his obedience?
Our ædiles smote? ourselves resisted?—come,—
    Men. Consider this:—he has been bred i' the wars
Since he could draw a sword, and is ill school'd
In bolted language; meal and bran together
He throws without distinction. Give me leave,
I'll go to him, and undertake to bring him
Where he shall answer, by a lawful form,
In peace, to his utmost peril.
    1 Sen.   Noble tribunes,
It is the humane way: the other course
Will prove too bloody; and the end of it
Unknown to the beginning.
    Sic.   Noble Menenius,
Be you then as the people's officer.—
Masters, lay down your weapons.
    Bru.   Go not home.
    Sic. Meet on the market-place.—We'll attend you there:
Where, if you bring not Marcius, we'll proceed
In our first way.
    Men.   I'll bring him to you.—
[*To the* Senators.] Let me desire your company: he must
Or what is worst will follow.   [come,
    1 Sen.   Pray you, let 's to him. [*Exeunt.*

SCENE II.—ROME.　*A Room in* CORIOLANUS'S *House.*

Enter CORIOLANUS *and* Patricians.

Cor. Let them pull all about mine ears ; present me
Death on the wheel, or at wild horses' heels ;
Or pile ten hills on the Tarpeian rock,
That the precipitation might down stretch
Below the beam of sight ; yet will I still
Be thus to them.
　　1 *Pat.*　　　　You do the nobler.
　　Cor. I muse my mother
Does not approve me further, who was wont
To call them woollen vassals, things created
To buy and sell with groats ; to show bare heads
In congregations, to yawn, be still, and wonder,
When one but of my ordinance stood up
To speak of peace or war.

Enter VOLUMNIA.

　　　　　　　I talk of you : [*To* VOLUMNIA.
Why did you wish me milder? Would you have me
False to my nature? Rather say, I play
The man I am.
　　Vol.　　　　O, sir, sir, sir,
I would have had you put your power well on
Before you had worn it out.
　　Cor.　　　　　　　Let go.
　　Vol. You might have been enough the man you are
With striving less to be so : lesser had been
The thwartings of your dispositions if
You had not show'd them how ye were dispos'd
Ere they lack'd power to cross you.
　　Cor.　　　　　　Let them hang.
　　Vol. Ay, and burn too.

Enter MENENIUS *and* Senators.

　　Men. Come, come, you have been too rough, something
You must return and mend it.　　　　　[too rough ;
　　1 *Sen.*　　　　　There's no remedy ;
Unless, by not so doing, our good city
Cleave in the midst, and perish.
　　Vol.　　　　　Pray, be counsell'd :
I have a heart as little apt as yours,
But yet a brain that leads my use of anger
To better vantage.
　　VOL. V.　　　　　　I

Men.   Well said, noble woman!
Before he should thus stoop to the herd, but that
The violent fit o' the time craves it as physic
For the whole state, I would put mine armour on,
Which I can scarcely bear.
  Cor. What must I do?
  Men. Return to the tribunes
  Cor. Well, what then? what then?
  Men. Repent what you have spoke.
  Cor. For them?—I cannot do it to the gods;
Must I then do't to them?
  Vol.   You are too absolute;
Though therein you can never be too noble
But when extremities speak. I have heard you say,
Honour and policy, like unsever'd friends,
I' the war do grow together: grant that, and tell me
In peace what each of them by th' other lose
That they combine not there.
  Cor.   Tush, tush!
  Men.   A good demand.
  Vol. If it be honour in your wars to seem
The same you are not,—which for your best ends
You adopt your policy,—how is it less or worse
That it shall hold companionship in peace
With honour as in war; since that to both
It stands in like request?
  Cor.   Why force you this?
  Vol. Because that now it lies you on to speak
To the people; not by your own instruction,
Nor by the matter which your heart prompts you,
But with such words that are but rooted in
Your tongue, though but bastards, and syllables
Of no allowance, to your bosom's truth.
Now, this no more dishonours you at all
Than to take in a town with gentle words,
Which else would put you to your fortune and
The hazard of much blood.
I would dissemble with my nature where
My fortunes and my friends at stake requir'd
I should do so in honour: I am in this
Your wife, your son, these senators, the nobles;
And you will rather show cur general louts
How you can frown, than spend a fawn upon 'em
For the inheritance of their loves and safeguard
Of what that want might ruin.
  Men.   Noble lady!—

Come, go with us; speak fair: you may salve so,
Not what is dangerous present, but the loss
Of what is past.
   Vol.   I pr'ythee now, my son,
Go to them with this bonnet in thy hand;
And thus far having stretch'd it,—here be with them,—
Thy knee bussing the stones,—for in such business
Action is eloquence, and the eyes of the ignorant
More learned than the ears,—waving thy head,
Which often, thus, correcting thy stout heart,
Now humble as the ripest mulberry
That will not hold the handling: or say to them
Thou art their soldier, and, being bred in broils,
Hast not the soft way which, thou dost confess,
Were fit for thee to use, as they to claim,
In asking their good loves; but thou wilt frame
Thyself, forsooth, hereafter theirs, so far
As thou hast power and person.
   Men.   This but done,
Even as she speaks, why, their hearts were yours:
For they have pardons, being ask'd, as free
As words to little purpose.
   Vol.   Pr'ythee now,
Go, and be rul'd: although I know thou had'st rather
Follow thine enemy in a fiery gulf
Than flatter him in a bower.   Here is Cominius.

        Enter COMINIUS.

   Com. I have been i' the market-place; and, sir, 'tis fit
You make strong party, or defend yourself
By calmness or by absence: all's in anger.
   Men. Only fair speech.
   Com.   I think 'twill serve, if he
Can thereto frame his spirit.
   Vol.   He must, and will.—
Pr'ythee now, say you will, and go about it.
   Cor. Must I go show them my unbarb'd sconce? must I,
With my base tongue, give to my noble heart
A lie, that it must bear?   Well, I will do't:
Yet, were there but this single plot to lose,
This mould of Marcius, they to dust should grind it,
And throw't against the wind.—To the market-place:—
You have put me now to such a part which never
I shall discharge to the life.
   Com.   Come, come, we'll prompt you.
   Vol. I pr'ythee now, sweet son,—as thou hast said

My praises made thee first a soldier, so,
To have my praise for this, perform a part
Thou hast not done before.

Cor.　　　　　　　　Well, I must do't:
Away, my disposition, and possess me
Some harlot's spirit!　My throat of war be turn'd,
Which quired with my drum, into a pipe
Small as an eunuch, or the virgin voice
That babies lulls asleep! the smiles of knaves
Tent in my cheeks; and school-boys' tears take up
The glasses of my sight! a beggar's tongue
Make motion through my lips; and my arm'd knees,
Who bow'd but in my stirrup, bend like his
That hath receiv'd an alms!—I will not do't;
Lest I surcease to honour mine own truth,
And by my body's action teach my mind
A most inherent baseness.

Vol.　　　　　　　　At thy choice, then:
To beg of thee, it is my more dishonour
Than thou of them.　Come all to ruin: let
Thy mother rather feel thy pride than fear
Thy dangerous stoutness; for I mock at death
With as big heart as thou.　Do as thou list.
Thy valiantness was mine, thou suck'dst it from me;
But owe thy pride thyself.

Cor.　　　　　　　　Pray, be content:
Mother, I am going to the market-place;
Chide me no more.　I'll mountebank their loves,
Cog their hearts from them, and come home belov'd
Of all the trades in Rome.　Look, I am going:
Commend me to my wife.　I'll return consul;
Or never trust to what my tongue can do
I' the way of flattery further.

Vol.　　　　　　　　Do your will.　　　*[Exit.*

Com. Away! the tribunes do attend you: arm yourself
To answer mildly; for they are prepar'd
With accusations, as I hear, more strong
Than are upon you yet.

Cor. The word is, mildly.—Pray you, let us go:
Let them accuse me by invention, I
Will answer in mine honour.

Men.　　　　　　　　Ay, but mildly.

Cor. Well mildly be it then; mildly.　　　*[Exeunt.*

SCENE III.—ROME. *The Forum.*

Enter SICINIUS *and* BRUTUS.

Bru. In this point charge him home, that he affects
Tyrannical power: if he evade us there,
Enforce him with his envy to the people;
And that the spoil got on the Antiates
Was ne'er distributed.

Enter an Ædile.

What, will he come?
  Æd.   He 's coming.
  Bru.   How accompanied?
  Æd. With old Menenius, and those senators
That always favour'd him.
  Sic.   Have you a catalogue
Of all the voices that we have procur'd,
Set down by the poll?
  Æd.   I have; 'tis ready.
  Sic. Have you collected them by tribes?
  Æd.   I have.
  Sic. Assemble presently the people hither:
And when they hear me say, *It shall be so*
I' the right and strength o' the commons, be it either
For death, for fine, or banishment, then let them,
If I say fine, cry *Fine,*—if death, cry *Death;*
Insisting on the old prerogative
And power i' the truth o' the cause.
  Æd.   I shall inform them.
  Bru. And when such time they have begun to cry,
Let them not cease, but with a din confus'd
Enforce the present execution
Of what we chance to sentence.
  Æd.   Very well.
  Sic. Make them be strong, and ready for this hint,
When we shall hap to give 't them.
  Bru.   Go about it.—
             [*Exit* Ædile.
Put him to choler straight: he hath been us'd
Ever to conquer, and to have his worth
Of contradiction: being once chaf'd, he cannot
Be rein'd again to temperance; then he speaks
What 's in his heart; and that is there which looks
With us to break his neck.
  Sic. Well, here he comes.

Enter CORIOLANUS, MENENIUS, COMINIUS, Senators,
and Patricians.

Men. Calmly, I do beseech you.
Cor. Ay, as an ostler, that for the poorest piece
Will bear the knave by the volume.—The honour'd gods
Keep Rome in safety, and the chairs of justice
Supplied with worthy men! plant love among 's!
Throng our large temples with the shows of peace,
And not our streets with war!
1 Sen.   Amen, amen!
Men. A noble wish.

Re-enter Ædile, *with* Citizens.

Sic. Draw near, ye people.
Æd. List to your tribunes; audience: peace, I say!
Cor. First, hear me speak.
Both Tri.   Well, say.—Peace, ho!
Cor. Shall I be charg'd no further than this present?
Must all determine here?
Sic.   I do demand,
If you submit you to the people's voices,
Allow their officers, and are content
To suffer lawful censure for such faults
As shall be proved upon you?
Cor.   I am content.
Men. Lo, citizens, he says he is content:
The warlike service he has done, consider; think
Upon the wounds his body bears, which show like
Graves i' the holy churchyard.
Cor.   Scratches with briers,
Scars to move laughter only.
Men.   Consider further,
That when he speaks not like a citizen,
You find him like a soldier: do not take
His rougher accents for malicious sounds,
But, as I say, such as become a soldier,
Rather than envy you.
Com.   Well, well, no more.
Cor. What is the matter,
That being pass'd for consul with full voice,
I am so dishonour'd that the very hour
You take it off again?
Sic.   Answer to us.
Cor. Say then: 'tis true, I ought so.
Sic. We charge you that you have contriv'd to take

From Rome all season'd office, and to wind
Yourself into a power tyrannical;
For which you are a traitor to the people.
   Cor. How! traitor!
   Men.   Nay, temperately; your promise.
   Cor. The fires i' the lowest hell fold in the people!
Call me their traitor!—Thou injurious tribune!
Within thine eyes sat twenty thousand deaths,
In thy hands clutch'd as many millions, in
Thy lying tongue both numbers, I would say,
Thou liest unto thee, with a voice as free
As I do pray the gods.
   Sic.   Mark you this, people?
   Citizens. To the rock, to the rock with him!
   Sic. Peace!
We need not put new matter to his charge:
What you have seen him do and heard him speak,
Beating your officers, cursing yourselves,
Opposing laws with strokes, and here defying
Those whose great power must try him; even this,
So criminal, and in such capital kind,
Deserves the extremest death.
   Bru.   But since he hath
Serv'd well for Rome,—
   Cor.   What, do you prate of service!
   Bru. I talk of that, that know it.
   Cor. You?
   Men. Is this the promise that you made your mother?
   Com. Know, I pray you,—
   Cor.   I'll know no further:
Let them pronounce the steep Tarpeian death,
Vagabond exile, flaying, pent to linger
But with a grain a day, I would not buy
Their mercy at the price of one fair word,
Nor check my courage for what they can give,
To have't with saying Good-morrow.
   Sic.   For that he has,—
As much as in him lies,—from time to time
Envied against the people, seeking means
To pluck away their power; as now at last
Given hostile strokes, and that not in the presence
Of dreaded justice, but on the ministers
That do distribute it;—in the name o' the people,
And in the power of us the tribunes, we,
Even from this instant, banish him our city;
In peril of precipitation

From off the rock Tarpeian, never more
To enter our Rome gates: i' the people's name,
I say it shall be so.

Citizens. It shall be so, it shall be so; let him away:
He's banished, and it shall be so.

Com. Hear me, my masters, and my common friends,—
Sic. He's sentenc'd; no more hearing.
Com.　　　　　　　　　　　　　Let me speak:
I have been consul, and can show for Rome
Her enemies' marks upon me. I do love
My country's good with a respect more tender,
More holy and profound, than mine own life,
My dear wife's estimate, her womb's increase,
And treasure of my loins; then if I would
Speak that,—
Sic.　　　　　We know your drift. Speak what?
Bru. There's no more to be said, but he is banish'd,
As enemy to the people and his country:
It shall be so.

Citizens. It shall be so, it shall be so.

Cor. You common cry of curs! whose breath I hate
As reek o' the rotten fens, whose loves I prize
As the dead carcasses of unburied men
That do corrupt my air,—I banish you;
And here remain with your uncertainty!
Let every feeble rumour shake your hearts!
Your enemies, with nodding of their plumes,
Fan you into despair! Have the power still
To banish your defenders; till at length
Your ignorance,—which finds not till it feels,—
Making not reservation of yourselves,—
Still your own foes,—deliver you, as most
Abated captives, to some nation
That won you without blows! Despising,
For you, the city, thus I turn my back:
There is a world elsewhere.
　　　　[*Exeunt* COR., COM., MEN., Senators, *and* Patricians.
Æd. The people's enemy is gone, is gone!

Citizens. Our enemy is banish'd! he is gone! Hoo! hoo!
　　　　　　　[*Shouting, and throwing up their caps.*
Sic. Go, see him out at gates, and follow him,
As he hath follow'd you, with all despite;
Give him deserv'd vexation. Let a guard
Attend us through the city.

Citizens. Come, come, let us see him out at gates; come.
The gods preserve our noble tribunes!—Come. [*Exeunt.*

ACT IV.

SCENE I.—ROME. *Before a Gate of the City.*

Enter CORIOLANUS, VOLUMNIA, VIRGILIA, MENENIUS,
  COMINIUS, *and several young* Patricians.

Cor. Come, leave your tears; a brief farewell:—the beast
With many heads butts me away.—Nay, mother,
Where is your ancient courage? you were us'd
To say extremity was the trier of spirits;
That common chances common men could bear;
That when the sea was calm all boats alike
Show'd mastership in floating; fortune's blows,
When most struck home, being gentle wounded, craves
A noble cunning: you were us'd to load me
With precepts that would make invincible
The heart that conn'd them.
  Vir. O heavens! O heavens!
  Cor.   Nay, I pr'ythee, woman,—
  Vol. Now the red pestilence strike all trades in Rome,
And occupations perish!
  Cor.   What, what, what!
I shall be lov'd when I am lack'd. Nay, mother,
Resume that spirit when you were wont to say,
If you had been the wife of Hercules,
Six of his labours you'd have done, and sav'd
Your husband so much sweat.—Cominius,
Droop not; adieu.—Farewell, my wife,—my mother:
I'll do well yet.—Thou old and true Menenius,
Thy tears are salter than a younger man's,
And venomous to thine eyes.—My some time general,
I have seen thee stern, and thou hast oft beheld
Heart-hard'ning spectacles; tell these sad women
'Tis fond to wail inevitable strokes
As 'tis to laugh at 'em.—My mother, you wot well
My hazards still have been your solace: and
Believe 't not lightly,—though I go alone,
Like to a lonely dragon, that his fen
Makes fear'd and talk'd of more than seen,—your son
Will or exceed the common or be caught
With cautelous baits and practice.
  Vol.   My first son,
Whither wilt thou go? Take good Cominius
With thee awhile: determine on some course

More than a wild exposture to each chance
That starts i' the way before thee.

Cor.   O the gods!

Com. I'll follow thee a month, devise with thee
Where thou shalt rest, that thou may'st hear of us,
And we of thee: so, if the time thrust forth
A cause for thy repeal, we shall not send
O'er the vast world to seek a single man ;
And lose advantage, which doth ever cool
I' the absence of the needer.

Cor.   Fare ye well:
Thou hast years upon thee; and thou art too full
Of the wars' surfeits to go rove with one
That's yet unbruis'd: bring me but out at gate. —
Come, my sweet wife, my dearest mother, and
My friends of noble touch; when I am forth,
Bid me farewell, and smile. I pray you, come.
While I remain above the ground, you shall
Hear from me still; and never of me aught
But what is like me formerly.

Men.   That's worthily
As any ear can hear.—Come, let's not weep.—
If I could shake off but one seven years
From these old arms and legs, by the good gods,
I'd with thee every foot.

Cor.   Give me thy hand:—
Come.   [*Exeunt.*

_____

SCENE II.—ROME. *A Street near the Gate.*

Enter SICINIUS, BRUTUS, *and an* Ædile.

Sic. Bid them all home; he's gone, and we'll no further.—
The nobility are vex'd, whom we see have sided
In his behalf.

Bru.   Now we have shown our power,
Let us seem humbler after it is done
Than when it was a-doing.

Sic.   Bid them home:
Say their great enemy is gone, and they
Stand in their ancient strength.

Bru.   Dismiss them home.
                              [*Exit* Ædile.

Here comes his mother.

Sic.   Let's not meet her.

Bru.   Why?

Sic. They say she's mad.

Bru. They have ta'en note of us: keep on your way.

Enter VOLUMNIA, VIRGILIA, *and* MENENIUS.

Vol. O, you're well met: the hoarded plague o' the gods
Requite your love!
Men.   Peace, peace, be not so loud.
Vol. If that I could for weeping, you should hear,—
Nay, and you shall hear some.—Will you be gone?
                                        [*To* BRUTUS.
Vir. You shall stay too [*to* SICINIUS]: I would I had the
To say so to my husband.   [power
Sic.   Are you mankind?
Vol. Ay, fool; is that a shame?—Note but this fool.—
Was not a man my father? Hadst thou foxship
To banish him that struck more blows for Rome
Than thou hast spoken words?—
Sic.   O blessed heavens!
Vol. More noble blows than ever thou wise words;
And for Rome's good.—I'll tell thee what;—yet go;—
Nay, but thou shalt stay too:—I would my son
Were in Arabia, and thy tribe before him,
His good sword in his hand.
Sic.   What then?
Vir.   What then!
He'd make an end of thy posterity.
Vol. Bastards and all.—
Good man, the wounds that he does bear for Rome!
Men. Come, come, peace.
Sic. I would he had continu'd to his country
As he began, and not unknit himself
The noble knot he made.
Bru.   I would he had.
Vol. I would he had! 'Twas you incens'd the rabble;—
Cats, that can judge as fitly of his worth
As I can of those mysteries which heaven
Will not have earth to know.
Bru.   Pray, let us go.
Vol. Now, pray, sir, get you gone:
You have done a brave deed. Ere you go, hear this,--
As far as doth the Capitol exceed
The meanest house in Rome, so far my son,—
This lady's husband here; this, do you see?—
Whom you have banish'd, does exceed you all.
Bru. Well, well, we'll leave you.
Sic.   Why stay we to be baited
With one that wants her wits!

Vol.   Take my prayers with you.—
I would the gods had nothing else to do [*Exeunt* Tribunes.
But to confirm my curses!   Could I meet 'em
But once a day, it would unclog my heart
Of what lies heavy to't.
  Men.   You have told them home,
And, by my troth, you have cause.   You'll sup with me?
    Vol. Anger's my meat; I sup upon myself,
And so shall starve with feeding.—Come, let's go:
Leave this faint puling, and lament as I do,
In anger, Juno-like.   Come, come, come.
    Men. Fie, fie, fie!   [*Exeunt.*

SCENE III.—*A Highway between Rome and Antium.*

Enter a Roman *and a* Volsce, *meeting.*

  Rom. I know you well, sir; and you know me: your
name, I think, is Adrian.
  Vols. It is so, sir: truly, I have forgot you.
  Rom. I am a Roman; and my services are, as you are,
against 'em: know you me yet?
  Vols. Nicanor? no.
  Rom. The same, sir.
  Vol's. You had more beard when I last saw you; but your
favour is well approved by your tongue.   What's the news
in Rome? I have a note from the Volscian state, to find you
out there: you have well saved me a day's journey.
  Rom. There hath been in Rome strange insurrections; the
people against the senators, patricians, and nobles.
  Vols. Hath been! is it ended, then? Our state thinks not
so ; they are in a most warlike preparation, and hope to come
upon them in the heat of their division.
  Rom. The main blaze of it is past, but a small thing would
make it flame again: for the nobles receive so to heart the
banishment of that worthy Coriolanus that they are in a ripe
aptness to take all power from the people, and to pluck from
them their tribunes for ever.   This lies glowing, I can
tell you, and is almost mature for the violent breaking
out.
  Vols. Coriolanus banished!
  Rom. Banished, sir.
  Vols. You will be welcome with this intelligence, Nicanor.
  Rom. The day serves well for them now.   I have heard it
said the fittest time to corrupt a man's wife is when she's
fallen out with her husband.   Your noble Tullus Aufidius

will appear well in these wars, his great opposer, Coriolanus,
being now in no request of his country.

Vols. He cannot choose. I am most fortunate thus
accidentally to encounter you : you have ended my business,
and I will merrily accompany you home.

Rom. I shall, between this and supper, tell you most
strange things from Rome; all tending to the good of their
adversaries. Have you an army ready, say you?

Vols. A most royal one; the centurions and their charges,
distinctly billeted, already in the entertainment, and to be
on foot at an hour's warning.

Rom. I am joyful to hear of their readiness, and am the
man, I think, that shall set them in present action. So, sir,
heartily well met, and most glad of your company.

Vols. You take my part from me, sir; I have the most
cause to be glad of yours.

Rom. Well, let us go together.   [*Exeunt.*

SCENE IV.—ANTIUM. *Before* AUFIDIUS'S *House.*

Enter CORIOLANUS, *in mean apparel, disguised and muffled.*

Cor. A goodly city is this Antium.—City,
'Tis I that made thy widows : many an heir
Of these fair edifices 'fore my wars
Have I heard groan and drop: then know me not,
Lest that thy wives with spits and boys with stones
In puny battle slay me.

Enter a Citizen.
Save you, sir.

Cit. And you.

Cor.   Direct me, if it be your will,
Where great Aufidius lies: is he in Antium?

Cit. He is, and feasts the nobles of the state
At his house this night.

Cor.   Which is his house, beseech you?

Cit. This, here, before you.

Cor.   Thank you, sir : farewell.
         [*Exit* Citizen

O world, thy slippery turns! Friends now fast sworn,
Whose double bosoms seem to wear one heart,
Whose house, whose bed, whose meal and exercis
Are still together, who twin, as 'twere, in love
Unseparable, shall within this hour,
On a dissension of a doit, break out

To bitterest enmity; so fellest foes,
Whose passions and whose plots have broke their sleep
To take the one the other, by some chance,
Some trick not worth an egg, shall grow dear friends
And interjoin their issues. So with me:—
My birthplace hate I, and my love's upon
This enemy town.—I'll enter: if he slay me,
He does fair justice; if he give me way,
I'll do his country service.   [*Exit.*

SCENE V.—ANTIUM. *A Hall in* AUFIDIUS'S *House.*

Music within.   Enter a Servant.

1 *Serv.* Wine, wine, wine!   What service is here!
I think our fellows are asleep.   [*Exit.*

Enter a second Servant.

2 *Serv.* Where's Cotus! my master calls for him.—
Cotus!   [*Exit.*

Enter CORIOLANUS.

Cor. A goodly house: the feast smells well; but I
Appear not like a guest.

Re-enter the first Servant.

1 *Serv.* What would you have, friend? whence are you?
Here's no place for you: pray, go to the door.
Cor. I have deserv'd no better entertainment
In being Coriolanus.

Re-enter second Servant.

2 *Serv.* Whence are you, sir? Has the porter his eyes
in his head, that he gives entrance to such companions?
Pray, get you out.
Cor. Away!
2 *Serv.* Away! Get you away.
Cor. Now thou art troublesome.
2 *Serv.* Are you so brave? I'll have you talked with anon.

Enter a third Servant.   *The first meets him.*

3 *Serv.* What fellow's this?
1 *Serv.* A strange one as ever I looked on: I cannot get
him out o' the house: pr'ythee, call my master to him.
3 *Serv.* What have you to do here, fellow? Pray you,
avoid the house.

Cor. Let me but stand; I will not hurt your hearth.

3 Serv. What are you?

Cor. A gentleman.

3 Serv. A marvellous poor one.

Cor. True, so I am.

3 Serv. Pray you, poor gentleman, take up some other station; here's no place for you; pray you, avoid: come.

Cor. Follow your function, go,
And batten on cold bits. [*Pushes him away.*

3 Serv. What, you will not?—Pr'ythee, tell my master what a strange guest he has here.

2 Serv. And I shall. [*Exit.*

3 Serv. Where dwellest thou?

Cor. Under the canopy.

3 Serv. Under the canopy!

Cor. Ay.

3 Serv. Where's that?

Cor. I' the city of kites and crows.

3 Serv. I' the city of kites and crows!—What an ass it is!—Then thou dwellest with daws too?

Cor. No, I serve not thy master.

3 Serv. How, sir! Do you meddle with my master?

Cor. Ay; 'tis an honester service than to meddle with
       thy mistress:
Thou prat'st and prat'st; serve with thy trencher, hence!
[*Beats him in*

Enter AUFIDIUS *and the second* Servant.

Auf. Where is this fellow?

2 Serv. Here, sir: I'd have beaten him like a dog, but for disturbing the lords within.

Auf. Whence comest thou? what wouldst thou? thy
       name?
Why speak'st not? speak, man: what's thy name?

Cor. If, Tullus, [*Unmuffling.*
Not yet thou know'st me, and, seeing me, dost not
Think me for the man I am, necessity
Commands me name myself.

Auf. What is thy name?
[*Servants retire.*

Cor. A name unmusical to the Volscians' ears,
And harsh in sound to thine.

Auf. Say, what's thy name?
Thou hast a grim appearance, and thy face
Bears a command in't; though thy tackle's torn,
Thou show'st a noble vessel: what's thy name?

Cor. Prepare thy brow to frown :—know'st thou me yet ?
Auf. I know thee not :—thy name?
Cor. My name is Caius Marcius, who hath done
To thee particularly, and to all the Volsces,
Great hurt and mischief; thereto witness may
My surname, Coriolanus : the painful service,
The extreme dangers, and the drops of blood
Shed for my thankless country, are requited
But with that surname; a good memory,
And witness of the malice and displeasure
Which thou shouldst bear me : only that name remains;
The cruelty and envy of the people,
Permitted by our dastard nobles, who
Have all forsook me, hath devour'd the rest,
And suffer'd me by the voice of slaves to be
Whoop'd out of Rome.   Now, this extremity
Hath brought me to thy hearth : not out of hope,
Mistake me not, to save my life; for if
I had fear'd death, of all the men i' the world
I would have 'voided thee; but in mere spite,
To be full quit of those my banishers,
Stand I before thee here.   Then if thou hast
A heart of wreak in thee, that wilt revenge
Thine own particular wrongs, and stop those maims
Of shame seen through thy country, speed thee straight,
And make my misery serve thy turn : so use it
That my revengeful services may prove
As benefits to thee; for I will fight
Against my canker'd country with the spleen
Of all the under fiends.   But if so be
Thou dar'st not this, and that to prove more fortunes
Thou 'rt tir'd, then, in a word, I also am
Longer to live most weary, and present
My throat to thee and to thy ancient malice;
Which not to cut would thee show but a fool,
Since I have ever follow'd thee with hate,
Drawn tuns of blood out of thy country's breast,
And cannot live but to thy shame, unless
It be to do thee service.
    Auf.   O Marcius, Marcius!
Each word thou hast spoke hath weeded from my heart
A root of ancient envy.   If Jupiter
Should from yond cloud speak divine things,
And say '*Tis true*, I'd not believe them more
Than thee, all noble Marcius.—Let me twine
Mine arms about that body, where against

My grained ash an hundred times hath broke,
And scar'd the moon with splinters: here I clip
The anvil of my sword, and do contest
As hotly and as nobly with thy love
As ever in ambitious strength I did
Contend against thy valour.   Know thou first,
I lov'd the maid I married; never man
Sighed truer breath; but that I see thee here,
Thou noble thing! more dances my rapt heart
Than when I first my wedded mistress saw
Bestride my threshold.   Why, thou Mars! I tell thee,
We have a power on foot; and I had purpose
Once more to hew thy target from thy brawn,
Or lose mine arm for't: thou hast beat me out
Twelve several times, and I have nightly since
Dreamt of encounters 'twixt thyself and me;
We have been down together in my sleep,
Unbuckling helms, fisting each other's throat,
And wak'd half dead with nothing.   Worthy Marcius,
Had we no other quarrel else to Rome, but that
Thou art thence banish'd, we would muster all
From twelve to seventy; and, pouring war
Into the bowels of ungrateful Rome,
Like a bold flood o'erbear.   O, come, go in,
And take our friendly senators by the hands;
Who now are here, taking their leaves of me,
Who am prepar'd against your territories,
Though not for Rome itself.
    Cor.   You bless me, gods!
    Auf. Therefore, most absolute sir, if thou wilt have
The leading of thine own revenges, take
The one half of my commission; and set down,—
As best thou art experienc'd, since thou know'st
Thy country's strength and weakness,—thine own ways;
Whether to knock against the gates of Rome,
Or rudely visit them in parts remote,
To fright them, ere destroy.   But come in:
Let me commend thee first to those that shall
Say yea to thy desires.   A thousand welcomes!
And more a friend than e'er an enemy;
Yet, Marcius, that was much.   Your hand: most welcome
                            [*Exeunt* COR. *and* AUF.

    1 *Serv.* [*advancing.*] Here's a strange alteration!
    2 *Serv.* By my hand, I had thought to have strucken
him with a cudgel; and yet my mind gave me his clothes
made a false report of him.

1 Serv. What an arm he has! He turned me about with his finger and his thumb, as one would set up a top.

2 Serv. Nay, I knew by his face that there was something in him: he had, sir, a kind of face, methought,—I cannot tell how to term it.

1 Serv. He had so; looking as it were,—would I were hanged, but I thought there was more in him than I could think.

2 Serv. So did I, I'll be sworn: he is simply the rarest man i' the world.

1 Serv. I think he is: but a greater soldier than he you wot on.

2 Serv. Who, my master?

1 Serv. Nay, it 's no matter for that.

2 Serv. Worth six on him.

1 Serv. Nay, not so neither: but I take him to be the greater soldier.

2 Serv. Faith, look you, one cannot tell how to say that: for the defence of a town our general is excellent.

1 Serv. Ay, and for an assault too.

Re-enter third Servant.

3 *Serv.* O slaves, I can tell you news,—news, you rascals!

1 and 2 *Serv.* What, what, what? let 's partake.

3 *Serv.* I would not be a Roman, of all nations; I had as lieve be a condemned man.

1 and 2 *Serv.* Wherefore? wherefore?

3 Serv. Why, here 's he that was wont to thwack our general,—Caius Marcius.

1 Serv. Why do you say, thwack our general?

3 Serv. I do not say, thwack our general; but he was always good enough for him.

2 Serv. Come, we are fellows and friends: he was ever too hard for him; I have heard him say so himself.

1 Serv. He was too hard for him directly, to say the troth on 't: before Corioli he scotched him and notched him like a carbouado.

2 Serv. An he had been cannibally given, he might have broiled and eaten him too.

1 Serv. But more of thy news?

3 Serv. Why, he is so made on here within as if he were son and heir to Mars; set at upper end o' the table; no question asked him by any of the senators, but they stand bald before him: our general himself makes a mistress of him; sanctifies himself with 's hand, and turns up the white o' the eye to his discourse. But the bottom of the

news is, our general is cut i' the middle, and but one half
of what he was yesterday; for the other has half, by the
entreaty and grant of the whole table. He'll go, he says, and
sowl the porter of Rome gates by the ears: he will mow
all down before him, and leave his passage polled.

2 Serv. And he's as like to do't as any man I can imagine.

3 Serv. Do't! he will do't; for, look you, sir, he has
as many friends as enemies; which friends, sir, as it were,
durst not, look you, sir, show themselves, as we term it, his
friends, whilst he's in dejectitude.

1 Serv. Dejectitude! what's that?

3 Serv. But when they shall see, sir, his crest up again,
and the man in blood, they will out of their burrows, like
conies after rain, and revel all with him.

1 Serv. But when goes this forward?

3 Serv. To-morrow; to-day; presently; you shall have the
drum struck up this afternoon: 'tis as it were a parcel of
their feast, and to be executed ere they wipe their lips.

2 Serv. Why, then we shall have a stirring world again.
This peace is good for nothing but to rust iron, increase
tailors, and breed ballad-makers.

1 Serv. Let me have war, say I; it exceeds peace as far as
day does night; it's spritely, waking, audible, and full of
vent. Peace is a very apoplexy, lethargy; mulled, deaf,
sleepy, insensible; a getter of more bastard children than
wars a destroyer of men.

2 Serv. 'Tis so: and as wars, in some sort, may be said
to be a ravisher, so it cannot be denied but peace is a great
maker of cuckolds.

1 Serv. Ay, and it makes men hate one another.

3 Serv. Reason; because they then less need one another.
The wars for my money. I hope to see Romans as cheap
as Volscians. They are rising, they are rising.

All. In, in, in, in!   [*Exeunt*

SCENE VI.—ROME.   *A public Place.*

Enter SICINIUS *and* BRUTUS.

Sic. We hear not of him, neither need we fear him;
His remedies are tame i' the present peace
And quietness of the people, which before
Were in wild hurry. Here do we make his friends
Blush that the world goes well; who rather had,
Though they themselves did suffer by't, behold
Dissentious numbers pestering streets than see

Our tradesmen singing in their shops, and going
About their functions friendly.

Bru. We stood to 't in good time.—Is this Menenius?

Sic. 'Tis he, 'tis he: O, he is grown most kind
Of late.

Enter MENENIUS.

Bru. Hail, sir!

Men.   Hail to you both!

Sic. Your Coriolanus is not much miss'd
But with his friends: the commonwealth doth stand;
And so would do, were he more angry at it.

Men. All 's well; and might have been much better if
He could have temporiz'd.

Sic.   Where is he, hear you?

Men. Nay, I hear nothing: his mother and his wife
Hear nothing from him.

Enter three or four Citizens.

Citizens. The gods preserve you both!

Sic.   God-den, our neighbours.

Bru. God-den to you all, god-den to you all.

1 Cit. Ourselves, our wives, and children, on our knees,
Are bound to pray for you both.

Sic.   Live and thrive!

Bru. Farewell, kind neighbours: we wish'd Coriolanus
Had lov'd you as we did.

Citizens.   Now the gods keep you!

Both Tri. Farewell, farewell.   [*Exeunt* Citizens.

Sic. This is a happier and more comely time
Than when these fellows ran about the streets
Crying confusion.

Bru.   Caius Marcius was
A worthy officer i' the war; but insolent,
O'ercome with pride, ambitious past all thinking,
Self-loving,—

Sic.   And affecting one sole throne,
Without assistance.

Men.   I think not so.

Sic. We should by this, to all our lamentation,
If he had gone forth consul, found it so.

Bru. The gods have well prevented it, and Rome
Sits safe and still without him.

Enter an Ædile.

Æd.   Worthy tribunes,

There is a slave, whom we have put in prison,
Reports,—the Volsces with two several powers
Are enter'd in the Roman territories;
And with the deepest malice of the war
Destroy what lies before 'em.
    Men.   'Tis Aufidius,
Who, hearing of our Marcius' banishment,
Thrusts forth his horns again into the world;
Which were inshell'd when Marcius stood for Rome,
And durst not once peep out.
    Sic.   Come, what talk you
Of Marcius?
    Bru. Go see this rumourer whipp'd.—It cannot be
The Volsces dare break with us.
    Men.   Cannot be!
We have record that very well it can;
And three examples of the like have been
Within my age.   But reason with the fellow,
Before you punish him, where he heard this:
Lest you shall chance to whip your information,
And beat the messenger who bids beware
Of what is to be dreaded.
    Sic.   Tell not me:
I know this cannot be.
    Bru.   Not possible.

Enter a Messenger.

    Mess. The nobles in great earnestness are going
All to the senate-house: some news is come
That turns their countenances.
    Sic.   'Tis this slave;—
Go whip him 'fore the people's eyes:—his raising;
Nothing but his report.
    Mess.   Yes, worthy sir,
The slave's report is seconded; and more,
More fearful, is deliver'd.
    Sic.   What more fearful?
    Mess. It is spoke freely out of many mouths,—
How probable I do not know,—that Marcius,
Join'd with Aufidius, leads a power 'gainst Rome,
And vows revenge as spacious as between
The young'st and oldest thing.
    Sic.   This is most likely!
    Bru. Rais'd only, that the weaker sort may wish
God Marcius home again.
    Sic.   The very trick on't.

Men. This is unlikely:
He and Aufidius can no more atone
Than violentest contrariety.

Enter a second Messenger.

2 Mess. You are sent for to the senate:
A fearful army, led by Caius Marcius
Associated with Aufidius, rages
Upon our territories; and have already
O'erborne their way, consum'd with fire, and took
What lay before them.

Enter COMINIUS.

Com. O, you have made good work!
Men.   What news? what news
Com. You have holp to ravish your own daughters, and
To melt the city leads upon your pates;
To see your wives dishonour'd to your noses,—
Men. What's the news? what's the news?
Com. Your temples burned in their cement; and
Your franchises, whereon you stood, confin'd
Into an auger's bore.
Men.   Pray now, your news?—
You have made fair work, I fear me.—Pray, your news?
If Marcius should be join'd with Volscians,—
Com.   If!
He is their god: he leads them like a thing
Made by some other deity than nature,
That shapes man better; and they follow him,
Against us brats, with no less confidence
Than boys pursuing summer butterflies,
Or butcher's killing flies.
Men.   You have made good work,
You and your apron men; you that stood so much
Upon the voice of occupation and
The breath of garlic-eaters!
Com.   He will shake
Your Rome about your ears.
Men.   As Hercules
Did shake down mellow fruit.—You have made fair work
Bru. But is this true, sir?
Com.   Ay; and you'll look pale
Before you find it other. All the regions
Do smilingly revolt; and who resist
Are only mock'd for valiant ignorance,

And perish constant fools.   Who is't can blame him?
Your enemies and his find something in him.
    Men. We are all undone unless
The noble man have mercy.
    Com.   Who shall ask it?
The tribunes cannot do't for shame; the people
Deserve such pity of him as the wolf
Does of the shepherds : for his best friends, if they
Should say, *Be good to Rome*, they charg'd him even
As those should do that had deserv'd his hate,
And therein show'd like enemies.
    Men.   'Tis true :
If he were putting to my house the brand
That should consume it, I have not the face
To say, *Beseech you, cease.*—You have made fair hands,
You and your crafts! you have crafted fair!
    Com.   You have brought
A trembling upon Rome, such as was never
So incapable of help.
    Both Tri.   Say not, we brought it.
    Men. How ! Was it we? we lov'd him ; but, like beasts,
And cowardly nobles, gave way unto your clusters,
Who did hoot him out o' the city.
    Com.   But I fear
They'll roar him in again.   Tullus Aufidius,
The second name of men, obeys his points
As if he were his officer :—desperation
Is all the policy, strength, and defence,
That Rome can make against them.

       Enter a troop of Citizens.

    Men.   Here comes the clusters.—
And is Aufidius with him?—You are they
That made the air unwholesome, when you cast
Your stinking greasy caps in hooting at
Coriolanus' exile.   Now he's coming ;
And not a hair upon a soldier's head
Which will not prove a whip : as many coxcombs
As you threw caps up will he tumble down,
And pay you for your voices.   'Tis no matter ;
If he could burn us all into one coal,
We have deserv'd it.
    Citizens. Faith, we hear fearful news.
    1 Cit.   For mine own part,
When I said banish him, I said 'twas pity.
    2 Cit. And so did I.

3 *Cit.* And so did I; and, to say the truth, so did very
many of us. That we did, we did for the best; and though
we willingly consented to his banishment, yet it was against
our will.

Com. You are goodly things, you voices!

Men.   You have made
Good work, you and your cry!—Shall 's to the Capitol?

Com.. O, ay; what else?   [*Exeunt* COM. *and* MEN.

Sic. Go, masters, get you home; be not dismay'd:
These are a side that would be glad to have
This true which they so seem to fear. Go home,
And show no sign of fear.

1 *Cit.* The gods be good to us!—Come, masters, let 's
home. I ever said we were i' the wrong when we banished
him.

2 *Cit.* So did we all. But come, let 's home.
                                         [*Exeunt* Citizens.

Bru. I do not like this news.

Sic. Nor I.

Bru. Let 's to the Capitol:—would half my wealth
Would buy this for a lie!

Sic.   Pray, let us go.   [*Exeunt.*

SCENE VII.—*A Camp at a small distance from Rome.*

Enter AUFIDIUS *and his* Lieutenant.

Auf. Do they still fly to the Roman?

Lieu. I do not know what witchcraft 's in him, but
Your soldiers use him as the grace 'fore meat,
Their talk at table, and their thanks at end;
And you are darken'd in this action, sir,
Even by your own.

Auf.   I cannot help it now,
Unless, by using means, I lame the foot
Of our design. He bears himself more proudlier,
Even to my person, than I thought he would
When first I did embrace him: yet his nature
In that 's no changeling; and I must excuse
What cannot be amended.

Lieu.   Yet I wish, sir,—
I mean, for your particular,—you had not
Join'd in commission with him; but either
Had borne the action of yourself, or else
To him had left it solely.

Auf. I understand thee well; and be thou sure,

When he shall come to his account, he knows not
What I can urge against him.   Although it seems,
And so he thinks, and is no less apparent
To the vulgar eye, that he bears all things fairly,
And shows good husbandry for the Volscian state,
Fights dragon-like, and does achieve as soon
As draw his sword: yet he hath left undone
That which shall break his neck or hazard mine
Whene'er we come to our account.

Lieu. Sir, I beseech you, think you he'll carry Rome?

Auf. All places yield to him ere he sits down;
And the nobility of Rome are his:
The senators and patricians love him too:
The tribunes are no soldiers; and their people
Will be as rash in the repeal as hasty
To expel him thence.   I think he'll be to Rome
As is the osprey to the fish, who takes it
By sovereignty of nature.   First he was
A noble servant to them; but he could not
Carry his honours even: whether 'twas pride,
Which out of daily fortune ever taints
The happy man; whether defect of judgment,
To fail in the disposing of those chances
Which he was lord of; or whether nature,
Not to be other than one thing, not moving
From the casque to the cushion, but commanding peace
Even with the same austerity and garb
As he controll'd the war; but one of these,—
As he hath spices of them all, not all,
For I dare so far free him,—made him fear'd,
So hated, and so banish'd: but he has a merit
To choke it in the utterance.   So our virtues
Lie in the interpretation of the time:
And power, unto itself most commendable,
Hath not a tomb so evident as a cheer
To extol what it hath done.
One fire drives out one fire; one nail, one nail;
Rights by rights falter, strengths by strengths do fail.
Come, let's away.   When, Caius, Rome is thine,
Thou art poor'st of all; then shortly art thou mine. [*Exeunt.*

ACT V.

SCENE I.—ROME. *A public Place.*

Enter MENENIUS, COMINIUS, SICINIUS, BRUTUS, *and others.*

Men. No, I'll not go: you hear what he hath said
Which was sometime his general; who lov'd him
In a most dear particular.   He call'd me father:
But what o' that?   Go, you that banish'd him;
A mile before his tent fall down, and knee
The way into his mercy: nay, if he coy'd
To hear Cominius speak, I'll keep at home.
  Com. He would not seem to know me.
  Men.   Do you hear?
  Com. Yet one time he did call me by my name:
I urg'd our old acquaintance, and the drops
That we have bled together.   Coriolanus
He would not answer to: forbad all names;
He was a kind of nothing, titleless,
Till he had forg'd himself a name o' the fire
Of burning Rome.
  Men.   Why, so,—you have made good work!
A pair of tribunes that have rack'd for Rome,
To make coals cheap,—a noble memory!
  Com. I minded him how royal 'twas to pardon
When it was less expected: he replied,
It was a bare petition of a state
To one whom they had punish'd.
  Men.   Very well:
Could he say less?
  Com. I offer'd to awaken his regard
For 's private friends: his answer to me was,
He could not stay to pick them in a pile
Of noisome musty chaff: he said 'twas folly
For one poor grain or two to leave unburnt,
And still to nose the offence.
  Men.   For one poor grain
Or two! I am one of those; his mother, wife,
His child, and this brave fellow too, we are the grains:
You are the musty chaff; and you are smelt
Above the moon: we must be burnt for you.
  Sic. Nay, pray, be patient: if you refuse your aid
In this so never-heeded help, yet do not

Upbraid's with our distress.   But, sure, if you
Would be your country's pleader, your good tongue,
More than the instant army we can make,
Might stop our countryman.
    Men.   No; I'll not meddle.
    Sic. Pray you, go to him.
    Men.   What should I do?
    Bru. Only make trial what your love can do
For Rome, towards Marcius.
    Men.   Well, and say that Marcius
Return me, as Cominius is return'd,
Unheard; what then?
But as a discontented friend, grief-shot
With his unkindness? Say't be so?
    Sic.   Yet your good-will
Must have that thanks from Rome, after the measure
As you intended well.
    Men.   I'll undertake't:
I think he'll hear me.   Yet to bite his lip
And hum at good Cominius much unhearts me.
He was not taken well: he had not din'd:
The veins unfill'd, our blood is cold, and then
We pout upon the morning, are unapt
To give or to forgive; but when we have stuff'd
These pipes and these conveyances of our blood
With wine and feeding, we have suppler souls
Than in our priest-like fasts: therefore I'll watch him
Till he be dieted to my request,
And then I'll set upon him.
    Bru. You know the very road into his kindness,
And cannot lose your way.
    Men.   Good faith, I'll prove him,
Speed how it will.   I shall ere long have knowledge
Of my success.   [*Exit*
    Com.   He'll never hear him.
    Sic.   Not?
    Com. I tell you, he does sit in gold, his eye
Red as 'twould burn Rome; and his injury
The gaoler to his pity.   I kneel'd before him;
'Twas very faintly he said *Rise;* dismiss'd me
Thus, with his speechless hand: what he would do,
He sent in writing after me; what he would not,
Bound with an oath to yield to his conditions:
So that all hope is vain,
Unless in 's noble mother and his wife;
Who, as I hear, mean to solicit him

For mercy to his country.   Therefore, let's hence,
And with our fair entreaties haste them on.

[Exeunt.

SCENE II.—*An advanced Post of the Volscian Camp before
Rome.   The* Guard *at their stations.*

Enter to them MENENIUS.

1 *G.* Stay: whence are you?
2 *G.*   Stand, and go back.
Men. You guard like men; 'tis well: but, by your leave,
I am an officer of state, and come
To speak with Coriolanus.
  1 *G.*   From whence?
  Men.   From Rome.
  1 *G* You may not pass, you must return: our general
Will no more hear from thence.
  2 *G.* You'll see your Rome embrac'd with fire before
You'll speak with Coriolanus.
  Men.   Good my friends,
If you have heard your general talk of Rome,
And of his friends there, it is lots to blanks
My name hath touch'd your ears: it is Menenius.
  1 *G.* Be it so; go back: the virtue of your name
Is not here passable.
  Men.   I tell thee, fellow,
Thy general is my lover: I have been
The book of his good acts, whence men have read
His fame unparallel'd, haply amplified;
For I have ever verified my friends,—
Of whom he's chief,—with all the size that verity
Would without lapsing suffer: nay, sometimes,
Like to a bowl upon a subtle ground,
I have tumbled past the throw: and in his praise
Have almost stamp'd the leasing: therefore, fellow,
I must have leave to pass.
  1 *G.* Faith, sir, if you had told as many lies in his behalf
as you have utter'd words in your own, you should not pass
here: no, though it were as virtuous to lie as to live chastely.
Therefore, go back.
  Men. Pr'ythee, fellow, remember my name is Menenius,
always factionary on the party of your general.
  2 *G.* Howsoever you have been his liar,—as you say you
have,—I am one that, telling true under him, must say, you
cannot pass. Therefore, go back.

Men. Has he dined, canst thou tell? for I would not speak with him till after dinner.

1 *G.* You are a Roman, are you?

Men. I am as thy general is.

1 *G.* Then you should hate Rome, as he does. Can you, when you have pushed out your gates the very defender of them, and, in a violent popular ignorance, given your enemy your shield, think to front his revenges with the easy groans of old women, the virginal palms of your daughters, or with the palsied intercession of such a decayed dotant as you seem to be? Can you think to blow out the intended fire your city is ready to flame in, with such weak breath as this? No, you are deceived; therefore, back to Rome, and prepare for your execution: you are condemned; our general has sworn you out of reprieve and pardon.

Men. Sirrah, if thy captain knew I were here he would use me with estimation.

2 *G.* Come, my captain knows you not.

Men. I mean thy general.

1 *G.* My general cares not for you. Back, I say; go, lest I let forth your half pint of blood;—back; that's the utmost of your having:—back.

Men. Nay, but, fellow, fellow,—

Enter CORIOLANUS *and* AUFIDIUS.

Cor. What's the matter?

Men. Now, you companion, I'll say an errand for you; you shall know now that I am in estimation; you shall perceive that a jack guardant cannot office me from my son Coriolanus: guess but by my entertainment with him if thou standest not i' the state of hanging, or of some death more long in spectatorship and crueller in suffering; behold now presently, and swoon for what's to come upon thee.— The glorious gods sit in hourly synod about thy particular prosperity, and love thee no worse than thy old father Menenius does! O my son! my son! thou art preparing fire for us; look thee, here's water to quench it. I was hardly moved to come to thee; but being assured none but myself could move thee, I have been blown out of your gates with sighs; and conjure thee to pardon Rome and thy petitionary countrymen. The good gods assuage thy wrath, and turn the dregs of it upon this varlet here; this, who, like a block, hath denied my access to thee.

Cor. Away!

Men. How! away!

Cor. Wife, mother, child, I know not. My affairs

Are servanted to others: though I owe
My revenge properly, my remission lies
In Volscian breasts. That we have been familiar,
Ingrate forgetfulness shall poison, rather
Than pity note how much.—Therefore, be gone.
Mine ears against your suits are stronger than
Your gates against my force. Yet, for I lov'd thee,
Take this along; I writ it for thy sake,

　　　　　　　　　　　　　　[*Gives a letter.*

And would have sent it. Another word, Menenius,
I will not hear thee speak.—This man, Aufidius,
Was my beloved in Rome: yet thou behold'st!

　　Auf. You keep a constant temper.

　　　　　　　　　　　　　[*Exeunt* COR. *and* AUF.

　　1 *G.* Now, sir, is your name Menenius?

　　2 *G.* 'Tis a spell, you see, of much power: you know the
way home again.

　　1 *G.* Do you hear how we are shent for keeping your
greatness back?

　　2 *G.* What cause, do you think, I have to swoon?

　　Men. I neither care for the world nor your general:
for such things as you, I can scarce think there's any, ye're
so slight. He that hath a will to die by himself fears it
not from another. Let your general do his worst. For
you, be that you are, long; and your misery increase with
your age! I say to you, as I was said to, Away! [*Exit.*

　　1 *G.* A noble fellow, I warrant him.

　　2 *G.* The worthy fellow is our general: he is the rock,
the oak not to be wind-shaken. 　　　　　　[*Exeunt*

　　　　　　　　　　　SCENE III.—*The Tent of* CORIOLANUS.

　　　　　Enter CORIOLANUS, AUFIDIUS, *and others.*

　　Cor. We will before the walls of Rome to-morrow
Set down our host.—My partner in this action,
You must report to the Volscian lords how plainly
I have borne this business.

　　Auf. 　　　　　　　　Only their ends
You have respected; stopp'd your ears against
The general suit of Rome; never admitted
A private whisper, no, not with such friends
That thought them sure of you.

　　Cor. 　　　　　　　　This last old man,
Whom with a crack'd heart I have sent to Rome,
Lov'd me above the measure of a father;

Nay, godded me, indeed.　Their latest refuge
Was to send him; for whose old love I have,—
Though I show'd sourly to him,—once more offer'd
The first conditions, which they did refuse,
And cannot now accept, to grace him only,
That thought he could do more, a very little
I have yielded to: fresh embassies and suits,
Nor from the state nor private friends, hereafter
Will I lend ear to.—Ha! what shout is this?

　　　　　　　　　　　　　　　　[Shout within.

Shall I be tempted to infringe my vow
In the same time 'tis made?　I will not.

Enter, in mourning habits, VIRGILIA, VOLUMNIA, *leading
　　young* MARCIUS, VALERIA, *and* Attendants.

My wife comes foremost; then the honour'd mould
Wherein this trunk was fram'd, and in her hand
The grandchild to her blood.　But, out, affection!
All bond and privilege of nature, break!
Let it be virtuous to be obstinate.—
What is that curt'sy worth? or those doves' eyes,
Which can make gods forsworn?—I melt, and am not
Of stronger earth than others.—My mother bows,
As if Olympus to a molehill should
In supplication nod: and my young boy
Hath an aspect of intercession which
Great nature cries, *Deny not.*—Let the Volsces
Plough Rome and harrow Italy: I'll never
Be such a gosling to obey instinct; but stand,
As if a man were author of himself,
And knew no other kin.

　　Vir.　　　　　　　My lord and husband!
　　Cor. These eyes are not the same I wore in Rome.
　　Vir. The sorrow that delivers us thus chang'd
Makes you think so.
　　Cor.　　　　　　Like a dull actor now,
I have forgot my part, and I am out,
Even to a full disgrace.　Best of my flesh,
Forgive my tyranny; but do not say,
For that, *Forgive our Romans.*—O, a kiss
Long as my exile, sweet as my revenge;
Now, by the jealous queen of heaven, that kiss
I carried from thee, dear; and my true lip
Hath virgin'd it e'er since.—You gods! I prate,
And the most noble mother of the world
Leave unsaluted: sink, my knee, i' the earth;　　　*[Kneels.*

Of thy deep duty more impression show
Than that of common sons.

Vol.   O, stand up bless'd!
Whilst, with no softer cushion than the flint,
I kneel before thee; and unproperly
Show duty, as mistaken all this while
Between the child and parent.   [*Kneels.*

Cor.   What is this?
Your knees to me? to your corrected son?
Then let the pebbles on the hungry beach
Fillip the stars; then let the mutinous winds
Strike the proud cedars 'gainst the fiery sun;
Murdering impossibility, to make
What cannot be, slight work.

Vol.   Thou art my warrior;
I holp to frame thee. Do you know this lady?

Cor. The noble sister of Publicola,
The moon of Rome; chaste as the icicle
That's curded by the frost from purest snow,
And hangs on Dian's temple:—dear Valeria!

Vol. This is a poor epitome of yours,
Which, by the interpretation of full time,
May show like all yourself.

Cor.   The god of soldiers,
With the consent of supreme Jove, inform
Thy thoughts with nobleness; that thou mayst prove
To shame unvulnerable, and stick i' the wars
Like a great sea-mark, standing every flaw,
And saving those that eye thee!

Vol.   Your knee, sirrah.

Cor. That's my brave boy.

Vol. Even he, your wife, this lady, and myself,
Are suitors to you.

Cor. I beseech you, peace:
Or, if you'd ask, remember this before,—
The things I have forsworn to grant may never
Be held by you denials. Do not bid me
Dismiss my soldiers, or capitulate
Again with Rome's mechanics.—Tell me not
Wherein I seem unnatural: desire not
To allay my rages and revenges with
Your colder reasons.

Vol.   O, no more, no more!
You have said you will not grant us anything;
For we have nothing else to ask but that
Which you deny already: yet we will ask;

That, if you fail in our request, the blame
May hang upon your hardness; therefore hear us.

Cor. Aufidius, and you Volsces, mark: for we'll
Hear naught from Rome in private.—Your request?

Vol. Should we be silent and not speak, our raiment
And state of bodies would bewray what life
We have led since thy exile.　Think with thyself,
How more unfortunate than all living women
Are we come hither: since that thy sight, which should
Make our eyes flow with joy, hearts dance with comfort,
Constrains them weep, and shake with fear and sorrow;
Making the mother, wife, and child to see
The son, the husband, and the father tearing
His country's bowels out.　And to poor we,
Thine enmity's most capital: thou barr'st us
Our prayers to the gods, which is a comfort
That all but we enjoy; for how can we,
Alas, how can we for our country pray,
Whereto we are bound,—together with thy victory,
Whereto we are bound? alack, or we must lose
The country, our dear nurse; or else thy person,
Our comfort in the country.　We must find
An evident calamity, though we had
Our wish, which side should win; for either thou
Must, as a foreign recreant, be led
With manacles thorough our streets, or else
Triumphantly tread on thy country's ruin,
And bear the palm for having bravely shed
Thy wife and children's blood.　For myself, son,
I purpose not to wait on fortune till
These wars determine: if I cannot persuade thee
Rather to show a noble grace to both parts
Than seek the end of one, thou shalt no sooner
March to assault thy country than to tread,—
Trust to't, thou shalt not,—on thy mother's womb,
That brought thee to this world.

Vir.　　　　　　　Ay, and mine,
That brought you forth this boy, to keep your name
Living to time.

Boy.　　　'A shall not tread on me;
I'll run away till I am bigger; but then I'll fight.

Cor. Not of a woman's tenderness to be,
Requires nor child nor woman's face to see.
I have sat too long.　　　　　　　　　　　*[Rising.*

Vol.　　　　Nay, go not from us thus.
If it were so that our request did tend

To save the Romans, thereby to destroy
The Volsces whom you serve, you might condemn us,
As poisonous of your honour: no; our suit
Is, that you reconcile them: while the Volsces
May say, *This mercy we have show'd;* the Romans,
This we receiv'd; and each in either side
Give thee all-hail to thee, and cry, *Be bless'd*
For making up this peace! Thou know'st, great son,
The end of war 's uncertain; but this certain,
That, if thou conquer Rome, the benefit
Which thou shalt thereby reap is such a name,
Whose repetition will be dogg'd with curses;
Whose chronicle thus writ,—*The man was noble,*
But with his last attempt he wip'd it out;
Destroy'd his country; and his name remains
To the ensuing age abhorr'd. Speak to me, son:
Thou hast affected the fine strains of honour,
To imitate the graces of the gods,
To tear with thunder the wide cheeks o' the air,
And yet to charge thy sulphur with a bolt
That should but rive an oak. Why dost not speak?
Think'st thou it honourable for a noble man
Still to remember wrongs?—Daughter, speak you:
He cares not for your weeping.—Speak thou, boy:
Perhaps thy childishness will move him more
Than can our reasons.—There 's no man in the world
More bound to his mother; yet here he lets me prate
Like one i' the stocks. Thou hast never in thy life
Show'd thy dear mother any courtesy;
When she,—poor hen,—fond of no second brood,
Has cluck'd thee to the wars, and safely home,
Loaden with honour. Say my request 's unjust,
And spurn me back: but if it be not so,
Thou art not honest; and the gods will plague thee,
That thou restrain'st from me the duty which
To a mother's part belongs.—He turns away:
Down, ladies; let us shame him with our knees.
To his surname Coriolanus 'longs more pride
Than pity to our prayers. Down: an end;
This is the last.—So we will home to Rome,
And die among our neighbours.—Nay, behold's·
This boy, that cannot tell what he would have,
But kneels and holds up hands for fellowship,
Does reason our petition with more strength
Than thou hast to deny't.—Come, let us go:
This fellow had a Volscian to his mother;

His wife is in Corioli, and his child
Like him by chance.—Yet give us our despatch :
I am hush'd until our city be afire,
And then I'll speak a little.
 Cor. [*after holding* VOLUMNIA *by the hands in silence.*]
   O mother, mother!
What have you done? Behold, the heavens do ope,
The gods look down, and this unnatural scene
They laugh at. O my mother, mother! O!
You have won a happy victory to Rome;
But for your son,—believe it, O, believe it,
Most dangerously you have with him prevail'd,
If not most mortal to him. But let it come.—
Aufidius, though I cannot make true wars,
I'll frame convenient peace. Now, good Aufidius,
If you were in my stead, would you have heard
A mother less? or granted less, Aufidius?
 Auf. I was mov'd withal.
 Cor.   I dare be sworn you were:
And, sir, it is no little thing to make
Mine eyes to sweat compassion. But, good sir,
What peace you'll make, advise me: for my part,
I'll not to Rome, I'll back with you ; and, pray you,
Stand to me in this cause.—O mother! wife!
 Auf. I am glad thou hast set thy mercy and thy honour
At difference in thee : out of that I'll work
Myself a former fortune.   [*Aside.*
     [*The* Ladies *make signs to* CORIOLANUS.
 Cor.   Ay, by and by;
      [*To* VOLUMNIA, VIRGILIA, *&c.*
But we'll drink together; and you shall hear
A better witness back than words, which we,
On like conditions, will have counter-seal'd.
Come, enter with us. Ladies, you deserve
To have a temple built you: all the swords
In Italy, and her confederate arms,
Could not have made this peace.   [*Exeunt.*

SCENE IV.—ROME. *A public Place.*

Enter MENENIUS *and* SICINIUS.

 Men. See you yond coigne o' the Capitol,--yond corner-
stone?
 Sic. Why, what of that?
 Men. If it be possible for you to displace it with your

little finger, there is some hope the ladies of Rome, especially
his mother, may prevail with him. But I say there is no
hope in't : our throats are sentenced, and stay upon execution.

Sic. Is't possible that so short a time can alter the condition of a man?

Men. There is differency between a grub and a butterfly ;
yet your butterfly was a grub. This Marcius is grown
from man to dragon : he has wings ; he 's more than a
creeping thing.

Sic. He loved his mother dearly.

Men. So did he me : and he no more remembers his mother
now than an eight-year-old horse. The tartness of his face
sours ripe grapes : when he walks, he moves like an engine,
and the ground shrinks before his treading : he is able to
pierce a corslet with his eye ; talks like a knell, and his hum
is a battery. He sits in his state as a thing made for Alexander. What he bids be done is finished with his bidding.
He wants nothing of a god but eternity, and a heaven to
throne in.

Sic. Yes, mercy, if you report him truly.

Men. I paint him in the character. Mark what mercy
his mother shall bring from him : there is no more mercy
in him than there is milk in a male tiger ; that shall our poor
city find : and all this is 'long of you.

Sic. The gods be good unto us !

Men. No, in such a case the gods will not be good unto
us. When we banished him we respected not them : and,
he returning to break our necks, they respect not us.

Enter a Messenger.

Mess. Sir, if you'd save your life, fly to your house :
The plebeians have got your fellow-tribune,
And hale him up and down ; all swearing, if
The Roman ladies bring not comfort home,
They'll give him death by inches.

Enter a second Messenger.

Sic.   What 's the news?

2 *Mess.* Good news, good news ;—the ladies have prevail'd,
The Volscians are dislodg'd and Marcius gone :
A merrier day did never yet greet Rome,
No, not the expulsion of the Tarquins.

Sic.   Friend,
Art thou certain this is true? is it most certain?

2 *Mess.* As certain as I know the sun is fire :
Where have you lurk'd, that you make doubt of it?

Ne'er through an arch so hurried the blown tide
As the recomforted through the gates.　Why, hark you!
　　　　　　　[*Trumpets and hautboys sounded, drums
　　　　　　　　　　beaten, and shouting within.*
The trumpets, sackbuts, psalteries, and fifes,
Tabors and cymbals, and the shouting Romans,
Make the sun dance.　Hark you!　　　[*Shouting again.*
　　Men.　　　　　　　　　This is good news.
I will go meet the ladies.　This Volumnia
Is worth of consuls, senators, patricians,
A city full: of tribunes such as you,
A sea and land full.　You have pray'd well to-day:
This morning, for ten thousand of your throats
I'd not have given a doit.　Hark, how they joy!
　　　　　　　　　　[*Shouting and music.*
　　Sic. First, the gods bless you for your tidings; next,
Accept my thankfulness.
　　2 Mess.　　　　　　Sir, we have all
Great cause to give great thanks.
　　Sic.　　　　　　They are near the city?
　　2 Mess. Almost at point to enter.
　　Sic.　　　　　　We will meet them,
And help the joy.　　　　　　　　　[*Exeunt.*

SCENE V.—Rome.　*A Street near the Gate.*

Enter Volumnia, Virgilia, Valeria, *&c., accompanied
by* Senators, Patricians, *and* Citizens.

　1 Sen. Behold our patroness, the life of Rome!
Call all your tribes together, praise the gods,
And make triumphant fires; strew flowers before them:
Unshout the noise that banish'd Marcius,
Repeal him with the welcome of his mother;
Cry, *Welcome, ladies, welcome!*—
　　All.　　　　　　　Welcome, ladies,
Welcome!　[*A flourish with drums and trumpets.　Exeunt.*

SCENE VI.—Antium.　*A public Place.*

Enter Tullus Aufidius, *with* Attendants.

　Auf. Go tell the lords of the city I am here:
Deliver them this paper; having read it,
Bid them repair to the market-place: where I,
Even in theirs and in the commons' ears,

Will vouch the truth of it.   Him I accuse
The city ports by this hath enter'd, and
Intends to appear before the people, hoping
To purge himself with words: despatch. [*Exeunt* Attendants.

Enter three or four Conspirators *of* AUFIDIUS'S *faction.*
Most welcome!
   1 *Con.* How is it with our general?
   Auf.   Even so
As with a man by his own alms empoison'd,
And with his charity slain.
   2 *Con.*   Most noble sir,
If you do hold the same intent wherein
You wish'd us parties, we'll deliver you
Of your great danger.
   Auf.   Sir, I cannot tell:
We must proceed as we do find the people.
   3 *Con.* The people will remain uncertain whilst
'Twixt you there's difference: but the fall of either
Makes the survivor heir of all.
   Auf.   I know it;
And my pretext to strike at him admits
A good construction. I rais'd him, and I pawn'd
Mine honour for his truth: who being so heighten'd,
He water'd his new plants with dews of flattery,
Seducing so my friends; and to this end
He bow'd his nature, never known before
But to be rough, unswayable, and free.
   3 *Con.* Sir, his stoutness,
When he did stand for consul, which he lost
By lack of stooping,—
   Auf.   That I would have spoke of:
Being banish'd for't, he came unto my hearth;
Presented to my knife his throat: I took him;
Made him joint-servant with me; gave him way
In all his own desires; nay, let him choose
Out of my files, his projects to accomplish,
My best and freshest men; serv'd his designments
In mine own person; holp to reap the fame
Which he made all his; and took some pride
To do myself this wrong: till, at the last,
I seem'd his follower, not partner; and
He wag'd me with his countenance as if
I had been mercenary.
   1 *Con.*   So he did, my lord:
The army marvell'd at it; and, in the last,

When he had carried Rome, and that we look'd
For no less spoil than glory,—
  Auf.   There was it;—
For which my sinews shall be stretch'd upon him.
At a few drops of women's rheum, which are
As cheap as lies, he sold the blood and labour
Of our great action : therefore shall he die,
And I'll renew me in his fall. But, hark!
      [*Drums and trumpets sound, with great*
        shouts of the people.
 1 *Con.* Your native town you enter'd like a post,
And had no welcomes home; but he returns
Splitting the air with noise.
 2 *Con*   And patient fools,
Whose children he hath slain, their base throats tear
With giving him glory.
 3 *Con.*   Therefore, at your vantage,
Ere he express himself, or move the people
With what he would say, let him feel your sword,
Which we will second. When he lies along,
After your way his tale pronounc'd shall bury
His reasons with his body.
 Auf.   Say no more :
Here come the lords.

    Enter the Lords *of the City.*

 Lords. You are most welcome home.
 Auf.   I have not deserv'd it.
But, worthy lords, have you with heed perus'd
What I have written to you?
 Lords.   We have.
 1 *Lord.*   And grieve to hear't.
What faults he made before the last, I think
Might have found easy fines : but there to end
Where he was to begin, and give away
The benefit of our levies, answering us
With our own charge : making a treaty where
There was a yielding.—This admits no excuse.
 Auf. He approaches : you shall hear him.

 Enter CORIOLANUS, *with drums and colours; a crowd of*
    Citizens *with him.*

 Cor. Hail, lords! I am return'd your soldier;
No more infected with my country's love
Than when I parted hence, but still subsisting
Under your great command. You are to know

That prosperously I have attempted, and
With bloody passage led your wars even to
The gates of Rome. Our spoils we have brought home
Do more than counterpoise a full third part
The charges of the action. We have made peace
With no less honour to the Antiates
Than shame to the Romans: and we here deliver,
Subscribed by the consuls and patricians,
Together with the seal o' the senate, what
We have compounded on.

    Auf.   Read it not, noble lords
But tell the traitor, in the highest degree
He hath abus'd your powers.

    Cor. Traitor!—How now!

    Auf.   Ay, traitor, Marcius.

    Cor.   Marcius!

    Auf. Ay, Marcius, Caius Marcius. Dost thou think
I'll grace thee with that robbery, thy stol'n name
Coriolanus in Corioli?—
You lords and heads o' the state, perfidiously
He has betray'd your business, and given up,
For certain drops of salt, your city Rome,—
I say your city,—to his wife and mother;
Breaking his oath and resolution, like
A twist of rotten silk; never admitting
Counsel o' the war; but at his nurse's tears
He whin'd and roar'd away your victory;
That pages blush'd at him, and men of heart
Look'd wondering each at other.

    Cor.   Hear'st thou, Mars?

    Auf. Name not the god, thou boy of tears,—

    Cor.   Ha!

    Auf. No more.

    Cor. Measureless liar, thou hast made my heart
Too great for what contains it. Boy! O slave!—
Pardon me, lords, 'tis the first time that ever
I was forc'd to scold. Your judgments, my grave lords,
Must give this cur the lie: and his own notion,—
Who wears my stripes impress'd upon him; that must bear
My beating to his grave,—shall join to thrust
The lie unto him.

    1 *Lord.*   Peace, both, and hear me speak.

    Cor. Cut me to pieces, Volsces; men and lads,
Stain all your edges on me.—Boy! False hound!
If you have writ your annals true, 'tis there,
That, like an eagle in a dove-cote, I

Flutter'd your Volscians in Corioli:
Alone I did it.—Boy!
   Auf.   Why, noble lords,
Will you be put in mind of his blind fortune,
Which was your shame, by this unholy braggart,
'Fore your own eyes and ears?
   Conspirators.   Let him die for't.
   Citizens. Tear him to pieces, do it presently:—he killed
my son;—my daughter;—he killed my cousin Marcus;—he
killed my father,—
   2 Lord. Peace, ho!—no outrage;—peace!
The man is noble, and his fame folds in
This orb o' the earth. His last offences to us
Shall have judicious hearing.—Stand, Aufidius,
And trouble not the peace.
   Cor.   O that I had him,
With six Aufidiuses, or more, his tribe,
To use my lawful sword!
   Auf.   Insolent villain!
   Conspirators. Kill, kill, kill, kill, kill him!
             [Auf. *and the* Conspirators *draw, and kill*
             Cor., *who falls:* Auf. *stands on him.*
   Lords.   Hold, hold, hold, hold!
   Auf. My noble masters, hear me speak.
   1 Lord.   O Tullus,—
   2 Lord. Thou hast done a deed whereat valour will weep.
   3 Lord. Tread not upon him.—Masters all, be quiet;
Put up your swords.
   Auf. My lords, when you shall know,—as in this rage,
Provok'd by him, you cannot,—the great danger
Which this man's life did owe you, you'll rejoice
That he is thus cut off. Please it your honours
To call me to your senate, I'll deliver
Myself your loyal servant, or endure
Your heaviest censure.
   1 Lord.   Bear from hence his body,
And mourn you for him. Let him be regarded
As the most noble corse that ever herald
Did follow to his urn.
   2 Lord.   His own impatience
Takes from Aufidius a great part of blame.
Let's make the best of it.
   Auf.   My rage is gone;
And I am struck with sorrow.—Take him up:—
Help, three o' the chiefest soldiers; I'll be one.—
Beat thou the drum, that it speak mournfully:

Trail your steel pikes.   Though in this city he
Hath widow'd and unchilded many a one,
Which to this hour bewail the injury,
Yet he shall have a noble memory.—
Assist.   [*Exeunt, bearing the body of* CORIOLANUS.
                    A dead march sounded.

JULIUS CÆSAR

PERSONS REPRESENTED.

JULIUS CÆSAR.

OCTAVIUS CÆSAR,
MARCUS ANTONIUS, } *Triumvirs after the death of* JULIUS
M. ÆMIL. LEPIDUS, } CÆSAR.

CICERO,
PUBLIUS, } *Senators.*
POPILIUS LENA,

MARCUS BRUTUS,
CASSIUS,
CASCA,
TREBONIUS, } *Conspirators against* JULIUS CÆSAR.
LIGARIUS,
DECIUS BRUTUS,
METELLUS CIMBER,
CINNA,

FLAVIUS *and* MARULLUS, *Tribunes.*
ARTEMIDORUS, *a Sophist of Cnidos.*
A Soothsayer.
CINNA, *a Poet.*
Another Poet.
LUCILIUS, TITINIUS, MESSALA, YOUNG CATO, *and* VOLUM-
NIUS,—*Friends to* BRUTUS *and* CASSIUS.
VARRO, CLITUS, CLAUDIUS, STRATO, LUCIUS, DARDANIUS,
—*Servants to* BRUTUS.
PINDARUS, *Servant to* CASSIUS.

CALPHURNIA, *Wife to* CÆSAR.
PORTIA, *Wife to* BRUTUS.

Senators, Citizens, Guards, Attendants, &c.

SCENE,—*During a great part of the Play at* ROME;
afterwards at SARDIS, *and near* PHILIPPI

JULIUS CÆSAR.

———— ◆ ————

ACT I.

SCENE I.—ROME. *A Street.*

Enter FLAVIUS, MARULLUS, *and a rabble of* Citizens.

Flav. Hence! home, you idle creatures, get you home:
Is this a holiday? What! know you not,
Being mechanical, you ought not walk
Upon a labouring day without the sign
Of your profession?—Speak, what trade art thou?

1 Cit. Why, sir, a carpenter.

Mar. Where is thy leather apron and thy rule?
What dost thou with thy best apparel on?—
You, sir, what trade are you?

2 Cit. Truly, sir, in respect of a fine workman,
I am but, as you would say, a cobbler.

Mar. But what trade art thou? answer me directly.

2 Cit. A trade, sir, that I hope I may use with a safe
conscience; which is indeed, sir, a mender of bad soles.

Mar. What trade, thou knave, thou naughty knave,
what trade?

2 Cit. Nay, I beseech you, sir, be not out with me: yet,
if you be out, sir, I can mend you.

Mar. What meanest thou by that? mend me, thou saucy
fellow!

2 Cit. Why, sir, cobble you.

Flav. Thou art a cobbler, art thou?

2 Cit. Truly, sir, all that I live by is with the awl: I
meddle with no tradesman's matters, nor women's matters,
but with awl. I am, indeed, sir, a surgeon to old shoes;
when they are in great danger, I re-cover them. As proper
men as ever trod upon neats-leather have gone upon my
handiwork.

Flav. But wherefore art not in thy shop to-day?
Why dost thou lead these men about the streets?

2 Cit. Truly, sir, to wear out their shoes, to get myself

into more work.   But, indeed, sir, we make holiday to see
Cæsar, and to rejoice in his triumph.

    Mar. Wherefore rejoice?   What conquest brings he home?
What tributaries follow him to Rome,
To grace in captive bonds his chariot wheels? ,
You blocks, you stones, you worse than senseless things!
O you hard hearts, you cruel men of Rome,
Knew you not Pompey?   Many a time and oft
Have you climb'd up to walls and battlements,
To towers and windows, yea, to chimney-tops,
Your infants in your arms, and there have sat
The live-long day, with patient expectation,
To see great Pompey pass the streets of Rome:
And when you saw his chariot but appear,
Have you not made an universal shout,
That Tiber trembled underneath her banks,
To hear the replication of your sounds
Made in her cancave shores?
And do you now put on your best attire?
And do you now cull out a holiday?
And do you now strew flowers in his way
That comes in triumph over Pompey's blood?
Be gone!
Run to your houses, fall upon your knees,
Pray to the gods to intermit the plague
That needs must light on this ingratitude.

    Flav. Go, go, good countrymen, and for this fault
Assemble all the poor men of your sort;
Draw them to Tiber banks, and weep your tears
Into the channel, till the lowest stream
Do kiss the most exalted shores of all.   [*Exeunt Citizens.*
See, whe'r their basest metal be not mov'd;
They vanish tongue-tied in their guiltiness.
Go you down that way towards the Capitol:
This way will I: disrobe the images
If you do find them deck'd with ceremonies.

    Mar. May we do so?
You know it is the feast of Lupercal.

    Flav. It is no matter; let no images
Be hung with Cæsar's trophies.   I'll about,
And drive away the vulgar from the streets:
So do you too, where you perceive them thick.
These growing feathers pluck'd from Cæsar's wing
Will make him fly an ordinary pitch;
Who else would soar above the view of men,
And keep us all in servile fearfulness.   [*E: :t.*

SCENE II.—ROME. *A public Place.*

Enter, in procession, with music, CÆSAR; ANTONY, *for the course;* CALPHURNIA, PORTIA, DECIUS, CICERO, BRUTUS, CASSIUS, *and* CASCA; *a great crowd following: among them a* Soothsayer.

Cæs. Calphurnia,—

Casca.   Peace, ho! Cæsar speaks.
                                                [Music ceases.

Cæs.   Calphurnia,—

Cal. Here, my lord.

Cæs. Stand you directly in Antonius' way
When he doth run his course.—Antonius.

Ant. Cæsar, my lord.

Cæs. Forget not, in your speed, Antonius,
To touch Calphurnia; for our elders say,
The barren, touched in this holy chase,
Shake off their sterile curse.

Ant.   I shall remember:
When Cæsar says, *Do this,* it is perform'd.

Cæs. Set on; and leave no ceremony out.   *[Music.*

Sooth. Cæsar!

Cæs. Ha! Who calls?

Casca. Bid every noise be still.—Peace yet again.
                                                [Music ceases.

Cæs. Who is it in the press that calls on me?
I hear a tongue, shriller than all the music,
Cry, *Cæsar.* Speak; Cæsar is turn'd to hear.

Sooth. Beware the ides of March.

Cæs.   What man is that

Bru. A soothsayer bids you beware the ides of March.

Cæs. Set him before me; let me see his face.

Cas. Fellow, come from the throng; look upon
          Cæsar.

Cæs. What say'st thou to me now? speak once again.

Sooth. Beware the ides of March.

Cæs. He is a dreamer; let us leave him.—Pass.
             [Sennet. Exeunt all but BRU. *and* CAS.

Cas. Will you go see the order of the course?

Bru. Not I.

Cas. I pray you do.

Bru. I am not gamesome: I do lack some part
Of that quick spirit that is in Antony.
Let me not hinder, Cassius, your desires;
I'll leave you.

Cas. Brutus, I do observe you now of late:
I have not from your eyes that gentleness
And show of love as I was wont to have:
You bear too stubborn and too strange a hand
Over your friend that loves you.
  Bru.   Cassius,
Be not deceiv'd: if I have vail'd my look,
I turn the trouble of my countenance
Merely upon myself.   Vexed I am
Of late with passions of some difference,
Conceptions only proper to myself,
Which gives some soil, perhaps, to my behaviours;
But let not therefore my good friends be griev'd,—
Among which number, Cassius, be you one,—
Nor construe any further my neglect
Than that poor Brutus, with himself at war,
Forgets the shows of love to other men.
  Cas. Then, Brutus, I have much mistook your passion;
By means whereof this breast of mine hath buried
Thoughts of great value, worthy cogitations.
Tell me, good Brutus, can you see your face?
  Bru. No, Cassius; for the eye sees not itself
But by reflection, by some other things.
  Cas. 'Tis just:
And it is very much lamented, Brutus,
That you have no such mirrors as will turn
Your hidden worthiness into your eye,
That you might see your shadow.   I have heard,
Where many of the best respect in Rome,—
Except immortal Cæsar,—speaking of Brutus,
And groaning underneath this age s yoke,
Have wish'd that noble Brutus had his eyes.
  Bru. Into what dangers would you lead me, Cassius,
That you would have me seek into myself
For that which is not in me?
  Cas. Therefore, good Brutus, be prepar'd to hear:
And, since you know you cannot see yourself
So well as by reflection, I, your glass,
Will modestly discover to yourself
That of yourself which you yet know not of.
And be not jealous on me, gentle Brutus:
Were I a common laugher, or did use
To stale with ordinary oaths my love
To every new protester; if you know
That I do fawn on men, and hug them hard,
And after scandal them; or if you know

That I profess myself in banqueting
To all the rout, then hold me dangerous.

                                  [Flourish and shout.

   Bru. What means this shouting? I do fear the people
Choose Cæsar for their king.

   Cas.   Ay, do you fear it?
Then must I think you would not have it so.

   Bru. I would not, Cassius; yet I love him well--
But wherefore do you hold me here so long?
What is it that you would impart to me?
If it be aught toward the general good,
Set honour in one eye and death i' the other,
And I will look on both indifferently;
For, let the gods so speed me as I love
The name of honour more than I fear death.

   Cas. I know that virtue to be in you, Brutus,
As well as I do know your outward favour.
Well, honour is the subject of my story.--
I cannot tell what you and other men
Think of this life; but, for my single self,
I had as lief not be as live to be
In awe of such a thing as I myself.
I was born free as Cæsar; so were you:
We both have fed as well; and we can both
Endure the winter's cold as well as he.
For once, upon a raw and gusty day,
The troubled Tiber chafing with her shores,
Cæsar said to me, *Dar'st thou, Cassius, now
Leap in with me into this angry flood,
And swim to yonder point?*--Upon the word,
Accoutred as I was, I plunged in,
And bade him follow: so indeed he did.
The torrent roar'd; and we did buffet it
With lusty sinews, throwing it aside
And stemming it with hearts of controversy:
But ere we could arrive the point propos'd,
Cæsar cried, *Help me, Cassius, or I sink!*
I, as Æneas, our great ancestor,
Did from the flames of Troy upon his shoulder
The old Anchises bear, so from the waves of Tiber
Did I the tired Cæsar: and this man
Is now become a god; and Cassius is
A wretched creature, and must bend his body
If Cæsar carelessly but nod on him.
He had a fever when he was in Spain,
And, when the fit was on him, I did mark

VOL. V.   N

How he did shake: 'tis true, this god did shake:
His coward lips did from their colour fly;
And that same eye, whose bend doth awe the world,
Did lose his lustre: I did hear him groan:
Ay, and that tongue of his, that bade the Romans
Mark him, and write his speeches in their books,
Alas! it cried, *Give me some drink, Titinius,*
As a sick girl.   Ye gods, it doth amaze me,
A man of such a feeble temper should
So get the start of the majestic world,
And bear the palm alone.   [*Shout: flourish.*

 Bru. Another general shout!
I do believe that these applauses are
For some new honours that are heap'd on Cæsar.

 Cas. Why, man, he doth bestride the narrow world
Like a Colossus; and we petty men
Walk under his huge legs, and peep about
To find ourselves dishonourable graves.
Men at some time are masters of their fates:
The fault, dear Brutus, is not in our stars,
But in ourselves, that we are underlings.
Brutus and Cæsar: what should be in that Cæsar'
Why should that name be sounded more than yours?
Write them together, yours is as fair a name;
Sound them, it doth become the mouth as well;
Weigh them, it is as heavy; conjure with 'em,
Brutus will start a spirit as soon as Cæsar.   [*Shout.*
Now, in the names of all the gods at once,
Upon what meat doth this our Cæsar feed,
That he is grown so great?   Age, thou art sham'd!
Rome, thou hast lost the breed of noble bloods!
When went there by an age, since the great flood,
But it was fam'd with more than with one man?
When could they say, till now, that talk'd of Rome,
That her wide walls encompass'd but one man?
Now is it Rome indeed, and room enough,
When there is in it but one only man.
O! you and I have heard our fathers say,
There was a Brutus once that would have brook'd
The eternal devil to keep his state in Rome
As easily as a king.

 Bru. That you do love me, I am nothing jealous;
What you would work me to, I have some aim:
How I have thought of this, and of these times,
I shall recount hereafter; for this present,
I would not, so with love I might entreat you,

Be any further mov'd. What you have said
I will consider; what you have to say
I will with patience hear: and find a time
Both meet to hear and answer such high things
Till then, my noble friend, chew upon this;
Brutus had rather be a villager
Than to repute himself a son of Rome
Under these hard conditions as this time
Is like to lay upon us.

Cas. I am glad that my weak words
Have struck but thus much show of fire from Brutus.

Bru. The games are done, and Cæsar is returning.

Cas. As they pass by, pluck Casca by the sleeve;
And he will, after his sour fashion, tell you
What hath proceeded worthy note to-day.

Re-enter CÆSAR *and his* Train.

Bru. I will do so.—But, look you, Cassius,
The angry spot doth glow on Cæsar's brow,
And all the rest look like a chidden train:
Calphurnia's cheek is pale; and Cicero
Looks with such ferret and such fiery eyes
As we have seen him in the Capitol,
Being cross'd in conference by some senators.

Cas. Casca will tell us what the matter is.

Cæs. Antonius.

Ant. Cæsar?

Cæs. Let me have men about me that are fat;
Sleek-headed men, and such as sleep o' nights:
Yond Cassius has a lean and hungry look;
He thinks too much: such men are dangerous.

Ant. Fear him not, Cæsar, he's not dangerous;
He is a noble Roman, and well given.

Cæs. Would he were fatter!—But I fear him not:
Yet if my name were liable to fear,
I do not know the man I should avoid
So soon as that spare Cassius. He reads much;
He is a great observer, and he looks
Quite through the deeds of men: he loves no plays,
As thou dost, Antony; he hears no music:
Seldom he smiles; and smiles in such a sort
As if he mock'd himself, and scorn'd his spirit
That could be mov'd to smile at anything.
Such men as he be never at heart's ease
Whiles they behold a greater than themselves;
And therefore are they very dangerous.

I rather tell thee what is to be fear'd
Than what I fear,—for always I am Cæsar.
Come on my right hand, for this ear is deaf,
And tell me truly what thou think'st of him.

[Exeunt CÆSAR *and his* Train. CASCA *stays behind.*

Casca. You pull'd me by the cloak; would you speak
    with me?

Bru. Ay, Casca; tell us, what hath chanc'd to-day,
That Cæsar looks so sad?

Casca. Why, you were with him, were you not?

Bru. I should not then ask Casca what had chanc'd.

Casca. Why, there was a crown offered him: and being
offered him, he put it by with the back of his hand, thus;
and then the people fell a-shouting.

Bru. What was the second noise for?

Casca. Why, for that too.

Cas. They shouted thrice: what was the last cry for?

Casca. Why, for that too.

Bru. Was the crown offer'd him thrice?

Casca. Ay, marry, was't, and he put it by thrice, every
time gentler than other; and at every putting by mine
honest neighbours shouted.

Cas. Who offered him the crown?

Casca. Why, Antony.

Bru. Tell us the manner of it, gentle Casca.

Casca. I can as well be hanged as tell the manner of it:
it was mere foolery; I did not mark it. I saw Mark
Antony offer him a crown;—yet 'twas not a crown neither,
'twas one of these coronets;—and, as I told you, he put it
by once: but, for all that, to my thinking, he would fain
have had it. Then he offered it to him again; then he put
it by again: but, to my thinking, he was very loth to
lay his fingers off it And then he offered it the third
time; he put it the third time by: and still, as he refused
it, the rabblement hooted, and clapped their chapped
hands, and threw up their sweaty night-caps, and uttered
such a deal of stinking breath because Cæsar refused the
crown, that it had almost choked Cæsar; for he swooned,
and fell down at it: and for mine own part I durst not
laugh, for fear of opening my lips and receiving the bad air.

Cas. But, soft, I pray you: what, did Cæsar swoon?

Casca. He fell down in the market-place, and foamed at
mouth, and was speechless.

Bru. 'Tis very like,—he hath the falling sickness.

Cas. No, Cæsar hath it not; but you, and I,
And honest Casca, we have the falling sickness.

Casca. I know not what you mean by that; but I am sure
Cæsar fell down. If the tag-rag people did not clap him
and hiss him, according as he pleased and displeased them,
as they use to do the players in the theatre, I am no true man.

Bru. What said he when he came unto himself?

Casca. Marry, before he fell down, when he perceived the
common herd was glad he refused the crown, he plucked
me ope his doublet, and offered them his throat to cut.—An
I had been a man of any occupation, if I would not have
taken him at a word, I would I might go to hell among
the rogues. And so he fell. When he came to himself
again, he said, If he had done or said anything amiss, he de-
sired their worships to think it was his infirmity. Three or
four wenches, where I stood, cried, *Alas, good soul!*—and
forgave him with all their hearts: but there's no heed to
be taken of them; if Cæsar had stabbed their mothers they
would have done no less.

Bru. And after that he came, thus sad, away?

Casca Ay.

Cas. Did Cicero say anything?

Casca. Ay, he spoke Greek.

Cas. To what effect?

Casca. Nay, an I tell you that, I'll ne'er look you i' the
face again: but those that understood him smiled at one
another, and shook their heads; but, for mine own part,
it was Greek to me. I could tell you more news too:
Marullus and Flavius, for pulling scarfs off Cæsar's images,
are put to silence. Fare you well. There was more foolery
yet, if I could remember it.

Cas. Will you sup with me to-night, Casca?

Casca. No, I am promised forth.

Cas. Will you dine with me to-morrow?

Casca. Ay, if I be alive, and your mind hold, and your
dinner worth the eating.

Cas. Good; I will expect you.

Casca Do so: farewell, both.   [*Exit.*

Bru. What a blunt fellow is this grown to be!
He was quick mettle when he went to school.

Cas. So is he now, in execution
Of any bold or noble enterprise,
However he puts on this tardy form.
This rudeness is a sauce to his good wit,
Which gives men stomach to digest his words
With better appetite.

Bru. And so it is. For this time I will leave you:
To-morrow, if you please to speak with me,

I will come home to you; or, if you will,
Come home to me, and I will wait for you.
   Cas. I will do so: till then, think of the world.

                          [Exit BRUTUS.

Well, Brutus, thou art noble; yet, I see,
Thy honourable metal may be wrought
From that it is dispos'd: therefore it is meet
That noble minds keep ever with their likes;
For who so firm that cannot be sedue'd?
Cæsar doth bear me hard; but he loves Brutus:
If I were Brutus now, and he were Cassius,
He should not humour me. I will this night,
In several hands, in at his windows throw,
As if they came from several citizens,
Writings, all tending to the great opinion
That Rome holds of his name; wherein obscurely
Cæsar's ambition shall be glanced at:
And, after this, let Cæsar seat him sure;
For we will shake him, or worse days endure.

                                 [Exit.

SCENE III.—ROME. *A Street.*

Thunder and Lightning. *Enter, from opposite sides,* CASCA,
      with his sword drawn, and CICERO.

   Cic. Good-even, Casca: brought you Cæsar home?
Why are you breathless? and why stare you so?
   Casca Are not you mov'd, when all the sway of earth
Shakes like a thing unfirm? O Cicero,
I have seen tempests, when the scolding winds
Have riv'd the knotty oaks; and I have seen
The ambitious ocean swell, and rage, and foam,
To be exalted with the threat'ning clouds:
But never till to-night, never till now,
Did I go through a tempest dropping fire.
Either there is a civil strife in heaven;
Or else the world, too saucy with the gods,
Incenses them to send destruction.
    Cic. Why, saw you anything more wonderful?
    Casca. A common slave,—you know him well by sight,—
Held up his left hand, which did flame and burn
Like twenty torches join'd; and yet his hand,
Not sensible of fire, remain'd unscorch'd.
Besides,—I ha' not since put up my sword,—
Against the Capitol I met a lion,
Who glar'd upon me, and went surly by,

Withont annoying me: and there were drawn
Upon a heap a hundred ghastly women,
Transformed with their fear; who swore they saw
Men, all in fire, walk up and down the streets.
And yesterday the bird of night did sit,
Even at noon-day, upon the market-place,
Hooting and shrieking.　When these prodigies
Do so conjointly meet, let not men say,
These are their reasons,—they are natural;
For I believe they are portentous things
Unto the climate that they point upon.

　　Cic. Indeed, it is a strange-disposed time:
But men may construe things after their fashion,
Clean from the purpose of the things themselves.
Comes Cæsar to the Capitol to-morrow?

　　Casca. He doth; for he did bid Antonius
Send word to you he would be there to-morrow.

　　Cic. Good-night, then, Casca: this disturbed sky
Is not to walk in.

　　Casca.　　　　Farewell, Cicero.　　　[*Exit* CICERO.

Enter CASSIUS.

　　Cas. Who's there?
　　Casca.　　　　A Roman.
　　Cas.　　　　　　　Casca, by your voice.
　　Casca. Your ear is good.　Cassius, what night is this!
　　Cas. A very pleasing night to honest men.
　　Casca. Who ever knew the heavens menace so?
　　Cas. Those that have known the earth so full of faults.
For my part, I have walk'd about the streets,
Submitting me unto the perilous night;
And, thus unbraced, Casca, as you see,
Have bar'd my bosom to the thunder-stone:
And when the cross-blue lightning seem'd to open
The breast of heaven, I did present myself
Even in the aim and very flash of it.

　　Casca. But wherefore did you so much tempt the heavens?
It is the part of men to fear and tremble
When the most mighty gods, by tokens, send
Such dreadful heralds to astonish us.

　　Cas. You are dull, Casca; and those sparks of life
That should be in a Roman you do want,
Or else you use not.　You look pale, and gaze,
And put on fear, and cast yourself in wonder,
To see the strange impatience of the heavens:
But if you would consider the true cause

Why all these fires, why all these gliding ghosts,
Why birds and beasts, from quality and kind;
Why old men fools, and children calculate;
Why all these things change, from their ordinance,
Their natures, and preformed faculties,
To monstrous quality;—why, you shall find
That heaven hath infus'd them with these spirits,
To make them instruments of fear and warning
Unto some monstrous state.
Now could I, Casca, name to thee a man
Most like this dreadful night
That thunders, lightens, opens graves, and roars
As doth the lion in the Capitol,—
A man no mightier than thyself or me
In personal action; yet prodigious grown,
And fearful, as these strange eruptions are.

 Casca. 'Tis Cæsar that you mean; is it not, Cassius?

 Cas. Let it be who it is: for Romans now
Have thews and limbs like to their ancestors;
But, woe the while! our fathers' minds are dead,
And we are govern'd with our mothers' spirits;
Our yoke and sufferance show us womanish.

 Casca. Indeed they say the senators to-morrow
Mean to establish Cæsar as a king;
And he shall wear his crown by sea and land,
In every place, save here in Italy.

 Cas. I know where I will wear this dagger then;
Cassius from bondage will deliver Cassius:
Therein, ye gods, you make the weak most strong;
Therein, ye gods, you tyrants do defeat:
Nor stony tower, nor walls of beaten brass,
Nor airless dungeon, nor strong links of iron,
Can be retentive to the strength of spirit;
But life, being weary of these worldly bars,
Never lacks power to dismiss itself.
If I know this, know all the world besides,
That part of tyranny that I do bear
I can shake off at pleasure.   [*Thunder still.*

 Casca.   So can I:
So every bondman in his own hand bears
The power to cancel his captivity.

 Cas. And why should Cæsar be a tyrant, then?
Poor man! I know he would not be a wolf,
But that he sees the Romans are but sheep:
He were no lion, were not Romans hinds.
Those that with haste will make a mighty fire

Begin it with weak straws: what trash is Rome,
What rubbish, and what offal, when it serves
For the base matter to illuminate
So vile a thing as Cæsar!　But, O grief,
Where hast thou led me?　I perhaps speak this
Before a willing bondman; then I know
My answer must be made: but I am arm'd,
And dangers are to me indifferent.

　　Casca. You speak to Casca; and to such a man
That is no fleering tell-tale.　Hold, my hand:
Be factious for redress of all these griefs;
And I will set this foot of mine as far
As who goes farthest.

　　Cas.　　　　　　There's a bargain made.
Now know you, Casca, I have mov'd already
Some certain of the noblest-minded Romans
To undergo with me an enterprise
Of honourable-dangerous consequence;
And I do know by this they stay for me
In Pompey's porch: for now, this fearful night,
There is no stir or walking in the streets;
And the complexion of the element
In favour's like the work we have in hand,
Most bloody, fiery, and most terrible.

　　Casca. Stand close awhile, for here comes one in haste.

　　Cas. 'Tis Cinna,—I do know him by his gait;
He is a friend.

Enter CINNA.

　　　　　　Cinna, where haste you so?

　　Cin. To find out you.　Who's that?　Metullus Cimber?

　　Cas. No, it is Casca; one incorporate
To our attempts.　Am I not stay'd for, Cinna?

　　Cin. I am glad on't.　What a fearful night is this!
There's two or three of us have seen strange sights.

　　Cas. Am I not stay'd for?　Tell me.

　　Cin.　　　　　　　　　Yes, you are.
O Cassius, if you could
But win the noble Brutus to our party,—

　　Cas. Be you content: good Cinna, take this paper,
And look you lay it in the prætor's chair,
Where Brutus may but find it; and throw this
In at his window; set this up with wax
Upon old Brutus' statue: all this done,
Repair to Pompey's porch, where you shall find us.
Is Decius Brutus and Trebonius there?

Cin. All but Metellus Cimber; and he's gone
To seek you at your house.   Well, I will hie,
And so bestow these papers as you bade me.
   Cas. That done, repair to Pompey's theatre. [*Exit* CINNA.
Come, Casca, you and I will yet, ere day,
See Brutus at his house: three parts of him
Is ours already; and the man entire,
Upon the next encounter, yields him ours.
   Casca. O, he sits high in all the people's hearts:
And that which would appear offence in us,
His countenance, like richest alchemy,
Will change to virtue and to worthiness.
   Cas. Him, and his worth, and our great need of him,
You have right well conceited.   Let us go,
For it is after midnight: and ere day
We will awake him, and be sure of him.   [*Exeunt.*

ACT II.

SCENE I.—ROME.   BRUTUS's *Orchard.*

Enter BRUTUS.

Bru. What, Lucius, ho!—
I cannot, by the progress of the stars,
Give guess how near to day.—Lucius, I say!—
I would it were my fault to sleep so soundly.—
When, Lucius, when? awake, I say! what, Lucius!

Enter LUCIUS.

Luc. Call'd you, my lord?
Bru. Get me a taper in my study, Lucius:
When it is lighted, come and call me here.
Luc. I will, my lord.   [*Exit.*
Bru. It must be by his death: and, for my part,
I know no personal cause to spurn at him,
But for the general.   He would be crown'd:
How that might change his nature, there's the question:
It is the bright day that brings forth the adder;
And that craves wary walking.   Crown him?—that—
And then, I grant, we put a sting in him,
That at his will he may do danger with.
The abuse of greatness is, when it disjoins
Remorse from power: and, to speak truth of Cæsar,

I have not known when his affections sway'd
More than his reason. But 'tis a common proof
That lowliness is young ambition's ladder,
Whereto the climber-upward turns his face;
But when he once attains the utmost round,
He then unto the ladder turns his back,
Looks in the clouds, scorning the base degrees
By which he did ascend. So Cæsar may;
Then, lest he may, prevent. And, since the quarrel
Will bear no colour for the thing he is,
Fashion it thus; that what he is, augmented,
Would run to these and these extremities:
And therefore think him as a serpent's egg,
Which, hatch'd, would as his kind grow mischievous;
And kill him in the shell.

Re-enter LUCIUS.

Luc. The taper burneth in your closet, sir.
Searching the window for a flint, I found
[Giving him a letter.
This paper, thus seal'd up; and I am sure
It did not lie there when I went to bed.
Bru. Get you to bed again, it is not day.
Is not to-morrow, boy, the ides of March?
Luc. I know not, sir.
Bru. Look in the calendar, and bring me word.
Luc. I will, sir.   [*Exit.*
Bru. The exhalations, whizzing in the air,
Give so much light that I may read by them.
[Opens the letter and reads.
Brutus, thou sleep'st: awake, and see thyself.
Shall Rome, &c. Speak, strike, redress!
Brutus, thou sleep'st: awake.—
Such instigations have been often dropp'd
Where I have took them up.
Shall Rome, &c. Thus must I piece it out,—
Shall Rome stand under one man's awe? What, Rome?
My ancestors did from the streets of Rome
The Tarquin drive, when he was call'd a king.
Speak, strike, redress!—Am I entreated then
To speak and strike! O Rome! I make thee promise,
If the redress will follow, thou receivest
Thy full petition at the hand of Brutus!

Re-enter LUCIUS.

Luc. Sir, March is wasted fourteen days. [*Knocking within.*

Bru. 'Tis good. Go to the gate ; somebody knocks.

[*Exit* LUCIUS.

Since Cassius first did whet me against Cæsar,
I have not slept.
Between the acting of a dreadful thing
And the first motion, all the interim is
Like a phantasma or a hideous dream :
The genius and the mortal instruments
Are then in council ; and the state of man,
Like to a little kingdom, suffers then
The nature of an insurrection.

Re-enter LUCIUS.

Luc. Sir, 'tis your brother Cassius at the door
Who doth desire to see you.
Bru.   Is he alone?
Luc. No, sir, there are more with him.
Bru.   Do you know them?
Luc. No, sir; their hats are pluck'd about their ears,
And half their faces buried in their cloaks,
That by no means I may discover them
By any mark of favour.
Bru.   Let 'em enter.   [*Exit* LUCIUS.
They are the faction. O conspiracy,
Sham'st thou to show thy dangerous brow by night,
When evils are most free? O, then, by day
Where wilt thou find a cavern dark enough
To mask thy monstrous visage ? Seek none, conspiracy;
Hide it in smiles and affability :
For if thou hath thy native semblance on,
Not Erebus itself were dim enough
To hide thee from prevention.

Enter CASSIUS, CASCA, DECIUS, CINNA, METELLUS CIMBER,
          and TREBONIUS.

Cas. I think we are too bold upon your rest :
Good-morrow, Brutus; do we trouble you?
Bru. I have been up this hour; awake all night.
Know I these men that come along with you?
Cas. Yes, every man of them; and no man here
But honours you; and every one doth wish
You had but that opinion of yourself
Which every noble Roman bears of you.
This is Trebonius.
Bru.   He is welcome hither.
Cas. This, Decius Brutus.

Bru.   He is welcome too.

Cas. This, Casca; this, Cinna;
And this, Metellus Cimber.

Bru.   They are all welcome.
What watchful cares do interpose themselves
Betwixt your eyes and night?

Cas. Shall I entreat a word?

                    [BRUTUS *and* CASSIUS *whisper.*

Dec. Here lies the east; doth not the day break
    here?

Casca. No.

Cin. O, pardon, sir, it doth; and yon grey lines
That fret the clouds are messengers of day:

Casca. You shall confess that you are both deceiv'd.
Here, as I point my sword, the sun arises;
Which is a great way growing on the south,
Weighing the youthful season of the year.
Some two months hence up higher toward the north
He first presents his fire; and the high east
Stands, as the Capitol, directly here.

Bru. Give me your hands all over, one by one.

Cas. And let us swear our resolution.

Bru. No, not an oath: if not the face of men,
The sufferance of our souls, the time's abuse,—
If these be motives weak, break off betimes,
And every man hence to his idle bed;
So let high-sighted tyranny range on,
Till each man drop by lottery.   But if these,
As I am sure they do, bear fire enough
To kindle cowards, and to steel with valour
The melting spirits of women; then, countrymen,
What need we any spur, but our own cause,
To prick us to redress? what other bond
Than secret Romans, that have spoke the word
And will not palter? and what other oath
Than honesty to honesty engag'd
That this shall be, or we will fall for it?
Swear priests, and cowards, and men cautelous,
Old feeble carrions, and such suffering souls
That welcome wrongs; unto bad causes swear
Such creatures as men doubt: but do not stain
The even virtue of our enterprise,
Nor the insuppressive mettle of our spirits,
To think that or our cause or our performance
Did need an oath; when every drop of blood
That every Roman bears, and nobly bears,

Is guilty of a several bastardy
If he do break the smallest particle
Of any promise that hath pass'd from him.
    Cas. But what of Cicero? shall we sound him?
I think he will stand very strong with us.
    Casca. Let us not leave him out.
    Cin.   No, by no means.
    Met. O, let us have him; for his silver hairs
Will purchase us a good opinion,
And buy men's voices to commend our deeds:
It shall be said his judgment rul'd our hands;
Our youths and wildness shall no whit appear,
But all be buried in his gravity.
    Bru. O, name him not: let us not break with him;
For he will never follow anything
That other men begin.
    Cas.   Then leave him out.
    Casca. Indeed he is not fit.
    Dec. Shall no man else be touch'd but only Cæsar?
    Cas. Decius, well urg'd.—I think it is not meet
Mark Antony, so well belov'd of Cæsar,
Should outlive Cæsar: we shall find of him
A shrewd contriver; and, you know, his means,
If he improve them, may well stretch so far
As to annoy us all: which to prevent,
Let Antony and Cæsar fall together.
    Bru. Our course will seem too bloody, Caius Cassius,
To cut the head off and then hack the limbs,—
Like wrath in death and envy afterwards;
For Antony is but a limb of Cæsar:
Let's be sacrificers, but not butchers, Caius.
We all stand up against the spirit of Cæsar;
And in the spirit of men there is no blood:
O that we, then, could come by Cæsar's spirit,
And not dismember Cæsar! But, alas,
Cæsar must bleed for it! And, gentle friends,
Let's kill him boldly, but not wrathfully;
Let's carve him as a dish fit for the gods,
Not hew him as a carcase fit for hounds:
And let our hearts, as subtle masters do,
Stir up their servants to an act of rage,
And after seem to chide 'em. This shall make
Our purpose necessary, and not envious:
Which so appearing to the common eyes,
We shall be call'd purgers, not murderers.
And for Mark Antony, think not of him;

For he can do no more than Cæsar's arm
When Cæsar's head is off.
    Cas.   Yet I fear him;
For in the engrafted love he bears to Cæsar,—
    Bru. Alas, good Cassius, do not think of him:
If he love Cæsar, all that he can do
Is to himself,—take thought and die for Cæsar:
And that were much he should ; for he is given
To sports, to wildness, and much company.
    Treb. There is no fear in him; let him not die;
For he will live, and laugh at this hereafter. [*Clock strikes.*
    Bru. Peace, count the clock.
    Cas.   The clock hath stricken three.
    Treb. 'Tis time to part.
    Cas.   But it is doubtful yet
Whether Cæsar will come forth to-day or no:
For he is superstitious grown of late ;
Quite from the main opinion he held once
Of fantasy, of dreams, and ceremonies :
It may be these apparent prodigies,
The unaccustom'd terror of this night,
And the persuasion of his augurers,
May hold him from the Capitol to-day.
    Dec. Never fear that: if he be so resolv'd
I can o'ersway him; for he loves to hear
That unicorns may be betray'd with trees,
And bears with glasses, elephants with holes,
Lions with toils, and men with flatterers:
But when I tell him he hates flatterers,
He says he does,—being then most flatter'd.
Let me work ;
For I can give his humour the true bent,
And I will bring him to the Capitol.
    Cas. Nay, we will all of us be there to fetch him.
    Bru. By the eighth hour: is that the uttermost?
    Cin. Be that the uttermost, and fail not then.
    Met. Caius Ligarius doth bear Cæsar hard,
Who rated him for speaking well of Pompey:
I wonder none of you have thought of him.
    Bru. Now, good Metellus, go along by him:
He loves me well, and I have given him reasons ;
Send him but hither, and I'll fashion him.
    Cas. The morning comes upon 's: we'll leave you, Brutus:
And, friends, disperse yourselves : but all remember
What you have said, and show yourselves true Romans.
    Bru. Good gentlemen, look fresh and merrily;

Let not our looks put on our purposes;
But bear it as our Roman actors do,
With untir'd spirits and formal constancy;
And so, good-morrow to you every one.

[Exeunt all but BRUTUS.

Boy! Lucius!—Fast asleep? it is no matter;
Enjoy the heavy honey-dew of slumber:
Thou hast no figures nor no fantasies
Which busy care draws in the brains of men;
Therefore thou sleep'st so sound.

Enter PORTIA.

Por.   Brutus, my lord!
Bru. Portia, what mean you? wherefore rise you now
It is not for your health thus to commit
Your weak condition to the raw cold morning.
Por. Nor for yours neither.   You have ungently, Brutus,
Stole from my bed: and yesternight, at supper,
You suddenly arose, and walk'd about,
Musing and sighing, with your arms across;
And when I ask'd you what the matter was,
You star'd upon me with ungentle looks:
I urg'd you further; then you scratch'd your head,
And too impatiently stamp'd with your foot:
Yet I insisted, yet you answer'd not;
But with an angry wafture of your hand
Gave sign for me to leave you: so I did;
Fearing to strengthen that impatience
Which seem'd too much enkindled; and withal
Hoping it was but an effect of humour,
Which sometime hath his hour with every man.
It will not let you eat, nor talk, nor sleep;
And, could it work so much upon your shape
As it hath much prevail'd on your condition,
I should not know you, Brutus.   Dear my lord,
Make me acquainted with your cause of grief.
Bru. I am not well in health, and that is all.
Por. Brutus is wise, and were he not in health,
He would embrace the means to come by it.
Bru. Why, so I do.—Good Portia, go to bed.
Por. Is Brutus sick? and is it physical
To walk unbraced, and suck up the humours
Of the dank morning?   What, is Brutus sick,—
And will he steal out of his wholesome bed,
To dare the vile contagion of the night,
And tempt the rheumy and unpurg'd **air**

To add unto his sickness? No, my Brutus;
You have some sick offence within your mind,
Which by the right and virtue of my place
I ought to know of: and upon my knees
I charm you, by my once-commended beauty,
By all your vows of love, and that great vow
Which did incorporate and make us one,
That you unfold to me, yourself, your half,
Why you are heavy; and what men to-night
Have had resort to you,—for here have been
Some six or seven, who did hide their faces
Even from darkness.
 Bru.   Kneel not, gentle Portia.
 Por. I should not need if you were gentle Brutus.
Within the bond of marriage, tell me, Brutus,
Is it excepted I should know no secrets
That appertain to you? Am I yourself
But as it were in sort or limitation,—
To keep with you at meals, comfort your bed,
And talk to you sometimes? Dwell I but in the suburbs
Of your good pleasure? If it be no more,
Portia is Brutus' harlot, not his wife.
 Bru. You are my true and honourable wife;
As dear to me as are the ruddy drops
That visit my sad heart.
 Por. If this were true, then should I know this secret.
I grant I am a woman; but withal
A woman that Lord Brutus took to wife:
I grant I am a woman; but withal
A woman well-reputed,—Cato's daughter.
Think you I am no stronger than my sex,
Being so father'd and so husbanded?
Tell me your counsels, I will not disclose 'em
I have made strong proof of my constancy,
Giving myself a voluntary wound
Here in the thigh: can I bear that with patience,
And not my husband's secrets?
 Bru.   O ye gods,
Render me worthy of this noble wife! [*Knocking within.*
Hark, hark! one knocks: Portia, go in awhile;
And by and by thy bosom shall partake
The secrets of my heart:
All my engagements I will construe to thee,
All the charactery of my sad brows.
Leave me with haste.   [*Exit* PORTIA.
    Lucius, who's that knocks?

Enter LUCIS *with* LIGARIUS.

Luc. Here is a sick man that would speak with you.
Bru. Caius Ligarius, that Metellus spake of.—
Boy, stand aside.—Caius Ligarius,—how!
Lig. Vouchsafe good-morrow from a feeble tongue.
Bru. O, what a time have you chose out, brave Caius,
To wear a kerchief! Would you were not sick!
Lig. I am not sick if Brutus have in hand
Any exploit worthy the name of honour.
Bru. Such an exploit have I in hand, Ligarius,
Had you a healthful ear to hear of it.
Lig. By all the gods that Romans bow before,
I here discard my sickness! Soul of Rome!
Brave son, deriv'd from honourable loins!
Thou, like an exorcist, hast conjur'd up
My mortified spirit. Now bid me run,
And I will strive with things impossible;
Yea, get the better of them. What's to do?
Bru. A piece of work that will make sick men whole.
Lig. But are not some whole that we must make sick?
Bru. That must we also. What it is, my Caius,
I shall unfold to thee, as we are going
To whom it must be done.
Lig.   Set on your foot;
And with a heart new fir'd I follow you
To do I know not what: but it sufficeth
That Brutus leads me on.
Bru.   Follow me, then.   [*Exeunt.*

SCENE II.—ROME.   *A Room in* CÆSAR'S *Palace.*

Thunder and lightning.   Enter CÆSAR *in his night-gown.*

Cæs. Nor heaven nor earth have been at peace to-night:
Thrice hath Calphurnia in her sleep cried out,
Help, ho! They murder Cæsar!—Who's within?

Enter a Servant.

Serv. My lord?
Cæs. Go bid the priests do present sacrifice,
And bring me their opinions of success.
Serv. I will, my lord.   [*Exit.*

Enter CALPHURNIA.

Cal. What mean you, Cæsar? Think you to walk forth?
You shall not stir out of your house to-day.

Cæs. Cæsar shall forth: the things that threaten'd me
Ne'er look'd but on my back; when they shall see
The face of Cæsar they are vanished.
 Cal. Cæsar, I never stood on ceremonies,
Yet now they fright me. There is one within,
Besides the things that we have heard and seen,
Recounts most horrid sights seen by the watch.
A lioness hath whelped in the streets;
And graves have yawn'd and yielded up their dead;
Fierce fiery warriors fight upon the clouds,
In ranks and squadrons and right form of war,
Which drizzled blood upon the Capitol;
The noise of battle hurtled in the air,
Horses did neigh, and dying men did groan;
And ghosts did shriek and squeal about the streets.
O Cæsar, these things are beyond all use,
And I do fear them!
 Cæs.   What can be avoided,
Whose end is purpos'd by the mighty gods?
Yet Cæsar shall go forth; for these predictions
Are to the world in general as to Cæsar.
 Cal. When beggars die there are no comets seen;
The heavens themselves blaze forth the death of princes.
 Cæs. Cowards die many times before their deaths;
The valiant never taste of death but once.
Of all the wonders that I yet have heard,
It seems to me most strange that men should fear;
Seeing that death, a necessary end,
Will come when it will come.

    Re-enter Servant.
       What say the augurers?
 Serv. They would not have you to stir forth to-day.
Plucking the entrails of an offering forth,
They could not find a heart within the beast.
 Cæs. The gods do this in shame of cowardice:
Cæsar should be a beast without a heart
If he should stay at home to-day for fear.
No, Cæsar shall not: danger knows full well
That Cæsar is more dangerous than he:
We are two lions litter'd in one day,
And I the elder and more terrible:—
And Cæsar shall go forth.
 Cal.   Alas, my lord,
Your wisdom is consum'd in confidence.
Do not go forth to-day: call it my fear

That keeps you in the house, and not your own.
We'll send Mark Antony to the senate-house;
And he shall say you are not well to-day:
Let me, upon my knee, prevail in this.

Cœs. Mark Antony shall say I am not well;
And for thy humour I will stay at home.

Enter DECIUS.

Here's Decius Brutus, he shall tell them so.

Dec. Cæsar, all hail! good-morrow, worthy Cæsar:
I come to fetch you to the senate-house.

Cœs. And you are come in very happy time,
To bear my greeting to the senators,
And tell them that I will not come to-day:
Cannot, is false; and that I dare not, falser:
I will not come to-day,—tell them so, Decius.

Cal. Say he is sick.

Cœs.   Shall Cæsar send a lie?
Have I in conquest stretch'd mine arm so far,
To be afeard to tell graybeards the truth?
Decius, go tell them Cæsar will not come.

Dec. Most mighty Cæsar, let me know some cause,
Lest I be laugh'd at when I tell them so.

Cœs. The cause is in my will;—I will not come;
That is enough to satisfy the senate.
But for your private satisfaction,
Because I love you, I will let you know,— ·
Calphurnia here, my wife, stays me at home:
She dreamt to-night she saw my statua,
Which, like a fountain with a hundred spouts,
Did run pure blood; and many lusty Romans
Came smiling and did bathe their hands in it:
And these does she apply for warnings and portents,
And evils imminent; and on her knee
Hath begg'd that I will stay at home to-day.

Dec. This dream is all amiss interpreted;
It was a vision fair and fortunate:
Your statue spouting blood in many pipes,
In which so many smiling Romans bath'd,
Signifies that from you great Rome shall suck
Reviving blood; and that great men shall press
For tinctures, stains, relics, and cognizance.
This by Calphurnia's dream is signified.

Cœs. And this way have you well expounded it.

Dec. I have, when you have heard what I can say:
And know it now,—the senate have concluded

To give this day a crown to mighty Cæsar.
If you shall send them word you will not come,
Their minds may change. Besides, it were a mock,
Apt to be render'd, for some one to say,
Break up the senate till another time,
When Cæsar's wife shall meet with better dreams.
If Cæsar hide himself, shall they not whisper,
Lo, Cæsar is afraid?
Pardon me, Cæsar; for my dear dear love
To your proceeding bids me tell you this;
And reason to my love is liable.
   Cæs. How foolish do your fears seem now, Calphurnia!
I am ashamed I did yield to them.—
Give me my robe, for I will go:

   Enter PUBLIUS, BRUTUS, LIGARIUS, METELLUS, CASCA,
       TREBONIUS, *and* CINNA.

And look where Publius is come to fetch me.
   Pub. Good-morrow, Cæsar.
   Cæs.   Welcome, Publius.—
What, Brutus, are you stirred so early too?—
Good-morrow, Casca.—Caius Ligarius,
Cæsar was ne'er so much your enemy
As that same ague which hath made you lean.—
What is't o'clock?
   Bru.   Cæsar, 'tis strucken eight.
   Cæs. I thank you for your pains and courtesy.

       Enter ANTONY.

See! Antony, that revels long o' nights
Is notwithstanding up.—
Good-morrow, Antony.
   Ant.   So to most noble Cæsar.
   Cæs. Bid them prepare within.
I am to blame to be thus waited for.—
Now, Cinna;—now, Metellus:—what, Trebonius!
I have an hour's talk in store for you;
Remember that you call on me to-day:
Be near me, that I may remember you.
   Treb. Cæsar, I will:—and so near will I be,   [*Aside.*
That your best friends shall wish I had been further.
   Cæs. Good friends, go in and taste some wine with me;
And we, like friends, will straightway go together.
   Bru. That every like is not the same, O Cæsar,
The heart of Brutus yearns to think upon!   [*Exeunt.*

SCENE III.—ROME.   *A Street near the Capitol.*

Enter ARTEMIDORUS *reading a paper.*

Art. Cæsar, beware of Brutus; take heed of Cassius,
come not near Casca; have an eye to Cinna; trust not Trebonius; mark well Metellus Cimber; Decius Brutus loves thee
not; thou hast wronged Caius Ligarius.   There is but one
mind in all these men, and it is bent against Cæsar.   If thou
beest not immortal, look about you: security gives way to
conspiracy.   The mighty gods defend thee! Thy lover,

ARTEMIDORUS.

Here will I stand till Cæsar pass along,
And as a suitor will I give him this.
My heart laments that virtue cannot live
Out of the teeth of emulation.
If thou read this, O Cæsar, thou mayst live;
If not, the fates with traitors do contrive.   [*Exit.*

***

SCENE IV.—ROME.   *Another part of the same Street,
before the House of* BRUTUS.

Enter PORTIA *and* LUCIUS.

Por. I pr'ythee, boy, run to the senate-house;
Stay not to answer me, but get thee gone:
Why dost thou stay?
    Luc.   To know my errand, madam.
    Por. I would have had thee there and here again
Ere I can tell thee what thou shouldst do there.—
O constancy, be strong upon my side!
Set a huge mountain 'tween my heart and tongue!
I have a man's mind, but a woman's might.
How hard it is for women to keep counsel!—
Art thou here yet?
    Luc.   Madam, what should I do?
Run to the Capitol, and nothing else?
And so return to you, and nothing else?
    Por. Yes, bring me word, boy, if thy lord look well,
For he went sickly forth: and take good note
What Cæsar doth, what suitors press to him.
Hark, boy! what noise is that?
    Luc. I hear none, madam.
    Por.   Pr'ythee, listen well:
I heard a bustling rumour, like a fray,
And the wind brings it from the Capitol.

Luc. Sooth, madam, I hear nothing.

Enter ARTEMIDORUS.

Por.   Come hither, fellow:
Which way hast thou been?
   Art.   At mine own house, good lady.
   Por. What is't o'clock?
   Art.   About the ninth hour, lady.
   Por Is Cæsar yet gone to the Capitol?
   Art. Madam, not yet: I go to take my stand,
To see him pass on to the Capitol.
   Por. Thou hast some suit to Cæsar, hast thou not?
   Art. That I have, lady: if it will please Cæsar
To be so good to Cæsar as to hear me,
I shall beseech him to befriend himself.   [him?
   Por. Why, know'st thou any harm's intended towards
   Art. None that I know will be, much that I fear may
Good-morrow to you.   Here the street is narrow : [chance.
The throng that follows Cæsar at the heels
Of senators, of prætors, common suitors,
Will crowd a feeble man almost to death :
I'll get me to a place more void, and there
Speak to great Cæsar as he comes along.   [*Exit.*
   Por. I must go in.—Ah me, how weak a thing
The heart of woman is!   O Brutus,
The heavens speed thee in thine enterprise!—
Sure the boy heard me.—Brutus hath a suit
That Cæsar will not grant.—O, I grow faint.—
Run, Lucius, and commend me to my lord;
Say I am merry: come to me again,
And bring me word what he doth say to thee.
                              [*Exeunt severally.*

ACT III.

SCENE I.—ROME.   *The Capitol; the* Senate *sitting.*

A crowd of People *in the street leading to the Capitol;
among them* ARTEMIDORUS *and the* Soothsayer. *Flourish.
Enter* CÆSAR, BRUTUS, CASSIUS, CASCA, DECIUS, ME-
TELLUS, TREBONIUS, CINNA, ANTONY, LEPIDUS, PO-
PILIUS, PUBLIUS, *and others.*

Cæs. The ides of March are come.
Sooth. Ay, Cæsar; but not gone.

Art. Hail, Cæsar! Read this schedule.

Dec. Trebonius doth desire you to o'er-read,
At your best leisure, this his humble suit.

Art. O Cæsar, read mine first; for mine 's a suit
That touches Cæsar nearer : read it, great Cæsar.

Cæs. What touches us ourself shall be last serv'd.

Art. Delay not, Cæsar; read it instantly.

Cæs. What, is the fellow mad?

Pub.   Sirrah, give place.

Cas. What, urge you your petitions in the street?
Come to the Capitol.

> CÆSAR *enters the Capitol, the rest following. All the*
> Senators *rise.*

Pop. I wish your enterprise to-day may thrive.

Cas. What enterprise, Popilius?

Pop.   Fare you well.
                    [*Advances to* CÆSAR.

Bru. What said Popilius Lena?

Cas. He wish'd to-day our enterprise might thrive.
I fear our purpose is discovered.

Bru. Look how he makes to Cæsar: mark him.

Cas. Casca, be sudden, for we fear prevention.—
Brutus, what shall be done? If this be known,
Cassius or Cæsar never shall turn back,
For I will slay myself.

Bru.   Cassius, be constant :
Popilius Lena speaks not of our purposes ;
For, look, he smiles, and Cæsar doth not change.

Cas. Trebonius knows his time; for, look you, Brutus,
He draws Mark Antony out of the way.
                    [*Exeunt* ANT. *and* TREB. CÆSAR *and the* Senators
                    take their seats.

Dec Where is Metellus Cimber? Let him go,
And presently prefer his suit to Cæsar.

Bru. He is address'd : press near and second him.

Cin. Casca, you are the first that rears your hand.

Casca. Are we all ready?

Cæs. What is now amiss
That Cæsar and his senate must redress?

Met. Most high, most mighty, and most puissant Cæsar,
Metellus Cimber throws before thy seat
An humble heart,—   [*Kneeling*

Cæs.   I must prevent thee, Cimber.
These couchings and these lowly courtesies
Might fire the blood of ordinary men,

And turn pre-ordinance and first decree
Into the law of children. Be not fond
To think that Cæsar bears such rebel blood
That will be thaw'd from the true quality
With that which melteth fools; I mean, sweet words,
Low crooked curt'sies, and base spaniel fawning.
Thy brother by decree is banished:
If thou dost bend, and pray, and fawn for him,
I spurn thee like a cur out of my way.
Know, Cæsar doth not wrong; nor without cause
Will he be satisfied.

  Met. Is there no voice more worthy than my own,
To sound more sweetly in great Cæsar's ear
For the repealing of my banish'd brother?

  Bru. I kiss thy hand, but not in flattery, Cæsar,
Desiring thee that Publius Cimber may
Have an immediate freedom of repeal.

  Cæs. What, Brutus!

  Cas.   Pardon, Cæsar; Cæsar, pardon:
As low as to thy foot doth Cassius fall,
To beg enfranchisement for Publius Cimber.

  Cæs. I could be well mov'd if I were as you;
If I could pray to move, prayers would move me:
But I am constant as the northern star,
Of whose true-fix'd and resting quality
There is no fellow in the firmament.
The skies are painted with unnumber'd sparks,—
They are all fire, and every one doth shine;
But there's but one in all doth hold his place:
So in the world,—'tis furnish'd well with men,
And men are flesh and blood, and apprehensive;
Yet in the number I do know but one
That unassailable holds on his rank,
Unshak'd of motion: and that I am he,
Let me a little show it even in this,—
That I was constant Cimber should be banish'd,
And constant do remain to keep him so.

  Cin. O Cæsar,—

  Cæs.   Hence! wilt thou lift up Olympus?

  Dec. Great Cæsar,—

  Cæs.   Doth not Brutus bootless kneel?

  Casca. Speak, hands, for me!

    [CASCA *stabs* CÆSAR *in the neck.* CÆSAR *catches
     hold of his arm. He is then stabbed by several
     other Conspirators, and at last by* MARCUS
     BRUTUS.*

Cæs *Et tu, Brute?*—Then fall, Cæsar!
     [*Dies. The* Senators *and* People *retire in confusion.*
Cin. Liberty! Freedom! Tyranny is dead!—
Run hence, proclaim, cry it about the streets.
Cas. Some to the common pulpits, and cry out,
Liberty, freedom, and enfranchisement!
Bru. People and senators! be not affrighted;
Fly not; stand still: ambition's debt is paid.
Casca. Go to the pulpit, Brutus.
Dec.   And Cassius too.
Bru. Where's Publius?
Cin. Here, quite confounded with this mutiny.
Met. Stand fast together, lest some friend of Cæsar's
Should chance,—
Bru. Talk not of standing.—Publius, good cheer;
There is no harm intended to your person,
Nor to no Roman else: so tell them, Publius.
Cas. And leave us, Publius; lest that the people,
Rushing on us, should do your age some mischief.
Bru. Do so: and let no man abide this deed,
But we the doers.

Re-enter TREBONIUS.

Cas. Where is Antony?
Tre.   Fled to his house amaz'd:
Men, wives, and children stare, cry out, and run,
As it were doomsday.
Bru. Fates, we will know your pleasures:—
That we shall die, we know; 'tis but the time,
And drawing days out, that men stand upon.
Cas. Why, he that cuts off twenty years of life
Cuts off so many years of fearing death.
Bru. Grant that, and then is death a benefit:
So are we Cæsar's friends, that have abridg'd
His time of fearing death —Stoop, Romans, stoop,
And let us bathe our hands in Cæsar's blood
Up to the elbows, and besmear our swords:
Then walk we forth even to the market-place,
And, waving our red weapons o'er our heads,
Let's all cry, *Peace, freedom, and liberty!*
Cas. Stoop then, and wash.—How many ages hence
Shall this our lofty scene be acted over,
In states unborn and accents yet unknown!
Bru. How many times shall Cæsar bleed **in sport,**
That now on Pompey's basis lies along
No worthier than the dust!

Cas.   So oft as that shall be,
So often shall the knot of us be call'd
The men that gave their country liberty.
    Dec. What, shall we forth?
    Cas.   Ay, every man away:
Brutus shall lead; and we will grace his heels
With the most boldest and best hearts of Rome.
    Bru. Soft! who comes here?

Enter a Servant.

                        A friend of Antony's.
    Serv. Thus, Brutus, did my master bid me kneel;
Thus did Mark Antony bid me fall down;
And, being prostrate, thus he bade me say:—
Brutus is noble, wise, valiant, and honest;
Cæsar was mighty, bold, royal, and loving:
Say I lov'd Brutus, and I honour him;
Say I fear'd Cæsar, honour'd him, and lov'd him.
If Brutus will vouchsafe that Antony
May safely come to him, and be resolv'd
How Cæsar hath deserv'd to lie in death,
Mark Antony shall not love Cæsar dead
So well as Brutus living; but will follow
The fortunes and affairs of noble Brutus
Thorough the hazards of this untrod state
With all true faith.   So says my master Antony.
    Bru. Thy master is a wise and valiant Roman:
I never thought him worse.
Tell him, so please him come unto this place,
He shall be satisfied; and, by my honour,
Depart untouch'd.
    Serv.   I'll fetch him presently.   [*Exit.*
    Bru. I know that we shall have him well to friend.
    Cas. I wish we may: but yet have I a mind
That fears him much; and my misgiving still
Falls shrewdly to the purpose.
    Bru. But here comes Antony.

Re-enter ANTONY.

                    Welcome, Mark Antony.
    Ant. O mighty Cæsar! dost thou lie so low?
Are all thy conquests, glories, triumphs, spoils,
Shrunk to this little measure?—Fare thee well.—
I know not, gentlemen, what you intend,
Who else must be let blood, who else is rank:
If I myself, there is no hour so fit

As Cæsar's death's hour; nor no instrument
Of half that worth as those your swords, made rich
With the most noble blood of all this world.
I do beseech ye, if you bear me hard,
Now, whilst your purpled hands do reek and smoke,
Fulfil your pleasure. Live a thousand years,
I shall not find myself so apt to die:
No place will please me so, no mean of death,
As here by Cæsar, and by you cut off,
The choice and master spirits of this age.

   Bru. O Antony! beg not your death of us.
Though now we must appear bloody and cruel,
As by our hands and this our present act
You see we do; yet see you but our hands,
And this the bleeding business they have done:
Our hearts you see not,—they are pitiful;
And pity to the general wrong of Rome,—
As fire drives out fire, so pity pity,—
Hath done this deed on Cæsar. For your part,
To you our swords have leaden points, Mark Antony:
Our arms no strength of malice, and our hearts,
Of brothers' temper, do receive you in
With all kind love, good thoughts, and reverence.

   Cas. Your voice shall be as strong as any man's
In the disposing of new dignities.

   Bru. Only be patient till we have appeas'd
The multitude, beside themselves with fear,
And then we will deliver you the cause
Why I, that did love Cæsar when I struck him,
Have thus proceeded.

   Ant.   I doubt not of your wisdom.
Let each man render me his bloody hand:
First, Marcus Brutus, will I shake with you;—
Next, Caius Cassius, do I take your hand;—
Now, Decius Brutus, yours;—now yours, Metellus:—
Yours, Cinna;—and, my valiant Casca, yours;—
Though last, not least in love, yours, good Trebonius.
Gentlemen all,—alas, what shall I say?
My credit now stands on such slippery ground
That one of two bad ways you must conceit me,
Either a coward or a flatterer.—
That I did love thee, Cæsar, O, 'tis true:
If, then, thy spirit look upon us now,
Shall it not grieve thee dearer than thy death
To see thy Antony making his peace,
Shaking the bloody fingers of thy foes,

Most noble! in the presence of thy corse?
Had I as many eyes as thou hast wounds,
Weeping as fast as they stream forth thy blood,
It would become me better than to close
In terms of friendship with thine enemies.
Pardon me, Julius!—Here wast thou bay'd, brave hart;
Here didst thou fall; and here thy hunters stand,
Sign'd in thy spoil, and crimson'd in thy Lethe.—
O world, thou wast the forest to this hart;
And this, indeed, O world, the heart of thee.—
How like a deer strucken by many princes
Dost thou here lie!
　　Cas. Mark Antony,—
　　Ant.　　　　　　　　Pardon me, Caius Cassius:
The enemies of Cæsar shall say this;
Then in a friend it is cold modesty.
　　Cas. I blame you not for praising Cæsar so;
But what compáct mean you to have with us?
Will you be prick'd in number of our friends;
Or shall we on, and not depend on you?
　　Ant. Therefore I took your hands; but was, indeed,
Sway'd from the point by looking down on Cæsar.
Friends am I with you all, and love you all;
Upon this hope, that you shall give me reasons
Why and wherein Cæsar was dangerous.
　　Bru. Or else were this a savage spectacle:
Our reasons are so full of good regard
That were you, Antony, the son of Cæsar,
You should be satisfied.
　　Ant.　　　　　　　That's all I seek:
And am moreover suitor that I may
Produce his body to the market-place;
And in the pulpit, as becomes a friend,
Speak in the order of his funeral.
　　Bru. You shall, Mark Antony.
　　Cas.　　　　　　　Brutus, a word with you.—
You know not what you do: do not consent [*Aside to* BRU.
That Antony speak in his funeral:
Know you how much the people may be mov'd
By that which he will utter?
　　Bru.　　　　　　　By your pardon;—
I will myself into the pulpit first,
And show the reason of our Cæsar's death:
What Antony shall speak, I will protest
He speaks by leave and by permission;
And that we are contented Cæsar shall

Have all true rites and lawful ceremonies.
It shall advantage more than do us wrong.
 Cas. I know not what may fall; I like it not.
 Bru. Mark Antony, here, take you Cæsar's body.
You shall not in your funeral speech blame us,
But speak all good you can devise of Cæsar;
And say you do't by our permission;
Else shall you not have any hand at all
About his funeral: and you shall speak
In the same pulpit whereto I am going,
After my speech is ended.
 Ant.   Be it so;
I do desire no more.
 Bru. Prepare the body then, and follow us.
       [*Exeunt al' but* ANTONY.
 Ant. O, pardon me, thou bleeding piece of earth,
That I am meek and gentle with these butchers!
Thou art the ruins of the noblest man
That ever lived in the tide of times.
Woe to the hand that shed this costly blood!
Over thy wounds now do I prophesy,—
Which like dumb mouths do ope their ruby lips,
To beg the voice and utterance of my tongue,—
A curse shall light upon the limbs of men;
Domestic fury and fierce civil strife
Shall cumber all the parts of Italy;
Blood and destruction shall be so in use,
And dreadful objects so familiar,
That mothers shall but smile when they behold
Their infants quarter'd with the hands of war;
All pity chok'd with custom of fell deeds:
And Cæsar's spirit, ranging for revenge,
With Até by his side come hot from hell,
Shall in these confines with a monarch's voice
Cry *Havoc*, and let slip the dogs of war;
That this foul deed shall smell above the earth
With carrion men, groaning for burial.

     Enter a Servant.

You serve Octavius Cæsar, do you not?
 Serv. I do, Mark Antony.
 Ant. Cæsar did write for him to come to Rome.
 Serv. He did receive his letters, and is coming;
And bid me say to you by word of mouth,—
O Cæsar!—   [*Seeing the body.*
 Ant. Thy heart is big, get thee apart and weep..

Passion, I see, is catching; for mine eyes,
Seeing those beads of sorrow stand in thine,
Began to water. Is thy master coming?
   Serv. He lies to-night within seven leagues of Rome.
   Ant. Post back with speed, and tell him what hath
      chanc'd:
Here is a mourning Rome, a dangerous Rome,
No Rome of safety for Octavius yet;
Hie hence and tell him so. Yet, stay awhile;
Thou shalt not back till I have borne this corse
Into the market-place: there shall I try,
In my oration, how the people take
The cruel issue of these bloody men;
According to the which thou shalt discourse
To young Octavius of the state of things.
Lend me your hand.   [*Exeunt with* CÆSAR'S *body.*

SCENE II.—ROME.   *The Forum.*

   Enter BRUTUS *and* CASSIUS, *and a throng of* Citizens.

   Citizens. We will be satisfied; let us be satisfied.
   Bru. Then follow me, and give me audience, friends.—
Cassius, go you into the other street,
And part the numbers.—
Those that will hear me speak, let 'em stay here;
Those that will follow Cassius, go with him;
And public reasons shall be rendered
Of Cæsar's death.
   1 Cit.   I will hear Brutus speak.
   2 Cit. I will hear Cassius; and compare their reasons,
When severally we hear them rendered.
      [*Exit* CASSIUS, *with some of the* Citizens. BRUTUS
           goes into the Rostrum.
   3 Cit. The noble Brutus is ascended: silence!
   Bru. Be patient till the last.
Romans, countrymen, and lovers! hear me for my cause;
and be silent, that you may hear: believe me for mine
honour; and have respect to mine honour, that you may
believe: censure me in your wisdom; and awake your
senses, that you may the better judge. If there be any in
this assembly, any dear friend of Cæsar's, to him I say
that Brutus' love to Cæsar was no less than his. If, then,
that friend demand why Brutus rose against Cæsar, this is
my answer,—Not that I loved Cæsar less, but that I loved
Rome more. Had you rather Cæsar were living, and die

all slaves, than that Cæsar were dead, to live all free
men? As Cæsar loved me, I weep for him; as he was
fortunate, I rejoice at it; as he was valiant, I honour him:
but, as he was ambitious, I slew him: there is tears for his
love; joy for his fortune; honour for his valour; and death
for his ambition. Who is here so base that would be a
bondman? If any, speak; for him have I offended. Who
is here so rude that would not be a Roman? If any,
speak; for him have I offended. Who is here so vile that
will not love his country? If any, speak; for him have I
offended. I pause for a reply.

Citizens. None, Brutus, none.

Bru. Then none have I offended. I have done no more
to Cæsar than you shall do to Brutus. The question of his
death is enrolled in the Capitol; his glory not extenuated,
wherein he was worthy; nor his offences enforced, for
which he suffered death. Here comes his body, mourned
by Mark Antony:

Enter ANTONY *and others with* CÆSAR'S *body.*

who, though he had no hand in his death, shall receive
the benefit of his dying,—a place in the commonwealth;
as which of you shall not? With this I depart,—that, as I
slew my best lover for the good of Rome, I have the same
dagger for myself, when it shall please my country to need
my death.

Citizens. Live, Brutus! live, live!

1 *Cit.* Bring him with triumph home unto his house.

2 *Cit.* Give him a statue with his ancestors.

3 *Cit.* Let him be Cæsar.

4 *Cit.*   Cæsar's better parts
Shall be crown'd in Brutus.

1 *Cit.* We'll bring him to his house with shouts and

Bru. My countrymen,—   [clamours.

2 *Cit.*   Peace, silence! Brutus speaks.

1 *Cit.* Peace, ho!

Bru. Good countrymen, let me depart alone,
And for my sake stay here with Antony:
Do grace to Cæsar's corse, and grace his speech
Tending to Cæsar's glories; which Mark Antony,
By our permission, is allow'd to make.
I do entreat you, not a man depart,
Save I alone, till Antony have spoke.   [*Exit.*

1 *Cit.* Stay, ho! and let us hear Mark Antony.

3 *Cit.* Let him go up into the public chair;
We'll hear him.—Noble Antony, go up.

Ant. For Brutus' sake I am beholden to you.   [*Goes up.*
4 *Cit.* What does he say of Brutus?
3 *Cit.*   He says, for Brutus' sake
He finds himself beholden to us all.
4 *Cit.* 'Twere best he speak no harm of Brutus here.
1 *Cit.* This Cæsar was a tyrant.
8 *Cit.*   Nay, that's certain:
We are bless'd that Rome is rid of him.
2 *Cit.* Peace! let us hear what Antony can say.
Ant. You gentle Romans,—
Citizens.   Peace, ho! let us hear him.
Ant. Friends, Romans, countrymen, lend me your ears;
I come to bury Cæsar, not to praise him.
The evil that men do lives after them;
The good is oft interred with their bones;
So let it be with Cæsar.   The noble Brutus
Hath told you Cæsar was ambitious:
If it were so, it was a grievous fault;
And grievously hath Cæsar answer'd it.
Here, under leave of Brutus and the rest,
For Brutus is an honourable man;
So are they all, all honourable men,—
Come I to speak in Cæsar's funeral.
He was my friend, faithful and just to me:
But Brutus says he was ambitious;
And Brutus is an honourable man.
He hath brought many captives home to Rome,
Whose ransoms did the general coffers fill:
Did this in Cæsar seem ambitious?
When that the poor have cried, Cæsar hath wept:
Ambition should be made of sterner stuff:
Yet Brutus says he was ambitious;
And Brutus is an honourable man.
You all did see that on the Lupercal
I thrice presented him a kingly crown,
Which he did thrice refuse: was this ambition?
Yet Brutus says he was ambitious;
And, sure, he is an honourable man.
I speak not to disprove what Brutus spoke,
But here I am to speak what I do know.
You all did love him once,—not without cause:
What cause withholds you, then, to mourn for him?
O judgment, thou art fled to brutish beasts,
And men have lost their reason!—Bear with me;
My heart is in the coffin there with Cæsar,
And I must pause till it come back to me.

1 *Cit.* Methinks there is much reason in his sayings.

2 *Cit.* If thou consider rightly of the matter,
Cæsar has had great wrong.

3 *Cit.*   Has he, masters?
I fear there will a worse come in his place.

4 *Cit.* Mark'd ye his words? He would not take the
Therefore 'tis certain he was not ambitious.   [crown;

1 *Cit.* If it be found so, some will dear abide it.

2 *Cit.* Poor soul! his eyes are red as fire with weeping.

3 *Cit.* There's not a nobler man in Rome than Antony.

4 *Cit.* Now mark him, he begins again to speak.

Ant. But yesterday the word of Cæsar might
Have stood against the world: now lies he there,
And none so poor to do him reverence.
O masters, if I were dispos'd to stir
Your hearts and minds to mutiny and rage,
I should do Brutus wrong, and Cassius wrong,
Who, you all know, are honourable men:
I will not do them wrong; I rather choose
To wrong the dead, to wrong myself and you,
Than I will wrong such honourable men.
But here's a parchment with the seal of Cæsar,—
I found it in his closet,—'tis his will:
Let but the commons hear this testament,—
Which, pardon me, I do not mean to read,—
And they would go and kiss dead Cæsar's wounds,
And dip their napkins in his sacred blood;
Yea, beg a hair of him for memory,
And, dying, mention it within their wills,
Bequeathing it as a rich legacy
Unto their issue.

4 *Cit.* We'll hear the will: read it, Mark Antony.

Citizens. The will, the will! we will hear Cæsar's will.

Ant. Have patience, gentle friends, I must not read it;
It is not meet you know how Cæsar lov'd you.
You are not wood, you are not stones, but men;
And, being men, hearing the will of Cæsar,
It will inflame you,—it will make you mad:
'Tis good you know not that you are his heirs;
For, if you should, O, what would come of it!

4 *Cit.* Read the will; we'll hear it, Antony;
You shall read us the will,—Cæsar's will.

Ant. Will you be patient? will you stay awhile?
I have o'ershot myself to tell you of it:
I fear I wrong the honourable men
Whose daggers have stabb'd Cæsar; I do fear it.

4 *Cit.* They were traitors: honourable men!

Citizens. The will! the testament!

2 *Cit.* They were villains, murderers: the will! read the will!

Ant. You will compel me, then, to read the will?
Then make a ring about the corse of Cæsar,
And let me show you him that made the will.
Shall I descend? and will you give me leave?

Citizens. Come down.

2 *Cit.* Descend.   [ANTONY *comes down.*

3 *Cit.* You shall have leave.

4 *Cit.* A ring; stand round.

1 *Cit.* Stand from the hearse, stand from the body.

2 *Cit.* Room for Antony,—most noble Antony!

Ant. Nay, press not so upon me; stand far off.

Citizens. Stand back; room; bear back!

Ant. If you have tears, prepare to shed them now.
You all do know this mantle: I remember
The first time ever Cæsar put it on;
'Twas on a summer's evening, in his tent,
That day he overcame the Nervii:—
Look! in this place ran Cassius' dagger through:
See what a rent the envious Casca made:
Through this the well-beloved Brutus stabb'd;
And, as he pluck'd his cursed steel away,
Mark how the blood of Cæsar follow'd it,
As rushing out of doors, to be resolv'd
If Brutus so unkindly knock'd or no;
For Brutus, as you know, was Cæsar's angel:
Judge, O you gods, how dearly Cæsar loved him!
This was the most unkindest cut of all;
For when the noble Cæsar saw him stab,
Ingratitude, more strong than traitors' arms,
Quite vanquish'd him: then burst his mighty heart;
And, in his mantle muffling up his face,
Even at the base of Pompey's statua,
Which all the while ran blood, great Cæsar fell.
O, what a fall was there, my countrymen!
Then I, and you, and all of us fell down,
Whilst bloody treason flourish'd over us.
O, now you weep; and I perceive you feel
The dint of pity: these are gracious drops.
Kind souls, what, weep you when you but behold
Our Cæsar's vesture wounded? Look you here,
Here is himself, marr'd, as you see, with traitors.

1 *Cit.* O piteous spectacle!

2 Cit. O noble Cæsar!

3 Cit. O woeful day!

4 Cit. O traitors, villains!

1 Cit. O most bloody sight!

2 Cit. We will be revenged: revenge,—about,—seek,—burn,—fire,—kill,—slay,—let not a traitor live.

Ant. Stay, countrymen.

1 Cit. Peace there! hear the noble Antony.

2 Cit. We'll hear him, we'll follow him, we'll die with
　　him.

Ant. Good friends, sweet friends, let me not stir you up
To such a sudden flood of mutiny.
They that have done this deed are honourable;—
What private griefs they have, alas, I know not,
That made them do it;—they are wise and honourable,
And will, no doubt, with reasons answer you.
I come not, friends, to steal away your hearts:
I am no orator, as Brutus is;
But, as you know me all, a plain blunt man,
That love my friend; and that they know full well
That gave me public leave to speak of him:
For I have neither wit, nor words, nor worth,
Action, nor utterance, nor the power of speech,
To stir men's blood: I only speak right on;
I tell you that which you yourselves do know;
Show you sweet Cæsar's wounds, poor poor dumb mouths,
And bid them speak for me: but were I Brutus,
And Brutus Antony, there were an Antony
Would ruffle up your spirits, and put a tongue
In every wound of Cæsar, that should move
The stones of Rome to rise and mutiny.

Citizens. We'll mutiny.

1 Cit. We'll burn the house of Brutus.

3 Cit. Away, then! come, seek the conspirators.

Ant. Yet hear me, countrymen; yet hear me speak.

Citizens. Peace, ho! hear Antony, most noble Antony.

Ant. Why, friends, you go to do you know not what:
Wherein hath Cæsar thus deserv'd your loves?
Alas, you know not,—I must tell you, then.—
You have forgot the will I told you of.

Citizens. Most true;—the will:—let 's stay and hear the
　　will.

Ant. Here is the will, and under Cæsar's seal
To every Roman citizen he gives,
To every several man, seventy-five drachmas.

2 Cit. Most noble Cæsar!—we'll revenge his death.

.

FROM A PHOTOGRAPH BY H. MICHAEL.

ALBERT I JULIUS AS MARK ANTONY

Julius Caesar, Act III, Scene II.

3 *Cit.* O royal Cæsar!
Ant. Hear me with patience.
Citizens. Peace, ho!
Ant. Moreover, he hath left you all his walks,
His private arbours, and new-planted orchards
On this side Tiber; he hath left them you,
And to your heirs for ever,—common pleasures,
To walk abroad and recreate yourselves.
Here was a Cæsar! when comes such another?
1 *Cit.* Never, never.—Come away, away!
We'll burn his body in the holy place,
And with the brands fire the traitors' houses.
Take up the body.
2 *Cit.* Go, fetch fire.
3 *Cit.* Pluck down benches.
4 *Cit.* Pluck down forms, windows, anything.
                    [*Exeunt* Citizens *with the body.*
Ant. Now let it work: mischief, thou art afoot.
Take thou what course thou wilt!

                    Enter a Servant.

                              How now, fellow!
Serv. Sir, Octavius is already come to Rome.
Ant. Where is he?
Serv. He and Lepidus are at Cæsar's house.
Ant. And thither will I straight to visit him:
He comes upon a wish. Fortune is merry,
And in this mood will give us anything.
Serv. I heard him say Brutus and Cassius
Are rid like madmen through the gates of Rome.
Ant. Belike they had some notice of the people,
How I had mov'd them. Bring me to Octavius.   [*Exeunt.*

SCENE III.—ROME. *A Street.*

                    Enter CINNA *the Poet.*

Cin. I dreamt to-night that I did feast with Cæsar,
And things unlucky charge my fantasy:
I have no will to wander forth of doors,
Yet something leads me forth.

                    Enter Citizens.

1 *Cit.* What is your name?
2 *Cit.* Whither are you going?
3 *Cit.* Where do you dwell?

4 Cit. Are you a married man or a bachelor?

2 Cit. Answer every man directly.

1 Cit. Ay, and briefly.

4 Cit. Ay, and wisely.

3 Cit. Ay, and truly, you were best.

Cin. What is my name? Whither am I going? Where do I dwell? Am I a married man or a bachelor? Then, to answer every man directly and briefly, wisely and truly. —Wisely, I say I am a bachelor.

2 Cit. That's as much as to say they are fools that marry: you'll bear me a bang for that, I fear. Proceed; directly.

Cin. Directly, I am going to Cæsar's funeral.

1 Cit. As a friend or an enemy?

Cin. As a friend.

2 Cit. That matter is answered directly.

4 Cit. For your dwelling,—briefly.

Cin. Briefly, I dwell by the Capitol.

3 Cit. Your name, sir, truly.

Cin. Truly, my name is Cinna.

1 Cit. Tear him to pieces; he's a conspirator.

Cin. I am Cinna the poet, I am Cinna the poet.

4 Cit. Tear him for his bad verses, tear him for his bad verses.

Cin. I am not Cinna the conspirator.

4 Cit. It is no matter, his name's Cinna; pluck but his name out of his heart, and turn him going.

3 Cit. Tear him, tear him! Come, brands, ho! fire-brands: to Brutus', to Cassius', burn all: some to Decius' house, and some to Casca's; some to Ligarius': away, go!

               [Exeunt.

ACT IV.

SCENE I.—ROME. *A Room in* ANTONY'S *House.*

ANTONY, OCTAVIUS, *and* LEPIDUS, *seated at a table.*

Ant. These many, then, shall die; their names are
  prick'd.

Oct. Your brother too must die; consent you, Lepidus?

Lep. I do consent.

Oct.   Prick him down, Antony.

Lep. Upon condition Publius shall not live,
Who is your sister's son, Mark Antony.

Ant. He shall not live; look, with a spot I damn him.
But, Lepidus, go you to Cæsar's house;
Fetch the will hither, and we shall determine
How to cut off some charge in legacies.

    Lep. What, shall I find you here?

    Oct. Or here or at the Capitol.   [*Exit* LEPIDUS.

    Ant. This is a slight unmeritable man,
Meet to be sent on errands: is it fit,
The threefold world divided, he should stand
One of the three to share it?

    Oct.   So you thought him;
And took his voice who should be prick'd to die,
In our black sentence and proscription.

    Ant. Octavius, I have seen more days than you:
And though we lay these honours on this man,
To ease ourselves of divers slanderous loads,
He shall but bear them as the ass bears gold,
To groan and sweat under the business,
Either led or driven, as we point the way;
And having brought our treasure where we will,
Then take we down his load, and turn him off,
Like to the empty ass, to shake his ears
And graze in commons.

    Oct.   You may do your will:
But he's a tried and valiant soldier.

    Ant. So is my horse, Octavius; and for that
I do appoint him store of provender:
It is a creature that I teach to fight,
To wind, to stop, to run directly on,—
His corporal motion govern'd by my spirit.
And, in some taste, is Lepidus but so;
He must be taught, and train'd, and bid go forth;—
A barren-spirited fellow; one that feeds
On abject orts and imitations,
Which, out of use and stal'd by other men,
Begin his fashion: do not talk of him
But as a property. And now, Octavius,
Listen great things.—Brutus and Cassius
Are levying powers: we must straight make head:
Therefore let our alliance be combin'd,
Our best friends made, our means stretch'd;
And let us presently go sit in council,
How covert matters may be best disclos'd,
And open perils surest answered.

    Oct. Let us do so: for we are at the stake,
And bay'd about with many enemies;

And some that smile have in their hearts, I fear,
Millions of mischiefs.   [*Exeunt.*

SCENE II.—*Before* Brutus's *Tent, in the Camp
near Sardis.*

Drum.   Enter Brutus, Lucilius, Lucius, *and* Soldiers;
Titinius *and* Pindarus *meeting them.*

Bru. Stand, ho!
Lucil. Give the word, ho! and stand.
Bru. What now, Lucilius! is Cassius near?
Lucil. He is at hand; and Pindarus is come
To do you salutation from his master.
                              [Pin. *gives a letter to* Bru.
Bru. He greets me well.—Your master, Pindarus,
In his own change, or by ill officers,
Hath given me some worthy cause to wish
Things done undone: but if he be at hand
I shall be satisfied.
Pin.   I do not doubt
But that my noble master will appear
Such as he is, full of regard and honour.
Bru. He is not doubted.—A word, Lucilius;
How he receiv'd you let me be resolv'd.
Lucil. With courtesy and with respect enough;
But not with such familiar instances,
Nor with such free and friendly conference
As he hath us'd of old.
Bru.   Thou hast describ'd
A hot friend cooling: ever note, Lucilius,
When love begins to sicken and decay,
It useth an enforced ceremony.
There are no tricks in plain and simple faith:
But hollow men, like horses hot at hand,
Make gallant show and promise of their mettle;
But when they should endure the bloody spur,
They fall their crests, and, like deceitful jades,
Sink in the trial.   Comes his army on?
Lucil. They mean this night in Sardis to be quarter'd;
The greater part, the horse in general,
Are come with Cassius.   [*March within*
Bru.   Hark! he is arriv'd:
March gently on to meet him.

                    Enter Cassius *and* Soldiers.

Cas. Stand, ho!

Bru. Stand, ho! speak the word along.
Within. Stand!
Within. Stand!
Within. Stand!
Cas. Most noble brother, you have done me wrong.
Bru. Judge me, you gods! wrong I mine enemies?
And, if not so, how should I wrong a brother?
Cas. Brutus, this sober form of yours hides wrongs;
And when you do them,—
Bru.　　　　　　　Cassius, be content;
Speak your griefs softly,—I do know you well:—
Before the eyes of both our armies here,
Which should perceive nothing but love from us,
Let us not wrangle: bid them move away;
Then in my tent, Cassius, enlarge your griefs,
And I will give you audience.
Cas.　　　　　　　Pindarus,
Bid our commanders lead their charges off
A little from this ground.
Bru. Lucilius, do you the like; and let no man
Come to our tent till we have done our conference.
Let Lucius and Titinius guard our door.　　[*Exeunt.*

SCENE III.—*Within the Tent of* BRUTUS.

Enter BRUTUS *and* CASSIUS.

Cas. That you have wrong'd me doth appear in this,—
You have condemn'd and noted Lucius Pella
For taking bribes here of the Sardians;
Wherein my letters, praying on his side,
Because I knew the man, were slighted off.
Bru. You wrong'd yourself, to write in such a case.
Cas. In such a time as this it is not meet
That every nice offence should bear his comment.
Bru. Let me tell you, Cassius, you yourself
Are much condemn'd to have an itching palm;
To sell and mart your offices for gold
To undeservers.
Cas.　　　　I an itching palm!
You know that you are Brutus that speak this,
Or, by the gods, this speech were else your last.
Bru. The name of Cassius honours this corruption,
And chastisement doth therefore hide his head.
Cas. Chastisement!
Bru. Remember March, the ides of March remember!

Did not great Julius bleed for justice' sake?
What villain touch'd his body, that did stab,
And not for justice?   What, shall one of us,
That struck the foremost man of all this world
But for supporting robbers, shall we now
Contaminate our fingers with base bribes,
And sell the mighty space of our large honours
For so much trash as may be grasped thus?—
I had rather be a dog, and bay the moon,
Than such a Roman.
    Cas.   Brutus, bay not me,—
I'll not endure it: you forget yourself
To hedge me in; I am a soldier, J,
Older in practice, abler than yourself
To make conditions.
    Bru.   Go to; you are not, Cassius.
    Cas. I am.
    Bru. I say you are not.
    Cas. Urge me no more, I shall forget myself;
Have mind upon your health, tempt me no further.
    Bru. Away, slight man!
    Cas. Is't possible?
    Bru.   Hear me, for I will speak.
Must I give way and room to your rash choler?
Shall I be frighted when a madman stares?
    Cas. O ye gods, ye gods! must I endure all this?
    Bru. All this! ay, more: fret till your proud heart
        break;
Go, show your slaves how choleric you are,
And make your bondmen tremble.   Must I budge?
Must I observe you?   Must I stand and crouch
Under your testy humour?   By the gods,
You shall digest the venom of your spleen
Though it do split you; for from this day forth
I'll use you for my mirth, yea, for my laughter,
When you are waspish.
    Cas.   Is it come to this?
    Bru. You say you are a better soldier:
Let it appear so; make your vaunting true,
And it shall please me well: for mine own part,
I shall be glad to learn of noble men.
    Cas. You wrong me every way; you wrong me, Brutus;
I said an elder soldier, not a better:
Did I say better?
    Bru.   If you did, I care not.
    Cas. When Cæsar liv'd, he durst not thus have mov'd me.

Bru Peace, peace! you durst not so have tempted him.
Cas. I durst not!
Bru. No.
Cas. What, durst not tempt him!
Bru.   For your life you durst not.
Cas. Do not presume too much upon my love ;
I may do that I shall be sorry for.
Bru. You have done that you should be sorry for.
There is no terror, Cassius, in your threats ;
For I am arm'd so strong in honesty
That they pass by me as the idle wind,
Which I respect not. I did send to you
For certain sums of gold, which you denied me ;—
For I can raise no money by vile means :
By heaven, I had rather coin my heart,
And drop my blood for drachmas, than to wring
From the hard hands of peasants their vile trash
By any indirection ;—I did send
To you for gold to pay my legions,
Which you denied me : was that done like Cassius?
Should I have answer'd Caius Cassius so?
When Marcus Brutus grows so covetous,
To lock such rascal counters from his friends,
Be ready, gods, with all your thunderbolts,
Dash him to pieces!
    Cas.   I denied you not.
Bru. You did.
Cas. I did not : he was but a fool that brought
My answer back.--Brutus hath riv'd my heart :
A friend should bear his friend's infirmities,
But Brutus makes mine greater than they are.
    Bru. I do not, till you practise them on me.
Cas. You love me not.
Bru.   I do not like your faults.
Cas. A friendly eye could never see such faults.
Bru. A flatterer's would not, though they do appear
As huge as high Olympus.
    Cas. Come, Antony, and young Octavius, come,
· Revenge yourselves alone on Cassius,
For Cassius is aweary of the world ;
Hated by one he loves ; brav'd by his brother ;
Check'd like a bondman ; all his faults observ'd,
Set in a notebook, learn'd, and conn'd by rote,
To cast into my teeth. O, I could weep
My spirit from mine eyes!—There is my dagger,
And here my naked breast ; within, a heart

Dearer than Plutus' mine, richer than gold:
If that thou be'st a Roman, take it forth;
I, that denied thee gold, will give my heart:
Strike, as thou didst at Cæsar; for I know,
When thou didst hate him worst, thou lov'dst him better
Than ever thou lov'dst Cassius.

Bru.   Sheathe your dagger:
Be angry when you will, it shall have scope;
Do what you will, dishonour shall be humour.
O Cassius, you are yoked with a lamb,
That carries anger as the flint bears fire;
Who, much enforced, shows a hasty spark,
And straight is cold again.

Cas.   Hath Cassius liv'd
To be but mirth and laughter to his Brutus,
When grief and blood ill-temper'd vexeth him?

Bru. When I spoke that I was ill-temper'd too.

Cas. Do you confess so much? Give me your hand.

Bru. And my heart too.

Cas.   O Brutus,—

Bru.   What's the matter?

Cas. Have not you love enough to bear with me,
When that rash humour which my mother gave me
Makes me forgetful?

Bru.   Yes, Cassius; and from henceforth,
When you are over-earnest with your Brutus,
He'll think your mother chides, and leave you so.

[*Noise within.*

Poet. [*within.*] Let me go in to see the generals;
There is some grudge between 'em; 'tis not meet
They be alone.

Lucil. [*within.*] You shall not come to them.

Poet. [*within.*] Nothing but death shall stay me.

Enter Poet, *followed by* LUCILIUS *and* TITINIUS.

Cas. How now! what's the matter?

Poet. For shame, you generals! what do you mean?
Love, and be friends, as two such men should be;
For I have seen more years, I'm sure, than ye.

Cas. Ha, ha! how vilely doth this cynic rhyme!

Bru. Get you hence, sirrah; saucy fellow, hence!

Cas. Bear with him, Brutus; 'tis his fashion.

Bru. I'll know his humour when he knows his time:
What should the wars do with these jigging fools?
Companion, hence!

Cas.   Away, away, be gone!   [*Exit* Poet.

Bru. Lucilius and Titinius, bid the commanders
Prepare to lodge their companies to-night.
Cas. And come yourselves, and bring Messala with you
Immediately to us.   [*Exeunt* LUCIL. *and* TIT.
Bru.   Lucius, a bowl of wine!
Cas. I did not think you could have been so angry.
Bru. O Cassius, I am sick of many griefs.
Cas. Of your philosophy you make no use
If you give place to accidental evils.
Bru. No man bears sorrow better.—Portia is dead.
Cas. Ha! Portia!
Bru. She is dead.
Cas. How scap'd I killing when I cross'd you so?—
O insupportable and touching loss!—
Upon what sickness?
Bru.   Impatient of my absence,
And grief that young Octavius with Mark Antony
Have made themselves so strong; for with her death
That tidings came;—with this she fell distract,
And, her attendants absent, swallow'd fire.
Cas. And died so?
Bru. Even so.
Cas. O ye immortal gods.

Enter LUCIUS *with wine and tapers.*

Bru. Speak no more of her.—Give me a bowl of wine.—
In this I bury all unkindness, Cassius.   [*Drinks.*
Cas. My heart is thirsty for that noble pledge.—
Fill, Lucius, till the wine o'erswell the cup;
I cannot drink too much of Brutus' love.   [*Drinks.*
Bru. Come in, Titinius!

Re-enter TITINIUS, *with* MESSALA.

                Welcome, good Messala!—
Now sit we close about this taper here,
And call in question our necessities.
Cas. Portia, art thou gone?
Bru.   No more, I pray you.—
Messala, I have here received letters,
That young Octavius and Mark Antony
Come down upon us with a mighty power,
Bending their expedition toward Philippi.
Mes. Myself have letters of the self-same tenor.
Bru. With what addition?
Mes. That, by proscription and bills of outlawry,

Octavius, Antony, and Lepidus
Have put to death an hundred senators.

Bru. Therein our letters do not well agree;
Mine speak of seventy senators that died
By their proscriptions, Cicero being one.

Cas. Cicero one!

Mes.   Cicero is dead,
And by that order of proscription.—
Had you your letters from your wife, my lord?

Bru. No, Messala.

Mes. Nor nothing in your letters writ of her?

Bru. Nothing, Messala.

Mes.   That, methinks, is strange.

Bru. Why ask you? hear you aught of her in yours?

Mes. No, my lord.

Bru. Now, as you are a Roman, tell me true.

Mes. Then like a Roman bear the truth I tell:
For certain she is dead, and by strange manner.

Bru. Why, farewell, Portia.—We must die, Messala:
With meditating that she must die once,
I have the patience to endure it now.

Mes. Even so great men great losses should endure.

Cas. I have as much of this in art as you,
But yet my nature could not bear it so.

Bru. Well, to our work alive.   What do you think
Of marching to Philippi presently!

Cas. I do not think it good.

Bru.   Your reason?

Cas.   This it is:
'Tis better that the enemy seek us:
So shall he waste his means, weary his soldiers,
Doing himself offence; whilst we, lying still,
Are full of rest, defence, and nimbleness.

Bru. Good reasons must, of force, give place to better.
The people 'twixt Philippi and this ground
Do stand but in a forc'd affection;
For they have grudg'd us contribution:
The enemy, marching along by them,
By them shall make a fuller number up,
Come on refresh'd, new-aided, and encourag'd;
From which advantage shall we cut him off
If at Philippi we do face him there,
These people at our back.

Cas.   Hear me, good brother.

Bru. Under your pardon.—You must note beside,
That we have tried the utmost of our friends,

Our legions are brimful, our cause is ripe:
The enemy increaseth every day;
We, at the height, are ready to decline.
There is a tide in the affairs of men
Which, taken at the flood, leads on to fortune;
Omitted, all the voyage of their life
Is bound in shallows and in miseries.
On such a full sea are we now afloat;
And we must take the current when it serves,
Or lose our ventures.
  Cas.   Then, with your will, go on;
We'll along ourselves, and meet them at Philippi
  Bru. The deep of night is crept upon our talk,
And nature must obey necessity;
Which we will niggard with a little rest.
There is no more to say?
  Cas.   No more. Good-night:
Early to-morrow will we rise, and hence.
  Bru. Lucius, my gown. [*Exit* LUCIUS.] Farewell, good
Good-night, Titinius;—noble, noble Cassius, [Messala:—
Good-night, and good repose.
  Cas.   O my dear brother!
This was an ill beginning of the night:
Never come such division 'tween our souls!
Let it not, Brutus.
  Bru.   Everything is well.
  Cas. Good-night, my lord.
  Bru.   Good-night, good brother.
  Tit. and Mes. Good-night, Lord Brutus.
  Bru.   Farewell, every one.
      [*Exeunt* CAS., TIT., *and* MES.

Re-enter LUCIUS *with the gown.*

Give me the gown.   Where is thy instrument?
  Luc. Here in the tent.
  Bru.   What, thou speak'st drowsily
Poor knave, I blame thee not; thou art o'er-watch'd.
Call Claudius and some other of my men;
I'll have them sleep on cushions in my tent.
  Luc. Varro and Claudius!

Enter VARRO *and* CLAUDIUS.

  Var. Calls my lord?
  Bru. I pray you, sirs, lie in my tent and sleep;
It may be I shall raise you by and by
On business to my brother Cassius.

Var. So please you, we will stand and watch your pleasure.

Bru. I will not have it so: lie down, good sirs;
It may be I shall otherwise bethink me.—
Look, Lucius, here 's the book I sought for so;
I put it in the pocket of my gown.

                              [VAR. *and* CLAUD. *lie down*

Luc. I was sure your lordship did not give it me.

Bru. Bear with me, good boy, I am much forgetful.
Canst thou hold up thy heavy eyes awhile,
And touch thy instrument a strain or two?

Luc. Ay, my lord, an't please you.

Bru.   It does, my boy:
I trouble thee too much, but thou art willing.

Luc. It is my duty, sir.

Bru. I should not urge thy duty past thy might;
I know young bloods look for a time of rest.

Luc. I have slept, my lord, already.

Bru. It was well done; and thou shalt sleep again;
I will not hold thee long: if I do live
I will be good to thee.   [*Music and a Song.*
This is a sleepy tune.—O murderous slumber,
Lay'st thou thy leaden mace upon my boy
That plays the music?—Gentle knave, good-night;
I will not do thee so much wrong to wake thee:
If thou dost nod, thou break'st thy instrument;
I'll take it from thee; and, good boy, good-night.—
Let me see, let me see;—is not the leaf turn'd down
Where I left reading? Here it is, I think.   [*Sits down.*

                Enter the Ghost *of* CÆSAR.

How ill this taper burns!—Ha! who comes here?
I think it is the weakness of mine eyes
That shapes this monstrous apparition.
It comes upon me.—Art thou anything?
Art thou some god, some angel, or some devil,
That mak'st my blood cold, and my hair to stare?
Speak to me what thou art.

Ghost. Thy evil spirit, Brutus.

Bru.   Why com'st thou?

Ghost. To tell thee thou shalt see me at Philippi.

Bru. Well;
Then I shall see thee again?

Ghost.   Ay, at Philippi.

Bru. Why, I will see thee at Philippi, then.—

                              [*Exit Ghost.*

Now, I have taken heart thou vanishest:
Ill spirit, I would hold more talk with thee.—
Boy Lucius!—Varro! Claudius!—sirs, awake!—
Claudius!

    Luc. The strings, my lord, are false.

    Bru. He thinks he still is at his instrument.—
Lucius, awake!

    Luc. My lord?

    Bru. Didst thou dream, Lucius, that thou so criedst out?

    Luc. My lord, I do not know that I did cry.

    Bru. Yes, that thou didst: didst thou see anything?

    Luc. Nothing, my lord.

    Bru. Sleep again, Lucius.—Sirrah, Claudius!
Fellow, thou, awake!

    Var. My lord?

    Clau. My lord?

    Bru. Why did you cry so out, sirs, in your sleep?

    Var. and Clau. Did we, my lord?

    Bru.   Ay: saw you anything?

    Var. No, my lord, I saw nothing.

    Clau.   Nor I, my lord.

    Bru. Go and commend me to my brother Cassius;
Bid him set on his powers betimes before,
And we will follow.

    Var. and Clau. It shall be done, my lord.   [*Exeunt.*

ACT V.

SCENE I.—*The Plains of Philippi.*

Enter OCTAVIUS, ANTONY, *and their* Army.

    Oct. Now, Antony, our hopes are answered:
You said the enemy would not come down,
But keep the hills and upper regions;
It proves not so: their battles are at hand;
They mean to warn us at Philippi here,
Answering before we do demand of them.

    Ant. Tut, I am in their bosoms, and I know
Wherefore they do it: they could be content
To visit other places; and come down
With fearful bravery, thinking by this face
To fasten in our thoughts that they have courage;
But 'tis not so.

    VOL. V.   P

Enter a Messenger.

Mess. Prepare you, generals:
The enemy comes on in gallant show;
Their bloody sign of battle is hung out,
And something to be done immediately.

Ant. Octavius, lead your battle softly on,
Upon the left hand of the even field.

Oct. Upon the right hand I; keep thou the left.

Ant. Why do you cross me in this exigent?

Oct. I do not cross you; but I will do so. [*March.*

Drum. Enter BRUTUS, CASSIUS, *and their* Army; LUCILIUS,
TITINIUS, MESSALA, *and others.*

Bru. They stand, and would have parley.

Cas. Stand fast, Titinius: we must out and talk.

Oct. Mark Antony, shall we give sign of battle?

Ant. No, Cæsar, we will answer on their charge.
Make forth; the generals would have some words.

Oct. Stir not until the signal.

Bru. Words before blows: is it so, countrymen?

Oct. Not that we love words better, as you do.

Bru. Good words are better than bad strokes, Octavius,

Ant. In your bad strokes, Brutus, you give good words:
Witness the hole you made in Cæsar's heart,
Crying, *Long live! hail, Cæsar!*

Cas. Antony,
The posture of your blows are yet unknown;
But for your words, they rob the Hybla bees,
And leave them honeyless.

Ant. Not stingless too.

Bru. O, yes, and soundless too;
For you have stol'n their buzzing, Antony,
And very wisely threat before you sting.

Ant. Villains, you did not so when your vile daggers
Hack'd one another in the sides of Cæsar:
You show'd your teeth like apes, and fawn'd like hounds,
And bow'd like bondmen, kissing Cæsar's feet;
Whilst damned Casca, like a cur, behind,
Struck Cæsar on the neck. O you flatterers!

Cas. Flatterers!—Now, Brutus, thank yourself:
This tongue had not offended so to-day
If Cassius might have rul'd.

Oct. Come, come, the cause: if arguing make us sweat,
The proof of it will turn to redder drops.
Look,—

I draw a sword against conspirators;
When think you that the sword goes up again?—
Never till Cæsar's three-and-thirty wounds
Be well aveng'd; or till another Cæsar
Have added slaughter to the sword of traitors.

Bru. Cæsar, thou canst not die by traitors' hands,
Unless thou bring'st them with thee.

Oct.   So I hope;
I was not born to die on Brutus' sword.

Bru. O, if thou wert the noblest of thy strain,
Young man, thou couldst not die more honourable.

Cas. A peevish school-boy, worthless of such honour
Join'd with a masker and a reveller!

Ant. Old Cassius still!

Oct.   Come, Antony; away!—
Defiance, traitors, hurl we in your teeth:
If you dare fight to-day, come to the field;
If not, when you have stomachs.

                    [*Exeunt* OCT., ANT., *and their* Army.

Cas. Why, now, blow wind, swell billow, and swim bark!
The storm is up, and all is on the hazard.

Bru. Ho, Lucilius! hark, a word with you.

Lucil.   My lord,

                    [BRU. *and* LUCIL. *converse apart.*

Cas. Messala,—

Mes.   What says my general?

Cas.   Messala,
This is my birth-day; as this very day
Was Cassius born.   Give me thy hand, Messala:
Be thou my witness that, against my will,
As Pompey was, am I compell'd to set
Upon one battle all our liberties.
You know that I held Epicurus strong,
And his opinion: now I change my mind,
And partly credit things that do presage.
Coming from Sardis, on our former ensign
Two mighty eagles fell; and there they perch'd,
Gorging and feeding from our soldiers' hands;
Who to Philippi here consorted us:
This morning are they fled away and gone,
And in their steads do ravens, crows, and kites
Fly o'er our heads, and downward look on us,
As we were sickly prey: their shadows seem
A canopy most fatal, under which
Our army lies, ready to give up the ghost.

Mes. Believe not so.

Cas.   I but believe it partly;
For I am fresh of spirit; and resolv'd
To meet all perils very constantly.
  Bru. Even so, Lucilius.
  Cas.   Now, most noble Brutus,
The gods to-day stand friendly, that we may,
Lovers in peace, lead on our days to age!
But, since the affairs of men rest still incertain,
Let 's reason with the worst that may befall.
If we do lose this battle, then is this
The very last time we shall speak together:
What are you, then, determined to do?
  Bru. Even by the rule of that philosophy
By which I did blame Cato for the death
Which he did give himself.—I know not how,
But I do find it cowardly and vile,
For fear of what might fall, so to prevent
The time of life:—arming myself with patience
To stay the providence of some high powers
That govern us below.
  Cas.   Then, if we lose this battle,
You are contented to be led in triumph
Thorough the streets of Rome?
  Bru. No, Cassius, no: think not, thou noble Roman,
That ever Brutus will go bound to Rome;
He bears too great a mind. But this same day
Must end that work the ides of March began;
And whether we shall meet again I know not.
Therefore our everlasting farewell take:
For ever, and for ever, farewell, Cassius!
If we do meet again, why, we shall smile;
If not, why, then, this parting was well made.
  Cas. For ever, and for ever, farewell, Brutus!
If we do meet again we'll smile indeed;
If not, 'tis true this parting was well made.
  Bru. Why, then, lead on.—O that a man might know
The end of this day's business ere it come?
But it sufficeth that the day will end,
And then the end is known.—Come, ho! away! [*Exeunt*

SCENE II.—The Plains of Philippi.   *The Field
of Battle.*

Alarum.   Enter Brutus *and* Messala.
  Bru. Ride, ride, Messala, ride, and give these bills

Unto the legions on the other side:　　　*[Loud alarum.*
Let them set on at once; for I perceive
But cold demeanour in Octavius' wing,
And sudden push gives them the overthrow.
Ride, ride, Messala: let them all come down.　　　*[Exeunt.*

SCENE III.—THE PLAINS OF PHILIPPI.　*Another part of the Field.*

Alarum.　Enter CASSIUS *and* TITINIUS.

Cas. O look, Titinius, look, the villains fly!
Myself have to mine own turn'd enemy:
This ensign here of mine was turning back;
I slew the coward, and did take it from him.
　Tit. O Cassius, Brutus gave the word too early;
Who, having some advantage on Octavius,
Took it too eagerly: his soldiers fell to spoil:
Whilst we by Antony are all enclos'd.

Enter PINDARUS.

Pin. Fly further off, my lord, fly further off;
Mark Antony is in your tents, my lord!
Fly, therefore, noble Cassius! fly far off.
　Cas. This hill is far enough.—Look, look, Titinius;
Are those my tents where I perceive the fire?
　Tit. They are, my lord.
　Cas.　　　　　　　　Titinius, if thou lov'st me,
Mount thou my horse, and hide thy spurs in him,
Till he have brought thee up to yonder troops
And here again, that I may rest assur'd
Whether yond troops are friend or enemy.
　Tit. I will be here again even with a thought.　　*[Exit.*
　Cas. Go, Pindarus, get higher on that hill;
My sight was ever thick; regard Titinius,
And tell me what thou not'st about the field.—
　　　　　　　　　　　　　　　　[Exit PINDARUS.
This day I breathed first: time is come round,
And where I did begin there shall I end;
My life is run his compass—Sirrah, what news?
　Pin. [*above.*] O my lord!
　Cas. What news?
　Pin. Titinius is enclosed round about
With horsemen, that make to him on the spur:—
Yet he spurs on.—Now they are almost on him;—

Now, Titinius!—now some 'light:—O, he 'lights too:—
He's ta'en;—and, hark! they shout for joy.   [*Shout.*
    Cas.   Come down, behold no more.
O, coward that I am, to live so long,
To see my best friend ta'en before my face!

Enter PINDARUS.

Come hither, sirrah:
In Parthia did I take thee prisoner;
And then I swore thee, saving of thy life,
That whatsoever I did bid thee do
Thou shouldst attempt it.   Come now, keep thine oath!
Now be a freeman; and with this good sword,
That ran through Cæsar's bowels. search this bosom.
Stand not to answer: here, take thou the hilts;
And when my face is cover'd, as 'tis now,
Guide thou the sword.—Cæsar, thou art reveng'd,
Even with the sword that kill'd thee.   [*Dies.*
    Pin. So, I am free; yet would not so have been,
Durst I have done my will.   O Cassius!
Far from this country Pindarus shall run,
Where never Roman shall take note of him.   [*Exit.*

Re-enter TITINIUS, *with* MESSALA.

    Mes. It is but change, Titinius; for Octavius
Is overthrown by noble Brutus' power,
As Cassius' legions are by Antony.
    Tit. These tidings will well comfort Cassius.
    Mes. Where did you leave him?
    Tit.   All disconsolate,
With Pindarus, his bondman, on this hill.
    Mes. Is not that he that lies upon the ground?
    Tit. He lies not like the living.   O my heart!
    Mes. Is not that he?
    Tit.   No, this was he, Messala,
But Cassius is no more.—O setting sun,
As in thy red rays thou dost sink to-night,
So in his red blood Cassius' day is set,—
The sun of Rome is set!   Our day is gone;
Clouds, dews, and dangers come; our deeds are done!
Mistrust of my success hath done this deed.
    Mes. Mistrust of good success hath done this deed.
O hateful error, melancholy's child,
Why dost thou show to the apt thoughts of men
The things that are not?   O error, soon conceiv'd,

Thou never com'st unto a happy birth,
But kill'st the mother that engender'd thee!

Tit. What, Pindarus! where art thou, Pindarus?

Mes. Seek him, Titinius: whilst I go to meet
The noble Brutus, thrusting this report
Into his ears: I may say, thrusting it;
For piercing steel and darts envenomed
Shall be as welcome to the ears of Brutus
As tidings of this sight.

Tit.   Hie you, Messala,
And I will seek for Pindarus the while.   [*Exit* MESSALA.
Why didst thou send me forth, brave Cassius?
Did I not meet thy friends? and did not they
Put on my brows this wreath of victory,
And bid me giv't thee? Didst thou not hear their
     shouts?
Alas, thou hast misconstru'd everything.
But, hold thee, take this garland on thy brow;
Thy Brutus bid me give it thee, and I
Will do his bidding.—Brutus, come apace,
And see how I regarded Caius Cassius.—
By your leave, gods.—This is a Roman's part:
Come, Cassius' sword, and find Titinius' heart.   [*Dies.*

Alarum. Re-enter MESSALA, *with* BRUTUS, YOUNG CATO,
          STRATO, VOLUMNIUS, *and* LUCILIUS.

Bru. Where, where, Messala, doth his body lie?
Mes. Lo, yonder; and Titinius mourning it.
Bru. Titinius' face is upward.
Cato.   He is slain.
Bru. O Julius Cæsar, thou art mighty yet!
Thy spirit walks abroad, and turns our swords
In our own proper entrails.   [*Low alarums.*
Cato.   Brave Titinius!
Look, whe'r he have not crown'd dead Cassius!
Bru. Are yet two Romans living such as these?—
The last of all the Romans, fare thee well!
It is impossible that ever Rome
Should breed thy fellow.—Friends, I owe more tears
To this dead man than you shall see me pay.—
I shall find time, Cassius, I shall find time.—
Come, therefore, and to Thassos send his body:
His funerals shall not be in our camp,
Lest it discomfort us.—Lucilius, come;—
And come, young Cato; let us to the field.—
Labeo and Flavius, set our battles on:—

'Tis three o'clock; and, Romans, yet ere night
We shall try fortune in a second fight.   [*Exeunt.*

SCENE IV.—*Another part of the Field.*

Alarum.   Enter, fighting, Soldiers *of both Armies; then*
BRUTUS, YOUNG CATO, LUCILIUS, *and others.*

Bru. Yet, countrymen, O, yet hold up your heads!
Cato. What bastard doth not? Who will go with me?
I will proclaim my name about the field :—
I am the son of Marcus Cato, ho!
A foe to tyrants, and my country's friend;
I am the son of Marcus Cato, ho!   [*Charges the enemy.*
Bru. And I am Brutus, Marcus Brutus, I;
Brutus, my country's friend; know me for Brutus!
                    [*Exit, charging the enemy.* YOUNG CATO
                         is overpowered, and falls.
Lucil. O young and noble Cato, art thou down?
Why, now thou diest as bravely as Titinius;
And mayst be honour'd, being Cato's son.
1 Sold. Yield, or thou diest.
Lucil.   Only I yield to die?
There is so much that thou wilt kill me straight;
                         [*Offering money.*
Kill Brutus, and be honour'd in his death.
1 Sold. We must not.—A noble prisoner!
2 Sold. Room, ho! Tell Antony Brutus is ta'en.
1 Sold. I'll tell the news.—Here comes the general.—

Enter ANTONY.

Brutus is ta'en, Brutus is ta'en, my lord.
Ant. Where is he?
Lucil. Safe, Antony; Brutus is safe enough:
I dare assure thee that no enemy
Shall ever take alive the noble Brutus:
The gods defend him from so great a shame!
When you do find him, or alive or dead,
He will be found like Brutus, like himself.
Ant. This is not Brutus, friend; but, I assure you,
A prize no less in worth: keep this man safe,
Give him all kindness: I had rather have
Such men my friends than enemies. Go on,
And see whe'r Brutus be alive or dead;
And bring us word unto Octavius' tent
How everything is chanc'd.   [*Exeunt.*

SCENE V.—*Another part of the Field.*

Enter BRUTUS, DARDANIUS, CLITUS, STRATO, *and*
VOLUMNIUS.

Bru. Come, poor remains of friends, rest on this rock.
Cli. Statilius show'd the torch-light; but, my lord,
He came not back: he is or ta'en or slain.
Bru. Sit thee down, Clitus: slaying is the word;
It is a deed in fashion.　Hark thee, Clitus.
　　　　　　　　　　　　　　　　[*Whispering him.*
Cli. What, I, my lord?　No, not for all the world.
Bru. Peace, then, no words.
Cli.　　　　　　　　　I'll rather kill myself.
Bru. Hark thee, Dardanius!　　　　[*Whispers him.*
Dar.　　　　　　　　Shall I do such a deed?
Cli. O Dardanius!
Dar. O Clitus!
Cli. What ill request did Brutus make to thee?
Dar. To kill him, Clitus.　Look, he meditates.
Cli. Now is that noble vessel full of grief,
That it runs over even at his eyes.
Bru. Come hither, good Volumnius; list a word.
Vol. What says my lord?
Bru.　　　　　　　Why, this, Volumnius:
The ghost of Cæsar hath appear'd to me
Two several times by night,—at Sardis once,
And this last night here in Philippi fields:
I know my hour is come.
Vol.　　　　　　　Not so, my lord.
Bru. Nay, I am sure it is, Volumnius.
Thou seest the world, Volumnius, how it goes;
Our enemies have beat us to the pit:　　[*Low alarums.*
It is more worthy to leap in ourselves
Than tarry till they push us.　Good Volumnius,
Thou know'st that we two went to school together:
Even for that our love of old, I pray thee,
Hold thou my sword-hilts whilst I run on it.
Vol. That 's not an office for a friend, my lord.
　　　　　　　　　　　　　　　　[*Alarum still.*
Cli. Fly, fly, my lord; there is no tarrying here.
Bru. Farewell to you;—and you;—and you, Volumnius.—
Strato, thou hast been all this while asleep;
Farewell to thee too, Strato.—Countrymen,
My heart doth joy that yet, in all my life,
I found no man but he was true to me.

I shall have glory by this losing day
More than Octavius and Mark Antony
By this vile conquest shall attain unto.
So, fare you well at once; for Brutus' tongue
Hath almost ended his life's history:
Night hangs upon mine eyes; my bones would rest,
That have but labour'd to attain this hour.

     [*Alarum. Cry within,* " Fly, fly, fly !"

Cli. Fly, my lord, fly.
Bru.   Hence! I will follow.

      [*Exeunt* CLI., DAR., *and* VOL.

I pr'ythee, Strato, stay thou by thy lord:
Thou art a fellow of a good respect;
Thy life hath had some smatch of honour in it:
Hold, then, my sword, and turn away thy face,
While I do run upon it. Wilt thou, Strato?

 Stra. Give me your hand first: fare you well, my
  lord.

 Bru. Farewell, good Strato —Cæsar, now be still:
I kill'd not thee with half so good a will.

     [*He runs on his sword, and dies.*

Alarum. Retreat. Enter OCTAVIUS, ANTONY, *and* Army;
  MESSALA *and* LUCILIUS, *prisoners.*

 Oct. What man is that?

 Mes. My master's man.—Strato, where is thy master?

 Stra. Free from the bondage you are in, Messala:
The conquerors can but make a fire of him;
For Brutus only overcame himself,
And no man else hath honour by his death.

 Lucil. So Brutus should be found.—I thank thee, Brutus
That thou hast prov'd Lucilius' saying true.

 Oct. All that serv'd Brutus I will entertain them.
Fellow, wilt thou bestow thy time with me?

 Stra. Ay, if Messala will prefer me to you.

 Oct. Do so, good Messala.

 Mes. How died my master, Strato?

 Stra. I held the sword, and he did run on it.

 Mes. Octavius, then take him to follow thee,
That did the latest service to my master.

 Ant. This was the noblest Roman of them all:
All the conspirators, save only he,
Did that they did in envy of great Cæsar;
He only, in a general honest thought,
And common good to all, made one of them.
His life was gentle; and the elements

So mix'd in him that Nature might stand up
And say to all the world, *This was a man!*
    Oct. According to his virtue, let us use him
With all respect and rites of burial.
Within my tent his bones to-night shall lie,
Most like a soldier, order'd honourably.—
So, call the field to rest: and let 's away,
To part the glories of this happy day.   [*Exeunt.*

ANTONY AND CLEOPATRA.

PERSONS REPRESENTED.

M. ANTONY,
OCTAVIUS CÆSAR, } *Triumvirs.*
M. ÆMIL. LEPIDUS,

SEXTUS POMPEIUS.

DOMITIUS ENOBARBUS,
VENTIDIUS,
EROS,
SCARUS, } *Friends to* ANTONY.
DERCETAS,
DEMETRIUS,
PHILO,

MECÆNAS,
AGRIPPA,
DOLABELLA, } *Friends to* CÆSAR.
PROCULEIUS,
THYREUS,
GALLUS,

MANAS,
MENECRATES, } *Friends to* POMPEY.
VARRIUS,

TAURUS, *Lieutenant-General to* CÆSAR.
CANIDIUS, *Lieutenant-General to* ANTONY.
SILIUS, *an Officer in* VENTIDIUS'S *Army.*
EUPHRONIUS, *an Ambassador from* ANTONY *to* CÆSAR.
ALEXAS, MARDIAN, SELEUCUS, *and* DIOMEDES, *Attendants*
     on CLEOPATRA.
A Soothsayer.   A Clown.

CLEOPATRA, *Queen of Egypt.*
OCTAVIA, *Sister to* CÆSAR *and Wife to* ANTONY.
CHARMIAN *and* IRAS, *Attendants on* CLEOPATRA.
Officers, Soldiers, Messengers, *and other* Attendants.

SCENE.—*Dispersed; in several parts of the Roman Empire.*

ANTONY AND CLEOPATRA.

---◆---

ACT I.

SCENE I.—ALEXANDRIA. *A Room in* CLEOPATRA *Palace.*

Enter DEMETRIUS *and* PHILO.

Phi. Nay, but this dotage of our general's
O'erflows the measure: those his goodly eyes,
That o'er the files and musters of the war
Have glow'd like plated Mars, now bend, now turn
The office and devotion of their view
Upon a tawny front: his captain's heart,
Which in the scuffles of great fights hath burst
The buckles on his breast, reneges all temper,
And is become the bellows and the fan
To cool a gipsy's lust. [*Flourish within.*] Look where
      they come:
Take but good note, and you shall see in him
The triple pillar of the world transform'd
Into a strumpet's fool: behold and see !

Enter ANTONY *and* CLEOPATRA, *with their* Trains; Eunuchs
fanning her.

Cleo. If it be love indeed, tell me how much.
Ant. There's beggary in the love that can be reckon'd.
Cleo. I'll set a bourn how far to be belov'd.
Ant. Then must thou needs find out new heaven, new
    earth.

Enter an Attendant.

Att. News, my good lord, from Rome.
Ant.   Grates me :—the sum.
Cleo. Nay, hear them, Antony:
Fulvia perchance is angry; or, who knows
If the scarce-bearded Cæsar have not sent
His powerful mandate to you, *Do this or this;*

Take in that kingdom and enfranchise that;
Perform't, or else we damn thee.
 Ant.   How, my love!
 Cleo. Perchance! nay, and most like :—
You must not stay here longer,—your dismission
Is come from Cæsar ; therefore hear it, Antony.—
Where 's Fulvia's process?—Cæsar's I would say?—both?—
Call in the messengers.—As I am Egypt's queen,
Thou blushest, Antony ; and that blood of thine
Is Cæsar's homager : else so thy cheek pays shame
When shrill-tongu'd Fulvia scolds.—The messengers!
 Ant. Let Rome in Tiber melt, and the wide arch
Of the rang'd empire fall!   Here is my space.
Kingdoms are clay : our dungy earth alike
Feeds beast as man : the nobleness of life
Is to do thus ; when such a mutual pair   *[Embracing.*
And such a twain can do't, in which I bind,
On pain of punishment, the world to weet
We stand up peerless.
 Cleo.   Excellent falsehood!
Why did he marry Fulvia, and not love her ?—
I'll seem the fool I am not; Antony
Will be himself.
 Ant.   But stirr'd by Cleopatra.—
Now, for the love of Love and her soft hours,
Let 's not confound the time with conference harsh :
There 's not a minute of our lives should stretch
Without some pleasure now :—what sport to-night?
 Cleo. Hear the ambassadors.
 Ant.   Fie, wrangling queen!
Whom everything becomes,—to chide, to laugh,
To weep ; whose every passion fully strives
To make itself in thee fair and admir'd !
No messenger ; but thine, and all alone,
To-night we'll wander through the streets, and note
The qualities of people.   Come, my queen ;
Last night you did desire it :—speak not to us.
    [Exeunt ANT. *and* CLEO., *with their* Trains.
 Dem. Is Cæsar with Antonius priz'd so slight ?
 Phi. Sir, sometimes, when he is not Antony,
He comes too short of that great property
Which still should go with Antony.
 Dem.   I am full sorry
That he approves the common liar, who
Thus speaks of him at Rome : but I will hope
Of better deeds to-morrow.   Rest you happy ! *[Exeunt.*

SCENE II.—ALEXANDRIA. *Another Room in* CLEOPATRA'S *Palace.*

Enter CHARMIAN, IRAS, ALEXAS, *and a* Soothsayer.

Char. Lord Alexas, sweet Alexas, most anything Alexas, almost most absolute Alexas, where's the soothsayer that you praised so to the queen? O that I knew this husband, which you say must charge his horns with garlands!

Alex. Soothsayer,—

Sooth. Your will?

Char. Is this the man?—Is't you, sir, that know things?

Sooth. In nature's infinite book of secrecy
A little I can read.

Alex.   Show him your hand.

Enter ENOBARBUS.

Eno. Bring in the banquet quickly; wine enough Cleopatra's health to drink.

Char. Good sir, give me good fortune.

Sooth. I make not, but foresee.

Char. Pray, then, foresee me one.

Sooth. You shall be yet far fairer than you are.

Char. He means in flesh.

Iras. No, you shall paint when you are old.

Char. Wrinkles forbid!

Alex. Vex not his prescience; be attentive.

Char. Hush!

Sooth. You shall be more beloving than beloved.

Char. I had rather heat my liver with drinking.

Alex. Nay, hear him.

Char. Good now, some excellent fortune! Let me be married to three kings in a forenoon, and widow them all: let me have a child at fifty, to whom Herod of Jewry may do homage : find me to marry me with Octavius Cæsar, and companion me with my mistress.

Sooth. You shall outlive the lady whom you serve.

Char. O excellent! I love long life better than figs.

Sooth. You have seen and prov'd a fairer former fortune Than that which is to approach.

Char. Then belike my children shall have no names:— pr'ythee, how many boys and wenches must I have?

Sooth. If every of your wishes had a womb, And fertile every wish, a million.

Char. Out, fool ! I forgive thee for a witch.

Alex. You think none but your sheets are privy to your wishes.

Char. Nay, come, tell Iras hers.

Alex. We'll know all our fortunes.

Eno. Mine, and most of our fortunes, to-night, shall be— drunk to bed.

Iras. There's a palm presages chastity, if nothing else.

Char. Even as the o'erflowing Nilus presageth famine.

Iras. Go, you wild bedfellow, you cannot soothsay.

Char. Nay, if an oily palm be not a fruitful prognostication, I cannot scratch mine ear.—Pr'ythee, tell her but a worky-day fortune.

Sooth. Your fortunes are alike.

Iras. But how, but how? give me particulars.

Sooth. I have said.

Iras. Am I not an inch of fortune better than she?

Char. Well, if you were but an inch of fortune better than I, where would you choose it?

Iras. Not in my husband's nose.

Char. Our worser thoughts heavens mend!—Alexas,— come, his fortune, his fortune!—O, let him marry a woman that cannot go, sweet Isis, I beseech thee! And let her die too, and give him a worse! and let worse follow worse, till the worst of all follow him laughing to his grave, fifty-fold a cuckold! Good Isis, hear me this prayer, though thou deny me a matter of more weight; good Isis, I beseech thee!

Iras. Amen. Dear goddess, hear that prayer of the people! for, as it is a heart-breaking to see a handsome man loose-wived, so it is a deadly sorrow to behold a foul knave uncuckolded: therefore, dear Isis, keep decorum, and fortune him accordingly!

Char. Amen.

Alex. Lo, now, if it lay in their hands to make me a cuckold, they would make themselves whores, but they'd do't!

Eno. Hush! here comes Antony.

Char.   Not he; the queen.

Enter CLEOPATRA.

Cleo. Saw you my lord?

Eno.   No, lady.

Cleo.   Was he not here?

Char. No, madam.

Cleo. He was dispos'd to mirth; but on the sudden A Roman thought hath struck him.—Enobarbus.—

Eno. Madam?

Cleo. Seek him, and bring him hither.—Where's Alexas?

Alex. Here, at your service.—My lord approaches.

Cleo. We will not look upon him: go with us.

[*Exeunt* CLEO., ENO., CHAR., IRAS, ALEX.,
and Soothsayer.

Enter ANTONY, *with a* Messenger *and* Attendants.

Mess. Fulvia thy wife first came into the field.

Ant. Against my brother Lucius?

Mess. Ay:
But soon that war had end, and the time's state
Made friends of them, jointing their force 'gainst Cæsar;
Whose better issue in the war, from Italy,
Upon the first encounter, drave them.

Ant. Well, what worst?

Mess. The nature of bad news infects the teller.

Ant. When it concerns the fool or coward.—On:—
Things that are past are done with me.—'Tis thus;
Who tells me true, though in his tale lie death,
I hear him as he flatter'd.

Mess.   Labienus,—
This is stiff news,—hath, with his Parthian force,
Extended Asia from Euphrates;
His conquering banner shook from Syria
To Lydia and to Ionia;
Whilst,—

Ant.   Antony, thou wouldst say,—

Mess.   O, my lord!

Ant. Speak to me home, mince not the general tongue:
Name Cleopatra as she is call'd in Rome;
Rail thou in Fulvia's phrase; and taunt my faults
With such full license as both truth and malice
Have power to utter. O, then we bring forth weeds
When our quick minds lie still: and our ills told us
Is as our earing. Fare thee well awhile.

Mess. At your noble pleasure.   [*Exit.*

Ant. From Sicyon, ho, the news! Speak there!

1 Att. The man from Sicyon,—is there such an one?

2 Att. He stays upon your will.

Ant.   Let him appear.—
These strong Egyptian fetters I must break,
Or lose myself in dotage.—

Enter a second Messenger.
What are you?

2 Mess. Fulvia thy wife is dead.

Ant.   Where died she?

2 Mess. In Sicyon:
Her length of sickness, with what else more serious
Importeth thee to know, this bears.   [*Gives a letter.*

Ant.   Forbear me.
                                   [*Exit second* Messenger.

There's a great spirit gone! Thus did I desire it:
What our contempts do often hurl from us,
We wish it ours again; the present pleasure,
By revolution lowering, does become
The opposite of itself: she's good, being gone;
The hand could pluck her back that shov'd her on.
I must from this enchanting queen break off:
Ten thousand harms, more than the ills I know,
My idleness doth hatch.—Ho, Enobarbus!

Re-enter ENOBARBUS.

Eno. What's your pleasure, sir?

Ant. I must with haste from hence.

Eno. Why, then, we kill all our women: we see how
mortal an unkindness is to them; if they suffer our
departure, death's the word.

Ant. I must be gone.

Eno. Under a compelling occasion, let women die: it
were pity to cast them away for nothing; though, between
them and a great cause, they should be esteemed nothing.
Cleopatra, catching but the least noise of this, dies instantly;
I have seen her die twenty times upon far poorer moment:
I do think there is mettle in death, which commits some
loving act upon her, she hath such a celerity in dying.

Ant. She is cunning past man's thought.

Eno. Alack, sir, no; her passions are made of nothing
but the finest part of pure love: we cannot call her winds
and waters, sighs and tears; they are greater storms and
tempests than almanacs can report: this cannot be cunning
in her; if it be, she makes a shower of rain as well as Jove.

Ant. Would I had never seen her!

Eno. O, sir, you had then left unseen a wonderful piece
of work; which not to have been blessed withal would
have discredited your travel.

Ant. Fulvia is dead.

Eno. Sir?

Ant. Fulvia is dead.

Eno. Fulvia!

Ant. Dead.

Eno. Why, sir, give the gods a thankful sacrifice.   When
it pleaseth their deities to take the wife of a man from him,
it shows to man the tailors of the earth; comforting therein
that when old robes are worn out there are members to
make new.   If there were no more women but Fulvia,
then had you indeed a cut, and the case to be lamented:
this grief is crowned with consolation; your old smock
brings forth a new petticoat:—and, indeed, the tears live
in an onion that should water this sorrow.

Ant. The business she hath broached in the state
Cannot endure my absence.

Eno. And the business you have broached here cannot be
without you; especially that of Cleopatra's, which wholly
depends on your abode.

Ant. No more light answers.   Let our officers
Have notice what we purpose.   I shall break
The cause of our expedience to the queen,
And get her leave to part.   For not alone
The death of Fulvia, with more urgent touches,
Do strongly speak to us; but the letters too
Of many our contriving friends in Rome
Petition us at home: Sextus Pompeius
Hath given the dare to Cæsar, and commands
The empire of the sea; our slippery people,—
Whose love is never link'd to the deserver
Till his deserts are past,—begin to throw
Pompey the Great, and all his dignities,
Upon his son; who, high in name and power,
Higher than both in blood and life, stands up
For the main soldier: whose quality, going on,
The sides o' the world may danger: much is breeding,
Which, like the courser's hair, hath yet but life,
And not a serpent's poison.   Say, our pleasure,
To such whose place is under us, requires
Our quick remove from hence.

Eno. I shall do't.   [*Exeunt*

SCENE III.—ALEXANDRIA.   *A Room in* CLEOPATRA'S
Palace.

Enter CLEOPATRA, CHARMIAN, IRAS, *and* ALEXAS.

Cleo. Where is he?

Char.   I did not see him since.

Cleo. See where he is, who's with him, what he does:—
I did not send you:—if you find him sad,

Say I am dancing; if in mirth, report
That I am sudden sick : quick, and return. [*Exit* ALEXAS.
 Char. Madam, methinks, if you did love him dearly,
You do not hold the method to enforce
The like from him.
  Cleo.   What should I do, I do not.
 Char. In each thing give him way; cross him in nothing.
 Cleo. Thou teachest like a fool,—the way to lose him.
 Char. Tempt him not so too far; I wish, forbear:
In time we hate that which we often fear.
But here comes Antony.
  Cleo.   I am sick and sullen.

Enter ANTONY.

 Ant. I am sorry to give breathing to my purpose,—
 Cleo. Help me away, dear Charmian; I shall fall:
It cannot be thus long, the sides of nature
Will not sustain it.
  Ant.   Now, my dearest queen,—
 Cleo. Pray you, stand further from me.
  Ant.   What's the matter?
 Cleo. I know, by that same eye, there's some good news.
What says the married woman?—You may go:
Would she had never given you leave to come!
Let her not say 'tis I that keep you here,—
I have no power upon you; hers you are.
  Ant. The gods best know,—
  Cleo.   O, never was there queen
So mightily betray'd! Yet at the first
I saw the treasons planted.
  Ant.   Cleopatra,—
 Cleo. Why should I think you can be mine and true,
Though you in swearing shake the throned gods,
Who have been false to Fulvia? Riotous madness,
To be entangled with those mouth-made vows,
Which break themselves in swearing!
  Ant.   Most sweet queen,—
 Cleo. Nay, pray you, seek no colour for your going,
But bid farewell, and go: when you su'd staying,
Then was the time for words: no going then;—
Eternity was in our lips and eyes,
Bliss in our brows' bent; none our parts so poor
But was a race of heaven: they are so still,
Or thou, the greatest soldier of the world,
Art turn'd the greatest liar.
  Ant.   How now, lady!

Cleo. I would I had thy inches; thou shouldst know
There were a heart in Egypt.

Ant. Fear me, queen:
The strong necessity of time commands
Our services awhile; but my full heart
Remains in use with you. Our Italy
Shines o'er with civil swords: Sextus Pompeius
Makes his approaches to the port of Rome:
Equality of two domestic powers
Breeds scrupulous faction: the hated, grown to strength,
Are newly grown to love: the condemn'd Pompey,
Rich in his father's honour, creeps apace
Into the hearts of such as have not thriv'd
Upon the present state, whose numbers threaten;
And quietness, grown sick of rest, would purge
By any desperate change. My more particular,
And that which most with you should safe my going,
Is Fulvia's death.

Cleo. Though age from folly could not give me freedom,
It does from childishness:—can Fulvia die?

Ant. She's dead, my queen:
Look here, and, at thy sovereign leisure, read
The garboils she awak'd; at the last, best.
See when and where she died.

Cleo. O most false love!
Where be the sacred vials thou shouldst fill
With sorrowful water? Now I see, I see,
In Fulvia's death how mine receiv'd shall be.

Ant. Quarrel no more, but be prepar'd to know
The purposes I bear; which are, or cease,
As you shall give the advice. By the fire
That quickens Nilus' slime, I go from hence
Thy soldier, servant; making peace or war
As thou affect'st.

Cleo. Cut my lace, Charmian, come;—
But let it be:—I am quickly ill and well,
So Antony loves.

Ant. My precious queen, forbear;
And give true evidence to his love, which stands
An honourable trial.

Cleo. So Fulvia told me.
I pr'ythee, turn aside and weep for her;
Then bid adieu to me, and say the tears
Belong to Egypt: good now, play one scene
Of excellent dissembling; and let it look
Like perfect honour.

Ant.   You'll heat my blood: no more.
Cleo. You can do better yet; but this is meetly.
Ant. Now, by my sword,—
Cleo.   And target.—Still he mends;
But this is not the best:—look, pr'ythee, Charmian,
How this Herculean Roman does become
The carriage of his chafe.
Ant.   I'll leave you, lady.
Cleo. Courteous lord, one word.
Sir, you and I must part,—but that's not it:
Sir, you and I have lov'd,—but there's not it;
That you know well: something it is I would,—
O, my oblivion is a very Antony,
And I am all forgotten.
Ant.   But that your royalty
Holds idleness your subject, I should take you
For idleness itself.
Cleo.   'Tis sweating labour
To bear such idleness so near the heart
As Cleopatra this.   But, sir, forgive me;
Since my becomings kill me, when they do not
Eye well to you: your honour calls you hence;
Therefore be deaf to my unpitied folly,
And all the gods go with you! upon your sword
Sit laurel victory! and smooth success
Be strew'd before your feet!
Ant.   .   Let us go.   Come;
Our separation so abides, and flies,
That thou, residing here, go'st yet with me,
And I, hence fleeting, here remain with thee.
Away !   [*Exeunt*

SCENE IV.—ROME.   *An Apartment in* CÆSAR'S *House.*

Enter OCTAVIUS CÆSAR, LEPIDUS, *and* Attendants.

Cæs. You may see, Lepidus, and henceforth know,
It is not Cæsar's natural vice to hate
Our great competitor.   From Alexandria
This is the news:—he fishes, drinks, and wastes
The lamps of night in revel: is not more manlike
Than Cleopatra; nor the queen of Ptolemy
More womanly than he: hardly gave audience, or
Vouchsaf'd to think he had partners: you shall find there
A man who is the abstract of all faults
That all men follow.

Lep.   I must not think there are
Evils enow to darken all his goodness:
His faults in him seem as the spots of heaven,
More fiery by night's blackness; hereditary
Rather than purchas'd; what he cannot change
Than what he chooses.

Cœs. You are too indulgent.   Let us grant it is not
Amiss to tumble on the bed of Ptolemy;
To give a kingdom for a mirth; to sit
And keep the turn of tippling with a slave; .
To reel the streets at noon, and stand the buffet
With knaves that smell of sweat: say this becomes him,—
As his composure must be rare indeed
Whom these things cannot blemish,—yet must Antony
No way excuse his soils when we do bear
So great weight in his lightness.   If he fill'd
His vacancy with his voluptuousness,
Full surfeits and the dryness of his bones
Call on him for't: but to confound such time,
That drums him from his sport, and speaks as loud
As his own state and ours,—'tis to be chid
As we rate boys, who, being mature in knowledge,
Pawn their experience to their present pleasure,
And so rebel to judgment.

Enter a Messenger.

Lep.   Here's more news.
Mes. Thy biddings have been done; and every hour,
Most noble Cæsar, shalt thou have report
How 'tis abroad.   Pompey is strong at sea;
And it appears he is belov'd of those
That only have fear'd Cæsar: to the ports
The discontents repair, and men's reports
Give him much wrong'd.
Cæs.   I should have known no less:
It hath been taught us from the primal state
That he which is was wish'd until he were;
And the ebb'd man, ne'er lov'd till ne'er worth love,
Comes dear'd by being lack'd.   This common body,
Like to a vagabond flag upon the stream,
Goes to and back, lackeying the varying tide,
To rot itself with motion.
Mess.   Cæsar, I bring thee word,
Menecrates and Menas, famous pirates,
Make the sea serve them, which they ear and wound
With keels of every kind: many hot inroads

They make in Italy; the borders maritime
Lack blood to think on't, and flush youth revolt:
No vessel can peep forth but 'tis as soon
Taken as seen; for Pompey's name strikes more
Than could his war resisted.

Cæs.   Antony,
Leave thy lascivious wassails.   When thou once
Wast beaten from Modena, where thou slew'st
Hirtius and Pansa, consuls, at thy heel
Did famine follow; whom thou fought'st against,
Though daintily brought up, with patience more
Than savages could suffer: thou didst drink
The stale of horses, and the gilded puddle
Which beasts would cough at: thy palate then did deign
The roughest berry on the rudest hedge;
Yea, like the stag, when snow the pasture sheets,
The barks of trees thou browsed'st; on the Alps
It is reported thou didst eat strange flesh,
Which some did die to look on: and all this,—
It wounds thine honour that I speak it now,—
Was borne so like a soldier that thy cheek
So much as lank'd not.

Lep.   'Tis pity of him.

Cæs. Let his shames quickly
Drive him to Rome: 'tis time we twain
Did show ourselves i' the field; and to that end
Assemble we immediate council: Pompey
Thrives in our idleness.

Lep.   To-morrow, Cæsar,
I shall be furnish'd to inform you rightly
Both what by sea and land I can be able
To front this present time.

Cæs.   Till which encounter
It is my business too.   Farewell.

Lep. Farewell, my lord: what you shall know meantime
Of stirs abroad, I shall beseech you, sir,
To let me be partaker.

Cæs.   Doubt not, sir;
I knew it for my bond.   [*Exeunt.*

SCENE V.—ALEXANDRIA.   *A Room in the Palace.*

Enter CLEOPATRA, CHARMIAN, IRAS, *and* MARDIAN.

Cleo. Charmian,—

Char. Madam?

Cleo. Ha, ha!—
Give me to drink mandragora.
   Char.   Why, madam?
   Cleo. That I might sleep out this great gap of time
My Antony is away.
   Char.   You think of him too much.
   Cleo. O, 'tis treason!
   Char.   Madam, I trust, not so.
   Cleo. Thou, eunuch Mardian!
   Mar.   What's your highness' pleasure?
   Cleo. Not now to hear thee sing; I take no pleasure
In aught an eunuch has: 'tis well for thee
That, being unseminar'd, thy freer thoughts
May not fly forth of Egypt. Hast thou affections?
   Mar. Yes, gracious madam.
   Cleo. Indeed!
   Mar. Not in deed, madam; for I can do nothing
But what indeed is honest to be done:
Yet have I fierce affections, and think
What Venus did with Mars.
   Cleo.   O Charmian,
Where think'st thou he is now? Stands he or sits
      he?
Or does he walk? or is he on his horse?
O happy horse, to bear the weight of Antony!
Do bravely, horse! for wott'st thou whom thou mov'st?
The demi-Atlas of this earth, the arm
And burgonet of men.—He's speaking now,
Or murmuring, *Where's my serpent of old Nile?*
For so he calls me.—Now I feed myself
With most delicious poison:—think on me,
That am with Phœbus' amorous pinches black,
And wrinkled deep in time? Broad-fronted Cæsar,
When thou wast here above the ground I was
A morsel for a monarch: and great Pompey
Would stand and make his eyes grow in my brow;
There would he anchor his aspect, and die
With looking on his life.

Enter ALEXAS.

   Alex.   Sovereign of Egypt, hail!
   Cleo. How much unlike art thou Mark Antony!
Yet, coming from him, that great medicine hath
With his tinct gilded thee.—
How goes it with my brave Mark Antony?
   Alex. Last thing he did, dear queen,

He kiss'd.—the last of many doubled kisses,—
This orient pearl:—his speech sticks in my heart.

Cleo. Mine ear must pluck it thence.

Alex.   *Good friend,* quoth he,
Say, the firm Roman to great Egypt sends
This treasure of an oyster; at whose foot,
To mend the petty present, I will piece
Her opulent throne with kingdoms; all the east,
Say thou, shall call her mistress.   So he nodded,
And soberly did mount an arm-girt steed,
Who neigh'd so high that what I would have spoke
Was beastly dumb'd by him.

Cleo.   What, was he sad or merry?

Alex. Like to the time o' the year between the extremes
Of hot and cold, he was nor sad nor merry.

Cleo. O well-divided disposition!—Note him,
Note him, good Charmian, 'tis the man; but note him:
He was not sad,—for he would shine on those
That make their looks by his; he was not merry,—
Which seem'd to tell them his remembrance lay
In Egypt with his joy; but between both:
O heavenly mingle!—Be'st thou sad or merry,
The violence of either thee becomes,
So does it no man else.—Mett'st thou my posts?

Alex. Ay, madam, twenty several messengers:
Why do you send so thick?

Cleo.   Who 's born that day
When I forget to send to Antony
Shall die a beggar.—Ink and paper, Charmian.—
Welcome, my good Alexas.—Did I, Charmian,
Ever love Cæsar so?

Char.   O that brave Cæsar!

Cleo. Be chok'd with such another emphasis!
Say, the brave Antony.

Char.   The valiant Cæsar!

Cleo. By Isis, I will give thee bloody teeth
If thou with Cæsar paragon again
My man of men.

Char.   By your most gracious pardon,
I sing but after you.

Cleo.   My salad days,
When I was green in judgment:—cold in blood,
To say as I said then!—but, come, away;
Get me ink and paper: he shall have every day
A several greeting, or I'll unpeople Egypt.   [*Exeunt.*

ACT II.

SCENE I.—MESSINA.   *A Room in* POMPEY'S *House.*

Enter POMPEY, MENECRATES, *and* MENAS.

Pom. If the great gods be just, they shall assist
The deeds of justest men.
Mene.   Know, worthy Pompey,
That what they do delay they not deny.
Pom. Whiles we are suitors to their throne, decays
The thing we sue for.
Mene.   We, ignorant of ourselves,
Beg often our own harms, which the wise powers
Deny us for our good; so find we profit
By losing of our prayers.
Pom.   I shall do well:
The people love me, and the sea is mine;
My powers are crescent, and my auguring hope
Says it will come to the full.   Mark Antony
In Egypt sits at dinner, and will make
No wars without doors: Cæsar gets money where
He loses hearts: Lepidus flatters both,
Of both is flatter'd; but he neither loves
Nor either cares for him.
Men.   Cæsar and Lepidus
Are in the field: a mighty strength they carry.
Pom. Where have you this? 'tis false.
Men.   From Silvius, sir.
Pom. He dreams: I know they are in Rome together,
Looking for Antony.   But all the charms of love,
Salt Cleopatra, soften thy wan'd lip!
Let witchcraft join with beauty, lust with both!
Tie up the libertine in a field of feasts,
Keep his brain fuming; Epicurean cooks
Sharpen with cloyless sauce his appetite;
That sleep and feeding may prorogue his honour
Even till a Lethe'd dullness.

Enter VARRIUS.

How now, Varrius!
Var. This is most certain that I shall deliver:—
Mark Antony is every hour in Rome
Expected: since he went from Egypt 'tis
A space for further travel.

Pom.   I could have given less matter
A better ear.—Menas, I did not think
This amorous surfeiter would have donn'd his helm
For such a petty war: his soldiership
Is twice the other twain: but let us rear
The higher our opinion, that our stirring
Can from the lap of Egypt's widow pluck
The ne'er lust-wearied Antony.
    Men.   I cannot hope
Cæsar and Antony shall well greet together:
His wife that's dead did trespasses to Cæsar;
His brother warr'd upon him; although, I think,
Not mov'd by Antony.
    Pom.   I know not, Menas,
How lesser enmities may give way to greater.
Were't not that we stand up against them all,
'Twere pregnant they should square between them-
    selves;
For they have entertained cause enough
To draw their swords: but how the fear of us
May cement their divisions, and bind up
The petty difference, we yet not know.
Be't as our gods will have't! It only stands
Our lives upon to use our strongest hands.
Come, Menas.
                                        [Exeunt.

SCENE II.—ROME.   *A Room in the House of* LEPIDUS.

Enter ENOBARBUS *and* LEPIDUS.

Lep. Good Enobarbus, 'tis a worthy deed,
And shall become you well, to entreat your captain
To soft and gentle speech.
    Eno.   I shall entreat him
To answer like himself: if Cæsar move him,
Let Antony look over Cæsar's head,
And speak as loud as Mars. By Jupiter,
Were I the wearer of Antonius' beard,
I would not shave't to-day.
    Lep.   'Tis not a time
For private stomaching.
    Eno.   Every time
Serves for the matter that is then born in't.
    Lep. But small to greater matters must give way.
    Eno. Not if the small come first.

Lep.   Your speech is passion:
But, pray you, stir no embers up.   Here comes
The noble Antony.

       Enter ANTONY *and* VENTIDIUS.
Eno.   And yonder Cæsar.

       Enter CÆSAR, MECÆNAS, *and* AGRIPPA.
Ant. If we compose well here, to Parthia:
Hark, Ventidius.
Cæs.   I do not know,
Mecænas; ask Agrippa.
Lep.   Noble friends,
That which combin'd us was most great, and let not
A leaner action rend us.   What's amiss,
May it be gently heard: when we debate
Our trivial difference loud, we do commit
Murder in healing wounds: then, noble partners,—
The rather for I earnestly beseech,—
Touch you the sourest points with sweetest terms,
Nor curstness grow to the matter.
Ant.   'Tis spoken well.
Were we before our armies, and to fight,
I should do thus.
Cæs. Welcome to Rome.
Ant.   Thank you.
Cæs.   Sit.
Ant.   Sit, sir.
Cæs.   Nay, then.
Ant. I learn, you take things ill which are not so,
Or being, concern you not.
Cæs.   I must be laugh'd at
If, or for nothing or a little, I
Should say myself offended, and with you
Chiefly i' the world; more laugh'd at that I should
Once name you derogately, when to sound your name
It not concern'd me.
Ant.   My being in Egypt, Cæsar,
What was't to you?
Cæs. No more than my residing here at Rome
Might be to you in Egypt: yet, if you there
Did practise on my state, your being in Egypt
Might be my question.
Ant.   How intend you, practis'd?
Cæs. You may be pleas'd to catch at mine intent
By what did here befall me.   Your wife and brother

Made wars upon me; and their contestation
Was theme for you, you were the word of war.

Ant. You do mistake your business; my brother never
Did urge me in his act: I did inquire it;
And have my learning from some true reports
That drew their swords with you. Did he not rather
Discredit my authority with yours;
And make the wars alike against my stomach,
Having alike your cause? Of this my letters
Before did satisfy you. If you'll patch a quarrel,
As matter whole you have not to make it with,
It must not be with this.

Cæs.   You praise yourself
By laying defects of judgment to me; but
You patch'd up your excuses.

Ant.   Not so, not so;
I know you could not lack, I am certain on't,
Very necessity of this thought, that I,
Your partner in the cause 'gainst which he fought,
Could not with graceful eyes attend those wars
Which 'fronted mine own peace. As for my wife,
I would you had her spirit in such another:
The third o' the world is yours; which with a snaffle
You may pace easy, but not such a wife.

Eno. Would we had all such wives, that the men
Might go to wars with the women!

Ant. So much uncurbable, her garboils, Cæsar,
Made out of her impatience,—which not wanted
Shrewdness of policy too,—I grieving grant
Did you too much disquiet: for that you must
But say I could not help it.

Cæs.   I wrote to you
When rioting in Alexandria; you
Did pocket up my letters, and with taunts
Did gibe my missive out of audience.

Ant.   Sir,
He fell upon me ere admitted: then
Three kings I had newly feasted, and did want
Of what I was i' the morning: but next day
I told him of myself; which was as much
As to have ask'd him pardon. Let this fellow
Be nothing of our strife; if we contend,
Out of our question wipe him.

Cæs.   You have broken
The article of your oath; which you shall never
Have tongue to charge me with.

Lep.   Soft, Cæsar!
Ant. No, Lepidus, let him speak:
The honour is sacred which he talks on now,
Supposing that I lack'd it.—But on, Cæsar;
The article of my oath.
    Cæs. To lend me arms and aid when I requir'd them;
The which you both denied.
    Ant.   Neglected, rather;
And then when poison'd hours had bound me up
From mine own knowledge. As nearly as I may,
I'll play the penitent to you: but mine honesty
Shall not make poor my greatness, nor my power
Work without it. Truth is, that Fulvia,
To have me out of Egypt, made wars here;
For which myself, the ignorant motive, do
So far ask pardon as befits mine honour
To stoop in such a case.
    Lep.   'Tis noble spoken.
    Mec. If it might please you to enforce no further
The griefs between ye: to forget them quite
Were to remember that the present need
Speaks to atone you.
    Lep.   Worthily spoken, Mecænas.
    Eno. Or, if you borrow one another's love for the instant,
you may, when you hear no more words of Pompey, return
it again: you shall have time to wrangle in when you have
nothing else to do.
    Ant. Thou art a soldier only: speak no more.
    Eno. That truth should be silent I had almost forgot.
    Ant. You wrong this presence; therefore speak no
        more.
    Eno. Go to, then; your considerate stone.
    Cæs. I do not much dislike the matter, but
The manner of his speech; for't cannot be
We shall remain in friendship, our conditions
So differing in their acts. Yet, if I knew
What hoop should hold us stanch, from edge to edge
O' the world I would pursue it.
    Agr.   Give me leave, Cæsar,—
    Cæs. Speak, Agrippa.
    Agr. Thou hast a sister by the mother's side,
Admir'd Octavia: great Mark Antony
Is now a widower.
    Cæs.   Say not so, Agrippa:
If Cleopatra heard you, your reproof
Were well deserv'd of rashness.
        VOL. V.   R

Ant. I am not married, Cæsar: let me hear
Agrippa further speak.

Agr. To hold you in perpetual amity,
To make you brothers, and to knit your hearts
With an unslipping knot, take Antony
Octavia to his wife; whose beauty claims
No worse a husband than the best of men;
Whose virtue and whose general graces speak
That which none else can utter. By this marriage,
All little jealousies, which now seem great,
And all great fears, which now import their dangers,
Would then be nothing: truths would then be tales,
Where now half tales be truths: her love to both
Would, each to other and all loves to both,
Draw after her. Pardon what I have spoke;
For 'tis a studied, not a present thought,
By duty ruminated.

Ant. Will Cæsar speak?

Cæs. Not till he hears how Antony is touch'd
With what is spoke already.

Ant. What power is in Agrippa,
If I would say, *Agrippa, be it so,*
To make this good?

Cæs. The power of Cæsar, and
His power unto Octavia.

Ant. May I never
To this good purpose, that so fairly shows,
Dream of impediment!—Let me have thy hand:
Further this act of grace; and from this hour
The heart of brothers govern in our loves
And sway our great designs!

Cæs. There is my hand.
A sister I bequeath you, whom no brother
Did ever love so dearly: let her live
To join our kingdoms and our hearts; and never
Fly off our loves again!

Lep. Happily, amen!

Ant. I did not think to draw my sword 'gainst Pompey;
For he hath laid strange courtesies and great
Of late upon me: I must thank him only,
Lest my remembrance suffer ill report;
At heel of that, defy him.

Lep. Time calls upon 's:
Of us must Pompey presently be sought,
Or else he seeks out us.

Ant. Where lies he?

Antony and Cleopatra. Act II, Scene II.

Cæs. About the Mount Miscnum.

Ant.   What 's his strength
By land?

Cæs. Great and increasing: but by sea
He is an absolute master.

Ant.   So is the fame.
Would we had spoke together!   Haste we for it:
Yet, ere we put ourselves in arms, despatch we
The business we have talk'd of.

Cæs.   With most gladness;
And do invite you to my sister's view,
Whither straight I'll lead you.

Ant.   Let us, Lepidus,
Not lack your company.

Lep.   Noble Antony,
Not sickness should detain me.

                [*Flourish.   Exeunt* CÆS., ANT., *and* LEP.

Mec. Welcome from Egypt, sir.

Eno. Half the heart of Cæsar, worthy Mecænas!—my
honourable friend, Agrippa!—

Agr. Good Enobarbus!

Mec. We have cause to be glad that matters are so well
digested.   You stay'd well by it in Egypt.

Eno. Ay, sir; we did sleep day out of countenance, and
made the night light with drinking.

Mec. Eight wild boars roasted whole at a breakfast, and
but twelve persons there; is this true?

Eno. This was but as a fly by an eagle: we had much
more monstrous matter of feasts, which worthily deserved
noting.

Mec. She's a most triumphant lady, if report be square
to her.

Eno. When she first met Mark Antony she pursed up
his heart, upon the river of Cydnus.

Agr. There she appeared indeed; or my reporter devised
well for her.

Eno. I will tell you.
The barge she sat in, like a burnish'd throne,
Burn'd on the water: the poop was beaten gold;
Purple the sails, and so perfumed that
The winds were love-sick with them; the oars were silver,
Which to the tune of flutes kept stroke, and made
The water which they beat to follow faster,
As amorous of their strokes.   For her own person,
It beggar'd all description: she did lie
In her pavilion,—cloth-of-gold of tissue,—

O'er-picturing that Venus where we see
The fancy out-work nature: on each side her
Stood pretty dimpled boys, like smiling Cupids,
With divers-colour'd fans, whose wind did seem
To glow the delicate cheeks which they did cool,
And what they undid did.

Agr.   O, rare for Antony!

Eno. Her gentlewomen, like the Nereïds,
So many mermaids, tended her i' the eyes,
And made their bends adornings: at the helm
A seeming mermaid steers: the silken tackle
Swell with the touches of those flower-soft hands
That yarely frame the office.   From the barge
A strange invisible perfume hits the sense
Of the adjacent wharfs.   The city cast
Her people out upon her; and Antony,
Enthron'd i' the market-place, did sit alone,
Whistling to the air; which, but for vacancy,
Had gone to gaze on Cleopatra too,
And made a gap in nature.

Agr.   Rare Egyptian!

Eno. Upon her landing, Antony sent to her,
Invited her to supper: she replied
It should be better he became her guest;
Which she entreated: our courteous Antony,
Whom ne'er the word of *No* woman heard speak,
Being barber'd ten times o'er, goes to the feast,
And, for his ordinary, pays his heart
For what his eyes eat only.

Agr.   Royal wench!
She made great Cæsar lay his sword to bed:
He plough'd her, and she cropp'd.

Eno.   I saw her once
Hop forty paces through the public street;
And having lost her breath, she spoke and panted,
That she did make defect perfection,
And, breathless, power breathe forth.

Mec. Now Antony must leave her utterly.

Eno. Never; he will not:
Age cannot wither her, nor custom stale
Her infinite variety: other women cloy
The appetites they feed; but she makes hungry
Where most she satisfies: for vilest things
Become themselves in her; that the holy priests
Bless her when she is riggish.

Mec. If beauty, wisdom, modesty, can settle

The heart of Antony, Octavia is
A blessed lottery to him.
 Agr.   Let us go.—
Good Enobarbus, make yourself my guest
Whilst you abide here.
 Eno.   Humbly, sir, I thank you. [*Exeunt.*

SCENE III.—ROME. *A Room in* CÆSAR'S *House.*

Enter CÆSAR, ANTONY, OCTAVIA *between them, and*
      Attendants.

 Ant. The world and my great office will sometimes
Divide me from your bosom.
 Octa.   All which time
Before the gods my knee shall bow my prayers
To them for you.
 Ant.   Good-night, sir.—My Octavia,
Read not my blemishes in the world's report:
I have not kept my square; but that to come
Shall all be done by the rule. Good-night, dear lady.—
 Octa. Good-night, sir.
 Cæs. Good-night.   [*Exeunt* CÆS. *and* OCTA.

    Enter Soothsayer.

 Ant. Now, sirrah, you do wish yourself in Egypt?
 Sooth. Would I had never come from thence, nor you
Thither!
 Ant. If you can, your reason?
 Sooth.   I see it in
My motion, have it not in my tongue: but yet
Hie you to Egypt again.
 Ant.   Say to me,
Whose fortunes shall rise higher, Cæsar's or mine?
 Sooth. Cæsar's.
Therefore, O Antony, stay not by his side:
Thy demon, that's thy spirit which keeps thee, is
Noble, courageous, high, unmatchable,
Where Cæsar's is not; but near him thy angel
Becomes afear'd, as being o'erpower'd: therefore
Make space enough between you.
 Ant.   Speak this no more.
 Sooth. To none but thee; no more but when to thee
If thou dost play with him at any game,
Thou art sure to lose; and of that natural luck
He beats thee 'gainst the odds: thy lustre thickens

When he shines by: I say again, thy spirit
Is all afraid to govern thee near him;
But, he away, 'tis noble.
   Ant.   Get thee gone:
Say to Ventidius I would speak with him:—   [*Exit* Scoth.
He shall to Parthia.—Be it art or hap,
He hath spoken true: the very dice obey him ;—
And in our sports my better cunning faints
Under his chance: if we draw lots he speeds;
His cocks do win the battle still of mine,
When it is all to naught; and his quails ever
Beat mine, inhoop'd, at odds. I will to Egypt:
And though I make this marriage for my peace,
I' the east my pleasure lies.

Enter VENTIDIUS.

                O, come, Ventidius,
You must to Parthia: your commission's ready;
Follow me and receive it.   [*Exeunt.*

SCENE IV.—ROME.   *A Street.*

Enter LEPIDUS, MECÆNAS, *and* AGRIPPA.

   Lep. Trouble yourselves no further: pray you, hasten
Your generals after.
   Agr.   Sir, Mark Antony
Will e'en but kiss Octavia, and we'll follow.
   Lep. Till I shall see you in your soldier's dress,
Which will become you both, farewell.
   Mec.   We shall,
As I conceive the journey, be at the mount
Before you, Lepidus.
   Lep.   Your way is shorter;
My purposes do draw me much about:
You'll win two days upon me.
   Mec. and Agr.   Sir, good success!
   Lep. Farewell.   [*Exeunt.*

SCENE V.—ALEXANDRIA.   *A Room in the Palace.*

Enter CLEOPATRA, CHARMIAN, IRAS, ALEXAS, *and* Attendants.

   Cleo. Give me some music,—music, moody food
Of us that trade in love.

Attend.   The music, ho!

Enter MARDIAN.

Cleo. Let it alone; let's to billiards:
Come, Charmian.
   Char. My arm is sore; best play with Mardian.
   Cleo. As well a woman with an eunuch play'd
As with a woman.—Come, you'll play with me, sir?
   Mar. As well as I can, madam.
   Cleo. And when good-will is show'd, though't come too
      short,
The actor may plead pardon.   I'll none now:—
Give me mine angle,—we'll to the river: there,
My music playing far off, I will betray
Tawny-finn'd fishes; my bended hook shall pierce
Their slimy jaws; and as I draw them up
I'll think them every one an Antony,
And say, *Ah ha! you're caught.*
   Char.   'Twas merry when
You wager'd on your angling; when your diver
Did hang a salt fish on his hook, which he
With fervency drew up.
   Cleo.   That time,—O times!—
I laugh'd him out of patience; and that night
I laugh'd him into patience: and next morn,
Ere the ninth hour, I drunk him to his bed;
Then put my tires and mantles on him, whilst
I wore his sword Philippan.

Enter a Messenger.

              O! from Italy!—
Ram thou thy fruitful tidings in mine ears,
That long time have been barren.
   Mess.   Madam, madam,—
   Cleo. Antony's dead!—
If thou say so, villain, thou kill'st thy mistress:
But well and free,
If thou so yield him, there is gold, and here
My bluest veins to kiss,—a hand that kings
Have lipp'd, and trembled kissing.
   Mess.   First, madam, he's well.
   Cleo. Why, there's more gold.   But, sirrah, mark, we use
To say the dead are well: bring it to that,
The gold I give thee will I melt and pour
Down thy ill-uttering throat.
   Mess. Good madam, hear me.

Cleo. Well, go to, I will;
But there's no goodness in thy face: if Antony
Be free and healthful,—why so tart a favour
To trumpet such good tidings! If not well,
Thou shouldst come like a fury crown'd with snakes,
Not like a formal man.

    Mess. Will't please you hear me?

    Cleo. I have a mind to strike thee ere thou speak'st:
Yet, if thou say Antony lives, is well,
Or friends with Cæsar, or not captive to him,
I'll set thee in a shower of gold, and hail
Rich pearls upon thee.

    Mess. Madam, he's well.

    Cleo. Well said.

    Mess. And friends with Cæsar.

    Cleo. Thou'rt an honest man.

    Mess. Cæsar and he are greater friends than ever.

    Cleo. Make thee a fortune from me.

    Mess. But yet, madam,—

    Cleo. I do not like *but yet*, it does allay
The good precedence; fie upon *but yet!*
But yet is as a gaoler to bring forth
Some monstrous malefactor. Pr'ythee, friend,
Pour out the pack of matter to mine ear,
The good and bad together: he's friends with Cæsar;
In state of health, thou say'st; and, thou say'st, free.

    Mess. Free, madam! no; I made no such report:
He's bound unto Octavia.

    Cleo. For what good turn?

    Mess. For the best turn i' the bed.

    Cleo. I am pale, Charmian.

    Mess. Madam, he's married to Octavia.

    Cleo. The most infectious pestilence upon thee!
        [Strikes him down.

    Mess. Good madam, patience.

    Cleo. What say you?—Hence,
        [Strikes him again.
Horrible villain! or I'll spurn thine eyes
Like balls before me; I'll unhair thy head:
        [She hales him up and down.
Thou shalt be whipp'd with wire and stew'd in brine,
Smarting in ling'ring pickle.

    Mess. Gracious madam,
I that do bring the news made not the match.

    Cleo. Say 'tis not so, a province I will give thee,
And make thy fortunes proud: the blow thou hadst

Shall make thy peace for moving me to rage;
And I will boot thee with what gift beside
Thy modesty can beg.
 Mess.   He's married, madam.
 Cleo. Rogue, thou hast liv'd too long. [*Draws a dagger.*
 Mess. Nay, then I'll run.—
What mean you, madam? I have made no fault. [*Exit.*
 Char. Good madam, keep yourself within yourself:
The man is innocent.
 Cleo. Some innocents scape not the thunderbolt.—
Melt Egypt into Nile! and kindly creatures—
Turn all to serpents!—Call the slave again :
Though I am mad, I will not bite him :—call.
 Char. He is afear'd to come.
 Cleo.   I will not hurt him.
           [*Exit* CHARMIAN.
These hands do lack nobility, that they strike
A meaner than myself; since I myself
Have given myself the cause.

   Re-enter CHARMIAN *and* Messenger.
       Come hither, sir.
Though it be honest, it is never good
To bring bad news : give to a gracious message
An host of tongues; but let ill tidings tell
Themselves when they be felt.
 Mess.   I have done my duty.
 Cleo. Is he married?
I cannot hate thee worser than I do
If thou again say *Yes.*
 Mess.   He is married, madam.
 Cleo. The gods confound thee! dost thou hold there still!
 Mess. Should I lie, madam?
 Cleo.   O, I would thou didst,
So half my Egypt were submerg'd, and made
A cistern for scal'd snakes! Go, get thee hence:
Hadst thou Narcissus in thy face, to me
Thou wouldst appear most ugly. He is married?
 Mess. I crave your highness' pardon.
 Cleo.   He is married?
 Mess. Take no offence that I would not offend you:
To punish me for what you make me do
Seems much unequal: he is married to Octavia.
 Cleo. O that his fault should make a knave of thee,
That art not what thou'rt sure of!—Get thee hence:
The merchandise which thou hast brought from Rome

Are all too dear for me : lie they upon thy hand,
And be undone by 'em! [*Exit* Messenger.
 Char.   Good your highness, patience.
 Cleo. In praising Antony I have disprais'd Cæsar.
 Char. Many times, madam.
 Cleo.   I am paid for't now.
Lead me from hence ;
I faint :—O Iras, Charmian !—'tis no matter.—
Go to the fellow, good Alexas ; bid him
Report the feature of Octavia, her years,
Her inclination, let him not leave out
The colour of her hair :—bring me word quickly.
           [*Exit* ALEXAS.
Let him for ever go :—let him not—Charmian,
Though he be painted one way like a Gorgon,
T'other way he's a Mars.—Bid you Alexas [*To* MARDIAN.
Bring me word how tall she is. —Pity me, Charmian,
But do not speak to me.—Lead me to my chamber. [*Exeunt.*

SCENE VI.—*Near Misenum.*

Flourish. *Enter* POMPEY *and* MENAS *at one side, with drum
 and trumpet: at the other,* CÆSAR, ANTONY, LEPIDUS,
 ENOBARBUS, MECÆNAS, *with* Soldiers *marching.*

 Pom. Your hostages I have, so have you mine ;
And we shall talk before we fight.
 Cæs.   Most meet
That first we come to words ; and therefore have we
Our written purposes before us sent ;
Which, if thou hast consider'd, let us know
If 'twill tie up thy discontented sword,
And carry back to Sicily much tall youth
That else must perish here.
 Pom.   To you all three,
The senators alone of this great world,
Chief factors for the gods,—I do not know
Wherefore my father should revengers want,
Having a son and friends ; since Julius Cæsar,
Who at Philippi the good Brutus ghosted,
There saw you labouring for him. What was't
That mov'd pale Cassius to conspire ; and what
Made the all-honour'd, honest Roman, Brutus,
With the arm'd rest, courtiers of beauteous freedom,
To drench the Capitol, but that they would
Have one man but a man? And that is it

Hath made me rig my navy; at whose burden
The anger'd ocean foams; with which I meant
To scourge the ingratitude that despiteful Rome
Cast on my noble father.
  Cæs.   Take your time.
  Ant. Thou canst not fear us, Pompey, with thy sails;
We'll speak with thee at sea: at land thou know'st
How much we do o'er-count thee.
  Pom.   At land, indeed,
Thou dost o'er-count me of my father's house:
But, since the cuckoo builds not for himself,
Remain in't as thou mayst.
  Lep.   Be pleas'd to tell us,—
For this is from the present,—how you take
The offers we have sent you.
  Cæs.   There's the point.
  Ant. Which do not be entreated to, but weigh
What it is worth embrac'd.
  Cæs.   And what may follow,
To try a larger fortune.
  Pom.   You have made me offer
Of Sicily, Sardinia; and I must
Rid all the sea of pirates; then to send
Measures of wheat to Rome; this 'greed upon,
To part with unhack'd edges, and bear back
Our targes undinted.
  Cæs., Ant., and Lep. That's our offer.
  Pom.   Know, then,
I came before you here a man prepar'd
To take this offer: but Mark Antony
Put me to some impatience:—though I lose
The praise of it by telling, you must know,
When Cæsar and your brother were at blows,
Your mother came to Sicily, and did find
Her welcome friendly.
  Ant.   I have heard it, Pompey·
And am well studied for a liberal thanks
Which I do owe you.
  Pom.   Let me have your hand:
I did not think, sir, to have met you here.
  Ant. The beds i' the east are soft; and, thanks to you,
That call'd me, timelier than my purpose, hither;
For I have gain'd by it.
  Cæs.   Since I saw you last
There is a change upon you.
  Pom.   Well, I know not

What counts harsh fortune casts upon my face;
But in my bosom shall she never come
To make my heart her vassal.

Lep.   Well met here.

Pom. I hope so, Lepidus.—Thus we are agreed:
I crave our composition may be written,
And seal'd between us.

Cæs.   That's the next to do.

Pom. We'll feast each other ere we part; and let's
Draw lots who shall begin.

Ant.   That will I, Pompey.

Pom. No, Antony, take the lot: but, first
Or last, your fine Egyptian cookery
Shall have the fame.   I have heard that Julius Cæsar
Grew fat with feasting there.

Ant.   You have heard much.

Pom. I have fair meanings, sir.

Ant.   And fair words to them.

Pom. Then so much have I heard:
And I have heard Apollodorus carried,—

Eno. No more of that:—he did so.

Pom.   What, I pray you?

Eno. A certain queen to Cæsar in a mattress.

Pom. I know thee now: how far'st thou, soldier?

Eno.   Well;
And well am like to do; for I perceive
Four feasts are toward.

Pom.   Let me shake thy hand;
I never hated thee: I have seen thee fight,
When I have envied thy behaviour.

Eno.   Sir,
I never lov'd you much; but I ha' prais'd ye,
When you have well deserv'd ten times as much
As I have said you did.

Pom.   Enjoy thy plainness,
It nothing ill becomes thee.—
Aboard my galley I invite you all:
Will you lead, lords!

Cæs., Ant., and Lep.   Show us the way, sir.

Pom.   Come.

                    [*Exeunt all but* MEN. *and* ENO.

Men. [*aside.*] Thy father, Pompey, would ne'er have made
this treaty.—You and I have known, sir.

Eno. At sea, I think.

Men. We have, sir.

Eno. You have done well by water.

Men. And you by land.

Eno. I will praise any man that will praise me; though it cannot be denied what I have done by land.

Men. Nor what I have done by water.

Eno. Yes, something you can deny for your own safety: you have been a great thief by sea.

Men. And you by land.

Eno. There I deny my land service. But give me your hand, Menas: if our eyes had authority, here they might take two thieves kissing.

Men. All men's faces are true, whatsoe'er their hands are.

Eno. But there is never a fair woman has a true face.

Men. No slander; they steal hearts.

Eno. We came hither to fight with you.

Men. For my part, I am sorry it is turned to a drinking. Pompey doth this day laugh away his fortune.

Eno. If he do, sure, he cannot weep it back again.

Men. You have said, sir. We looked not for Mark Antony here: pray you, is he married to Cleopatra?

Eno. Cæsar's sister is called Octavia.

Men. True, sir; she was the wife of Caius Marcellus.

Eno. But she is now the wife of Marcus Antonius.

Men. Pray you, sir?

Eno. 'Tis true.

Men. Then is Cæsar and he for ever knit together.

Eno. If I were bound to divine of this unity, I would not prophesy so.

Men. I think the policy of that purpose made more in the marriage than the love of the parties.

Eno. I think so too. But you shall find the band that seems to tie their friendship together will be the very strangler of their amity: Octavia is of a holy, cold, and still conversation.

Men. Who would not have his wife so?

Eno. Not he that himself is not so; which is Mark Antony. He will to his Egyptian dish again: then shall the sighs of Octavia blow the fire up in Cæsar; and, as I said before, that which is the strength of their amity shall prove the immediate author of their variance. Antony will use his affection where it is: he married but his occasion here.

Men. And thus it may be. Come, sir, will you aboard? I have a health for you.

Eno. I shall take it, sir: we have used our throats in Egypt.

Men. Come, let's away.   [*Exeunt.*

SCENE VII.—*On board* POMPEY's *Galley, lying
near Misenum.*

Music.   Enter two or three Servants *with a banquet.*

1 *Serv.* Here they'll be, man.   Some o' their plants are
ill-rooted already; the least wind i' the world will blow
them down.

2 *Serv.* Lepidus is high-coloured.

1 *Serv.* They have made him drink alms-drink.

2 *Serv.* As they pinch one another by the disposition,
he cries out, *no more;* reconciles them to his entreaty and
himself to the drink.

1 *Serv.* But it raises the greater war between him and
his discretion.

2 *Serv.* Why, this it is to have a name in great men's
fellowship: I had as lief have a reed that will do me no
service as a partizan I could not heave.

1 *Serv.* To be called into a huge sphere, and not to be
seen to move in't, are the holes where eyes should be,
which pitifully disaster the cheeks.

A sennet sounded.   Enter CÆSAR, ANTONY, LEPIDUS, POM-
PEY, AGRIPPA, MECÆNAS, ENOBARBUS, MENAS, *with
other* Captains.

Ant. [*to* CÆSAR.] Thus do they, sir: they take the flow
        o' the Nile
By certain scales i' the pyramid; they know,
By the height, the lowness, or the mean, if dearth
Or foison follow: the higher Nilus swells
The more it promises: as it ebbs, the seedsman
Upon the slime and ooze scatters his grain,
And shortly comes to harvest.

Lep. You've strange serpents there.

Ant. Ay, Lepidus.

Lep. Your serpent of Egypt is bred now of your mud by
the operation of your sun: so is your crocodile.

Ant. They are so.

Pom. Sit,—and some wine!—A health to Lepidus!

Lep. I am not so well as I should be, but I'll ne'er out.

Eno. Not till you have slept; I fear me you'll be in till
then.

Lep. Nay, certainly, I have heard the Ptolemies' pyra-
mises are very goodly things; without contradiction, I have
heard that.

Men. [*aside to* POM.] Pompey, a word.

Pom. [*aside to* MEN.] Say in mine ear: what is't?

Men. [*aside to* POM.] Forsake thy seat, I do beseech
    thee, captain,
And hear me speak a word.

Pom. [*aside to* MEN.] Forbear me till anon.—
This wine for Lepidus!

Lep. What manner o' thing is your crocodile?

Ant. It is shaped, sir, like itself; and it is as broad as
it hath breadth: it is just so high as it is, and moves with
its own organs: it lives by that which nourisheth it; and,
the elements once out of it, it transmigrates.

Lep. What colour is it of?

Ant. Of its own colour too.

Lep. 'Tis a strange serpent.

Ant. 'Tis so.   And the tears of it are wet.

Cæs. Will this description satisfy him?

Ant. With the health that Pompey gives him, else he is
a very epicure.

Pom. [*aside to* MEN.] Go, hang, sir, hang! Tell me of
    that? away!
Do as I bid you.—Where's this cup I call'd for?

Men. [*aside to* POM.] If for the sake of merit thou wilt
    hear me,
Rise from thy stool.

Pom. [*aside to* MEN.] I think thou'rt mad.   The matter?
                       [*Rises and walks aside.*

Men. I have ever held my cap off to thy fortunes.

Pom. Thou hast serv'd me with much faith.   What's
    else to say?—
Be jolly, lords.

Ant.   These quicksands, Lepidus,
Keep off them, for you sink.

Men. Wilt thou be lord of all the world?

Pom.   What say'st thou?

Men. Wilt thou be lord of the whole world?   That's
    twice.

Pom. How should that be?

Men.   But entertain it, and,
Although thou think me poor, I am the man
Will give thee all the world.

Pom.   Hast thou drunk well?

Men. No, Pompey, I have kept me from the cup.
Thou art, if thou dar'st be, the earthly Jove:
Whate'er the ocean pales or sky inclips
Is thine, if thou wilt hav't.

Pom.   Show me which way.

Men. These three world-sharers, these competitors,
Are in thy vessel: let me cut the cable;
And, when we are put off, fall to their throats:
All then is thine.

Pom.   Ah, this thou shouldst have done,
And not have spoke on't! In me 'tis villany;
In thee't had been good service. Thou must know
'Tis not my profit that does lead mine honour;
Mine honour it. Repent that e'er thy tongue
Hath so betray'd thine act: being done unknown,
I should have found it afterwards well done;
But must condemn it now. Desist, and drink.

Men. [*aside.*] For this
I'll never follow thy pall'd fortunes more.
Who seeks, and will not take when once 'tis offer'd,
Shall never find it more.

Pom.   This health to Lepidus!

Ant. Bear him ashore.—I'll pledge it for him, Pompey.

Eno. Here 's to thee, Menas!

Men.   Enobarbus, welcome!

Pom. Fill till the cup be hid.

Eno. There 's a strong fellow, Menas.
               [*Pointing to the* Attendant *who carries off* LEP.

Men.   Why?

Eno.   'A bears
The third part of the world, man; see'st not?

Men. The third part, then, is drunk: would it were
               all,
That it might go on wheels!

Eno. Drink thou; increase the reels.

Men. Come.

Pom. This is not yet an Alexandrian feast.

Ant It ripens towards it.—Strike the vessels, ho!—
Here is to Cæsar!

Cæs.   I could well forbear't.
It 's monstrous labour when I wash my brain
And it grows fouler.

Ant.   Be a child o' the time.

Cæs. Possess it, I'll make answer:
But I had rather fast from all four days
Than drink so much in one.

Eno.   Ha, my brave emperor! [*To* ANTONY,
Shall we dance now the Egyptian Bacchanals,
And celebrate our drink?

Pom.   Let 's ha't, good soldier.

Ant. Come, let 's all take hands,

Till that the conquering wine hath steep'd our sense
In soft and delicate Lethe.
Eno.   All take hands.—
Make battery to our ears with the loud music:—
The while I'll place you: then the boy shall sing;
The holding every man shall beat as loud
As his strong sides can volley.
                    [*Music plays.* ENO. *places them hand in hand.*

SONG.

Come, thou monarch of the vine,
Plumpy Bacchus with pink eyne!
In thy fats our cares be drown'd,
With thy grapes our hairs be crown'd
Cup us, till the world go round,
Cup us, till the world go round!

Cæs. What would you more?—Pompey, good-night.
            Good brother,
Let me request you off: our graver business
Frowns at this levity.—Gentle lords, let 's part;
You see we have burnt our cheeks: strong Enobarb
Is weaker than the wine; and mine own tongue
Splits what it speaks: the wild disguise hath almost
Antick'd us all. What needs more words? Good-night.—
Good Antony, your hand.
Pom.   I'll try you on the shore.
Ant. And shall, sir: give 's your hand.
Pom.   O Antony,
You have my father's house,—but, what? we are friends.
Come, down into the boat.
Eno.   Take heed you fall not.
            [*Exeunt* POM., CÆS., ANT., *and* Attendants.
Menas, I'll not on shore.
Men.   No, to my cabin.—
These drums!—these trumpets, flutes! what!—
Let Neptune hear we bid a loud farewell
To these great fellows: sound and be hang'd, sound out!
                    [*A flourish of trumpets. with drums.*
Eno. Hoo! says 'a.—There 's my cap.
Men. Hoo!—noble captain, come.   [*Exeunt.*

ACT III.

SCENE I.—*A Plain in Syria.*

Enter VENTIDIUS, *in triumph, with* SILIUS *and other* Romans, Officers, *and* Soldiers; *the dead body of* PACORUS *borne in front.*

Ven. Now, darting Parthia, art thou struck; and now
Pleas'd fortune does of Marcus Crassus' death
Make me revenger.—Bear the king's son's body
Before our army —Thy Pacorus, Orodes,
Pays this for Marcus Crassus.

    Sil.   Noble Ventidius,
Whilst yet with Parthian blood thy sword is warm
The fugitive Parthians follow; spur through Media,
Mesopotamia, and the shelters whither
The routed fly: so thy grand captain Antony
Shall set thee on triumphant chariots, and
Put garlands on thy head.

    Ven.   O Silius, Silius,
I have done enough: a lower place, note well,
May make too great an act; for learn this, Silius,—
Better to leave undone, than by our deed
Acquire too high a fame when him we serve 's away.
Cæsar and Antony have ever won
More in their officer than person: Sossius,
One of my place in Syria, his lieutenant,
For quick accumulation of renown,
Which he achiev'd by the minute, lost his favour.
Who does i' the wars more than his captain can
Becomes his captain's captain: and ambition,
The soldier's virtue, rather makes choice of loss
Than gain which darkens him.
I could do more to do Antonius good,
But 'twould offend him; and in his offence
Should my performance perish.

    Sil.   Thou hast, Ventidius, that
Without the which a soldier and his sword
Grants scarce distinction.   Thou wilt write to Antony?

    Ven. I'll humbly signify what in his name,
That magical word of war, we have effected;
How, with his banners and his well-paid ranks,
The ne'er-yet-beaten horse of Parthia
We have jaded out o' the field.

Sil.   Where is he now?

Ven. He purposeth to Athens: whither, with what haste
The weight we must convey with's will permit.
We shall appear before him.—On, there; pass along!

> [*Exeunt*

SCENE II.—ROME.   *An Ante-Chamber in* CÆSAR'S *House.*

Enter AGRIPPA *and* ENOBARBUS *meeting.*

Agr. What, are the brothers parted?

Eno. They have despatch'd with Pompey, he is gone;
The other three are scaling.   Octavia weeps
To part from Rome: Cæsar is sad; and Lepidus,
Since Pompey's feast, as Menas says, is troubled
With the green sickness.

Agr.   'Tis a noble Lepidus.

Eno. A very fine one: O, how he loves Cæsar!

Agr. Nay, but how dearly he adores Mark Antony!

Eno. Cæsar? Why he's the Jupiter of men.

Agr. What's Antony?   The god of Jupiter.

Eno. Speak you of Cæsar? How! the nonpareil!

Agr. Of Antony.   O thou Arabian bird!

Eno. Would you praise Cæsar, say *Cæsar*,—go no further.

Agr. Indeed, he plied them both with excellent praises.

Eno. But he loves Cæsar best;—yet he loves Antony:
Hoo! hearts, tongues, figures, scribes, bards, poets cannot
Think, speak, cast, write, sing, number,—hoo!—
His love to Antony.   But as for Cæsar,
Kneel down, kneel down, and wonder.

Agr.   Both he loves.

Eno. They are his shards, and he their beetle. [*Trumpets within*].   So,—
This is to horse.—Adieu, noble Agrippa.

Agr. Good fortune, worthy soldier; and farewell.

Enter CÆSAR, ANTONY, LEPIDUS, *and* OCTAVIA.

Ant. No further, sir.

Cæs. You take from me a great part of myself;
Use me well in't.—Sister, prove such a wife
As my thoughts make thee, and as my furthest band
Shall pass on thy approof.—Most noble Antony,
Let not the piece of virtue which is set
Betwixt us as the cement of our love,
To keep it builded, be the ram to batter

The fortress of it; for better might we
Have lov'd without this mean if on both parts
This be not cherish'd.

Ant.   Make me not offended
In your distrust.

Cæs.   I have said.

Ant.   You shall not find,
Though you be therein curious, the least cause
For what you seem to fear: so, the gods keep you,
And make the hearts of Romans serve your ends!
We will here part.

Cæs. Farewell, my dearest sister, fare thee well:
The elements be kind to thee, and make
Thy spirits all of comfort!   Fare thee well.

Octa. My noble brother!—

Ant. The April's in her eyes: it is love's spring,
And these the showers to bring it on—Be cheerful.

Octa. Sir, look well to my husband's house; and—

Cæs.   What,
Octavia?

Octa. I'll tell you in your ear.

Ant. Her tongue will not obey her heart, nor can
Her heart inform her tongue,—the swan's down feather,
That stands upon the swell at the full of tide,
And neither way inclines.

Eno. [*aside to* AGRIPPA.] Will Cæsar weep?

Agr. [*aside to* ENO.] He has a cloud in 's face.

Eno. [*aside to* AGRIPPA.] He were the worse for that,
                were he a horse;
So is he, being a man.

Agr. [*aside to* ENO.] Why, Enobarbus,
When Antony found Julius Cæsar dead,
He cried almost to roaring; and he wept
When at Philippi he found Brutus slain.

Eno. [*aside to* AGRIPPA.] That year, indeed, he was
                troubled with a rheum;
What willingly he did confound he wail'd:
Believe 't till I weep too.

Cæs.   No, sweet Octavia,
You shall hear from me still; the time shall not
Out-go my thinking on you.

Ant.   Come, sir, come;
I'll wrestle with you in my strength of love:
Look, here I have you; thus I let you go,
And give you to the gods.

Cæs.   Adieu; be happy!

Lep. Let all the number of the stars give light
To thy fair way!
   Cæs.   Farewell, farewell!   [*Kisses* OCTAVIA.
   Ant.   Farewell!
           [*Trumpets sound within. Exeunt.*

SCENE III.—ALEXANDRIA.   *A Room in the Palace.*

   Enter CLEOPATRA, CHARMIAN, IRAS, *and* ALEXAS.

   Cleo. Where is the fellow?
   Alex.   Half afear'd to come.
   Cleo. Go to, go to.

            Enter a Messenger.
            Come hither, sir.
   Alex.   Good majesty,
Herod of Jewry dare not look upon you
But when you are well pleas'd.
   Cleo.   That Herod's head
I'll have: but how? when Antony is gone,
Through whom I might command it?—Come thou near.
   Mess. Most gracious majesty,—
   Cleo.   Didst thou behold
Octavia?
   Mess. Ay, dread queen.
   Cleo.   Where?
   Mess.   Madam, in Rome
I look'd her in the face, and saw her led
Between her brother and Mark Antony.
   Cleo. Is she as tall as me?
   Mess.   She is not, madam.
   Cleo. Didst hear her speak? is she shrill-tongu'd or low?
   Mess. Madam, I heard her speak; she is low-voic'd.
   Cleo. That's not so good:—he cannot like her long.
   Char. Like her! O Isis! 'tis impossible.
   Cleo. I think so, Charmian: dull of tongue and
        dwarfish!—
What majesty is in her gait? Remember,
If e'er thou look'dst on majesty.
   Mess.   She creeps,—
Her motion and her station are as one;
She shows a body rather than a life,
A statue than a breather.
   Cleo.   Is this certain?
   Mess. Or I have no observance.

Char.   Three in Egypt
Cannot make better note.
    Cleo.   He's very knowing;
I do perceive't:—there's nothing in her yet:—
The fellow has good judgment.
    Char.   Excellent.
    Cleo. Guess at her years, I pr'ythee.
    Mess.   Madam,
She was a widow.
    Cleo.   Widow!—Charmian, hark!
    Mess. And I do think she's thirty.
    Cleo. Bear'st thou her face in mind? is't long or round?
    Mess. Round even to faultiness.
    Cleo. For the most part, too, they are foolish that are so.—·
Her hair, what colour?
    Mess. Brown, madam: and her forehead
As low as she would wish it.
    Cleo.   There's gold for thee.
Thou must not take my former sharpness ill:—
I will employ thee back again; I find thee
Most fit for business: go make thee ready;
Our letters are prepar'd.   [*Exit* Messenger.
    Char.   A proper man.
    Cleo. Indeed, he is so: I repent me much
That so I harried him. Why, methinks, by him
This creature's no such thing.
    Char.   Nothing, madam.
    Cleo. The man hath seen some majesty, and should know.
    Char. Hath he seen majesty? Isis else defend,
And serving you so long!
    Cleo. I have one thing more to ask him yet, good Charmian:
But 'tis no matter; thou shalt bring him to me
Where I will write. All may be well enough.
    Char. I warrant you, madam.   [*Exeunt.*

SCENE IV.—ATHENS. *A Room in* ANTONY'S *House.*

Enter ANTONY *and* OCTAVIA.

    Ant. Nay, nay, Octavia, not only that,—
That were excusable, that and thousands more
Of semblable import,—'mt he hath wag'd
New wars 'gainst Pompey; made his will, and read it
To public ear:
Spoke scantly of me: when perforce he could not
But pay me terms of honour, cold and sickly

He vented them; most narrow measure lent me:
When the best hint was given him, he not took't,
Or did it from his teeth.
  Octa.   O my good lord,
Believe not all; or, if you must believe,
Stomach not all.   A more unhappy lady,
If this division chance, ne'er stood between,
Praying for both parts:
Sure the good gods will mock me presently
When I shall pray, O, *bless my lord and husband!*
Undo that prayer, by crying out as loud,
O, bless my brother!   Husband win, win brother,
Prays and destroys the prayer; no midway
'Twixt these extremes at all.
  Ant.   Gentle Octavia,
Let your best love draw to that point which seeks
Best to preserve it: if I lose mine honour
I lose myself: better I were not yours
Than yours so branchless.   But, as you requested,
Yourself shall go between 's: the meantime, lady,
I'll raise the preparation of a war
Shall stain your brother: make your soonest haste;
So your desires are yours.
  Octa.   Thanks to my lord.
The Jove of power make me, most weak, most weak,
Your reconciler! Wars 'twixt you twain would be
As if the world should cleave, and that slain men
Should solder up the rift.
  Ant. When it appears to you where this begins,
Turn your displeasure that way; for our faults
Can never be so equal that your love
Can equally move with them.   Provide your going;
Choose your own company, and command what cost
Your heart has mind to.   [*Exeunt.*

SCENE V.—ATHENS.   *Another Room in* ANTONY'S *House.*

Enter ENOBARBUS *and* EROS, *meeting.*

Eno. How now, friend Eros!
Eros. There's strange news come, sir.
Eno. What, man?
Eros. Cæsar and Lepidus have made wars upon Pompey.
Eno. This is old: what is the success?
Eros. Cæsar, having made use of him in the wars 'gainst
Pompey, presently denied him rivality; would not let him

partake in the glory of the action: and not resting here,
accuses him of letters he had formerly wrote to Pompey;
upon his own appeal seizes him: so the poor third is up,
till death enlarge his confine.

Eno. Then world, thou hast a pair of chaps, no more;
And throw between them all the food thou hast,
They'll grind the one the other. Where 's Antony?

Eros. He 's walking in the garden—thus: and spurns
The rush that lies before him; cries, *Fool Lepidus!*
And threats the throat of that his officer
That murder'd Pompey.

Eno.   Our great navy 's rigg'd.

Eros. For Italy and Cæsar. More, Domitius;
My lord desires you presently: my news
I might have told hereafter.

Eno.   'Twill be naught:
But let it be.—Bring me to Antony.

Eros. Come, sir.   [*Exeunt.*

SCENE VI.—ROME.   *A Room in* CÆSAR'S *House.*

Enter CÆSAR, AGRIPPA, *and* MECÆNAS.

Cæs. Contemning Rome, he has done all this, and
     more,
In Alexandria: here 's the manner of't:—
I' the market-place, on a tribunal silver'd,
Cleopatra and himself in chairs of gold
Were publicly enthron'd: at the feet sat
Cæsarion, whom they call my father's son,
And all the unlawful issue that their lust
Since then hath made between them.   Unto her
He gave the 'stablishment of Egypt; made her
Of Lower Syria, Cyprus, Lydia,
Absolute queen.

Mec.   This in the public eye?

Cæs. I' the common show-place, where they exercise.
His sons he there proclaim'd the kings of kings:
Great Media, Parthia, and Armenia
He gave to Alexander; to Ptolemy he assign'd
Syria, Cilicia, and Phœnicia: she
In the habiliments of the goddess Isis
That day appear'd; and oft before gave audience
As 'tis reported, so.

Mec.   Let Rome be thus
Inform'd.

Agr.   Who, queasy with his insolence
Already, will their good thoughts call from him.
  Cœs. The people know it: and have now receiv'd
His accusations.
  Agr.   Who does he accuse?
  Cœs. Cæsar: and that, having in Sicily
Sextus Pompeius spoil'd, we had not rated him
His part o' the isle: then does he say he lent me
Some shipping, unrestor'd: lastly, he frets
That Lepidus of the triumvirate
Should be depos'd; and, being, that we detain
All his revenue.
  Agr.   Sir, this should be answer'd.
  Cœs. 'Tis done already, and the messenger gone.
I have told him Lepidus was grown too cruel;
That he his high authority abus'd,
And did deserve his change: for what I have conquer'd
I grant him part; but then, in his Armenia
And other of his conquer'd kingdoms, I
Demand the like.
  Mec.   He'll never yield to that.
  Cœs. Nor must not, then, be yielded to in this.

Enter OCTAVIA, *with her* Train.

  Octa. Hail, Cæsar, and my lord! hail, most dear
          Cæsar!
  Cœs. That ever I should call thee castaway!
  Octa. You have not call'd me so, nor have you cause.
  Cœs. Why have you stol'n upon us thus? You come
          not
Like Cæsar's sister: the wife of Antony
Should have an army for an usher, and
The neighs of horse to tell of her approach
Long ere she did appear; the trees by the way
Should have borne men; and expectation fainted,
Longing for what it had not; nay, the dust
Should have ascended to the roof of heaven,
Rais'd by your populous troops: but you are come
A market-maid to Rome; and have prevented
The ostentation of our love, which left unshown
Is often left unlov'd: we should have met you
By sea and land; supplying every stage
With an augmented greeting.
  Octa.   Good my lord,
To come thus was I not constrain'd, but did it
On my free-will. My lord, Mark Antony,

Hearing that you prepar'd for war, acquainted
My grieved ear withal: whereon I begg'd
His pardon for return.

Cæs. Which soon he granted,
Being an obstruct 'tween his lust and him.

Octa. Do not say so, my lord.

Cæs. I have eyes upon him,
And his affairs come to me on the wind.
Where is he now?

Octa. My lord, in Athens.

Cæs. No, my most wronged sister; Cleopatra
Hath nodded him to her. He hath given his empire
Up to a whore; who now are levying
The kings o' the earth for war: he hath assembled
Bocchus, the king of Lybia; Archelaus
Of Cappadocia; Philadelphos, king
Of Paphlagonia; the Thracian king, Adallas;
King Malchus of Arabia; King of Pont;
Herod of Jewry; Mithridates, king
Of Comagene; Polemon and Amyntas,
The kings of Mede and Lycaonia, with a
More larger list of sceptres.

Octa. Ay me, most wretched,
That have my heart parted betwixt two friends
That do afflict each other!

Cæs. Welcome hither:
Your letters did withhold our breaking forth,
Till we perceiv'd both how you were wrong led
And we in negligent danger. Cheer your heart:
Be you not troubled with the time, which drives
O'er your content these strong necessities;
But let determin'd things to destiny
Hold unbewail'd their way. Welcome to Rome;
Nothing more dear to me. You are abus'd
Beyond the mark of thought: and the high gods,
To do you justice, make their ministers
Of us and those that love you. Best of comfort;
And ever welcome to us.

Agr. Welcome, lady.

Mec. Welcome, dear madam.
Each heart in Rome does love and pity you:
Only the adulterous Antony, most large
In his abominations, turns you off;
And gives his potent regiment to a trull
That noises it against us.

Octa. Is it so, sir?

Cæs. Most certain.   Sister, welcome: pray you
Be ever known to patience: my dear'st sister!   [*Exeunt.*

SCENE VII.—ANTONY's *Camp near the Promontory
of Actium.*

Enter CLEOPATRA *and* ENOBARBUS.

Cleo. I will be even with thee, doubt it not.
Eno. But why, why, why?
Cleo. Thou hast forspoke my being in these wars,
And say'st it is not fit.
Eno.   Well, is it, is it?
Cleo. If not denounc'd against us, why should not we
Be there in person?
Eno. [*aside.*]   Well, I could reply:—
If we should serve with horse and mares together,
The horse were merely lost; the mares would bear
A soldier and his horse.
Cleo.   What is't you say!
Eno. Your presence needs must puzzle Antony;
Take from his heart, take from his brain, from 's time,
What should not then be spar'd.   He is already
Traduc'd for levity; and 'tis said in Rome
That Photinus an eunuch and your maids
Manage this war.
Cleo.   Sink Rome, and their tongues rot
That speak against us!   A charge we bear i' the war,
And, as the president of my kingdom, will
Appear there for a man.   Speak not against it;
I will not stay behind.
Eno.   Nay, I have done.
Here comes the emperor.

Enter ANTONY *and* CANIDIUS.

Ant.   Is it not strange, Canidius,
That from Tarentum and Brundusium
He could so quickly cut the Ionian sea,
And take in Toryne?—You have heard on't, sweet?
Cleo. Celerity is never more admir'd
Than by the negligent.
Ant.   A good rebuke,
Which might have well become the best of men
To taunt at slackness.—Canidius, we
Will fight with him by sea.
Cleo.   By sea! what else!

Can. Why will my lord do so?

Ant.   For that he dares us to't.

Eno. So hath my lord dar'd him to single fight.

Can. Ay, and to wage this battle at Pharsalia.
Where Cæsar fought with Pompey: but these offers,
Which serve not for his vantage, he shakes off;
And so should you.

Eno.   Your ships are not well mann'd:
Your mariners are muleteers, reapers, people
Ingross'd by swift impress; in Cæsar's fleet
Are those that often have 'gainst Pompey fought:
Their ships are yare; yours heavy: no disgrace
Shall fall you for refusing him at sea,
Being prepar'd for land.

Ant.   By sea, by sea.

Eno. Most worthy sir, you therein throw away
The absolute soldiership you have by land;
Distract your army, which doth most consist
Of war-mark'd footmen; leave unexecuted
Your own renowned knowledge; quite forego
The way which promises assurance; and
Give up yourself merely to chance and hazard
From firm security.

Ant.   I'll fight at sea.

Cleo. I have sixty sails, Cæsar none better.

Ant. Our overplus of shipping will we burn;
And, with the rest full-mann'd, from the head of Actium
Beat the approaching Cæsar.   But if we fail
We then can do't at land.

Enter a Messenger.

                    Thy business?

Mess. The news is true, my lord; he is descried;
Cæsar has taken Toryne.

Ant. Can he be there in person? 'tis impossible;
Strange that his power should be.—Canidius,
Our nineteen legions thou shalt hold by land,
And our twelve thousand horse.—We'll to our ship:
Away, my Thetis!

Enter a Soldier.

                    How now, worthy soldier?

Sold. O noble emperor, do not fight by sea;
Trust not to rotten planks: do you misdoubt
This sword and these my wounds?   Let the Egyptians
And the Phœnicians go a-ducking: we

Have used to conquer standing on the earth
And fighting foot to foot.
 Ant.   Well, well:—away.
     [*Exeunt* ANT., CLEO., *and* ENO.
 Sold. By Hercules, I think I am i' the right.
 Can. Soldier, thou art: but his whole action grows
Not in the power on't: so our leader's led,
And we are women's men.
 Sold.   You keep by land
The legions and the horse whole, do you not?
 Can. Marcus Octavius, Marcius Justeius,
Publicola, and Cælius are for sea:
But we keep whole by land.   This speed of Cæsar's
Carries beyond belief.
 Sold.   While he was yet in Rome
His power went out in such distractions as
Beguil'd all spies.
 Can.   Who's his lieutenant, hear you?
 Sold. They say one Taurus.
 Can.   Well I know the man.

     Enter a Messenger.

 Mess. The emperor calls Canidius.
 Can. With news the time's with labour: and throes forth
Each minute some.   [*Exeunt.*

     ———

   SCENE VIII.—*A Plain near Actium.*

  Enter CÆSAR, TAURUS, Officers, *and others.*

 Cæs. Taurus,—
 Taur.   My lord?
 Cæs. Strike not by land; keep whole; provoke not battle
Till we have done at sea.   Do not exceed
The prescript of this scroll: our fortune lies
Upon this jump.   [*Exeunt.*

     ———

   SCENE IX.—*Another part of the Plain.*

   Enter ANTONY *and* ENOBARBUS.

 Ant. Set we our squadrons on yon side o' the hill,
In eye of Cæsar's battle; from which place
We may the number of the ships behold,
And so proceed accordingly.   [*Exeunt.*

SCENE X.—*Another part of the Plain.*

Enter CANIDIUS, *marching with his land* Army *one way;
and* TAURUS, *the* Lieutenant *of* CÆSAR, *with his* Army,
*the other way. After their going in, is heard the noise of
a sea-fight.*

Alarum. Enter ENOBARBUS.

Eno. Naught, naught, all naught! I can behold no
The Antoniad, the Egyptian Admiral,   [longer:
With all their sixty, fly and turn the rudder:
To see't mine eyes are blasted.

Enter SCARUS.

Scar.   Gods and goddesses,
All the whole synod of them!
Eno.   What's thy passion?
Scar. The greater cantle of the world is lost
With very ignorance; we have kiss'd away
Kingdoms and provinces.
Eno.   How appears the fight?
Scar. On our side like the token'd pestilence,
Where death is sure.   Yon ribaudred nag of Egypt,—
Whom leprosy o'ertake!—i' the midst o' the fight,
When vantage like a pair of twins appear'd,
Both as the same, or rather ours the elder,—
The breese upon her, like a cow in June,—
Hoists sails and flies.
Eno.   That I beheld:
Mine eyes did sicken at the sight, and could not
Endure a further view.
Scar.   She once being loof'd,
The noble ruin of her magic, Antony,
Claps on his sea-wing, and, like a doting mallard,
Leaving the fight in height, flies after her:
I never saw an action of such shame;
Experience, manhood, honour, ne'er before
Did violate so itself.
Eno.   Alack, alack!

Enter CANIDIUS.

Can. Our fortune on the sea is out of breath,
And sinks most lamentably. Had our general
Been what he knew himself, it had gone well:
O, he has given example for our flight
Most grossly by his own!

Eno. Ay, are you thereabouts?
Why, then, good-night indeed.
  Can. Toward Peloponnesus are they fled.
  Scar. 'Tis easy to't; and there I will attend
What further comes.
  Can.   To Cæsar will I render
My legions and my horse; six kings already
Show me the way of yielding.
  Eno.   I'll yet follow
The wounded chance of Antony, though my reason
Sits in the wind against me.   [*Exeunt.*

SCENE XI.—ALEXANDRIA.   *A Room in the Palace.*

Enter ANTONY *and* Attendants.

  Ant. Hark! the land bids me tread no more upon't,--
It is asham'd to bear me!—Friends, come hither:
I am so lated in the world that I
Have lost my way for ever:—I have a ship
Laden with gold, take that, divide it; fly,
And make your peace with Cæsar.
  All.   Fly! not we.
  Ant. I have fled myself, and have instructed cowards
To run and show their shoulders.—Friends, be gone;
I have myself resolv'd upon a course
Which has no need of you; begone:
My treasure's in the harbour, take it.—O,
I follow'd that I blush to look upon:
My very hairs do mutiny; for the white   '
Reprove the brown for rashness, and they them
For fear and doting.—Friends, be gone: you shall
Have letters from me to some friends that will
Sweep your way for you.   Pray you, look not sad,
Nor make replies of loathness: take the hint
Which my despair proclaims; let that be left
Which leaves itself: to the sea-side straightway:
I will possess you of that ship and treasure.
Leave me, I pray, a little: pray you now:—
Nay, do so; for, indeed, I have lost command,
Therefore I pray you:—I'll see you by and by. [*Sits down.*

Enter CLEOPATRA *led by* CHARMIAN *and* IRAS,
EROS *following.*

  Eros. Nay, gentle madam, to him,—comfort him.

Iras. Do, most dear queen.

Char. Do! why, what else?

Cleo. Let me sit down. O Juno!

Ant. No, no, no, no, no.

Eros. See you here, sir?

Ant. O fie, fie, fie!

Char. Madam,—

Iras. Madam, O good empress,—

Eros. Sir, sir,—

Ant. Yes, my lord, yes;—he at Philippi kept
His sword e'en like a dancer; while I struck
The lean and wrinkled Cassius; and 'twas I
That the mad Brutus ended; he alone
Dealt on lieutenantry, and no practice had
In the brave squares of war: yet now—no matter.

Cleo. Ah, stand by.

Eros. The queen, my lord, the queen.

Iras. Go to him, madam, speak to him:
He is unqualitied with very shame.

Cleo. Well then,—sustain me:—O!

Eros. Most noble sir, arise; the queen approaches:
Her head's declin'd, and death will seize her, but
Your comfort make the rescue.

Ant. I have offended reputation,—
A most unnoble swerving.

Eros.   Sir, the queen.

Ant. O, whither hast thou led me, Egypt?   See
How I convey my shame out of thine eyes
By looking back, what I have left behind
'Stroy'd in dishonour.

Cleo.   O my lord, my lord,
Forgive my fearful sails! I little thought
You would have follow'd.

Ant.   Egypt, thou knew'st too well
My heart was to thy rudder tied by the strings,
And thou shouldst tow me after: o'er my spirit
Thy full supremacy thou knew'st, and that
Thy beck might from the bidding of the gods
Command me.

Cleo.   O, my pardon!

Ant.   Now I must
To the young man send humble treaties, dodge
And palter in the shifts of lowness; who
With half the bulk o' the world play'd as I pleas'd,
Making and marring fortunes. You did know
How much you were my conqueror; and that

My sword, made weak by my affection, would
Obey it on all cause.
    Cleo.   Pardon, pardon!
    Ant. Fall not a tear, I say; one of them rates
All that is won and lost: give me a kiss;
Even this repays me.—We sent our schoolmaster;
Is he come back?—Love, I am full of lead.—
Some wine, within there, and our viands!—Fortune knows
We scorn her most when most she offers blows.   [*Exeunt.*

SCENE XII.—Cæsar's *Camp in Egypt.*

Enter CÆSAR, DOLABELLA, THYREUS, *and others*

    Cæs. Let him appear that's come from Antony.—
Know you him?
    Dol.   Cæsar, 'tis his schoolmaster:
An argument that he is pluck'd, when hither
He sends so poor a pinion of his wing,
Which had superfluous kings for messengers
Not many moons gone by.

Enter EUPHRONIUS.

    Cæs.   Approach, and speak.
    Eup. Such as I am, I come from Antony:
I was of late as petty to his ends
As is the morn-dew on the myrtle leaf
To his grand sea.
    Cæs.   Be't so: declare thine office.
    Eup. Lord of his fortunes he salutes thee, and
Requires to live in Egypt: which not granted,
He lessens his requests; and to thee sues
To let him breathe between the heavens and earth,
A private man in Athens: this for him.
Next, Cleopatra does confess thy greatness;
Submits her to thy might; and of thee craves
The circle of the Ptolemies for her heirs,
Now hazarded to thy grace.
    Cæs.   For Antony,
I have no ears to his request   The queen
Of audience nor desire shall fail; so she
From Egypt drive her all-disgraced friend,
Or take his life there: this if she perform
She shall not sue unheard.   So to them both.
    Eup. Fortune pursue thee!
    VOL. V.   T

Cæs.   Bring him through the bands.
                      [*Exit* EUPHRONIUS.
To try thy eloquence, now 'tis time: despatch;
 From Antony win Cleopatra: promise,   [*To* THYREUS.
And in our name, what she requires; add more,
From thine invention, offers: women are not
In their best fortunes strong; but want will perjure
The ne'er-touch'd vestal: try thy cunning, Thyreus;
Make thine own edict for thy pains, which we
Will answer as a law.
     Thyr.   Cæsar, I go.
     Cæs. Observe how Antony becomes his flaw,
And what thou think'st his very action speaks
In every power that moves.
     Thyr.   Cæsar, I shall   [*Exeunt.*

SCENE XIII.—ALEXANDRIA.   *A Room in the Palace.*

Enter CLEOPATRA, ENOBARBUS, CHARMIAN, *and* IRAS.

     Cleo. What shall we do, Enobarbus?
     Eno.   Think, and die.
     Cleo. Is Antony or we in fault for this?
     Eno. Antony only, that would make his will
Lord of his reason. What though you fled
From that great face of war, whose several ranges
Frighted each other? why should he follow?
The itch of his affection should not then
Have nick'd his captainship; at such a point,
When half to half the world oppos'd, he being
The mered question: 'twas a shame no less
Than was his loss to course your flying flags
And leave his navy gazing.
     Cleo.   Pr'ythee, peace.

Enter ANTONY, *with* EUPHRONIUS.

     Ant. Is that his answer?
     Eup. Ay, my lord.
     Ant. The queen shall then have courtesy, so she
Will yield us up.
     Eup.   He says so.
     Ant.   Let her know't.—
To the boy Cæsar send this grizzled head,
And he will fill thy wishes to the brim
With principalities.
     Cleo.   That head, my lord?

Ant. To him again: tell him he wears the rose
Of youth upon him; from which the world should note
Something particular: his coins, ships, legions,
May be a coward's; whose ministers would prevail
Under the service of a child as soon
As i' the command of Cæsar: I dare him therefore
To lay his gay comparisons apart,
And answer me declin'd, sword against sword,
Ourselves alone.   I'll write it: follow me.
                              [*Exeunt* ANTONY *and* EUPHRONIUS.
  Eno. Yes, like enough, high-battled Cæsar will
Unstate his happiness, and be stag'd to the show
Against a sworder.—I see men's judgments are
A parcel of their fortunes; and things outward
Do draw the inward quality after them,
To suffer all alike.   That he should dream,
Knowing all measures, the full Cæsar will
Answer his emptiness!—Cæsar, thou hast subdu'd
His judgment too.

                   Enter an Attendant.
  Att.   A messenger from Cæsar.
  Cleo. What, no more ceremony?—See, my women!—
Against the blown rose may they stop their nose
That kneel'd unto the buds.—Admit him, sir.
                              [*Exit* Attendant.
  Eno. [*aside*] Mine honesty and I begin to square.
The loyalty well held to fools does make
Our faith mere folly:—yet he that can endure
To follow with allegiance a fallen lord
Does conquer him that did his master conquer,
And earns a place i' the story.

                   Enter THYREUS.
  Cleo.   Cæsar's will?
  Thyr. Hear it apart.
  Cleo.   None but friends: say boldly.
  Thyr. So, haply, are they friends to Antony.
  Eno. He needs as many, sir, as Cæsar has;
Or needs not us.   If Cæsar please, our master
Will leap to be his friend: for us, you know
Whose he is we are, and that is Cæsar's.
  Thyr.   So.—
Thus then, thou most renown'd: Cæsar entreats
Not to consider in what case thou stand'st,
Further than he is Cæsar.

Cleo. Go on: right royal.

Thyr. He knows that you embrace not Antony
As you did love, but as you fear'd him.

Cleo. O!

Thyr. The scars upon your honour, therefore, he
Does pity, as constrained blemishes,
Not as deserv'd.

Cleo. He is a god, and knows
What is most right: mine honour was not yielded,
But conquer'd merely.

Eno. [*aside.*] To be sure of that,
I will ask Antony.—Sir, sir, thou art so leaky
That we must leave thee to thy sinking, for
Thy dearest quit thee.   [*Exit*

Thyr. Shall I say to Cæsar
What you require of him? for he partly begs
To be desir'd to give. It much would please him
That of his fortunes you should make a staff
To lean upon: but it would warm his spirits
To hear from me you had left Antony,
And put yourself under his shroud, who is
The universal landlord.

Cleo. What 's your name?

Thyr. My name is Thyreus.

Cleo. Most kind messenger,
Say to great Cæsar this:—in deputation
I kiss his conquering hand: tell him I am prompt
To lay my crown at 's feet, and there to kneel:
Tell him, from his all-obeying breath I hear
The doom of Egypt.

Thyr. 'Tis your noblest course.
Wisdom and fortune combating together,
If that the former dare but what it can,
No chance may shake it. Give me grace to lay
My duty on your hand.

Cleo. Your Cæsar's father
Oft, when he hath mus'd of taking kingdoms in,
Bestow'd his lips on that unworthy place,
As it rain'd kisses.

Re-enter ANTONY *and* ENOBARBUS.

Ant. Favours, by Jove that thunders!—
What art thou, fellow?

Thyr. One that but performs
The bidding of the fullest man, and worthiest
To have command obey'd.

Eno. [*aside.*]   You will be whipp'd.
Ant. Approach there!—Ay, you kite!—Now, gods and
          devils!
Authority melts from me: of late, when I cried, *Ho!*
Like boys unto a muss, kings would start forth
And cry, *Your will?* Have you no ears? I am
Antony yet.

Enter Attendants.

          Take hence this Jack, and whip him.
Eno. 'Tis better playing with a lion's whelp
Than with an old one dying.
          Ant.   Moon and stars!
Whip him.—Were't twenty of the greatest tributaries
That do acknowledge Cæsar, should I find them
So saucy with the hand of she here,—what's her name
Since she was Cleopatra?—Whip him, fellows,
Till, like a boy, you see him cringe his face,
And whine aloud for mercy: take him hence.
          Thyr. Mark Antony,—
          Ant.   Tug him away: being whipp'd,
Bring him again.—This Jack of Cæsar's shall
Bear us an errand to him.—
                              [*Exeunt* Attend. *with* THYR.
You were half blasted ere I knew you.—Ha!
Have I my pillow left unpress'd in Rome,
Forborne the getting of a lawful race,
And by a gem of women, to be abus'd
By one that looks on feeders?
          Cleo.   Good my lord,—
          Ant. You have been a boggler ever:—
But when we in our viciousness grow hard,—
O misery on't!—the wise gods seal our eyes;
In our own filth drop our clear judgments; make us
Adore our errors; laugh at 's, while we strut
To our confusion.
          Cleo.   O, is't come to this?
          Ant. I found you as a morsel cold upon
Dead Cæsar's trencher; nay, you were a fragment
Of Cneius Pompey's; besides what hotter hours,
Unregister'd in vulgar fame, you have
Luxuriously pick'd out:—for I am sure,
Though you can guess what temperance should be,
You know not what it is.
          Cleo.   Wherefore is this?
          Ant. To let a fellow that will take rewards.

And say, *God quit you!* be familiar with
My playfellow, your hand; this kingly seal
And plighter of high hearts!—O that I were
Upon the hill of Basan, to outroar
The horned herd! for I have savage cause;
And to proclaim it civilly were like
A halter'd neck which does the hangman thank
For being yare about him.

Re-enter Attendants *with* THYREUS.
                                Is he whipp'd?
  1 *Att.* Soundly, my lord.
  Ant.   Cried he? and begg'd he pardon!
  1 *Att.* He did ask favour.
  Ant. If that thy father live, let him repent
Thou wast not made his daughter; and be thou sorry
To follow Cæsar in his triumph, since
Thou hast been whipp'd for following him: henceforth
The white hand of a lady fever thee,
Shake thou to look on't.—Get thee back to Cæsar,
Tell him thy entertainment: look thou say
He makes me angry with him; for he seems
Proud and disdainful, harping on what I am,
Not what he knew I was: he makes me angry;
And at this time most easy 'tis to do't,
When my good stars, that were my former guides,
Have empty left their orbs, and shot their fires
Into the abysm of hell.   If he mislike
My speech and what is done, tell him he has
Hipparchus, my enfranchis'd bondman, whom
He may at pleasure whip, or hang, or torture,
As he shall like, to quit me: urge it thou:
Hence with thy stripes, be gone.   [*Exit* THYREUS
  Cleo. Have you done yet?
  Ant.   Alack, our terrene moon
Is now eclips'd; and it portends alone
The fall of Antony!
  Cleo.   I must stay his time.
  Ant. To flatter Cæsar, would you mingle eyes
With one that ties his points?
  Cleo.   Not know me yet?
  Ant. Cold-hearted toward me?
  Cleo.   Ah, dear, if I be so,
From my cold heart let heaven engender hail,
And poison it in the source; and the first stone
Drop in my neck: as it determines, so

Dissolve my life! The next Cæsarion smite!
Till, by degrees, the memory of my womb,
Together with my brave Egyptians all,
By the discandying of this pelleted storm,
Lie graveless,—till the flies and gnats of Nile
Have buried them for prey!

Ant.   I am satisfied.
Cæsar sits down in Alexandria; where
I will oppose his fate. Our force by land
Hath nobly held : our sever'd navy too
Have knit again, and fleet, threat'ning most sealike.
Where hast thou been, my heart?—Dost thou hear, lady?
If from the field I shall return once more
To kiss these lips, I will appear in blood :
I and my sword will earn our chronicle :
There 's hope in't yet.

Cleo.   That 's my brave lord!
Ant. I will be treble-sinew'd, hearted, breath'd,
And fight maliciously : for when mine hours
Were nice and lucky, men did ransom lives
Of me for jests ; but now I'll set my teeth,
And send to darkness all that stop me.—Come,
Let 's have one other gaudy night : call to me
All my sad captains, fill our bowls ; once more
Let 's mock the midnight bell.

Cleo.   It is my birthday :
I had thought to have held it poor ; but since my lord
Is Antony again I will be Cleopatra.

Ant. We will yet do well.
Cleo. Call all his noble captains to my lord.
Ant. Do so ; we'll speak to them : and to-night I'll force
The wine peep through their scars.—Come on, my queen ;
There 's sap in't yet. The next time I do fight
I'll make death love me ; for I will contend
Even with his pestilent scythe.   [*Exeunt all but* ENO.

Eno. Now he'll outstare the lightning. To be furious
Is to be frighted out of fear ; and in that mood
The dove will peck the estridge ; and I see still
A diminution in our captain's brain
Restores his heart : when valour preys on reason
It eats the sword it fights with. I will seek
Some way to leave him.   [*Exit.*

ACT IV.

SCENE I.—Cæsar's *Camp at Alexandria.*

Enter Cæsar *reading a letter;* Agrippa, Mecænas, *and others.*

Cæs. He calls me boy; and chides as he had power
To beat me out of Egypt; my messenger
He hath whipp'd with rods; dares me to personal combat,
Cæsar to Antony:—let the old ruffian know
I have many other ways to die; meantime
Laugh at his challenge.
  Mec.   Cæsar must think,
When one so great begins to rage, he 's hunted
Even to falling. Give him no breath, but now
Make boot of his distraction:—never anger
Made good guard for itself.
  Cæs.   Let our best heads
Know that to-morrow the last of many battles
We mean to fight.—Within our files there are,
Of those that serv'd Mark Antony but late,
Enough to fetch him in. See it done:
And feast the army: we have store to do't,
And they have earn'd the waste. Poor Antony! [*Exeunt.*

———

SCENE II.—Alexandria. *A Room in the Palace.*

Enter Antony, Cleopatra, Enobarbus, Charmian, Iras, Alexas, *and others.*

Ant. He will not fight with me, Domitius.
Eno.   No.
Ant. Why should he not?
Eno. He thinks, being twenty times of better fortune,
He is twenty men to one.
  Ant.   To-morrow, soldier,
By sea and land I'll fight: or I will live,
Or bathe my dying honour in the blood
Shall make it live again. Woo't thou fight well?
  Eno. I'll strike, and cry, *Take all.*
  Ant.   Well said; come on.—
Call forth my household servants: let 's to-night
Be bounteous at our meal.—

Enter Servants.

                      Give me thy hand,
Thou hast been rightly honest;—so hast thou;—
Thou,—and thou,—and thou;—you have serv'd me well,
And kings have been your fellows.
    Cleo. [*aside to* ENO.]   What means this?
    Eno. [*aside to* CLEO.] 'Tis one of those odd tricks which
        sorrow shoots
Out of the mind.
    Ant.   And thou art honest too.
I wish I could be made so many men,
And all of you clapp'd up together in
An Antony, that I might do you service
So good as you have done.
    Serv.   The gods forbid!
    Ant. Well, my good fellows, wait on me to-night:
Scant not my cups; and make as much of me
As when mine empire was your fellow too,
And suffer'd my command.
    Cleo. [*aside to* ENO.]   What does he mean?
    Eno. [*aside to* CLEO.] To make his followers weep.
    Ant.   Tend me to-night;
May be it is the period of your duty:
Haply you shall not see me more; or if,
A mangled shadow: perchance to-morrow
You'll serve another master. I look on you
As one that takes his leave. Mine honest friends,
I turn you not away; but, like a master
Married to your good service, stay till death:
Tend me to-night two hours, I ask no more,
And the gods yield you for't!
    Eno.   What mean you, sir,
To give them this discomfort? Look, they weep;
And I, an ass, am onion-ey'd: for shame,
Transform us not to women.
    Ant.   Ho, ho, ho!
Now the witch take me, if I meant it thus!
Grace grow where those drops fall! My hearty friends,
You take me in too dolorous a sense;
For I spake to you for your comfort,—did desire you
To burn this night with torches: know, my hearts,
I hope well of to-morrow; and will lead you
Where rather I'll expect victorious life
Than death and honour. Let's to supper; come,
And drown consideration.   [*Exeunt.*

SCENE III.—ALEXANDRIA. *Before the Palace.*

Enter two Soldiers *to their guard.*

1 *Sold.* Brother, good-night: to-morrow is the day.
2 *Sold.* It will determine one way: fare you well.
Heard you of nothing strange about the streets?
1 *Sold.* Nothing. What news?
2 *Sold.* Belike 'tis but a rumour. Good-night to you.
1 *Sold.* Well, sir, good-night.

Enter two other Soldiers.

2 *Sold.* Soldiers, have careful watch.
3 *Sold.* And you. Good-night, good-night.
              [*The first two place themselves at their posts*
4 *Sold.* Here we: [*The third and fourth take their posts.*]
      and if to-morrow
Our navy thrive, I have an absolute hope
Our landmen will stand up.
3 *Sold.*   'Tis a brave army,
And full of purpose.
              [*Music as of hautboys under the stage.*
4 *Sold.*   Peace, what noise?
1 *Sold.*   List, list!
2 *Sold.* Hark!
1 *Sold.* Music i' the air.
3 *Sold.*   Under the earth.
4 *Sold.* It signs well, does it not?
3 *Sold.*   No.
1 *Sold.*   Peace, I say!
What should this mean?
2 *Sold.* 'Tis the god Hercules, whom Antony lov'd,
Now leaves him.
1 *Sold.*   Walk; let's see if other watchmen
Do hear what we do.   [*They advance to another post.*
2 *Sold.*   How now, masters!
Soldiers. [*speaking together.*]   How now!
How now! do your hear this?
1 *Sold.*   Ay; is't not strange?
3 *Sold.* Do you hear, masters? do you hear?
1 *Sold.* Follow the noise so far as we have quarter;
Let 's see how't will give off.
Soldiers. [*speaking together.*] Content. 'Tis strange.
                                        [*Exeunt.*

SCENE IV.—ALEXANDRIA.   *A Room in the Palace.*

Enter ANTONY *and* CLEOPATRA; CHARMIAN, IRAS, *and others attending.*

Ant. Eros! mine armour, Eros!
Cleo.   Sleep a little.
Ant. No, my chuck.—Eros, come; mine armour, Eros!

Enter EROS *with armour.*

Come, good fellow, put mine iron on.—
If fortune be not ours to-day, it is
Because we brave her.—Come.
  Cleo.   Nay, I'll help too.
What 's this for?
  Ant.   Ah, let be, let be! thou art
The armourer of my heart.   False, false; this, this.
  Cleo. Sooth, la, I'll help: thus it must be.
  Ant.   Well, well;
We shall thrive now.—Seest thou, my good fellow?
Go put on thy defences.
  Eros.   Briefly, sir.
  Cleo. Is not this buckled well?
  Ant.   Rarely, rarely:
He that unbuckles this, till we do please
To doff 't for our repose, shall hear a storm.—
Thou fumblest, Eros; and my queen 's a squire
More tight at this than thou: despatch.—O love,
That thou couldst see my wars to-day, and knew'st
The royal occupation! thou shouldst see
A workman in 't.—

Enter an Officer, *armed.*

                Good-morrow to thee; welcome:
Thou look'st like him that knows a warlike charge
To business that we love we rise betime,
And go to't with delight.
  Off.   A thousand, sir,
Early though it be, have on their riveted trim,
And at the port expect you.
                   [*Shout. Flourish of Trumpets within.*

Enter other Officers *and* Soldiers.

2 *Off.* The morn is fair.—Good-morrow, general.
All. Good-morrow, general.
Ant.   "Tis well blown, lads;

This morning, like the spirit of a youth
That means to be of note, begins betimes.—
So, so; come, give me that: this way; well said.—
Fare thee well, dame, whate'er becomes of me:
This is a soldier's kiss: rebukable,   [*Kisses her.*
And worthy shameful check it were, to stand
On more mechanic compliment; I'll leave thee
Now, like a man of steel.—You that will fight,
Follow me close; I'll bring you to't.—Adieu.

    [*Exeunt* ANT., EROS, Officers, *and* Soldiers.

  Char. Please you, retire to your chamber.
  Cleo.   Lead me.
He goes forth gallantly. That he and Cæsar might
Determine this great war in single fight!
Then, Antony,—but now—Well, on.   [*Exeunt.*

SCENE V.—ANTONY'S *Camp near Alexandria.*

Trumpets sound within. Enter ANTONY *and* EROS,
    a Soldier *meeting them.*

  Sold. The gods make this a happy day to Antony! -
  Ant. Would thou and those thy scars had once prevail'd
To make me fight at land!
  Sold.   Hadst thou done so,
The kings that have revolted, and the soldier
That has this morning left thee, would have still
Follow'd thy heels.
  Ant.   Who's gone this morning?
  Sold.   Who!
One ever near thee: call for Enobarbus,
He shall not hear thee; or from Cæsar's camp
Say, *I am none of thine.*
  Ant.   What say'st thou?
  Sold.   Sir,
He is with Cæsar.
  Eros.   Sir, his chests and treasure
He has not with him.
  Ant.   Is he gone?
  Sold.   Most certain.
  Ant. Go, Eros, send his treasure after; do it;
Detain no jot, I charge thee; write to him,—
I will subscribe,—gentle adieus and greetings;
Say that I wish he never find more cause
To change a master.—O, my fortunes have
Corrupted honest men!—Eros, despatch.   [*Exeunt.*

SCENE VI.—Cæsar's *Camp before Alexandria.*

Flourish.   Enter Cæsar, *with* Agrippa, Enobarbus, *and others.*

Cæs. Go forth, Agrippa, and begin the fight:
Our will is Antony be took alive;
Make it so known.
   Agr.   Cæsar, I shall.   [*Exit.*
   Cæs. The time of universal peace is near
Prove this a prosperous day, the three-nook'd world
Shall bear the olive freely.

                Enter a Messenger.

   Mess.   Antony
Is come into the field.
   Cæs.   Go charge Agrippa
Plant those that have revolted in the van,
That Antony may seem to spend his fury
Upon himself.   [*Exeunt* Cæsar *and his* Train.
   Eno. Alexas did revolt; and went to Jewry
On affairs of Antony; there did persuade
Great Herod to incline himself to Cæsar,
And leave his master Antony: for this pains
Cæsar hath hang'd him.   Canidius, and the rest
That fell away, have entertainment, but
No honourable trust.   I have done ill;
Of which I do accuse myself so sorely
That I will joy no more.

           Enter a Soldier *of* Cæsar's.

   Sold.   Enobarbus, Antony
Hath after thee sent all thy treasure, with
His bounty overplus: the messenger
Came on my guard, and at thy tent is now
Unloading of his mules.
   Eno. I give it you.
   Sold.   Mock not, Enobarbus.
I tell you true: best you saf'd the bringer
Out of the host; I must attend mine office,
Or would have done't myself.   Your emperor
Continues still a Jove.   [*Exit.*
   Eno. I am alone the villain of the earth,
And feel I am so most.   O Antony,
Thou mine of bounty, how wouldst thou have paid
My better service, when my turpitude

Thou dost so crown with gold! This blows my heart:
If swift thought break it not, a swifter mean
Shall outstrike thought: but thought will do't, I feel.
I fight against thee!—No: I will go seek
Some ditch wherein to die; the foul'st best fits
My latter part of life. [*Exit.*

SCENE VII.—*Field of Battle between the Camps.*

Alarum. Drums and trumpets. Enter AGRIPPA *and others.*

Agr. Retire, we have engag'd ourselves too far:
Cæsar himself has work, and our oppression
Exceeds what we expected. [*Exeunt.*

Alarum. Enter ANTONY, *and* SCARUS *wounded.*

Scar. O my brave emperor, this is fought indeed!
Had we done so at first, we had driven them home
With clouts about their heads.
Ant. Thou bleed'st apace.
Scar. I had a wound here that was like a T,
But now 'tis made an H.
Ant. They do retire.
Scar. We'll beat 'em into bench-holes: I have yet
Room for six scotches more.

Enter EROS.

Eros. They are beaten, sir; and our advantage serves
For a fair victory.
Scar. Let us score their backs,
And snatch 'em up, as we take hares, behind:
'Tis sport to maul a runner.
Ant. I will reward thee
Once for thy spritely comfort, and tenfold
For thy good valour. Come thee on.
Scar. I'll halt after. [*Exeunt.*

SCENE VIII. *Under the Walls of Alexandria.*

Alarum. Enter ANTONY *marching;* SCARUS *and* Forces.

Ant. We have beat him to his camp. Run one before,
And let the queen know of our gests.—To-morrow,
Before the sun shall see us, we'll spill the blood
That has to-day escap'd. I thank you all;
For doughty-handed are you, and have fought

Not as you serv'd the cause, but as 't had been
Each man's like mine; you have shown all Hectors.
Enter the city, clip your wifes, your friends,
Tell them your feats; whilst they with joyful tears
Wash the congealment from your wounds, and kiss
The honour'd gashes whole.—Give me thy hand;

[To SCARUS.

Enter CLEOPATRA, attended.

To this great fairy I'll commend thy acts,
Make her thanks bless thee.   O thou day o' the world,
Chain mine arm'd neck; leap thou, attire and all,
Through proof of harness to my heart, and there
Ride on the pants triumphing.
 Cleo.   Lord of lords!
O infinite virtue, com'st thou smiling from
The world's great snare uncaught?
 Ant.   My nightingale,
We have beat them to their beds.   What, girl! though gray
Do something mingle with our younger brown; yet ha' we
A brain that nourishes our nerves, and can
Get goal for goal of youth.   Behold this man;
Commend unto his lips thy favouring hand;—
Kiss it, my warrior: he hath fought to-day
As if a god, in hate of mankind, had
Destroy'd in such a shape.
 Cleo.   I'll give thee, friend,
An armour all of gold; it was a king's.
 Ant. He has deserv'd it, were it carbuncled
Like holy Phœbus' car.—Give me thy hand:
Through Alexandria make a jolly march;
Bear our hack'd targets like the men that owe them:
Had our great palace the capacity
To camp this host, we all would sup together,
And drink carouses to the next day's fate,
Which promises royal peril.—Trumpeters,
With brazen din blast you the city's ear;
Make mingle with our rattling tabourines;
That heaven and earth may strike their sounds together,
Applauding our approach.   [Exeunt.

<hr>

SCENE IX.—CÆSAR's Camp.

Sentinels at their Post.

1 Sold. If we be not reliev'd within this hour,
We must return to the court of guard: the night

Is shiny; and they say we shall embattle
By the second hour i' the morn.

2 *Sold.*   This last day was
A shrewd one to 's.

Enter ENOBARBUS.

Eno.   O, bear me witness, night.—

3 *Sold.* What man is this?

2 *Sold.*   Stand close and list to him.

Eno. Be witness to me, O thou blessed moon,
When men revolted shall upon record
Bear hateful memory, poor Enobarbus did
Before thy face repent!—

1 *Sold.*   Enobarbus!

3 *Sold.*   Peace!
Hark further.

Eno. O sovereign mistress of true melancholy,
The poisonous damp of night disponge upon me,
That life, a very rebel to my will,
May hang no longer on me: throw my heart
Against the flint and hardness of my fault;
Which, being dried with grief, will break to powder,
And finish all foul thoughts. O Antony,
Nobler than my revolt is infamous,
Forgive me in thine own particular;
But let the world rank me in register
A master-leaver and a fugitive:
O Antony! O Antony!   [*Dies.*

2 *Sold.*   Let's speak
To him.

1 *Sold.* Let's hear him, for the things he speaks
May concern Cæsar.

3 *Sold.*   Let's do so.   But he sleeps.

1 *Sold.* Swoons rather; for so bad a prayer as his
Was never yet fore sleep.

2 *Sold.*   Go we to him.

3 *Sold.* Awake, sir, awake; speak to us.

2 *Sold.*   Hear you, sir?

1 *Sold.* The hand of death hath raught him. [*Drums afar
off.*] Hark! the drums
Do merrily wake the sleepers.   Let us bear him
To the court of guard; he is of note: our hour
Is fully out.

3 *Sold.*   Come on, then;
He may recover yet.   [*Exeunt with the body.*

SCENE X.—*Ground between the two Camps.*

Enter ANTONY *and* SCARUS, *with* Forces, *marching.*

Ant. Their preparation is to-day by sea;
We please them not by land.
    Scar.   For both, my lord.
    Ant. I would they 'd fight i' the fire or i' the air;
We 'd fight there too.   But this it is; our foot
Upon the hills adjoining to the city
Shall stay with us:—order for sea is given;
They have put forth the haven:—forward now,
Where their appointment we may best discover,
And look on their endeavour.   [*Exeunt.*

SCENE XI.—*Another part of the Ground.*

Enter CÆSAR, *with his* Forces, *marching.*

Cæs. But being charg'd, we will be still by land,
Which, as I take't, we shall; for his best force
Is forth to man his galleys.   To the vales,
And hold our best advantage.   [*Exeunt.*

SCENE XII.—*Another part of the Ground.*

Enter ANTONY *and* SCARUS.

Ant. Yet they're not join'd: where yond pine does stand
I shall discover all: I'll bring thee word
Straight how 'tis like to go.   [*Exeunt.*
    Scar.   Swallows have built
In Cleopatra's sails their nests: the augurers
Say they know not,—they cannot tell;—look grimly,
And dare not speak their knowledge.   Antony
Is valiant and dejected; and, by starts,
His fretted fortunes give him hope and fear
Of what he has and has not.
            [*Alarum afar off, as at a sea-fight.*

Re-enter ANTONY.

    Ant.   All is lost;
This foul Egyptian hath betrayed me:
My fleet hath yielded to the foe; and yonder
They cast their caps up, and carouse together
Like friends long lost.—Triple-turn'd whore! 'tis thou

VOL. V.   U

Hast sold me to this novice; and my heart
Makes only wars on thee.—Bid them all fly;
For when I am reveng'd upon my charm,
I have done all.—Bid them all fly; begone.   [*Exit* SCARUS.
O sun, thy uprise shall I see no more:
Fortune and Antony part here; even here
Do we shake hands.—All come to this!—The hearts
That spaniel'd me at heels, to whom I gave
Their wishes, do discandy, melt their sweets
On blossoming Cæsar; and this pine is bark'd
That overtopp'd them all.   Betray'd I am:
O this false soul of Egypt! this grave charm,
Whose eye beck'd forth my wars and call'd them home;
Whose bosom was my crownet, my chief end,—
Like a right gipsy, hath, at fast and loose,
Beguil'd me to the very heart of loss.—
What, Eros, Eros!

Enter CLEOPATRA.

                Ah, thou spell! Avaunt!
Cleo. Why is my lord enrag'd against his love?
Ant. Vanish; or I shall give thee thy deserving,
And blemish Cæsar's triumph.   Let him take thee,
And hoist thee up to the shouting plebeians:
Follow his chariot, like the greatest spot
Of all thy sex; most monster-like, be shown
For poor'st diminutives, for doits; and let
Patient Octavia plough thy visage up
With her prepared nails. [*Exit* CLEOPATRA.] 'Tis well thou'rt
        gone,
If it be well to live; but better 'twere
Thou fell'st into my fury, for one death
Might have prevented many.—Eros, ho!—
The shirt of Nessus is upon me: teach me,
Alcides, thou mine ancestor, thy rage:
Let me lodge Lichas on the horns o' the moon;
And with those hands, that grasp'd the heaviest club,
Subdue my worthiest self.   The witch shall die:
To the young Roman boy she hath sold me, and I fall
Under this plot: she dies for 't.—Eros, ho!   [*Exit.*

SCENE XIII.—ALEXANDRIA.   *A Room in the Palace.*

Enter CLEOPATRA, CHARMIAN, IRAS, *and* MARDIAN.

Cleo. Help me, my women! O, he is more mad

Than Telamon for his shield; the boar of Thessaly
Was never so emboss'd.
 Char.   To the monument!
There lock yourself, and send him word you are dead.
The soul and body rive not more in parting
Than greatness going off.
 Cleo.   To the monument!—
Mardian, go tell him I have slain myself;
Say that the last I spoke was *Antony*,
And word it, pr'ythee, piteously: hence, Mardian;
And bring me how he takes my death.—
To the monument!   [*Exeunt.*

SCENE XIV.—ALEXANDRIA. *Another Room.*

Enter ANTONY *and* EROS.

 Ant. Eros, thou yet behold'st me?
 Eros.   Ay, noble lord.
 Ant. Sometime we see a cloud that's dragonish;
A vapour sometime like a bear or lion,
A tower'd citadel, a pendant rock,
A forked mountain, or blue promontory
With trees upon't, that nod unto the world,
And mock our eyes with air: thou hast seen these signs;
They are black vesper's pageants.
 Eros.   Ay, my lord.
 Ant. That which is now a horse, even with a thought
The rack dislimns; and makes it indistinct,
As water is in water.
 Eros.   It does, my lord.
 Ant. My good knave Eros, now thy captain is
Even such a body: here I am Antony;
Yet cannot hold this visible shape, my knave.
I made these wars for Egypt; and the queen,—
Whose heart I thought I had, for she had mine;
Which, whilst it was mine, had annex'd unto't
A million more now lost,—she, Eros, has
Pack'd cards with Cæsar, and false-play'd my glory
Unto an enemy's triumph.—
Nay, weep not, gentle Eros; there is left us
Ourselves to end ourselves.—

Enter MARDIAN.
     O, thy **vile lady!**
She **has robb'd me of my sword.**

Mar.   No, Antony;
My mistress lov'd thee, and her fortunes mingled
With thine entirely.
    Ant.   Hence, saucy eunuch; peace!
She hath betray'd me, and shall die the death.
    Mar. Death of one person can be paid but once,
And that she has discharg'd: what thou wouldst do
Is done unto thy hand: the last she spake
Was, *Antony! most noble Antony!*
Then in the midst a tearing groan did break
The name of Antony; it was divided
Between her heart and lips: she render'd life,
Thy name so buried in her.
    Ant.   Dead, then?
    Mar.   Dead.
    Ant. Unarm, Eros; the long day's task is done,
And we must sleep.—That thou depart'st hence safe
Does pay thy labour richly; go.   [*Exit* MARDIAN.
                     Off, pluck off;—
The sevenfold shield of Ajax cannot keep
The battery from my heart.   O, cleave, my sides!
Heart, once be stronger than thy continent,
Crack thy frail case!—Apace, Eros, apace.—
No more a soldier.—Bruised pieces, go;
You have been nobly borne.—From me awhile.—
                                [*Exit* EROS.
I will o'ertake thee, Cleopatra, and
Weep for my pardon.   So it must be, for now
All length is torture.—Since the torch is out,
Lie down, and stray no further: now all labour
Mars what it does; yea, very force entangles
Itself with strength: seal then, and all is done.—
Eros!—I come, my queen.—Eros!—Stay for me:
Where souls do couch on flowers, we'll hand in hand,
And with our sprightly port make the ghosts gaze:
Dido and her Æneas shall want troops,
And all the haunt be ours.—Come, Eros, Eros!

                  Re-enter EROS.

    Eros. What would my lord?
    Ant.   Since Cleopatra died,
I have liv'd in such dishonour that the gods
Detest my baseness.   I, that with my sword
Quarter'd the world, and o'er green Neptune's back
With ships made cities, condemn myself to lack
The courage of a woman; less noble mind

Than she which by her death our Cæsar tells,
I am conqueror of myself. Thou art sworn, Eros,
That, when the exigent should come,—which now
Is come, indeed—when I should see behind me　　·
The inevitable prosecution of
Disgrace and horror, that, on my command,
Thou then wouldst kill me: do't; the time is come:
Thou strik'st not me, 'tis Cæsar thou defeat'st.
Put colour in thy cheek.
  Eros.   The gods withhold me!
Shall I do that which all the Parthian darts,
Though enemy, lost aim, and could not?
  Ant.   Eros,
Wouldst thou be window'd in great Rome, and see
Thy master thus with pleach'd arms, bending down
His corrigible neck, his face subdu'd
To penetrative shame; whilst the wheel'd seat
Of fortunate Cæsar, drawn before him, branded
His baseness that ensu'd?
  Eros.   I would not see't.
  Ant. Come, then; for with a wound I must be cur'd.
Draw that thy honest sword, which thou hast worn
Most useful for thy country.
  Eros.   O, sir, pardon me!
  Ant. When I did make thee free, swor'st thou not then
To do this when I bade thee? Do it at once;
Or thy precedent services are all
But accidents unpurpos'd. Draw, and come.
  Eros. Turn from me then that noble countenance,
Wherein the worship of the whole world lies.
  Ant. Lo thee!   [*Turning from him.*
  Eros. My sword is drawn.
  Ant.   Then let it do at once
The thing why thou hast drawn it.
  Eros.   My dear master,
My captain and my emperor, let me say,
Before I strike this bloody stroke, farewell.
  Ant. 'Tis said, man;—and farewell.
  Eros. Farewell, great chief. Shall I strike now?
  Ant.   Now, Eros.
  Eros. Why, there then [*falls on his sword*]:—thus do ·
  escape the sorrow
Of Antony's death.   [*Dies*
  Ant.   Thrice nobler than myself!
Thou teachest me, O valiant Eros, what
I should, and thou couldst not. My queen and Eros

Have, by their brave instruction, got upon me
A nobleness on record : but I will be
A bridegroom in my death, and run into't
As to a lover's bed.   Come, then; and, Eros,
Thy master dies thy scholar: to do thus
                                   [*Falling on his sword.*
I learn'd of thee.   How! not dead? not dead?—
The guard, ho!—O, despatch me!

Enter DERCETAS *and* Guard.

1 *Guard.*   What's the noise?
Ant. I have done my work ill, friends : O, make an
          end
Of what I have begun.
  2 *Guard.*   The star is fallen.
  1 *Guard.* And time is at his period.
  All.   Alas, and woe!
  Ant. Let him that loves me strike me dead.
  1 *Guard.*   Not I.
  2 *Guard.* Nor I.
  3 *Guard.* Nor any one.   [*Exeunt* Guard.
  Der. Thy death and fortunes bid thy followers fly.
This sword but shown to Cæsar, with this tidings,
Shall enter me with him.

Enter DIOMEDES.

  Dio. Where's Antony?
  Der.   There, Diomed, there.
  Dio.   Lives he?
Wilt thou not answer, man?   [*Exit* DERCETAS.
  Ant. Art thou there, Diomed? Draw thy sword, and
          give me
Sufficing strokes for death.
  Dio.   Most absolute lord,
My mistress Cleopatra sent me to thee.
  Ant. When did she send thee?
  Dio.   Now, my lord.
  Ant.   Where is she?
  Dio. Lock'd in her monument.   She had a prophesying
Of what hath come to pass: for when she saw,—   [fear
Which never shall be found,—you did suspect
She had dispos'd with Cæsar, and that your rage
Would not be purg'd, she sent you word she was dead;
But, fearing since how it might work, hath sent
Me to proclaim the truth; and I am come,
I dread, too late.

Ant. Too late, good Diomed.—Call my guard, I pr'ythee.
Dio. What, ho! the emperor's guard!   The guard,
    what, ho!
Come, your lord calls!

Enter some of the Guard.

Ant. Bear me, good friends, where Cleopatra bides;
'Tis the last service that I shall command you.
1 *Guard.* Woe, woe are we, sir, you may not live to wear
All your true followers out.
All.   Most heavy day!
Ant. Nay, good my fellows, do not please sharp fate
To grace it with your sorrows: bid that welcome
Which comes to punish us, and we punish it,
Seeming to bear it lightly.   Take me up:
I have led you oft: carry me now, good friends,
And have my thanks for all.   [*Exeunt, bearing* ANTONY.

SCENE XV.—ALEXANDRIA. *A Monument.*

Enter, above, CLEOPATRA, CHARMIAN, *and* IRAS.

Cleo. O Charmian, I will never go from hence.
Char. Be comforted, dear madam.
Cleo.   No, I will not:
All strange and terrible events are welcome,
But comforts we despise; our size of sorrow,
Proportion'd to our cause, must be as great
As that which makes it.—

Enter, below, DIOMEDES.

                              How now! is he dead?
Dio. His death's upon him, but not dead.
Look out o' the other side your monument;
His guard have brought him thither.

Enter, below, ANTONY, *borne by the* Guard.

Cleo.   O sun,
Burn the great sphere thou mov'st in!—darkling stand
The varying shore o' the world.—O Antony,
Antony, Antony!—Help, Charmian; help, Iras, help,—
Help, friends below;—let's draw him hither.
Ant.   Peace!
Not Cæsar's valour hath o'erthrown Antony,
But Antony's hath triumph'd on itself.

Cleo. So it should be, that none but Antony
Should conquer Antony; but woe 'tis so

Ant. I am dying, Egypt, dying; only
I here impórtune death awhile, until
Of many thousand kisses the poor last
I lay upon thy lips.

   Cleo.   I dare not, dear,—
Dear my lord, pardon,—I dare not,
Lest I be taken: not the imperious show
Of the full-fortun'd Cæsar ever shall
Be brooch'd with me; if knife, drugs, serpents have
Edge, sting, or operation, I am safe;
Your wife Octavia, with her modest eyes
And still conclusion, shall acquire no honour
Demuring upon me.—But come, come, Antony,—
Help me, my women,—we must draw thee up;—
Assist, good friends.

   Ant.   O, quick, or I am gone.

   Cleo. Here's sport indeed!—How heavy weighs my
Our strength is all gone into heaviness,   [lord!
That makes the weight: had I great Juno's power,
The strong-wing'd Mercury should fetch thee up,
And set thee by Jove's side. Yet come a little,—
Wishers were ever fools,—O, come, come, come;
                  [*They draw* ANTONY *up.*
And welcome, welcome! die where thou hast liv'd:
Quicken with kissing: had my lips that power,
Thus would I wear them out.

   All.   A heavy sight!

   Ant. I am dying, Egypt, dying:
Give me some wine, and let me speak a little.

   Cleo. No, let me speak; and let me rail so high
That the false housewife Fortune break her wheel,
Provok'd by my offence.

   Ant.   One word, sweet queen:
Of Cæsar seek your honour, with your safety.—O!

   Cleo. They do not go together.

   Ant.   Gentle, hear me:
None about Cæsar trust but Proculeius.

   Cleo. My resolution and my hands I'll trust;
None about Cæsar.

   Ant. The miserable change now at my end
Lament nor sorrow at: but please your thoughts
In feeding them with those my former fortunes
Wherein I liv'd, the greatest prince o' the world,
The noblest; and do now not basely die,

Not cowardly put off my helmet to
My countryman, a Roman by a Roman
Valiantly vanquish'd.   Now my spirit is going:
I can no more.
  Cleo.   Noblest of men, woo't die?
Hast thou no care of me? shall I abide
In this dull world, which in thy absence is
No better than a sty?—O, see, my women,   [ANTONY *dies.*
The crown o' the earth doth melt.—My lord!—
O, wither'd is the garland of the war,
The soldier's pole is fallen: young boys and girls
Are level now with men: the odds is gone,
And there is nothing left remarkable
Beneath the visiting moon.   [*Faints.*
  Char.   O, quietness, lady!
  Iras. She is dead too, our sovereign.
  Char.   Lady,—
  Iras.   Madam,—
  Char. O madam, madam, madam,—
  Iras.   Royal Egypt,
Empress,—
  Char. Peace, peace, Iras!
  Cleo. No more, but e'en a woman, and commanded
By such poor passion as the maid that milks
And does the meanest chares.—It were for me
To throw my sceptre at the injurious gods;
To tell them that this world did equal theirs
Till they had stol'n our jewel.   All's but naught;
Patience is sottish, and impatience does
Become a dog that's mad: then is it sin
To rush into the secret house of death
Ere death dare come to us?—How do you, women?
What, what! good cheer!   Why, how now, Charmian!
My noble girls!—Ah, women, women, look,
Our lamp is spent, it's out!—Good sirs, take heart:—
We'll bury him; and then, what's brave, what's noble,
Let's do it after the high Roman fashion,
And make death proud to take us   Come, away:
This case of that huge spirit now is cold:
Ah, women, women!—Come; we have no friend
But resolution, and the briefest end.
    [*Exeunt; those above bearing off* ANTONY'S *body.*

ACT V.

SCENE I.—Cæsar's *Camp before Alexandria.*

Enter Cæsar, Agrippa, Dolabella, Mecænas, Gallus,
Proculeius, *and others.*

Cæs. Go to him, Dolabella, bid him yield;
Being so frustrate, tell him that he mocks
The pauses that he makes.

  Dol.   Cæsar, I shall.   [*Exit.*

Enter Dercetas *with the sword of* Antony.

  Cæs. Wherefore is that? and what art thou that dar'st
Appear thus to us?

  Der.   I am call'd Dercetas;
Mark Antony I serv'd, who best was worthy
Best to be serv'd: whilst he stood up and spoke,
He was my master; and I wore my life
To spend upon his haters. If thou please
To take me to thee, as I was to him
I'll be to Cæsar; if thou pleasest not,
I yield thee up my life.

  Cæs.   What is't thou say'st?

  Der. I say, O Cæsar, Antony is dead.

  Cæs. The breaking of so great a thing should make
A greater crack: the round world
Should have shook lions into civil streets,
And citizens to their dens. The death of Antony
Is not a single doom; in the name lay
A moiety of the world.

  Der.   He is dead, Cæsar;
Not by a public minister of justice,
Nor by a hired knife; but that self hand
Which writ his honour in the acts it did
Hath, with the courage which the heart did lend it,
Splitted the heart.—This is his sword;
I robb'd his wound of it; behold it stain'd
With his most noble blood.

  Cæs.   Look you sad, friends?
The gods rebuke me, but it is tidings
To wash the eyes of kings.

  Agr.   And strange it is
That nature must compel us to lament
Our most persisted deeds.

Mec.   His taints and honours
Weigh'd equal with him.
Agr.   A rarer spirit never
Did steer humanity: but you, gods, will give us
Some faults to make us men.   Cæsar is touch'd.
Mec. When such a spacious mirror's set before him,
He needs must see himself.
Cæs.   O Antony!
I have follow'd thee to this.—But we do lance
Diseases in our bodies: I must perforce
Have shown to thee such a declining day
Or look on thine; we could not stall together
In the whole world: but yet let me lament,
With tears as sovereign as the blood of hearts,
That thou, my brother, my competitor
In top of all design, my mate in empire,
Friend and companion in the front of war,
The arm of mine own body, and the heart
Where mine his thoughts did kindle,—that our stars,
Unreconciliable, should divide
Our equalness to this.—Hear me, good friends,—
But I will tell you at some meeter season:

Enter a Messenger.

The business of this man looks out of him;
We'll hear him what he says.—Whence are you?
Mess. A poor Egyptian yet.   The queen my mistress,
Confin'd in all she has, her monument,
Of thy intents desires instruction,
That she preparedly may frame herself
To the way she's forc'd to.
Cæs.   Bid her have good heart:
She soon shall know of us, by some of ours,
How honourable and how kindly we
Determine for her; for Cæsar cannot learn
To be ungentle.
Mess.   So the gods preserve thee!   [*Exit*
Cæs. Come hither, Proculeius.   Go, and say
We purpose her no shame: give her what comforts
The quality of her passion shall require,
Lest, in her greatness, by some mortal stroke
She do defeat us; for her life in Rome
Would be eternal in our triumph: go,
And with your speediest bring us what she says,
And how you find of her.
Pro.   Cæsar, I shall.   [*Exit*

Cæs. Gallus, go you along.—[*Exit* GALLUS.] Where's
     Dolabella,
To second Proculeius?
    Agr. and Mec.   Dolabella!
    Cæs. Let him alone, for I remember now
How he's employ'd: he shall in time be ready.
Go with me to my tent; where you shall see
How hardly I was drawn into this war;
How calm and gentle I proceeded still
In all my writings: go with me, and see
What I can show in this.   [*Exeunt.*

SCENE II.—ALEXANDRIA.   *A Room in the Monument.*

Enter CLEOPATRA, CHARMIAN, *and* IRAS.

    Cleo. My desolation does begin to make
A better life. 'Tis paltry to be Cæsar;
Not being Fortune, he's but Fortune's knave,
A minister of her will: and it is great
To do that thing that ends all other deeds;
Which shackles accidents and bolts up change;
Which sleeps, and never palates more the dug,
The beggar's nurse and Cæsar's.

Enter, to the gates of the Monument, PROCULEIUS, GALLUS,
               and Soldiers.

    Pro. Cæsar sends greeting to the Queen of Egypt;
And bids thee study on what fair demands
Thou mean'st to have him grant thee.
    Cleo.   What's thy name?
    Pro. My name is Proculeius.
    Cleo.   Antony
Did tell me of you, bade me trust you; but
I do not greatly care to be deceiv'd,
That have no use for trusting. If your master
Would have a queen his beggar, you must tell him
That majesty, to keep decorum, must
No less beg than a kingdom: if he please
To give me conquer'd Egypt for my son,
He gives me so much of mine own as I
Will kneel to him with thanks.
    Pro.   Be of good cheer;
You are fallen into a princely hand, fear nothing:
Make your full reference freely to my lord,
Who is so full of grace that it flows over

On all that need: let me report to him
Your sweet dependency; and you shall find
A conqueror that will pray in aid for kindness
Where he for grace is kneel'd to.
 Cleo.   Pray you, tell him
I am his fortune's vassal, and I send him
The greatness he has got.   I hourly learn
A doctrine of obedience; and would gladly
Look him i' the face.
 Pro.   This I'll report, dear lady.
Have comfort, for I know your plight is pitied
Of him that caus'd it.
 Gal. You see how easily she may be surpris'd:
    [*Here* PROCULEIUS *and two of the* Guard *ascend the
    Monument by a ladder placed against a window,
    and, having descended, come behind* CLEOPATRA.
    Some of the* Guard *unbar and open the gates.*
Guard her till Cæsar come. [*To* PRO. *and the* Guard. *Exit.*
 Iras. Royal queen!
 Char. O Cleopatra! thou art taken, queen!
 Cleo. Quick, quick, good hands. [*Drawing a dagger.*
 Pro.   Hold, worthy lady, hold:
       [*Seizes and disarms her.*
Do not yourself such wrong, who are in this
Reliev'd, but not betray'd.
 Cleo.   What, of death too,
That rids our dogs of languish?
 Pro.   Cleopatra,
Do not abuse my master's bounty by
The undoing of yourself: let the world see
His nobleness well acted, which your death
Will never let come forth.
 Cleo.   Where art thou, death?
Come hither, come! come, come, and take a queen
Worth many babes and beggars!
 Pro.   O, temperance, lady!
 Cleo. Sir, I will eat no meat, I'll not drink, sir;
If idle talk will once be accessary,
I'll not sleep neither: this mortal house I'll ruin,
Do Cæsar what he can.   Know, sir, that I
Will not wait pinion'd at your master's court;
Nor once be chástis d with the sober eye
Of dull Octavia.   Shall they hoist me up,
And show me to the shouting varletry
Of censuring Rome?   Rather a ditch in Egypt
Be gentle grave unto me! rather on Nilus' mud

Lay me stark nak'd, and let the water-flies
Blow me into abhorring! rather make
My country's high pyramides my gibbet,
And hang me up in chains!

Pro.   You do extend
These thoughts of horror further than you shall
Find cause in Cæsar.

Enter DOLABELLA.

Dol.   Proculeius,
What thou hast done thy master Cæsar knows,
And he hath sent for thee: as for the queen,
I'll take her to my guard.

Pro.   So, Dolabella,
It shall content me best: be gentle to her.—
To Cæsar I will speak what you shall please,
                                   [*To* CLEOPATRA.
If you'll employ me to him.

Cleo.   Say I would die.
                    [*Exeunt* PROCULEIUS *and* Soldiers.
Dol. Most noble empress, you have heard of me?
Cleo. I cannot tell.
Dol.   Assuredly you know me.
Cleo. No matter, sir, what I have heard or known.
You laugh when boys or women tell their dreams;
Is't not your trick?
Dol.   I understand not, madam.
Cleo. I dream'd there was an emperor Antony:—
O, such another sleep, that I might see
But such another man!
Dol.   If it might please you,—
Cleo. His face was as the heavens; and therein stuck
A sun and moon, which kept their course, and lighted
The little O, the earth.
Dol.   Most sovereign creature,—
Cleo. His legs bestrid the ocean: his rear'd arm
Crested the world: his voice was propertied
As all the tuned spheres, and that to friends;
But when he meant to quail and shake the orb,
He was as rattling thunder.   For his bounty,
There was no winter in't; an autumn 'twas
That grew the more by reaping: his delights
Were dolpin-like; they show'd his back above
The element they liv'd in: in his livery
Walk'd crowns and crownets; realms and islands were
As plates dropp'd from his pocket.

Dol.   Cleopatra,—
Cleo. Think you there was or might be such a man
As this I dream'd of?
Dol.   Gentle madam, no.
Cleo. You lie, up to the hearing of the gods.
But if there be, or ever were, one such,
It's past the size of dreaming: nature wants stuff
To vie strange forms with fancy: yet to imagine
An Antony were nature's piece 'gainst fancy,
Condemning shadows quite.
Dol.   Hear me, good madam.
Your loss is, as yourself, great; and you bear it
As answering to the weight: would I might never
O'ertake pursu'd success, but I do feel,
By the rebound of yours, a grief that smites
My very heart at root.
Cleo.   I thank you, sir.
Know you what Cæsar means to do with me?
Dol. I am loth to tell you what I would you knew.
Cleo. Nay, pray you, sir,—
Dol.   Though he be honourable,—
Cleo. He'll lead me, then, in triumph?
Dol.   Madam, he will;
I know it.   [*Flourish within.*
Within. Make way there,—Cæsar!

Enter CÆSAR, GALLUS, PROCULEIUS, MECÆNAS, SELEUCUS,
      and Attendants.

Cæs. Which is the Queen of Egypt?
Dol. It is the emperor, madam.   [CLEOPATRA *kneels.*
Cæs. Arise, you shall not kneel:—
I pray you rise; rise, Egypt.
Cleo.   Sir, the gods
Will have it thus; my master and my lord
I must obey.
Cæs.   Take to you no hard thoughts:
The record of what injuries you did us,
Though written in our flesh, we shall remember
As things but done by chance.
Cleo.   Sole sir o' the world,
I cannot project mine own cause so well
To make it clear: but do confess I have
Been laden with like frailties which before
Have often sham'd our sex.
Cæs.   Cleopatra, know
We will extenuate rather than enforce:

If you apply yourself to our intents,—
Which towards you are most gentle,—you shall find
A benefit in this change; but if you seek
To lay on me a cruelty, by taking
Antony's course, you shall bereave yourself
Of my good purposes, and put your children
To that destruction which I'll guard them from,
If thereon you rely.   I'll take my leave.

Cleo. And may, through all the world: 'tis yours; and we,
Your scutcheons and your signs of conquest, shall
Hang in what place you please.   Here, my good lord.

Cæs. You shall advise me in all for Cleopatra.

Cleo. This is the brief of money, plate, and jewels
I am possess'd of: 'tis exactly valued;
Not petty things admitted.—Where 's Seleucus?

Sel. Here, madam.

Cleo. This is my treasurer: let him speak, my lord,
Upon his peril, that I have reserv'd
To myself nothing.   Speak the truth, Seleucus.

Sel. Madam,
I had rather seal my lips than to my peril
Speak that which is not.

Cleo.   What have I kept back?

Sel. Enough to purchase what you have made known.

Cæs. Nay, blush not, Cleopatra; I approve
Your wisdom in the deed.

Cleo.   See, Cæsar! O, behold,
How pomp is follow'd! mine will now be yours;
And, should we shift estates, yours would be mine.
The ingratitude of this Seleucus does
Even make me wild: O slave, of no more trust
Than love that 's hir'd!—What, goest thou back? thou shalt
Go back, I warrant thee; but I'll catch thine eyes
Though they had wings; slave, soulless villain, dog!
O rarely base!

Cæs.   Good queen, let us entreat you.

Cleo. O Cæsar, what a wounding shame is this,—
That thou, vouchsafing here to visit me,
Doing the honour of thy lordliness
To one so meek, that mine own servant should
Parcel the sum of my disgraces by
Addition of his envy!   Say, good Cæsar,
That I some lady trifles have reserv'd,
Immoment toys, things of such dignity
As we greet modern friends withal; and say,
Some nobler token I have kept apart

For Livia and Octavia, to induce
Their mediation; must I be unfolded
With one that I have bred? The gods! It smites me
Beneath the fall I have.   Pr'ythee, go hence;

[To SELEUCUS.

Or I shall show the cinders of my spirits
Through the ashes of my chance.—Wert thou a man,
Thou wouldst have mercy on me.
  Cæs.   Forbear, Seleucus.

[Exit SELEUCUS.

 Cleo. Be it known that we, the greatest, are misthought
For things that others do; and when we fall
We answer others' merits in our name,
And therefore to be pitied.
  Cæs.   Cleopatra,
Not what you have reserv'd, nor what acknowledg'd,
Put we i' the roll of conquest: still be't yours,
Bestow it at your pleasure; and believe
Cæsar 's no merchant, to make prize with you
Of things that merchants sold.   Therefore be cheer'd;
Make not your thoughts your prisons: no, dear queen;
For we intend so to dispose you as
Yourself shall give us counsel.   Feed and sleep:
Our care and pity is so much upon you
That we remain your friend; and so, adieu.
 Cleo. My master and my lord!
  Cæs.   Not so.   Adieu.

[Flourish.   Exeunt CÆSAR and his Train.

 Cleo. He words me, girls, he words me, that I should not
Be noble to myself: but hark thee, Charmian!

[Whispers CHARMIAN.

 Iras. Finish, good lady; the bright day is done,
And we are for the dark.
  Cleo.   Hie thee again:
I have spoke already, and it is provided;
Go put it to the haste.
  Char.   Madam, I will.

Re-enter DOLABELLA.

 Dol. Where is the queen?
  Char.   Behold, sir.   [<i>Exit</i>
  Cleo.   Dolabella!
 Dol. Madam, as thereto sworn by your command,
Which my love makes religion to obey,
I tell you this: Cæsar through Syria
Intends his journey; and within three days

You with your children will he send before:
Make your best use of this: I have perform'd
Your pleasure and my promise.
 Cleo.   Dolabella,
I shall remain your debtor.
 Dol.   I your servant.
Adieu, good queen; I must attend on Cæsar.
 Cleo. Farewell, and thanks.   [*Exit* DOLABELLA.
Now, Iras, what think'st thou?
Thou, an Egyptian puppet, shalt be shown
In Rome as well as I: mechanic slaves,
With greasy aprons, rules, and hammers, shall
Uplift us to the view; in their thick breaths,
Rank of gross diet, shall we be enclouded,
And forc'd to drink their vapour.
 Iras.   The gods forbid!
 Cleo. Nay, 'tis most certain, Iras :—saucy lictors
Will catch at us like strumpets; and scald rhymers
Ballad us out o' tune: the quick comedians
Extemporally will stage us, and present
Our Alexandrian revels; Antony
Shall be brought drunken forth, and I shall see
Some squeaking Cleopatra boy my greatness
I' the posture of a whore.
 Iras.   O the good gods!
 Cleo. Nay, that's certain.
 Iras. I'll never see't; for I am sure my nails
Are stronger than mine eyes.
 Cleo.   Why, that's the way
To fool their preparation and to conquer
Their most absurd intents.

Enter CHARMIAN.

      Now, Charmian!—
Show me, my women, like a queen.—Go fetch
My best attires;—I am again for Cydnus,
To meet Mark Antony :—sirrah, Iras, go.—
Now, noble Charmian, we'll despatch indeed;
And when thou hast done this chare, I'll give thee leave
To play till doomsday —Bring our crown and all.
Wherefore's this noise? [*Exit* IRAS. *A noise within*

Enter one of the Guard.

 Guard.   Here is a rural fellow
That will not be denied your highness' presence:
He brings you figs.

Cleo. Let him come in.   [*Exit* Guard.
What poor an instrument
May do a noble deed! he brings me liberty.
My resolution 's plac'd, and I have nothing
Of woman in me: now from head to foot
I am marble-constant; now the fleeting moon
No planet is of mine.

  Re-enter Guard, *with* Clown *bringing a basket.*

Guard.   This is the man.   .
Cleo. Avoid, and leave him.   [*Exit* Guard.
Hast thou the pretty worm of Nilus there
That kills and pains not?

Clown. Truly, I have him: but I would not be the party
that should desire you to touch him, for his biting is immortal; those that do die of it do seldom or never recover.

Cleo. Remember'st thou any that have died on't?

Clown. Very many, men and women too.   I heard of one
of them no longer than yesterday: a very honest woman,
but something given to lie; as a woman should not do but
in the way of honesty: how she died of the biting of it,
what pain she felt,—truly she makes a very good report o'
the worm; but he that will believe all that they say shall
never be saved by half that they do: but this is most fallible,
the worm 's an odd worm.

Cleo. Get thee hence; farewell.

Clown. I wish you all joy of the worm.
        [*Sets down the basket.*

Cleo. Farewell.

Clown. You must think this, look you, that the worm
will do his kind.

Cleo. Ay, ay; farewell.

Clown. Look you, the worm is not to be trusted but in
the keeping of wise people; for indeed there is no goodness in the worm.

Cleo. Take thou no care; it shall be heeded.

Clown. Very good.   Give it nothing, I pray you, for it is
not worth the feeding.

Cleo. Will it eat me?

Clown. You must not think I am so simple but I know
the devil himself will not eat a woman: I know that a
woman is a dish for the gods, if the devil dress her not.
But, truly, these same whoreson devils do the gods great
harm in their women, for in every ten that they make the
devils mar five.

Cleo. Well, get thee gone; farewell.

Clown. Yes, forsooth: I wish you joy o' the worm. [*Exit.*

Re-enter IRAS, with a robe, crown, &c.

Cleo. Give me my robe, put on my crown; I have
Immortal longings in me: now no more
The juice of Egypt's grape shall moist this lip:—
Yare, yare, good Iras; quick.—Methinks I hear
Antony call; I see him rouse himself
To praise my noble act; I hear him mock
The luck of Cæsar, which the gods give men
To excuse their after wrath. Husband, I come:
Now to that name my courage prove my title!
I am fire and air; my other elements
I give to baser life.—So,—have you done?
Come then, and take the last warmth of my lips.
Farewell, kind Charmian;—Iras, long farewell.
[Kisses them. IRAS falls and dies.
Have I the aspic in my lips? Dost fall?
If thou and nature can so gently part,
The stroke of death is as a lover's pinch,
Which hurts and is desir'd. Dost thou lie still?
If thus thou vanishest, thou tell'st the world
It is not worth leave-taking.

Char. Dissolve, thick cloud, and rain; that I may say
The gods themselves do weep!

Cleo.   This proves me base: ·
If she first meet the curled Antony,
He'll make demand of her, and spend that kiss
Which is my heaven to have.—Come, thou mortal wretch,
[To an asp, which she applies to her breast.
With thy sharp teeth this knot intrinsicate
Of life at once untie: poor venomous fool,
Be angry, and despatch. O couldst thou speak,
That I might hear thee call great Cæsar ass
Unpolicied!

Char.   O eastern star!

Cleo.   Peace, peace!
Dost thou not see my baby at my breast
That sucks the nurse asleep?

Char.   O, break! O, break!

Cleo. As sweet as balm, as soft as air, as gentle:—
O Antony!—Nay, I will take thee too:—
[Applying another asp to her arm.
What, should I stay,—   [Falls on a bed and dies.

Char. In this vile world?—So, fare thee well.—
Now boast thee, death, in thy possession lies

A lass unparallel'd.—Downy windows, close;
And golden Phœbus never be beheld
Of eyes again so royal!   Your crown 's awry;
I'll mend it and then play.

Enter the Guard, *rushing in.*

1 *Guard.* Where is the queen?
Char.   Speak softly, wake her not.
1 *Guard.* Cæsar hath sent,—
Char.   Too slow a messenger.
                               [*Applies an asp.*
O, come apace, despatch: I partly feel thee.
   1 *Guard.* Approach, ho! all 's not well: Cæsar's beguil'd.
   2 *Guard.* There 's Dolabella sent from Cæsar; call him.
   1 *Guard.* What work is here!—Charmian, is this well
        done?
Char. It is well done, and fitting for a princess
Descended of so many royal kings.
Ah, soldier!   [*Dies.*

Re-enter DOLABELLA.

Dol. How goes it here?
2 *Guard.*   All dead.
Dol.   Cæsar, thy thoughts
Touch their effects in this: thyself art coming
To see perform'd the dreaded act which thou
So sought'st to hinder.
Within.   A way there, a way for Cæsar!

Re-enter CÆSAR *and his* Train.

Dol. O, sir, you are too sure an augurer;
That you did fear is done.
Cæs.   Bravest at the last,
She levell'd at our purposes, and, being royal,
Took her own way.—The manner of their deaths?
I do not see them bleed.
Dol.   Who was last with them?
   1 *Guard.* A simple countryman that brought her figs.
This was his basket.
Cæs.   Poison'd then.
   1 *Guard.*   O Cæsar,
This Charmian liv'd but now; she stood and spake:
I found her trimming up the diadem
On her dead mistress; tremblingly she stood,
And on the sudden dropp'd.
Cæs.   O noble weakness!—

If they had swallow'd poison 'twould appear
By external swelling: but she looks like sleep,--
As she would catch another Antony
In her strong toil of grace.

Dol.   Here on her breast
There is a vent of blood, and something blown:
The like is on her arm.

1 *Guard.* This is an aspic's trail: and these fig-leaves
Have slime upon them, such as the aspic leaves
Upon the caves of Nile.

Cæs.   Most probable
That so she died; for her physician tells me
She hath pursu'd conclusions infinite
Of easy ways to die.—Take up her bed,
And bear her women from the monument:—
She shall be buried by her Antony:
No grave upon the earth shall clip in it
A pair so famous. High events as these
Strike those that make them; and their story is
No less in pity than his glory which
Brought them to be lamented. Our army shall
In solemn show attend this funeral;
And then to Rome.—Come, Dolabella, see
High order in this great solemnity.   [*Exeunt.*

CYMBELINE

PERSONS REPRESENTED.

CYMBELINE, *King of Britain.*

CLOTEN, *Son to the Queen by a former Husband.*

POSTHUMUS LEONATUS, *a Gentleman, Husband to* IMOGEN.

BELARIUS, *a banished Lord, disguised under the name of* MORGAN.

GUIDERIUS, } *Sons to* CYMBELINE, *disguised under the*
ARVIRAGUS, } *names of* POLYDORE *and* CADWAL, *supposed Sons to* BELARIUS.

PHILARIO, *Friend to* POSTHUMUS, } *Italians.*
LACHIMO, *Friend to* PHILARIO,

A French Gentleman, *Friend to* PHILARIO.

CAIUS LUCIUS, *General of the Roman Forces.*

A Roman Captain.

Two British Captains.

PISANIO, *Servant to* POSTHUMUS.

CORNELIUS, *a Physician.*

Two Lords of CYMBELINE'S *Court.*

Two Gentlemen *of the same.*

Two Gaolers.

QUEEN, *Wife to* CYMBELINE.

IMOGEN, *Daughter to* CYMBELINE *by a former Queen.*

HELEN, *Woman to* IMOGEN.

Lords, Ladies, Roman Senators, Tribunes, Apparitions, a Soothsayer, a Dutch Gentleman, a Spanish Gentleman, Musicians, Officers, Captains, Soldiers, Messengers, *and other* Attendants.

SCENE,—*Sometimes in* BRITAIN; *sometimes in* ITALY.

CYMBELINE.

ACT I.

SCENE I.—BRITAIN. *The Garden behind* CYMBELINE'S *Palace.*

Enter two Gentlemen.

1 *Gent.* You do not meet a man but frowns : our bloods
No more obey the heavens than our courtiers
Still seem as does the king.
    2 *Gent.*   But what 's the matter?
    1 *Gent.* His daughter, and the heir of 's kingdom, whom
He purpos'd to his wife's sole son,— a widow
That late he married,—hath referr'd herself
Unto a poor but worthy gentleman. She's wedded;
Her husband banish'd; she imprison'd : all
Is outward sorrow; though I think the king
Be touch'd at very heart.
    2 *Gent.*   None but the king?
    1 *Gent.* He that hath lost her too : so is the queen,
That most desir'd the match. But not a courtier,
Although they wear their faces to the bent
Of the king's looks, hath a heart that is not
Glad at the thing they scowl at.
    2 *Gent.*   And why so?
    1 *Gent.* He that hath miss'd the princess is a thing
Too bad for bad report : and he that hath her,—
I mean that married her—alack, good man!—
And therefore banish'd,—is a creature such
As, to seek through the regions of the earth
For one his like, there would be something failing
In him that should compare. I do not think
So fair an outward and such stuff within
Endows a man but he.
    2 *Gent.*   You speak him far.
    1 *Gent.* I do extend him, sir, within himself;

Crush him together, rather than unfold
His measure duly.

  2 Gent.   What 's his name and birth

  1 Gent. I cannot delve him to the root : his father
Was call'd Sicilius, who did join his honour,
Against the Romans, with Cassibelan,
But had his titles by Tenantius, whom
He serv'd with glory and admir'd success,—
So gain'd the sur-addition Leouatus :
And had, besides this gentleman in question,
Two other sons, who, in the wars o' the time,
Died with their swords in hand; for which their
   father,—
Then old and fond of issue,—took such sorrow
That he quit being; and his gentle lady,
Big of this gentleman, our theme, deceas'd
As he was born. The king he takes the babe
To his protection; calls him Posthumus Leonatus;
Breeds him, and makes him of his bedchamber:
Puts to him all the learnings that his time
Could make him the receiver of; which he took,
As we do air, fast as 'twas minister'd;
And in 's spring became a harvest: liv'd in court,—
Which rare it is to do,—most prais'd, most lov'd;
A sample to the youngest; to the more mature
A glass that feated them; and to the graver
A child that guided dotards: to his mistress,
For whom he now is banish'd,—her own price
Proclaims how she esteem'd him and his virtue;
By her election may be truly read
What kind of man he is.

  2 Gent.   I honour him
Even out of your report. But, pray you, tell me,
Is she sole child to the king?

  1 Gent.   His only child.
He had two sons,—if this be worth your hearing,
Mark it,—the eldest of them at three years old,
I' the swathing clothes the other, from their nursery
Were stol'n; and to this hour no guess in knowledge
Which way they went.

  2 Gent.   How long is this ago?

  1 Gent. Some twenty years.

  2 Gent. That a king's children should be so convey'd!
So slackly guarded! And the search so slow
That could not trace them!

  1 Gent.   Howsoe'er 'tis strange,

Or that the negligence may well be laugh'd at,
Yet is it true, sir.
   2 Gent.   I do well believe you.
   1 Gent. We must forbear: here comes the gentleman,
The queen, and princess.   [*Exeunt.*

Enter the QUEEN, POSTHUMUS, *and* IMOGEN.

   Queen. No, be assur'd you shall not find me, daughter,
After the slander of most stepmothers,
Evil-ey'd unto you: you're my prisoner, but
Your gaoler shall deliver you the keys
That lock up your restraint.—For you, Posthumus,
So soon as I can win the offended king,
I will be known your advocate: marry, yet
The fire of rage is in him; and 'twere good
You lean'd unto his sentence with what patience
Your wisdom may inform you.
   Post.   Please your highness,
I will from hence to-day.
   Queen.   You know the peril.—
I'll fetch a turn about the garden, pitying
The pangs of barr'd affections; though the king
Hath charg'd you should not speak together.   [*Exit.*
   Imo.   O
Dissembling courtesy! How fine this tyrant
Can tickle where she wounds!—My dearest husband,
I something fear my father's wrath; but nothing,—
Always reserv'd my holy duty,—what
His rage can do on me. You must be gone;
And I shall here abide the hourly shot
Of angry eyes; not comforted to live,
But that there is this jewel in the world
That I may see again.
   Post. My queen! my mistress!
O lady, weep no more, lest I give cause
To be suspected of more tenderness
Than doth become a man! I will remain
The loyal'st husband that did e'er plight troth:
My residence in Rome at one Philario's,
Who to my father was a friend, to me
Known but by letter: thither write, my queen,
And with mine eyes I'll drink the words you send,
Though ink be made of gall.

Re-enter QUEEN.

   Queen.   Be brief, I pray you:

If the king come I shall incur I know not
How much of his displeasure.—[*Aside.*] Yet I'll move him
To walk this way: I never do him wrong
But he does buy my injuries to be friends,—
Pays dear for my offences. [*Exit.*
    Post.   Should we be taking leave
As long a term as yet we have to live,
The loathness to depart would grow. Adieu!
    Imo. Nay, stay a little:
Were you but riding forth to air yourself,
Such parting were too petty. Look here, love;
This diamond was my mother's: take it, heart;
But keep it till you woo another wife,
When Imogen is dead.
    Post. How, how! another?—
You gentle gods, give me but this I have,
And sear up my embracements from a next
With bonds of death!—Remain, remain thou here
                              [*Putting on the •ing.*
While sense can keep it on! And, sweetest, fairest,
As I my poor self did exchange for you,
To your so infinite loss, so in our trifles
I still win of you: for my sake wear this;
It is a manacle of love; I'll place it
Upon this fairest prisoner. [*Putting a bracelet on her arm.*
    Imo.   O the gods!
When shall we see again?
    Post.   Alack, the king!

Enter CYMBELINE *and* Lords.

    Cym. Thou basest thing, avoid! hence from my sight?
If after this command thou fraught the court
With thy unworthiness, thou diest: away!
Thou art poison to my blood.
    Post.   The gods protect you!
And bless the good remainders of the court!
I am gone. [*Exit.*
    Imo. There cannot be a pinch in death
More sharp than this is.
    Cym.   O disloyal thing,
That shouldst repair my youth, thou heapest
A year's age on me!
    Imo.   I beseech you, sir,
Harm not yourself with your vexation: I
Am senseless of your wrath; a touch more rare
Subdues all pangs, all fears.

Cym.   Past grace? obedience?
Imo. Past hope, and in despair; that way past grace.
Cym. That might'st have had the sole son of my queen!
Imo. O bless'd that I might not! I chose an eagle,
And did avoid a puttock.
   Cym. Thou took'st a beggar; wouldst have made my throne
      throne
A seat for baseness.
   Imo   No; I rather added
A lustre to it.
   Cym.   O thou vile one!
   Imo.   Sir,
It is your fault that I have lov'd Posthumus:
You bred him as my playfellow; and he is
A man worth any woman; overbuys me
Almost the sum he pays.
   Cym.   What, art thou mad?
   Imo. Almost, sir: heaven restore me!—Would I were
A neat-herd's daughter, and my Leonatus
Our neighbour shepherd's son!
   Cym.   Thou foolish thing!—

Re-enter QUEEN.

They were again together: you have done   [*To the Queen.*
Not after our command.   Away with her,
And pen her up.
   Queen.   Beseech your patience.—Peace,
Dear lady daughter, peace!—Sweet sovereign,
Leave us to ourselves; and make yourself some comfort
Out of your best advice.
   Cym.   Nay, let her languish
A drop of blood a day; and, being aged,
Die of this folly!   [*Exit, with* Lords.
   Queen.   Fie! you must give way.

Enter PISANIO.

Here is your servant.—How now, sir!   What news?
   Pis. My lord your son drew on my master.
   Queen.   Ha!
No harm, I trust, is done!
   Pis.   There might have been,
But that my master rather play'd than fought,
And had no help of anger: they were parted
By gentlemen at hand.
   Queen.   I am very glad on't.
   Imo. Your son's my father's friend; he takes his part.—

To draw upon an exile!—O brave sir!—
I would they were in Afric both together;
Myself by with a needle, that I might prick
The goer back.—Why came you from your master?

    Pis. On his command: he would not suffer me
To bring him to the haven: left these notes
Of what commands I should be subject to,
When't pleas'd you to employ me.

    Queen.   This hath been
Your faithful servant: I dare lay mine honour
He will remain so.

    Pis.   I humbly thank your highness.

    Queen. Pray, walk awhile.

    Imo.   About some half hour hence,
I pray you, speak with me: you shall at least
Go see my lord aboard: for this time leave me.   [*Exeunt.*

SCENE II.—BRITAIN. *A public Place.*

Enter CLOTEN *and two* Lords.

    1 *Lord.* Sir, I would advise you to shift a shirt; the
violence of action hath made you reek as a sacrifice: where
air comes out air comes in: there's none abroad so wholesome as that you vent.

    Clo. If my shirt were bloody, then to shift it.—Have I
hurt him?

    2 *Lord.* [*aside.*] No, faith; not so much as his patience.

    1 *Lord.* Hurt him! His body's a passable carcass if he
be not hurt: it is a throughfare for steel if it be not hurt.

    2 *Lord.* [*aside.*] His steel was in debt; it went o' the
back side the town.

    Clo. The villain would not stand me.

    2 *Lord.* [*aside.*] No; but he fled forward still, toward
your face.

    1 *Lord.* Stand you! You have land enough of your own:
but he added to your having; gave you some ground.

    2 *Lord.* [*aside.*] As many inches as you have oceans.—
Puppies!

    Clo. I would they had not come between us.

    2 *Lord.* [*aside.*] So would I, till you had measured how
long a fool you were upon the ground.

    Clo. And that she should love this fellow, and refuse me!

    2 *Lord.* [*aside.*] If it be a sin to make a true election,
she is damned.

    1 *Lord.* Sir, as I told you always, her beauty and her

brain go not together: she's a good sign, but I have seen
small reflection of her wit.

2 Lord. [*aside.*] She shines not upon fools, lest the reflection should hurt her.

Clo. Come, I'll to my chamber. Would there had been
some hurt done!

2 Lord. [*aside.*] I wish not so; unless it had been the fall
of an ass, which is no great hurt.

Clo. You'll go with us?

1 Lord. I'll attend your lordship.

Clo. Nay, come, let's go together.

2 Lord. Well, my lord.   [*Exeunt.*

SCENE III.—BRITAIN.   *A Room in* CYMBELINE'S *Palace.*

Enter IMOGEN *and* PISANIO.

Imo. I would thou grew'st unto the shores o' the haven,
And questioned'st every sail: if he should write,
And I not have it, 'twere a paper lost,
As offer'd mercy is. What was the last
That he spake to thee?

Pis.   It was, *His queen, his queen!*

Imo. Then wav'd his handkerchief?

Pis.   And kiss'd it, madam.

Imo. Senseless linen! happier therein than I!—
And that was all?

Pis.   No, madam; for so long
As he could make me with this eye or ear
Distinguish him from others, he did keep
The deck, with glove, or hat, or handkerchief
Still waving, as the fits and stirs of 's mind
Could best express how slow his soul sail'd on,
How swift his ship.

Imo.   Thou shouldst have made him
As little as a crow, or less, ere left
To after-eye him.

Pis.   Madam, so I did.

Imo. I would have broke mine eye-strings, crack'd them,
To look upon him, till the diminution   [but
Of space had pointed him sharp as my needle;
Nay, follow'd him till he had melted from
The smallness of a gnat to air; and then
Have turn'd mine eye and wept.—But, good Pisanio,
When shall we hear from him?

Pis.   Be assur'd, madam,
With his next vantage.

Imo. I did not take my leave of him, but had
Most pretty things to say: ere I could tell him
How I would think on him, at certain hours,
Such thoughts and such; or I could make him swear
The shes of Italy should not betray
Mine interest and his honour; or have charg'd him
At the sixth hour of morn, at noon, at midnight,
To encounter me with orisons, for then
I am in heaven for him; or ere I could
Give him that parting kiss which I had set
Betwixt two charming words, comes in my father,
And like the tyrannous breathing of the north
Shakes all our buds from growing.

Enter a Lady.

Lady.   The queen, madam,
Desires your highness' company.

Imo. Those things I bid you do, get them despatch'd.—
I will attend the queen.

Pis.   Madam, I shall.   [*Exeunt.*

SCENE IV.—ROME.   *An Apartment in* PHILARIO'S *House.*

Enter PHILARIO, IACHIMO, *a* Frenchman, *a* Dutchman, *and*
a Spaniard.

Iach. Believe it, sir, I have seen him in Britain: he was
then of a crescent note; expected to prove so worthy as
since he hath been allowed the name of: but I could then
have looked on him without the help of admiration; though
the catalogue of his endowments had been tabled by his
side, and I to peruse him by items.

Phi. You speak of him when he was less furnished than
now he is with that which makes him both without and
within.

French. I have seen him in France: we had very many
there could behold the sun with as firm eyes as he.

Iach. This matter of marrying his king's daughter,—
wherein he must be weighed rather by her value than his
own,—words him, I doubt not, a great deal from the matter.

French. And then his banishment,—

Iach. Ay, and the approbation of those that weep this
lamentable divorce, under her colours, are wonderfully to
extend him; be it but to fortify her judgment, which else

an easy battery might lay flat, for taking a beggar without less quality. But how comes it he is to sojourn with you? How creeps acquaintance?

Phi. His father and I were soldiers together; to whom I have been often bound for no less than my life.—Here comes the Briton: let him be so entertained amongst you as suits with gentlemen of your knowing to a stranger of his quality.

Enter POSTHUMUS.

I beseech you all, be better known to this gentleman; whom I commend to you as a noble friend of mine: how worthy he is I will leave to appear hereafter, rather than story him in his own hearing.

French. Sir, we have known together in Orleans.

Post. Since when I have been debtor to you for courtesies, which I will be ever to pay and yet pay still.

French. Sir, you o'errate my poor kindness: I was glad I did atone my countryman and you; it had been pity you should have been put together with so mortal a purpose as then each bore, upon importance of so slight and trivial a nature.

Post. By your pardon, sir, I was then a young traveller; rather shunned to go even with what I heard than in my every action to be guided by others' experiences: but, upon my mended judgment,—if I offend not to say it is mended, —my quarrel was not altogether slight.

French. Faith, yes, to be put to the arbitrement of swords; and by such two that would, by all likelihood, have confounded one the other, or have fallen both.

Iach. Can we, with manners, ask what was the difference?

French. Safely, I think: 'twas a contention in public, which may, without contradiction, suffer the report. It was much like an argument that fell out last night, where each of us fell in praise of our country mistresses; this gentleman at that time vouching,—and upon warrant of bloody affirmation,—his to be more fair, virtuous, wise, chaste, constant-qualified, and less attemptible than any the rarest of our ladies in France.

Iach. That lady is not now living; or this gentleman's opinion, by this, worn out.

Post. She holds her virtue still, and I my mind.

Iach. You must not so far prefer her fore ours of Italy.

Post. Being so far provoked as I was in France, I would abate her nothing; though I profess myself her adorer, not her friend.

Iach. As fair and as good,—a kind of hand-in-hand comparison,—had been something too fair and too good for any lady in Brittany. If she went before others I have seen, as that diamond of yours out-lustres many I have beheld, I could not but believe she excelled many: but I have not seen the most precious diamond that is, nor you the lady.

Post. I praised her as I rated her: so do I my stone.

Iach. What do you esteem it at?

Post. More than the world enjoys.

Iach. Either your unparagoned mistress is dead, or she's outprized by a trifle.

Post. You are mistaken: the one may be sold or given, if there were wealth enough for the purchase or merit for the gift: the other is not a thing for sale, and only the gift of the gods.

Iach. Which the gods have given you?

Post. Which, by their graces, I will keep.

Iach. You may wear her in title yours: but, you know, strange fowl light upon neighbouring ponds. Your ring may be stolen too: so your brace of unprizeable estimations, the one is but frail and the other casual; a cunning thief or a that-way-accomplished courtier would hazard the winning both of first and last.

Post. Your Italy contains none so accomplished a courtier to convince the honour of my mistress, if in the holding or loss of that you term her frail. I do nothing doubt you have store of thieves; notwithstanding I fear not my ring.

Phi. Let us leave here, gentlemen.

Post. Sir, with all my heart. This worthy signior, I thank him, makes no stranger of me; we are familiar at first.

Iach. With five times so much conversation I should get ground of your fair mistress; make her go back even to the yielding, had I admittance and opportunity to friend.

Post. No, no.

Iach. I dare thereupon pawn the moiety of my estate to your ring; which, in my opinion, o'ervalues it something: but I make my wager rather against your confidence than her reputation: and, to bar your offence herein too, I durst attempt it against any lady in the world.

Post. You are a great deal abused in too bold a persuasion; and I doubt not you sustain what you're worthy of by your attempt.

Iach. What's that?

Post. A repulse: though your attempt, as you call it, deserve more,—a punishment too.

Phil. Gentlemen, enough of this: it came in too suddenly; let it die as it was born, and, I pray you, be better acquainted.

Iach. Would I had put my estate and my neighbour's on the approbation of what I have spoke!

Post. What lady would you choose to assail?

Iach. Yours; whom in constancy you think stands so safe. I will lay you ten thousand ducats to your ring that commend me to the court where your lady is, with no more advantage than the opportunity of a second conference, and I will bring from thence that honour of hers which you imagine so reserved.

Post. I will wage against your gold gold to it: my ring I hold dear as my finger; 'tis part of it.

Iach. You are afraid, and therein the wiser. If you buy ladies' flesh at a million a dram, you cannot preserve it from tainting: but I see you have some religion in you, that you fear.

Post. This is but a custom in your tongue; you bear a graver purpose, I hope.

Iach. I am the master of my speeches; and would undergo what's spoken, I swear.

Post. Will you?—I shall but lend my diamond till your return:—let there be covenants drawn between us: my mistress exceeds in goodness the hugeness of your unworthy thinking: I dare you to this match: here's my ring.

Phi. I will have it no lay.

Iach. By the gods, it is one.—If I bring you no sufficient testimony that I have enjoyed the dearest bodily part of your mistress, my ten thousand ducats are yours; so is your diamond too: if I come off, and leave her in such honour as you have trust in, she your jewel, this your jewel, and my gold are yours;—provided I have your commendation for my more free entertainment.

Post. I embrace these conditions; let us have articles betwixt us.—Only, thus far you shall answer: if you make your voyage upon her, and give me directly to understand you have prevail'd, I am no further your enemy; she is not worth our debate: if she remain unseduced,—you not making it appear otherwise,—for your ill opinion and the assault you have made to her chastity you shall answer me with your sword.

Iach. Your hand,—a covenant: we will have these things set down by lawful counsel, and straight away for Britain, lest the bargain should catch cold and starve: I will fetch my gold, and have our two wagers recorded.

Post. Agreed. [*Exeunt* POST. *and* IACH.

French. Will this hold, think you?

Phi. Signior Iachimo will not from it. Pray, let us
follow 'em.   [*Exeunt.*

SCENE V.—BRITAIN. *A Room in* CYMBELINE'S *Palace.*

Enter QUEEN, Ladies, *and* CORNELIUS.

Queen. Whiles yet the dew's on ground gather those
    flowers;
Make haste: who has the note of them?
    1 *Lady.*   I, madam.
    Queen. Despatch.—   [*Exeunt* Ladies.
Now, master doctor, have you brought those drugs?
    Cor. Pleaseth your highness, ay: here they are, madam:
                            [*Presenting a small box.*
But I beseech your grace, without offence,—
My conscience bids me ask,—wherefore you have
Commanded of me these most poisonous compounds,
Which are the movers of a languishing death;
But, though slow, deadly?
    Queen.   I wonder, doctor,
Thou ask'st me such a question. Have I not been
Thy pupil long? Hast thou not learn'd me how
To make perfumes? distil? preserve? yea, so
That our great king himself doth woo me oft
For my confections? Having thus far proceeded,—
Unless thou think'st me devilish,—is't not meet
That I did amplify my judgment in
Other conclusions? I will try the forces
Of these thy compounds on such creatures as
We count not worth the hanging,—but none human,—
To try the vigour of them, and apply
Allayments to their act; and by them gather
Their several virtues and effects.
    Cor.   Your highness
Shall from this practice but make hard your heart:
Besides, the seeing these effects will be
Both noisome and infectious.
    Queen.   O, content thee.—
Here comes a flattering rascal; upon him   [*Aside*
Will I first work: he's for his master,
And enemy to my son.—

Enter PISANIO.

How now, Pisanio!—

Doctor, your service for this time is ended;
Take your own way.

 Cor. [*aside.*] I do suspect you, madam;
But you shall do no harm.

 Queen.   Hark thee, a word. [*To* PISANIO.

 Cor. [*aside.*] I do not like her. She doth think she has
Strange lingering poisons: I do know her spirit,
And will not trust one of her malice with
A drug of such damn'd nature. Those she has
Will stupify and dull the sense awhile;
Which first perchance she'll prove on cats and dogs,
Then afterward up higher: but there is
No danger in what show of death it makes,
More than the locking up the spirits a time,
To be more fresh, reviving. She is fool'd
With a most false effect; and I the truer
So to be false with her.

 Queen.   No further service, doctor,
Until I send for thee.

 Cor.   I humbly take my leave.   [*Exit.*

 Queen. Weeps she still, say'st thou? Dost thou think in
   time
She will not quench, and let instructions enter
Where folly now possesses? Do thou work:
When thou shalt bring me word she loves my son,
I'll tell thee on the instant thou art then
As great as is thy master; greater,—for
His fortunes all lie speechless, and his name
Is at last gasp: return he cannot, nor
Continue where he is: to shift his being
Is to exchange one misery with another;
And every day that comes comes to decay
A day's work in him. What shalt thou expect,
To be depender on a thing that leans,—
Who cannot be new built, nor has no friends
    [*The* QUEEN *drops the box:* PISANIO *takes it up.*
So much as but to prop him?—Thou tak'st up
Thou know'st not what; but take it for thy labour:
It is a thing I made, which hath the king
Five times redeem'd from death: I do not know
What is more cordial:—nay, I pr'ythee, take it;
It is an earnest of a further good
That I mean to thee. Tell thy mistress how
The case stands with her; do't as from thyself.
Think what a chance thou changest on; but think
Thou hast thy mistress still,—to boot, my son,

Who shall take notice of thee: I'll move the king
To any shape of thy preferment, such
As thou'lt desire ; and then myself, I chiefly,
That set thee on to this desert, am bound
To load thy merit richly.   Call my women:
Think on my words.   [*Exit* PISANIO.
                    A sly and constant knave;
Not to be shak'd: the agent for his master;
And the remembrancer of her to hold
The hand-fast to her lord.—I have given him that
Which, if he take, shall quite unpeople her
Of liegers for her sweet ; and which she after,
Except she bend her humour, shall be assur'd
To taste of too.

                Re-enter PISANIO *and* Ladies.

So, so;—well done, well done :
The violets, cowslips, and the primroses,
Bear to my closet.—Fare thee well, Pisanio ;
Think on my words.   [*Exeunt* QUEEN *and* Ladies.
     Pis.   And shall do :
But when to my good lord I prove untrue
I'll choke myself: there's all I'll do for you.   [*Exit.*

———

SCENE VI.—BRITAIN.   *Another Room in the Palace.*

                Enter IMOGEN.

     Imo. A father cruel and a step-dame false;
A foolish suitor to a wedded lady,
That hath her husband banish'd ;—O, that husband!
My supreme crown of grief! and those repeated
Vexations of it! Had I been thief-stolen,
As my two brothers, happy! but most miserable
Is the desire that's glorious: bless'd be those,
How mean soe'er, that have their honest wills,
Which seasons comfort.—Who may this be? Fie!

                Enter PISANIO *and* IACHIMO.

     Pis. Madam, a noble gentleman of Rome
Comes from my lord with letters.
     Iach.   Change you, madam ?
The worthy Leonatus is in safety,
And greets your highness dearly.   [*Presents a letter*
     Imo.   Thanks, good sir:
You're kindly welcome.

Iach. [*aside.*] All of her that is out of door most rich!
If she be furnish'd with a mind so rare,
She is alone the Arabian bird; and I
Have lost the wager. Boldness be my friend!
Arm me, audacity, from head to foot!
Or, like the Parthian, I shall flying fight;
Rather directly fly.

    Imo. [reads.] *He is one of the noblest note, to whose
kindnesses I am most infinitely tied. Reflect upon him
accordingly, as you value your truest*   LEONATUS.
So far I read aloud:
But even the very middle of my heart
Is warm'd by the rest, and takes it thankfully.—
You are as welcome, worthy sir, as I
Have words to bid you; and shall find it so
In all that I can do.

    Iach.   Thanks, fairest lady.—
What, are men mad? Hath nature given them eyes
To see this vaulted arch, and the rich cope
Of sea and land, which can distinguish 'twixt
The fiery orbs above and the twinn'd stones
Upon th' unnumber'd beach? and can we not
Partition make with spectacles so precious
'Twixt fair and foul?

    Imo.   What makes your admiration?

    Iach. It cannot be i' the eye; for apes and monkeys,
'Twixt two such shes, would chatter this way and
Contemn with mows the other: nor i' the judgment;
For idiots in this case of favour would
Be wisely definite: nor i' the appetite;
Sluttery, to such neat excellence oppos'd,
Should make desire vomit emptiness,
Not so allur'd to feed.

    Imo. What is the matter, trow?

    Iach.   The cloyed will,—
That satiate yet unsatisfied desire,
That tub both fill'd and running,—ravening first
The lamb, longs after for the garbage.

    Imo.   What, dear sir,
Thus raps you? Are you well?

    Iach. Thanks, madam; well.—Beseech you, sir, desire
                         [*To* PISANIO.
My man's abode where I did leave him: he
Is strange and peevish.

    Pis.   I was going, sir,
To give him welcome.   [*Exit.*

Imo. Continues well my lord? His health, beseech you?

Iach. Well, madam.

Imo. Is he dispos'd to mirth? I hope he is.

Iach. Exceeding pleasant; none a stranger there
So merry and so gamesome: he is call'd
The Briton reveller.

Imo.   When he was here
He did incline to sadness; and ofttimes
Not knowing why.

Iach.   I never saw him sad.
There is a Frenchman his companion, one
An eminent monsieur, that, it seems, much loves
A Gallian girl at home: he furnaces
The thick sighs from him; whiles the jolly Briton,—
Your lord, I mean,—laughs from 's free lungs, cries, *O,
Can my sides hold, to think that man,--who knows
By history, report, or his own proof,
What woman is, yea, what she cannot choose
But must be,—will his free hours languish for
Assured bondage?*

Imo.   Will my lord say so?

Iach. Ay, madam; with his eyes in flood with laughter.
It is a recreation to be by
And hear him mock the Frenchman. But, heavens know,
Some men are much to blame.

Imo.   Not he, I hope.

Iach. Not he: but yet heaven's bounty towards him might
Be us'd more thankfully. In himself 'tis much;
In you,—which I count his, beyond all talents,—
Whilst I am bound to wonder I am bound
To pity too.

Imo.   What do you pity, sir?

Iach. Two creatures heartily.

Imo.   Am I one, sir?
You look on me: what wreck discern you in me
Deserves your pity?

Iach.   Lamentable! What,
To hide me from the radiant sun, and solace
I' the dungeon by a snuff?

Imo.   I pray you, sir,
Deliver with more openness your answers
To my demands. Why do you pity me?

Iach. That others do,
I was about to say, enjoy your——But
It is an office of the gods to venge it,
Not mine to speak on 't.

Imo.   You do seem to know
Something of me, or what concerns me: pray you,—
Since doubting things go ill often hurts more
Than to be sure they do; for certainties
Either are past remedies, or, timely knowing,
The remedy then born,—discover to me
What both you spur and stop.
Iach.   Had I this cheek
To bathe my lips upon; this hand, whose touch,
Whose every touch, would force the feeler's soul
To the oath of loyalty; this object, which
Takes prisoner the wild motion of mine eye,
Fixing it only here;—should I,—damn'd then,—
Slaver with lips at common as the stairs
That mount the Capitol; join gripes with hands
Made hard with hourly falsehood,—falsehood as
With labour,—then bo-peeping in an eye
Base and unlustrous as the smoky light
That's fed with stinking tallow,—it were fit
That all the plagues of hell should at one time
Encounter such revolt.
Imo.   My lord, I fear,
Has forgot Britain.
Iach.   And himself.   Not I,
Inclin'd to this intelligence, pronounce
The beggary of his change; but 'tis your graces
That from my mutest conscience to my tongue
Charms this report out.
Imo.   Let me hear no more.
Iach. O dearest soul! your cause doth strike my heart
With pity that doth make me sick!   A lady
So fair, and fasten'd to an empery,
Would make the great'st king double,—to be partner'd
With tomboys, hir'd with that self-exhibition
Which your own coffers yield! with diseas'd ventures,
That play with all infirmities for gold
Which rottenness can lend nature! such boil'd stuff
As well might poison poison!   Be reveng'd;
Or she that bore you was no queen, and you
Recoil from your great stock.
Imo.   Reveng'd!
How should I be reveng'd?   If this be true,—
As I have such a heart that both mine ears
Must not in haste abuse,—if it be true,
How should I be reveng'd?
Iach.   Should he make me

Live like Diana's priest betwixt cold sheets,
Whiles he is vaulting variable ramps,
In your despite, upon your purse? Revenge it.
I dedicate myself to your sweet pleasure;
More noble than that runagate to your bed;
And will continue fast to your affection,
Still close as sure.
    Imo.   What, ho, Pisanio!
    Iach. Let me my service tender on your lips.
    Imo. Away!—I do condemn mine ears that have
So long attended thee.—If thou wert honourable
Thou wouldst have told this tale for virtue, not
For such an end thou seek'st,—as base as strange.
Thou wrong'st a gentleman who is as far
From thy report as thou from honour; and
Solicit'st here a lady that disdains
Thee and the devil alike.—What, ho, Pisanio!—
The king my father shall be made acquainted
Of thy assault: if he shall think it fit
A saucy stranger in his court to mart
As in a Romish stew, and to expound
His beastly mind to us,—he hath a court
He little cares for, and a daughter who
He not respects at all.—What, ho, Pisanio!—
    Iach. O happy Leonatus! I may say:
The credit that thy lady hath of thee
Deserves thy trust; and thy most perfect goodness
Her assur'd credit!—Blessed live you long!
A lady to the worthiest sir that ever
Country call'd his! and you his mistress, only
For the most worthiest fit! Give me your pardon.
I have spoke this to know if your alliance
Were deeply rooted; and shall make your lord
That which he is new o'er: and he is one
The truest manner'd; such a holy witch
That he enchants societies unto him;
Half all men's hearts are his.
    Imo.   You make amends.
    Iach. He sits 'mongst men like a descended god:
He hath a kind of honour sets him off
More than a mortal seeming. Be not angry,
Most mighty princess, that I have adventur'd
To try your taking of a false report; which hath
Honour'd with confirmation your great judgment
In the election of a sir so rare,
Which you know cannot err: the love I bear him

Made me to fan you thus; but the gods made you,
Unlike all others, chaffless.   Pray, your pardon.
    Imo. All's well, sir: take my power i' the court for yours.
    Iach. My humble thanks.   I had almost forgot
To entreat your grace but in a small request,
And yet of moment too, for it concerns
Your lord, myself, and other noble friends,
Are partners in the business.
    Imo.   Pray, what is't?
    Iach. Some dozen Romans of us, and your lord,—
The best feather of our wing,—have mingled sums
To buy a present for the emperor;
Which I, the factor for the rest, have done
In France: 'tis plate of rare device; and jewels
Of rich and exquisite form; their value's great;
And I am something curious, being strange,
To have them in safe stowage: may it please you
To take them in protection?
    Imo.   Willingly;
And pawn mine honour for their safety; since
My lord hath interest in them, I will keep them
In my bedchamber.
    Iach.   They are in a trunk,
Attended by my men: I will make bold
To send them to you only for this night;
I must aboard to-morrow.
    Imo.   O, no, no.
    Iach. Yes, I beseech; or I shall short my word
By length'ning my return.   From Gallia
I cross'd the seas on purpose and on promise
To see your grace.
    Imo.   I thank you for your pains:
But not away to-morrow!
    Iach.   O, I must, madam:
Therefore I shall beseech you, if you please
To greet your lord with writing, do't to-night:
I have outstood my time; which is material
To the tender of our present.
    Imo.   I will write.
Send your trunk to me; it shall safe be kept
And truly yielded you.   You're very welcome.   [*Exeunt.*

ACT II.

SCENE I.—BRITAIN. *Court before* CYMBELINE'S *Palace*

Enter CLOTEN *and two* Lords.

Clo. Was there ever man had such luck! when I kissed the jack, upon an up-cast to bet it away! I had a hundred pound ou't : and then a whoreson jackanapes must take me up for swearing; as if I borrowed mine oaths from him, and might not spend them at my pleasure.

1 Lord. What got he by that? You have broke his pate with your bowl.

2 Lord. [*aside.*] If his wit had been like him that broke it, it would have run all out.

Clo. When a gentleman is disposed to swear, it is not for any standers-by to curtail his oaths, ha?

2 Lord. No, my lord; [*aside*] nor crop the ears of them.

Clo. Whoreson dog!—I give him satisfaction? Would he had been one of my rank!

2 Lord. [*aside.*] To have smelt like a fool.

Clo. I am not vexed more at anything in the earth,— a pox on't! I had rather not be so noble as I am; they dare not fight with me, because of the queen my mother: every jack-slave hath his belly full of fighting, and I must go up and down like a cock that nobody can match.

2 Lord. [*aside.*] You are cock and capon too; and you crow, cock, with your comb on.

Clo. Sayest thou?

1 Lord. It is not fit your lordship should undertake every companion that you give offence to.

Clo. No, I know that : but it is fit I should commit offence to my inferiors.

2 Lord. Ay, it is fit for your lordship only.

Clo. Why, so I say.

1 Lord. Did you hear of a stranger that's come to court to-night?

Clo. A stranger, and I not know on't!

2 Lord. [*aside.*] He's a strange fellow himself, and knows it not.

1 Lord. There's an Italian come; and, 'tis thought, one of Leonatus' friends.

Clo. Leonatus! a banished rascal; and he's another, whatsoever he be. Who told you of this stranger?

1 Lord. One of your lordship's pages.

Clo. Is it fit I went to look upon him? Is there no deroga-
1 *Lord.* You cannot derogate, my lord.   [tion in't.
Clo. Not easily, I think.
2 *Lord.* [*aside.*] You are a fool granted; therefore your
issues, being foolish, do not derogate.
Clo. Come, I'll go see this Italian: what I have lost to-
day at bowls I'll win to-night of him. Come, go.
2 *Lord.* I'll attend your lordship.

                    [*Exeunt* CLOTEN *and first* Lord.
That such a crafty devil as is his mother
Should yield the world this ass! a woman that
Bears all down with her brain; and this her son
Cannot take two from twenty, for his heart,
And leave eighteen. Alas, poor princess,
Thou divine Imogen, what thou endur'st,—
Betwixt a father by thy stepdame govern'd:
A mother hourly coining plots; a wooer
More hateful than the foul expulsion is
Of thy dear husband, than that horrid act
Of the divorce he'd make! The heavens hold firm
The walls of thy dear honour; keep unshak'd
That temple, thy fair mind; that thou mayst stand
To enjoy thy banish'd lord and this great land!   [*Exit.*

SCENE II.—BRITAIN. IMOGEN's *Bedchamber; in one
part of it a Trunk.*

IMOGEN *in bed reading; a* Lady *attending.*

Imo. Who's there? my woman Helen?
Lady.   Please you, madam.
Imo. What hour is it?
Lady.   Almost midnight, madam.
Imo. I have read three hours, then: mine eyes are weak:
Fold down the leaf where I have left: to bed:
Take not away the taper, leave it burning;
And if thou canst awake by four o' the clock,
I pr'ythee, call me. Sleep hath seiz'd me wholly. [*Exit* Lady.
To your protection I commend me, gods!
From fairies and the tempters of the night
Guard me, beseech ye! [*Sleeps.* IACH. *comes from the trunk*
   Iach. The crickets sing, and man's o'er-labour'd sense
Repairs itself by rest. Our Tarquin thus
Did softly press the rushes ere he waken'd
The chastity he wounded.—Cytherea,
How bravely thou becom'st thy bed! fresh lily!

And whiter than the sheets! That I might touch!
But kiss; one kiss!—Rubies unparagon'd,
How dearly they do't!—'Tis her breathing that
Perfumes the chamber thus: the flame o' the taper
Bows toward her, and would underpeep her lids,
To see the enclosed lights, now canopied
Under these windows, white and azure, lac'd
With blue of heaven's own tinct.—But my design
To note the chamber:—I will write all down:—
Such and such pictures;—there the window:—such
The adornment of her bed;—the arras, figures,
Why, such and such;—and the contents o' the story,—
Ah, but some natural notes about her body
Above ten thousand meaner movables
Would testify, to enrich mine inventory.
O sleep, thou ape of death, lie dull upon her!
And be her sense but as a monument,
Thus in a chapel lying!—Come off, come off;
                              [*Taking off her bracelet.*
As slippery as the Gordian knot was hard!—
'Tis mine; and this will witness outwardly,
As strongly as the conscience does within,
To the madding of her lord. On her left breast
A mole cinque-spotted, like the crimson drops
I' the bottom of a cowslip. Here's a voucher
Stronger than ever law could make: this secret
Will force him think I have pick'd the lock, and ta'en
The treasure of her honour. No more. To what end?
Why should I write this down, that's riveted,
Screw'd to my memory?—She hath been reading late
The tale of Tereus; here the leaf's turn'd down
Where Philomel gave up.—I have enough: ·.
To the trunk again, and shut the spring of it.
Swift, swift, you dragons of the night, that dawning
May bare the raven's eye! I lodge in fear;
Though this a heavenly angel, hell is here. [*Clock strikes*
One, two, three,—Time, time!
                              [*Goes into the trunk. Scene closes.*

SCENE III.—BRITAIN. *An Ante-chamber adjoining*
        IMOGEN'S *Apartment.*

Enter CLOTEN *and* Lords.

1 *Lord.* Your lordship is the most patient man in loss,
the most coldest that ever turned up ace.

Clo. It would make any man cold to lose.

1 *Lord.* But not every man patient after the noble temper of your lordship. You are most hot and furious when you win.

Clo. Winning will put any man into courage. If I could get this foolish Imogen, I should have gold enough. It's almost morning, is't not?

1 *Lord.* Day, my lord.

Clo. I would this music would come: I am advised to give her music o' mornings; they say it will penetrate.

Enter Musicians.

Come on; tune: if you can penetrate her with your fingering, so; we'll try with tongue too: if none will do, let her remain; but I'll never give o'er. First, a very excellent good-conceited thing; after a wonderful sweet air, with admirable rich words to it,—and then let her consider.

SONG.

Hark, hark! the lark at heaven's gate sings,
 And Phœbus 'gins arise,
His steeds to water at those springs
 On chalic'd flowers that lies;
And winking Mary-buds begin
 To ope their golden eyes;
With everything that pretty is:
 My lady sweet, arise;
  Arise, arise!

So, get you gone. If this penetrate, I will consider your music the better: if it do not, it is a vice in her ears; which horse-hairs and calves' guts, nor the voice of unpaved eunuch to boot, can never amend. [*Exeunt* Musicians.

2 *Lord.* Here comes the king.

Clo. I am glad I was up so late; for that's the reason I was up so early: he cannot choose but take this service I have done fatherly.—

Enter CYMBELINE *and* QUEEN.

Good-morrow to your majesty and to my gracious mother.

Cym. Attend you here the door of our stern daughter? Will she not forth?

Clo. I have assailed her with music, but she vouchsafes no notice.

Cym. The exile of her minion is too new;
She hath not yet forgot him: some more time
Must wear the print of his remembrance out,
And then she's yours.

Queen.   You are most bound to the king,

Who lets go by no vantages that may
Prefer you to his daughter.   Frame yourself
To orderly solicits, and be friended
With aptness of the season; make denials
Increase your services; so seem as if
You were inspir'd to do those duties w'ich
You tender to her; that you in all obey her,
Save when command to your dismission tends,
And therein you are senseless.
  Clo.   Senseless! not so.
     Enter a Messenger.

 Mess. So like you, sir, ambassadors from Rome;
The one is Caius Lucius.
  Cym.   A worthy fellow,
Albeit he comes on angry purpose now;
But that's no fault of his: we must receive him
According to the honour of his sender;
And towards himself, his goodness forespent on us,
We must extend our notice.—Our dear son,
When you have given good-morning to your mistress,
Attend the queen and us; we shall have need
To employ you towards this Roman.—Come, our queen.
     [*Exeunt* CYM., QUEEN, Lords, *and* Mess.
  Clo. If she be up, I'll speak with her; if not,
Let her lie still and dream.—By your leave, ho!—[*Knocks.*
I know her women are about her: what
If I do line one of their hands? 'Tis gold
Which buys admittance; oft it doth; yea, and makes
Diana's rangers false themselves, yield up
Their deer to the stand o' the stealer; and 'tis gold
Which makes the true man kill'd and saves the thief;
Nay, sometimes hangs both thief and true man: what
Can it not do and undo? I will make
One of her women lawyer to me; for
I yet not understand the case myself.
By your leave.   [*Knocks.*
     Enter a Lady.

 Lady. Who's there that knocks?
 Clo.   A gentleman.
 Lady.   No more?
 Clo. Yes, and a gentlewoman's son.
 Lady.   That's more
Than some, whose tailors are as dear as yours, *who gave*
Can justly boast of.   What's your lordship's pleasure?
 Clo. Your lady's person: is she ready?

Lady.   Ay,
To keep her chamber.

Clo. There is gold for you; sell me your good report.

Lady. How! my good name? or to report of you
What I shall think is good?—The princess!

Enter IMOGEN.

Clo. Good-morrow, fairest: sister, your sweet hand.
                                        [*Exit* Lady.

Imo. Good-morrow, sir.   You lay out too much pains
For purchasing but trouble: the thanks I give
Is telling you that I am poor of thanks,
And scarce can spare them.

Clo.   Still, I swear I love you.

Imo. If you but said so, 'twere as deep with me:
If you swear still, your recompense is still
That I regard it not.

Clo.   This is no answer.

Imo. But that you shall not say I yield, being silent,
I would not speak.   I pray you, spare me: faith,
I shall unfold equal discourtesy
To your best kindness: one of your great knowing
Should learn, being taught, forbearance.

Clo. To leave you in your madness, 'twere my sin:
I will not.

Imo. Fools are not mad folks.

Clo.   Do you call me fool?

Imo. As I am mad, I do:
If you'll be patient I'll no more be mad;
That cures us both.   I am much sorry, sir,
You put me to forget a lady's manners
By being so verbal: and learn now, for all,
That I, which know my heart, do here pronounce,
By the very truth of it, I care not for you;
And am so near the lack of charity,—
To accuse myself,—I hate you; which I had rather
You felt than make't my boast.

Clo.   You sin against
Obedience, which you owe your father.   For
The contract you pretend with that base wretch,—
One bred of alms and foster'd with cold dishes,
With scraps o' the court,—it is no contract, none:
And though it be allow'd in meaner parties,—
Yet who than he more mean?—to knit their souls,—
On whom there is no more dependency
But brats and beggary,—in self-figur'd knot,

VOL. V.   Z

Yet you are curb'd from that enlargement by
The consequence o' the crown; and must not soil
The precious note of it with a base slave,
A hilding for a livery, a squire's cloth,
A pantler,—not so eminent.
   Imo.   Profane fellow!
Wert thou the son of Jupiter, and no more
But what thou art besides, thou wert too base
To be his groom: thou wert dignified enough,
Even to the point of envy, if 'twere made
Comparative for your virtues, to be styl'd
The under-hangman of his kingdom; and hated
For being preferr'd so well.
   Clo.   The south fog rot him!
   Imo. He never can meet more mischance than come
To be but nam'd of thee. His meanest garment,
That ever hath but clipp'd his body, is dearer
In my respect than all the hairs above thee,
Were they all made such men.

Enter PISANIO.

                 How now,. Pisanio!
   Clo. His garment! Now, the devil,—
   Imo. To Dorothy my woman hie thee presently,--
   Clo. His garment!
   Imo.   I am sprited with a fool;
Frighted, and anger'd worse.—Go bid my woman
Search for a jewel that too casually
Hath left mine arm: it was thy master's; shrew me
If I would lose it for a revenue
Of any king's in Europe. I do think
I saw't this morning: confident I am
Last night 'twas on mine arm; I kiss'd it:
I hope it be not gone to tell my lord
That I kiss aught but he.
   Pis.   'Twill not be lost.
   Imo. I hope so: go and search. [*Exit* PISANIO.
   Clo.   You have abus'd me.—
His meanest garment?
   Imo.   Ay, I said so, sir:
If you will make't an action, call witness to't.
   Clo. I will inform your father.
   Imo.   Your mother too:
She's my good lady; and will conceive, I hope,
But the worse of me. So I leave you, sir,
To the worst of discontent.

Clo.   I'll be reveng'd :—
His meanest garment!—Well.   [*Exit.*

SCENE IV.—Rome. *An Apartment in* Philario's *House.*

Enter Posthumus *and* Philario.

Post. Fear it not, sir: I would I were so sure
To win the king as I am bold her honour
Will remain hers.
   Phi.   What means do you make to him?
   Post. Not any; but abide the change of time;
Quake in the present winter's state, and wish
That warmer days would come: in these sear'd hopes
I barely gratify your love; they failing,
I must die much your debtor.
   Phi. Your very goodness and your company
O'erpays all I can do.   By this your king
Hath heard of great Augustus: Caius Lucius
Will do 's commission throughly: and I think
He'll grant the tribute, send the arrearages,
Or look upon our Romans, whose remembrance
Is yet fresh in their grief.
   Post.   I do believe,—
Statist though I am none, nor like to be,—
That this will prove a war; and you shall hear
The legions now in Gallia sooner landed
In our not-fearing Britain than have tidings
Of any penny tribute paid.   Our countrymen
Are men more ordered than when Julius Cæsar
Smil'd at their lack of skill, but found their courage
Worthy his frowning at: their discipline,—
Now mingled with their courage,—will make known
To their approvers they are people such
That mend upon the world.
   Phi.   See! Iachimo!

Enter Iachimo.

   Post. The swiftest harts have posted you by land,
And winds of all the corners kiss'd your sails,
To make your vessel nimble.
   Phi.   Welcome, sir.
   Post. I hope the briefness of your answer made
The speediness of your return.
   Iach.   Your lady
Is one of the fairest that I have look'd upon

Post. And therewithal the best; or let her beauty
Look through a casement to allure false hearts,
And be false with them.

Iach.   Here are letters for you.

Post. Their tenor good, I trust.

Iach.   'Tis very like.

Phi. Was Caius Lucius in the Britain court
When you were there?

Iach.   He was expected then,
But not approach'd.

Post.   All is well yet.—
Sparkles this stone as it was wont? or is't not
Too dull for your good wearing?

Iach.   If I had lost it
I should have lost the worth of it in gold.
I'll make a journey twice as far, to enjoy
A second night of such sweet shortness which
Was mine in Britain; for the ring is won.

Post. The stone's too hard to come by.

Iach.   Not a whit,
Your lady being so easy.

Post.   Make not, sir,
Your loss your sport: I hope you know that we
Must not continue friends.

Iach.   Good sir, we must,
If you keep covenant. Had I not brought
The knowledge of your mistress home, I grant
We were to question further: but I now
Profess myself the winner of her honour,
Together with your ring; and not the wronger
Of her or you, having proceeded but
By both your wills.

Post.   If you can make't apparent
That you have tasted her in bed, my hand
And ring is yours: if not, the foul opinion
You had of her pure honour gains or loses
Your sword or mine, or masterless leaves both
To who shall find them.

Iach.   Sir, my circumstances,
Being so near the truth as I will make them,
Must first induce you to believe: whose strength
I will confirm with oath; which I doubt not
You'll give me leave to spare when you shall find
You need it not.

Post.   Proceed.

Iach.   First, her bedchamber,—

Where, I confess, I slept not; but profess
Had that was well worth watching,—it was hang'd
With tapestry of silk and silver; the story
Proud Cleopatra, when she met her Roman,
And Cydnus swell'd above the banks, or for
The press of boats or pride: a piece of work
So bravely done, so rich, that it did strive
In workmanship and value; which I wonder'd
Could be so rarely and exactly wrought,
Since the true life on't was,—

  Post.   This is true;
And this you might have heard of here, by me
Or by some other.

  Iach.   More particulars
Must justify my knowledge.

  Post.   So they must,
Or do your honour injury.

  Iach.   The chimney
Is south the chamber; and the chimney-piece
Chaste Dian bathing: never saw I figures
So likely to report themselves: the cutter
Was, as another nature, dumb; outwent her,
Motion and breath left out.

  Post.   This is a thing
Which you might from relation likewise reap;
Being, as it is, much spoke of.

  Iach.   The roof o' the chamber
With golden cherubins is fretted: her andirons,—
I had forgot them,—were two winking Cupids
Of silver, each on one foot standing, nicely
Depending on their brands

  Post.   This is her honour!—
Let it be granted you have seen all this,—and praise
Be given to your remembrance,—the description
Of what is in her chamber nothing saves
The wager you have laid.

  Iach.   Then, if you can,
        [*Pulling out the bracelet.*
Be pale; I beg but leave to air this jewel; see!—
And now 'tis up again: it must be married
To that your diamond; I'll keep them.

  Post.   Jove!—
Once more let me behold it: is it that
Which I left with her?

  Iach.   Sir,—I thank her,—that:
She stripp'd it from her arm; I see her yet;

Her pretty action did outsell her gift,
And yet enrich'd it too: she gave it me, and said
She priz'd it once.
Post.   May be she pluck'd it off
To send it me.
    Iach.   She writes so to you? doth she?
    Post. O, no, no, no! 'tis true.   Here, take this too;
                                    [*Gives the ring*
It is a basilisk unto mine eye,
Kills me to look on't.—Let there be no honour
Where there is beauty; truth where semblance; love
Where there's another man: the vows of women
Of no more bondage be to where they are made
Than they are to their virtues; which is nothing.—
O, above measure false!
    Phi.   Have patience, sir,
And take your ring again; 'tis not yet won:
It may be probable she lost it; or,
Who knows if one o' her women, being corrupted,
Hath stolen it from her?
    Post.   Very true;
And so I hope he came by't.—Back my ring:
Render to me some corporal sign about her,
More evident than this; for this was stolen.
    Iach By Jupiter, I had it from her arm.
    Post. Hark you, he swears; by Jupiter he swears.
'Tis true,—nay, keep the ring,—'tis true: I am sure
She would not lose it: her attendants are
All sworn and honourable:—they induc'd to steal it!
And by a stranger!—No, he hath enjoy'd her:
The cognizance of her incontinency
Is this,—she hath bought the name of whore thus dearly.—
There, take thy hire; and all the fiends of hell
Divide themselves between you!
    Phi.   Sir, be patient:
This is not strong enough to be believ'd
Of one persuaded well of,—
    Post.   Never talk on't;
She hath been colted by him.
    Iach.   If you seek
For further satisfying, under her breast,—
Worthy the pressing,—lies a mole, right proud
Of that most delicate lodging: by my life,
I kiss'd it; and it gave me present hunger
To feed again, though full.   You do remember
This stain upon her?

Post.   Ay, and it doth confirm
Another stain, as big as hell can hold,
Were there no more but it.
   Iach.   Will you hear more?
   Post. Spare your arithmetic: never count the turns;
Once, and a million!
   Iach.   I'll be sworn,—
   Post.   No swearing.
If you will swear you have not done't, you lie;
And I will kill thee if thou dost deny
Thou'st made me cuckold.
   Iach.   I'll deny nothing.
   Post. O, that I had her here, to tear her limbmeal!
I will go there and do't; i' the court; before
Her father: I'll do something,—   [*Exit.*
   Phi.   Quite besides
The government of patience!—You have won:
Let's follow him, and pervert the present wrath
He hath against himself.
   Iach.   With all my heart.   [*Exeunt.*

SCENE V.—ROME.   *Another Room in* PHILARIO'S *House.*

Enter POSTHUMUS.

   Post. Is there no way for men to be, but women
Must be half-workers? We are all bastards;
And that most venerable man which I
Did call my father was I know not where
When I was stamp'd; some coiner with his tools
Made me a counterfeit: yet my mother seem'd
The Dian of that time: so doth my wife
The nonpareil of this.—O, vengeance, vengeance!—
Me of my lawful pleasure she restrain'd,
And pray'd me oft forbearance: did it with
A pudency so rosy, the sweet view on't
Might well have warm'd old Saturn; that I thought her
As chaste as unsunn'd snow.—O, all the devils!—
This yellow Iachimo in an hour,—was't not?
Or less,—at first?—Perchance he spoke not, but,
Like a full-acorn'd boar, a German one,
Cried *O!* and mounted: found no opposition
But what he look'd for should oppose, and she
Should from encounter guard. Could I find out
The woman's part in me! For there's no motion
That tends to vice in man but I affirm

It is the woman's part: be it lying, note it,
The woman's; flattering, hers; deceiving, hers;
Lust and rank thoughts, hers, hers; revenges, hers;
Ambitions, covetings, change of prides, disdain,
Nice longing, slanders, mutability,
All faults that have a name, nay, that hell knows,
Why, hers, in part or all; but rather all;
For ev'n to vice
They are not constant, but are changing still
One vice, but of a minute old, for one
Not half so old as that.   I'll write against them,
Detest them, curse them.—Yet 'tis greater skill
In a true hate to pray they have their will:
The very devils cannot plague them better.   [*Exit.*

ACT III.

SCENE I.—BRITAIN.   *A Room of State in* CYMBELINE'S *Palace.*

Enter, at one side, CYMBELINE, QUEEN, CLOTEN, *and* Lords; *at the other,* CAIUS LUCIUS *and* Attendants.

Cym. Now say, what would Augustus Cæsar with us?
Luc. When Julius Cæsar,—whose remembrance yet
Lives in men's eyes, and will to ears and tongues
Be theme and hearing ever,—was in this Britain,
And conquer'd it, Cassibelan, thine uncle,—
Famous in Cæsar's praises no whit less
Than in his feats deserving it,—for him
And his succession granted Rome a tribute,
Yearly three thousand pounds; which by thee lately
Is left untender'd.
Queen.   And, to kill the marvel,
Shall be so ever.
Clo.   There be many Cæsars
Ere such another Julius.   Britain is
A world by itself; and we will nothing pay
For wearing our own noses.
Queen.   That opportunity,
Which then they had to take from 's, to resume
We have again.—Remember, sir, my liege,
The kings your ancestors; together with
The natural bravery of your isle, which stands

As Neptune's park, ribbed and paled in
With rocks unscaleable and roaring waters;
With sands that will not bear your enemies' boats,
But suck them up to the top-mast.   A kind of conquest
Cæsar made here; but made not here his brag
Of *came,* and *saw,* and *overcame:* with shame,—
The first that ever touch'd him,—he was carried
From off our coast, twice beaten; and his shipping,—
Poor ignorant baubles!—on our terrible seas,
Like egg-shells mov'd upon their surges, crack'd
As easily 'gainst our rocks: for joy whereof
The fam'd Cassibelan, who was once at point,—
O, giglot fortune!—to master Cæsar's sword,
Made Lud's town with rejoicing fires bright
And Britons strut with courage.

    Clo. Come, there's no more tribute to be paid: our king-
dom is stronger than it was at that time; and, as I said,
there is no more such Cæsars: other of them may have
crooked noses; but to owe such straight arms, none.

    Cym. Son, let your mother end.

    Clo. We have yet many among us can gripe as hard as
Cassibelan: I do not say I am one; but I have a hand.—
Why tribute? why should we pay tribute? If Cæsar can
hide the sun from us with a blanket, or put the moon in his
pocket, we will pay him tribute for light; else, sir, no more
tribute, pray you now.

    Cym. You must know,
Till the injurious Romans did extort
This tribute from us, we were free: Cæsar's ambition,—
Which swell'd so much that it did almost stretch
The sides o' the world,—against all colour, here
Did put the yoke upon 's ; which to shake off
Becomes a warlike people, whom we reckon
Ourselves to be.

    Clo.   We do.

    Cym.   Say then to Cæsar,
Our ancestor was that Mulmutius which
Ordain'd our laws,—whose use the sword of Cæsar
Hath too much mangled; whose repair and franchise
Shall, by the power we hold, be our good deed,
Though Rome be therefore angry:—Mulmutius made our
        laws,
Who was the first of Britain which did put
His brows within a golden crown, and call'd
Himself a king.

    Luc.   I am sorry, Cymbeline,

That I am to pronounce Augustus Cæsar,—
Cæsar, that hath more kings his servants than
Thyself domestic officers,—thine enemy:
Receive it from me, then:—War and confusion
In Cæsar's name pronounce I 'gainst thee: look
For fury not to be resisted.—Thus defied,
I thank thee for myself.

    Cym.   Thou art welcome, Caius.
Thy Cæsar knighted me; my youth I spent
Much under him; of him I gather'd honour;
Which he to seek of me again, perforce,
Behoves me keep at utterance. I am perfect
That the Pannonians and Dalmatians for
Their liberties are now in arms,—a precedent
Which not to read would show the Britons cold:
So Cæsar shall not find them.

    Luc.   Let proof speak.

    Clo. His majesty bids you welcome. Make pastime with
us a day or two, or longer: if you seek us afterwards in
other terms, you shall find us in our salt-water girdle: if
you beat us out of it, it is yours; if you fall in the adventure,
our crows shall fare the better for you; and there's
an end.

    Luc. So, sir.

    Cym. I know your master's pleasure, and he mine:
All the remain is, welcome.   [*Exeunt.*

SCENE II.—BRITAIN. *Another Room in the Palace.*

Enter PISANIO *with a letter.*

    Pis. How! of adultery? Wherefore write you not
What monster's her accuser?—Leonatus!
O master! what a strange infection
Is fallen into thy ear! What false Italian,—
As poisonous tongu'd as handed,—hath prevail'd
On thy too ready hearing?—Disloyal! No:
She's punish'd for her truth; and undergoes,
More goddess-like than wife-like, such assaults
As would take in some virtue.—O my master!
Thy mind to her is now as low as were
Thy fortunes.—How! that I should murder her?
Upon the love, and truth, and vows which I
Have made to thy command?—I, her?—her blood?
If it be so to do good service, never
Let me be counted serviceable. How look I,

That I should seem to lack humanity
So much as this fact comes to? [*Reading.*] *Do't: the letter*
That I have sent her, by her own command
Shall give thee opportunity:—O damn'd paper!
Black as the ink that's on thee! Senseless bauble,
Art thou a fedary for this act, and look'st
So virgin-like without? Lo, here she comes.
I am ignorant in what I am commanded.

Enter IMOGEN.

Imo. How now, Pisanio!
Pis. Madam, here is a letter from my lord.
Imo. Who? thy lord? that is my lord,—Leonatus?
O, learn'd indeed were that astronomer
That knew the stars as I his characters;
He'd lay the future open.—You good gods,
Let what is here contain'd relish of love,
Of my lord's health, of his content,—yet not
That we two are asunder,—let that grieve him;—
Some griefs are med'cinable; that is one of them,
For it doth physic love;—of his content
All but in that!—Good wax, thy leave:—bless'd be
You bees that make these locks of counsel! Lovers
And men in dangerous bonds pray not alike:
Though forfeiters you cast in prison, yet
You clasp young Cupid's tables.—Good news, gods! [*Reads.*

Justice, and your father's wrath, should he take me in his
dominion, could not be so cruel to me, as you, O the dearest of
creatures, would even renew me with your eyes. Take notice
that I am in Cambria, at Milford-Haven: what your own love
will, out of this, advise you, follow. So he wishes you all hap-
piness that remains loyal to his vow, and your, increasing in
love, LEONATUS POSTHUMUS.
O for a horse with wings!—Hear'st thou, Pisanio?
He is at Milford-Haven: read, and tell me
How far 'tis thither. If one of mean affairs
May plod it in a week, why may not I
Glide thither in a day?—Then, true Pisanio,—
Who long'st, like me, to see thy lord; who long'st—
O, let me 'bate—but not like me; yet long'st,
But in a fainter kind: O, not like me;
For mine's beyond beyond,—say, and speak thick,—
Love's counsellor should fill the bores of hearing
To the smothering of the sense,—how far it is
To this same blessed Milford: and, by the way,
Tell me how Wales was made so happy as

To inherit such a haven: but, first of all,
How we may steal from hence; and for the gap
That we shall make in time, from our hence-going
And our return, to excuse. But first, how get hence:
Why should excuse be born or e'er begot?
We'll talk of that hereafter. Pr'ythee, speak,
How many score of miles may we well ride
'Twixt hour and hour?

 Pis.   One score 'twixt sun and sun,
Madam,'s enough for you, and too much too.

 Imo. Why, one that rode to 's execution, man,
Could never go so slow: I have heard of riding wagers,
Where horses have been nimbler than the sands
That run i' the clock's behalf;—but this is foolery:
Go bid my woman feign a sickness; say
She'll home to her father: and provide me presently
A riding suit no costlier than would fit
A franklin's housewife.

 Pis.   Madam, you're best consider.

 Imo. I see before me, man, nor here, nor here,
Nor what ensues; but have a fog in them
That I cannot look through. Away, I pr'ythee;
Do as I bid thee: there's no more to say;
Accessible is none but Milford way.   [*Exeunt.*

SCENE III.—WALES. *A mountainous Country with a
         Cave.*

Enter BELARIUS, GUIDERIUS, *and* ARVIRAGUS.

 Bel. A goodly day not to keep house, with such
Whose roof's as low as ours! Stoop, boys: this gate
Instructs you how to adore the heavens, and bows you
To morning's holy office: the gates of monarchs
Are arch'd so high that giants may jet through,
And keep their impious turbans on, without
Good-morrow to the sun.—Hail, thou fair heaven!
We house i' the rock, yet use thee not so hardly
As prouder livers do.

 Gui.   Hail, heaven!

 Arv.   Hail, heaven!

 Bel. Now for our mountain sport: up to yond hill,
Your legs are young; I'll tread these flats. Consider,
When you above perceive me like a crow,
That it is place which lessens and sets off:
And you may then revolve what tales I have told you

Of courts, of princes, of the tricks in war:
This service is not service so being done,
But being so allow'd: to apprehend thus
Draws us a profit from all things we see;
And often, to our comfort, shall we find
The sharded beetle in a safer hold
Than is the full-wing'd eagle. O, this life
Is nobler than attending for a check,
Richer than doing nothing for a bauble,
Prouder than rustling in unpaid-for silk:
Such gain the cap of him that makes 'em fine,
Yet keeps his book uncross'd: no life to ours.

　　Gui. Out of your proof you speak: we, poor unfledg'd,
Have never wing'd from view o' the nest; nor know not
What air's from home. Haply this life is best,
If quiet life be best; sweeter to you
That have a sharper known; well corresponding
With your stiff age: but unto us it is
A cell of ignorance; travelling abed;
A prison for a debtor, that not dares
To stride a limit.

　　Arv.　　　　　　What should we speak of
When we are old as you? when we shall hear
The rain and wind beat dark December, how,
In this our pinching cave, shall we discourse
The freezing hours away? We have seen nothing:
We are beastly; subtle as the fox for prey;
Like warlike as the wolf for what we eat:
Our valour is to chase what flies; our cage
We make a quire, as doth the prison'd bird,
And sing our bondage freely.

　　Bel.　　　　　　　　How you speak!
Did you but know the city's usuries,
And felt them knowingly: the art o' the court,
As hard to leave as keep; whose top to climb
Is certain falling, or so slippery that
The fear's as bad as falling: the toil o' the war,
A pain that only seems to seek out danger
I' the name of fame and honour; which dies i' the search
And hath as oft a slanderous epitaph
As record of fair act; nay, many times
Doth ill deserve by doing well; what's worse,
Must court'sy at the censure.—O, boys, this story
The world may read in me: my body's mark'd
With Roman swords; and my report was once
First with the best of note: Cymbeline lov'd me,

And when a soldier was the theme, my name
Was not far off: then was I as a tree
Whose boughs did bend with fruit: but in one night
A storm or robbery, call it what you will,
Shook down my mellow hangings, nay, my leaves,
And left me bare to weather.

 Gui.   Uncertain favour?

 Bel. My fault being nothing,—as I have told you oft,—
But that two villains, whose false oaths prevail'd
Before my perfect honour, swore to Cymbeline
I was confederate with the Romans: so
Follow'd my banishment; and this twenty years
This rock and these demesnes have been my world:
Where I have liv'd at honest freedom; paid
More pious debts to heaven than in all
The fore-end of my time.—But up to the mountains!
This is not hunters' language.—He that strikes
The venison first shall be the lord o' the feast;
To him the other two shall minister;
And we will fear no poison, which attends
In place of greater state. I'll meet you in the valleys.

         [*Exeunt* GUI. *and* ARV.

How hard it is to hide the sparks of nature!
These boys know little they are sons to the king;
Nor Cymbeline dreams that they are alive.
They think they are mine: and though train'd up thus
   meanly
I' the cave wherein they bow, their thoughts do hit
The roofs of palaces; and nature prompts them,
In simple and low things, to prince it much
Beyond the trick of others. This Polydore,—
The heir of Cymbeline and Britain, who
The king his father call'd Guiderius,—Jove!
When on my three-foot stool I sit, and tell
The warlike feats I have done, his spirits fly out
Into my story: say, *Thus mine enemy fell,
And thus I set my foot on's neck;* even then
The princely blood flows in his cheek, he sweats,
Strains his young nerves, and puts himself in posture
That acts my words. The younger brother, Cadwal,—
Once Arviragus,—in as like a figure
Strikes life into my speech, and shows much more
His own conceiving. Hark, the game is rous'd!—
O Cymbeline! heaven and my conscience knows
Thou didst unjustly banish me: whereon,
At three and two years old, I stole these babes;

Thinking to bar thee of succession, as
Thou reft'st me of my lands.   Euriphile,
Thou wast their nurse; they took thee for their mother,
And every day do honour to her grave:
Myself, Belarius, that am Morgan call'd,
They take for natural father.   The game is up.   [*Exit.*

SCENE IV.— *Wales, near Milford-Haven.*

·   *Enter* PISANIO *and* IMOGEN.

Imo. Thou told'st me, when we came from horse, the place
Was near at hand. —Ne'er long'd my mother so
To see me first as I have now.—Pisanio!   Man!
Where is Posthumus?   What is in thy mind
That makes thee stare thus? Wherefore breaks that sigh
From the inward of thee?   One but painted thus
Would be interpreted a thing perplex'd
Beyond self-explication: put thyself
Into a 'haviour of less fear, ere wildness
Vanquish my steadier senses.   What's the matter?
Why tender'st thou that paper to me, with
A look untender?   If't be summer news,
Smile to't before; if winterly, thou need'st
But keep that countenance still.—My husband's hand!
That drug-damn'd Italy hath out-crafticd him,
And he's at some hard point.—Speak, man; thy tongue
May take off some extremity, which to read
Would be even mortal to me.
    Pis.   Please you, read;
And you shall find me, wretched man, a thing
The most disdain'd of fortune.
    Imo. [reads.] *Thy mistress, Pisanio, hath played the*
strumpet in my bed; the testimonies whereof lie bleeding in
me.   I speak not out of weak surmises; but from proof as
strong as my grief and as certain as I expect my revenge.
That part thou, Pisanio, must act for me, if thy faith be not
tainted with the breach of hers.   Let thine own hands take
away her life; I shall give thee opportunity at Milford-Haven:
she hath my letter for the purpose: where, if thou fear to
strike, and to make me certain it is done, thou art the pander
to her dishonour, and equally to me disloyal.
    Pis. What, shall I need to draw my sword? the paper
Hath cut her throat already.—No, 'tis slander;
Whose edge is sharper than the sword; whose tongue
Outvenoms all the worms of Nile; whose breath

Rides on the posting winds, and doth belie
All corners of the world: kings, queens, and states,
Maids, matrons, nay, the secrets of the grave
This viperous slander enters.—What cheer, madam?

Imo. False to his bed? What is it to be false?
To lie in watch there, and to think on him?
To weep 'twixt clock and clock? if sleep charge nature,
To break it with a fearful dream of him,
And cry myself awake? that 's false to his bed,
Is it?

Pis. Alas, good lady!

Imo. I false! Thy conscience witness:—Iachimo,
Thou didst accuse him of incontinency;
Thou then look'dst like a villain; now, methinks,
Thy favour 's good enough.—Some jay of Italy,
Whose mother was her painting, hath betray'd him:
Poor I am stale, a garment out of fashion;
And for I am richer than to hang by the walls
I must be ripp'd: to pieces with me!—O,
Men's vows are women's traitors! All good seeming,
By thy revolt, O husband, shall be thought
Put on for villany,—not born where't grows,
But worn a bait for ladies.

Pis.   Good madam, hear me.

Imo. True honest men being heard, like false Æneas,
Were, in his time, thought false: and Sinon's weeping
Did scandal many a holy tear; took pity
From most true wretchedness: so thou, Posthumus,
Wilt lay the leaven on all proper men;
Goodly and gallant shall be false and perjur'd
From thy great fail.—Come, fellow, be thou honest:
Do thou thy master's bidding: when thou see'st him,
A little witness my obedience: look!
I draw the sword myself: take it, and hit
The innocent mansion of my love, my heart:
Fear not; 'tis empty of all things but grief:
Thy master is not there; who was indeed
The riches of it: do his bidding; strike.
Thou mayst be valiant in a better cause;
But now thou seem'st a coward.

Pis.   Hence, vile instrument!
Thou shalt not damn my hand.

Imo.   Why, I must die;
And if I do not by thy hand, thou art
No servant of thy master's: against self-slaughter
There is a prohibition so divine

That cravens my weak hand. Come, here's my heart:
Something's afore't.—Soft, soft! we'll no defence;
Obedient as the scabbard.—What is here?
The scriptures of the loyal Leonatus
All turn'd to heresy? Away, away,
Corrupters of my faith! you shall no more
Be stomachers to my heart. Thus may poor fools
Believe false teachers: though those that are betray'd
Do feel the treason sharply, yet the traitor
Stands in worse case of woe.
And thou, Posthumus, that didst set up
My disobedience 'gainst the king my father,
And make me put into contempt the suits
Of princely fellows, shalt hereafter find
It is no act of common passage, but
A strain of rareness: and I grieve myself
To think, when thou shalt be disedg'd by her
That now thou tir'st on, how thy memory
Will then be pang'd by me.—Pr'ythee, despatch:
The lamb entreats the butcher: where's thy knife?
Thou art too slow to do thy master's bidding,
When I desire it too.
  Pis.   O gracious lady,
Since I receiv'd command to do this business
I have not slept one wink.
  Imo.   Do't, and to bed then.
  Pis. I'll wake mine eyeballs blind first.
  Imo.   Wherefore then
Didst undertake it? Why hast thou abus'd
So many miles with a pretence? this place?
Mine action and thine own? our horses' labour?
The time inviting thee? the perturb'd court,
For my being absent; whereunto I never
Purpose return? Why hast thou gone so far,
To be unbent when thou hast ta'en thy stand,
The elected deer before thee?
  Pis.   But to win time
To lose so bad employment; in the which
I have consider'd of a course. Good lady,
Hear me with patience.
  Imo.   Talk thy tongue weary: speak:
I have heard I am a strumpet; and mine ear,
Therein false struck, can take no greater wound,
Nor tent to bottom that. But speak.
  Pis.   Then, madam,
I thought you would not back again.

Imo. .   Most like,—
Bringing me here to kill me.
    Pis.   Not so neither:
But if I were as wise as honest, then
My purpose would prove well.   It cannot be
But that my master is abus'd:
Some villain, ay, and singular in his art,
Hath done you both this cursed injury.
    Imo. Some Roman courtezan.
    Pis.   No, on my life:
I'll give but notice you are dead, and send him
Some bloody sign of it; for 'tis commanded
I should do so: you shall be miss'd at court,
And that will well confirm it.
    Imo.   Why, good fellow,
What shall I do the while? where bide? how live?
Or in my life what comfort when I am
Dead to my husband?
    Pis.   If you'll back to the court,—
    Imo. No court, no father; nor no more ado
With that harsh, noble, simple nothing,—
That Cloten, whose love-suit hath been to me
As fearful as a siege.
    Pis.   If not at court,
Then not in Britain must you bide.
    Imo.   Where then?
Hath Britain all the sun that shines?   Day, night,
Are they not but in Britain?   I' the world's volume
Our Britain seems as of it, but not in't;
In a great pool a swan's nest: pr'ythee, think
There's livers out of Britain.
    Pis.   I am most glad
You think of other place.   The ambassador,
Lucius the Roman, comes to Milford-Haven
To-morrow: now, if you could wear a mind
Dark as your fortune is, and but disguise
That which to appear itself must not yet be,
But by self-danger, you should tread a course
Privy and full of view; yea, haply, near
The residence of Posthumus,—so nigh at least
That though his actions were not visible, yet
Report should render him hourly to your ear,
As truly as he moves.
    Imo.   O, for such means,
Though peril to my modesty, not death on't,
I would adventure.

Pis.   Well then, here's the point:
You must forget to be a woman; change
Command into obedience; fear and niceness,—
The handmaids of all women, or, more truly,
Woman its pretty self,—into a waggish courage;
Ready in gibes, quick-answer'd, saucy, and
As quarrelous as the weasel; nay, you must
Forget that rarest treasure of your cheek,
Exposing it,—but, O, the harder heart!
Alack, no remedy!—to the greedy touch
Of common-kissing Titan; and forget
Your laboursome and dainty trims, wherein
You made great Juno angry.
   Imo.   Nay, be brief;
I see into thy end, and am almost
A man already.
   Pis.   First, make yourself but like one.
Fore-thinking this, I have already fit,—
'Tis in my cloak-bag,—doublet, hat, hose, all
That answer to them: would you, in their serving,
And with what imitation you can borrow
From youth of such a season, 'fore noble Lucius
Present yourself, desire his service, tell him
Wherein you are happy,—which you'll make him know
If that his head have ear in music,—doubtless
With joy he will embrace you; for he's honourable
And, doubling that, most holy. Your means abroad
You have me, rich; and I will never fail
Beginning nor supplyment.
   Imo.   Thou art all the comfort
The gods will diet me with. Pr'ythee, away:
There's more to be consider'd; but we'll even
All that good time will give us: this attempt
I am soldier to, and will abide it with
A prince's courage. Away, I pr'ythee.
   Pis. Well, madam, we must take a short farewell,
Lest, being miss'd, I be suspected of
Your carriage from the court. My noble mistress,
Here is a box; I had it from the queen;
What's in't is precious; if you are sick at sea
Or stomach-qualm'd at land, a dram of this
Will drive away distemper.—To some shade,
And fit you to your manhood:—may the gods
Direct you to the best!
   Imo.   Amen: I thank thee.   [*Exeunt.*

SCENE V.—Britain. *A Room in* Cymbeline's
Palace.

Enter Cymbeline, Queen, Cloten, Lucius, *and* Lords.

Cym. Thus far; and so farewell.
Luc.   Thanks, royal sir.
My emperor hath wrote; I must from hence;
And am right sorry that I must report ye
My master's enemy.
Cym.   Our subjects, sir,
Will not endure his yoke; and for ourself
To show less sovereignty than they, must needs
Appear unkinglike.
Luc.   So, sir, I desire of you
A conduct over-land to Milford-Haven.—
Madam, all joy befall his grace and you!
Cym. My lords, you are appointed for that office;
The due of honour in no point omit.—
So farewell, noble Lucius.
Luc.   Your hand, my lord.
Clo. Receive it friendly: but from this time forth
I wear it as your enemy.
Luc.   Sir, the event
Is yet to name the winner: fare you well.
Cym. Leave not the worthy Lucius, good my lords,
Till he have cross'd the Severn.—Happiness!

[*Exeunt* Lucius *and* Lords

Queen. He goes hence frowning: but it honours us
That we have given him cause.
Clo.   'Tis all the better;
Your valiant Britons have their wishes in it.
Cym. Lucius hath wrote already to the emperor
How it goes here.   It fits us therefore ripely
Our chariots and our horsemen be in readiness:
The powers that he already hath in Gallia
Will soon be drawn to head, from whence he moves
His war for Britain.
Queen.   'Tis not sleepy business;
But must be look'd to speedily and strongly.
Cym. Our expectation that it would be thus
Hath made us forward.   But, my gentle queen,
Where is our daughter?   She hath not appear'd
Before the Roman, nor to us hath tender'd
The duty of the day: she looks us like
A thing more made of malice than of duty:

We have noted it.—Call her before us; for
We have been too slight in sufferance. [*Exit an* Attendant.
 Queen.   Royal sir,
Since the exile of Posthumus, most retir'd
Hath her life been; the cure whereof, my lord,
'Tis time must do. Beseech your majesty,
Forbear sharp speeches to her: she's a lady
So tender of rebukes that words are strokes,
And strokes death to her.

     Re-enter Attendant.

 Cym.   Where is she, sir? How
Can her contempt be answer'd?
 Atten.   Please you, sir,
Her chambers are all lock'd; and there's no answer
That will be given to the loud'st of noise we make.
 Queen. My lord, when last I went to visit her,
She pray'd me to excuse her keeping close;
Whereto constrain'd by her infirmity
She should that duty leave unpaid to you
Which daily she was bound to proffer: this
She wish'd me to make known; but our great court
Made me to blame in memory.
 Cym.   Her door's lock'd?
Not seen of late? Grant, heavens, that which I fear
Prove false!   [*Exit.*
 Queen. Son, I say, follow the king.
 Clo. That man of hers, Pisanio, her old servant,
I have not seen these two days.
 Queen.   Go, look after.—
          [*Exit* CLOTEN.
Pisanio, thou that stand'st so for Posthumus!—
He hath a drug of mine; I pray his absence
Proceed by swallowing that; for he believes
It is a thing most precious. But for her,
Where is she gone? Haply despair hath seiz'd her;
Or, wing'd with fervour of her love, she's flown
To her desir'd Posthumus: gone she is
To death or to dishonour; and my end
Can make good use of either: she being down,
I have the placing of the British crown.

     Re-enter CLOTEN.

How now, my son!
 Clo.   'Tis certain she is fled.

Go in and cheer the king: he rages; none
Dare come about him.
 Queen.   All the better: may
This night forestall him of the coming day!   [*Exit.*
 Clo. I love and hate her: for she s fair and royal,
And that she hath all courtly parts more exquisite
Than lady, ladies, woman; from every one
The best she hath, and she, of all compounded,
Outsells them all.—I love her therefore: but,
Disdaining me, and throwing favours on
The low Posthumus, slanders so her judgment
That what's else rare is chok'd; and in that point
I will conclude to hate her, nay, indeed,
To be reveng'd upon her. For when fools shall—

Enter PISANIO.

Who is here? What, are you packing, sirrah?
Come hither: ah, you precious pander! Villain,
Where is thy lady? In a word; or else
Thou art straightway with the fiends.
 Pis.   O, good my lord!
 Clo. Where is thy lady? or, by Jupiter—
I will not ask again. Close villain,
I'll have this secret from thy heart, or rip
Thy heart to find it. Is she with Posthumus?
From whose so many weights of baseness cannot
A dram of worth be drawn.
 Pis.   Alas, my lord,
How can she be with him? When was she miss'd?
He is in Rome.
 Clo.   Where is she, sir? Come nearer;
No further halting: satisfy me home
What is become of her.
 Pis. O, my all-worthy lord!
 Clo.   All-worthy villain!
Discover where thy mistress is at once,
At the next word,—no more of worthy lord,—
Speak, or thy silence on the instant is
Thy condemnation and thy death.
 Pis.   Then, sir,
This paper is the history of my knowledge
Touching her flight.   [*Presenting a letter.*
 Clo.   Let's see't.—I will pursue her
Even to Augustus' throne.
 Pis. [*aside.*]   Or this or perish.

She 's far enough; and what he learns by this
May prove his travel, not her danger.

Clo.   Hum!

Pis. [aside] I'll write to my lord she 's dead. O Imogen,
Safe mayst thou wander, safe return again!

Clo. Sirrah, is this letter true?

Pis. Sir, as I think.

Clo. It is Posthumus' hand; I know't.—Sirrah, if thou
wouldst not be a villain, but do me true service, undergo
those employments wherein I should have cause to use thee
with a serious industry,—that is, what villany soe'er I bid
thee do, to perform it directly and truly,—I would think
thee an honest man: thou shouldst neither want my means
for thy relief nor my voice for thy preferment.

Pis. Well, my good lord.

Clo. Wilt thou serve me?—for since patiently and constantly thou hast stuck to the bare fortune of that beggar
Posthumus, thou canst not, in the course of gratitude, but
be a diligent follower of mine,—wilt thou serve me?

Pis. Sir, I will.

Clo. Give me thy hand; here's my purse. Hast any of
thy late master's garments in thy possession?

Pis. I have, my lord, at my lodging, the same suit he
wore when he took leave of my lady and mistress.

Clo. The first service thou dost me, fetch that suit
hither: let it be thy first service; go.

Pis. I shall, my lord.   [*Exit.*

Clo. Meet thee at Milford-Haven!—I forgot to ask him
one thing; I'll remember't anon: even there, thou villain
Posthumus, will I kill thee.—I would these garments were
come. She said upon a time,—the bitterness of it I now
belch from my heart,—that she held the very garment of
Posthumus in more respect than my noble and natural person, together with the adornment of my qualities. With
that suit upon my back will I ravish her: first kill him,
and in her eyes; there shall she see my valour, which will
then be a torment to her contempt. He on the ground, my
speech of insultment ended on his dead body,—and when my
lust hath dined,—which, as I say, to vex her, I will execute
in the clothes that she so praised,—to the court I'll knock
her back, foot her home again. She hath despised me re-
joicingly, and I'll be merry in my revenge.

Re-enter PISANIO *with the clothes.*

Be those the garments?

Pis. Ay, my noble lord.

C'o. How long is't since she went to Milford-Haven?

Pis. She can scarce be there yet.

Clo. Bring this apparel to my chamber; that is the second thing that I have commanded thee: the third is, that thou wilt be a voluntary mute to my design. Be but duteous, and true preferment shall tender itself to thee.—My revenge is now at Milford: would I had wings to follow it!—Come, and be true.   [*Exit.*

Pis. Thou bidd'st me to my loss: for true to thee
Were to prove false, which I will never be,
To him that is most true. To Milford go,
And find not her whom thou pursu'st.—Flow, flow,
You heavenly blessings, on her!—This fool's speed
Be cross'd with slowness; labour be his meed!   [*Exit*

SCENE VI.—WALES.   *Before the Cave of* BELARIUS.

Enter IMOGEN, *in boy's clothes.*

Imo. I see a man's life is a tedious one:
I have tir'd myself; and for two nights together
Have made the ground my bed. I should be sick,
But that my resolution helps me.—Milford,
When from the mountain-top Pisanio show'd thee,
Thou wast within a ken: O Jove! I think
Foundations fly the wretched; such, I mean,
Where they should be reliev'd. Two beggars told me
I could not miss my way: will poor folks lie,
That have afflictions on them, knowing 'tis
A punishment or trial? Yes; no wonder,
When rich ones scarce tell true: to lapse in fullness
Is sorer than to lie for need; and falsehood
Is worse in kings than beggars.—My dear lord!
Thou art one o' the false ones: now I think on thee
My hunger's gone; but even before, I was
At point to sink for food.—But what is this?
Here is a path to't: 'tis some savage hold:
I were best not call; I dare not call: yet famine,
Ere clean it o'erthrow nature, makes it valiant.
Plenty and peace breeds cowards; hardness ever
Of hardiness is mother.—Ho! who's here?
If anything that's civil, speak; if savage,
Take or lend.—Ho!—No answer? then I'll enter.
Best draw my sword; and if mine enemy
But fear the sword like me, he'll scarcely look on't.
Such a foe, good heavens!   [*Goes into the cave.*

Enter BELARIUS, GUIDERIUS, *and* ARVIRAGUS.

Bel. You, Polydore, have prov'd best woodman, and
Are master of the feast: Cadwal and I
Will play the cook and servant; 'tis our match:
The sweat of industry would dry and die
But for the end it works to. Come; our stomachs
Will make what's homely savoury: weariness
Can snore upon the flint, when restive sloth
Finds the down pillow hard.—Now, peace be here,
Poor house, that keep'st thyself!
  Gui.   I am throughly weary.
  Arv. I am weak with toil, yet strong in appetite.
  Gui. There is cold meat i' the cave; we'll browse on that
Whilst what we have kill'd be cook'd.
  Bel.   Stay; come not in.
                    [*Looking into the cave.*
But that it eats our victuals, I should think
Here were a fairy.
  Gui.   What's the matter, sir?
  Bel. By Jupiter, an angel! or, if not,
An earthly paragon!—Behold divineness
No elder than a boy!

Re-enter IMOGEN.

  Imo. Good masters, harm me not:
Before I enter'd here I call'd; and thought
To have begg'd or bought what I have took: good troth,
I have stol'n naught; nor would not, though I had
            found
Gold strew'd o' the floor.   Here's money for my meat:
I would have left it on the board, so soon
As I had made my meal; and parted
With prayers for the provider.
  Gui.   Money, youth?
  Arv. All gold and silver rather turn to dirt!
And 'tis no better reckon'd, but of these
Who worship dirty gods.
  Imo.   I see you are angry:
Know, if you kill me for my fault, I should
Have died had I not made it.
  Bel.   Whither bound?
  Imo. To Milford-Haven.
  Bel.   What's your name?
  Imo. Fidele, sir.   I have a kinsman who
Is bound for Italy; he embark'd at Milford;

To whom being going, almost spent with hunger,
I am fallen in this offence.

Bel.   Pr'ythee, fair youth,
Think us no churls, nor measure our good minds
By this rude place we live in.   Well encounter'd!
'Tis almost night : you shall have better cheer
Ere you depart ; and thanks to stay and eat it.—
Boys, bid him welcome.

Gui.   Were you a woman, youth,
I should woo hard but be your groom.—In honesty
I'd bid for you as I do buy.

Arv.   I'll make't my comfort
He is a man ; I'll love him as my brother :—
And such a welcome as I'd give to him,
After long absence, such as yours :—most welcome !
Be sprightly, for you fall 'mongst friends.

Imo.   'Mongst friends,
If brothers.—[*Aside.*] Would it had been so that they
Had been my father's sons ! then had my prize
Been less ; and so more equal ballasting
To thee, Posthumus.

Bel.   He wrings at some distress.

Gui. Would I could free't !

Arv.   Or I ; whate'er it be,
What pain it cost, what danger ! gods !

Bel.   Hark, boys. [*Whispering.*

Imo. Great men,
That had a court no bigger than this cave,
That did attend themselves, and had the virtue
Which their own conscience seal'd them,—laying by
That nothing gift of differing multitudes,—
Could not out-peer these twain. Pardon me, gods !
I'd change my sex to be companion with them,
Since Leonatus' false.

Bel.   It shall be so.
Boys, we'll go dress our hunt.—Fair youth, come in :
Discourse is heavy, fasting ; when we have supp'd
We'll mannerly demand thee of thy story,
So far as thou wilt speak it.

Gui.   Pray, draw near.

Arv. The night to the owl and morn to the lark less wel-
      come.

Imo. Thanks, sir.

Arv.   I pray, draw near.   [*Exeunt.*

SCENE VII.—ROME.   *A public Place.*

Enter two Senators *and* Tribunes.

1 *Sen.* This is the tenor of the Emperor's writ:
That since the common men are now in action
'Gainst the Pannonians and Dalmatians,
And that the legions now in Gallia are
Full weak to undertake our wars against
The fallen-off Britons, that we do incite
The gentry to this business.   He creates
Lucius pro-consul : and to you, the tribunes,
For this immediate levy, he commends
His absolute commission.   Long live Cæsar!
   1 *Tri.* Is Lucius general of the forces?
   2 *Sen.*   Ay.
   1 *Tri.* Remaining now in Gallia?
   1 *Sen.*   With those legions
Which I have spoke of, whereunto your levy
Must be supplyant : the words of your commission
Will tie you to the numbers, and the time
Of their despatch.
   1 *Tri.*   We will discharge our duty.   [*Exeunt.*

ACT IV.

SCENE I.—WALES.   *The Forest near the Cave of* BELARIUS.

Enter CLOTEN.

Clo. I am near to the place where they should meet, if
Pisanio have mapped it truly.   How fit his garments serve
me !   Why should his mistress, who was made by him that
made the tailor, not be fit too? the rather,—saving reverence
of the word,—for 'tis said a woman's fitness comes by fits.
Therein I must play the workman.   I dare speak it to myself,—for it is not vainglory for a man and his glass to confer
in his own chamber,—I mean, the lines of my body are as
well drawn as his ; no less young, more strong, not beneath
him in fortunes, beyond him in the advantage of the time,
above him in birth, alike conversant in general services,
and more remarkable in single oppositions : yet this imper-
ceiverant thing loves him in my despite.   What mortality
is !   Posthumus, thy head, which now is growing upon thy

shoulders, shall within this hour be off, thy mistress enforced
thy garments cut to pieces before thy face; and all this done,
spurn her home to her father, who may haply be a little
angry for my so rough usage; but my mother, having power
of his testiness, shall turn all into my commendations.
My horse is tied up safe: out, sword, and to a sore purpose!
Fortune, put them into my hand! This is the very description of their meeting-place: and the fellow dares not
deceive me.   [*Exit.*

SCENE II.—WALES.   *Before the Cave.*

Enter, from the Cave, BELARIUS, GUIDERIUS, ARVIRAGUS,
      and IMOGEN.

Bel. [*to* IMOGEN.] You are not well: remain here in the
We'll come to you after hunting.   [cave,
      Arv. [*to* IMOGEN.]   Brother, stay here:
Are we not brothers?
      Imo.   So man and man should be;
But clay and clay differs in dignity,
Whose dust is both alike.   I am very sick.
      Gui. Go you to hunting, I'll abide with him.
      Imo. So sick I am not,—yet I am not well;
But not so citizen a wanton as
To seem to die ere sick: so please you, leave me;
Stick to your journal course: the breach of custom
Is breach of all.   I am ill; but your being by me
Cannot amend me: society is no comfort
To one not sociable: I am not very sick,
Since I can reason of it.   Pray you, trust me here:
I'll rob none but myself; and let me die,
Stealing so poorly.
      Gui.   I love thee; I have spoke it:
How much the quantity, the weight as much,
As I do love my father.
      Bel.   What? how! how!
      Arv. If it be sin to say so, sir, I yoke me
In my good brother's fault: I know not why
I love this youth; and I have heard you say
Love's reason 's without reason: the bier at door,
And a demand who is't shall die, I'd say
My father, not this youth.
      Bel. [*aside.*]   O noble strain!
O worthiness of nature! breed of greatness!
Cowards father cowards, and base things sire base:

Nature hath meal and bran, contempt and grace.
I'm not their father; yet who this should be
Doth miracle itself, lov'd before me.—
'Tis the ninth hour o' the morn.

Arv. Brother, farewell.

Imo. I wish ye sport.

Arv. You health,—so please you, sir.

Imo. [aside.] These are kind creatures. Gods, what lies
  I have heard!
Our courtiers say all's savage but at court:
Experience, O, thou disprov'st report!
The imperious seas breed monsters; for the dish,
Poor tributary rivers as sweet fish.
I am sick still; heart-sick.—Pisanio,
I'll now taste of thy drug.   *[Swallows some.*

Gui. I could not stir him:
He said he was gentle, but unfortunate;
Dishonestly afflicted, but yet honest.

Arv. Thus did he answer me: yet said hereafter
I might know more.

Bel. To the field, to the field!—
We'll leave you for this time: go in and rest.

Arv. We'll not be long away.

Bel. Pray, be not sick,
For you must be our housewife.

Imo. Well or ill,
I am bound to you.

Bel. And shalt be ever.
    [Exit IMOGEN *into the Cave.*
This youth, howe'er distress'd, appears he hath had
Good ancestors.

Arv. How angel-like he sings!

Gui. But his neat cookery! He cut our roots in char-
  acters;
And sauc'd our broths as Juno had been sick,
And he her dieter.

Arv. Nobly he yokes
A smiling with a sigh,—as if the sigh
Was that it was for not being such a smile;
The smile mocking the sigh that it would fly
From so divine a temple to commix
With winds that sailors rail at.

Gui. I do note,
That grief and patience, rooted in him both,
Mingle their spurs together.

Arv. Grow, patience!

And let the stinking elder, grief, untwine
His perishing root with the increasing vine!
   Bel. It is great morning. Come, away!—Who's there?

Enter CLOTEN.

   Clo. I cannot find those runagates; that villain
Hath mock'd me.—I am faint.
   Bel.   Those runagates!
Means he not us? I partly know him; 'tis
Cloten, the son o' the queen. I fear some ambush.
I saw him not these many years, and yet
I know 'tis he.—We are held as outlaws: hence!
   Gui. He is but one: you and my brother search
What companies are near: pray you, away;
Let me alone with him.   [*Exeunt* BEL. *and* ARV.
   Clo.   Soft!—What are you
That fly me thus? some villain mountaineers?
I have heard of such.—What slave art thou?
   Gui.   A thing
More slavish did I ne'er than answering
A slave without a knock.
   Clo.   Thou art a robber,
A law-breaker, a villain: yield thee, thief.
   Gui. To whom? to thee? What art thou? Have not I
An arm as big as thine? a heart as big?
Thy words, I grant, are bigger; for I wear not
My dagger in my mouth. Say what thou art,
Why I should yield to thee?
   Clo.   Thou villain base,
Know'st me not by my clothes?
   Gui.   No, nor thy tailor, rascal,
Who is thy grandfather: he made those clothes,
Which, as it seems, make thee.
   Clo.   Thou precious varlet,
My tailor made them not.
   Gui.   Hence, then, and thank
The man that gave them thee. Thou art some fool;
I am loth to beat thee.
   Clo.   Thou injurious thief,
Hear but my name, and tremble.
   Gui.   What's thy name?
   Clo. Cloten, thou villain.
   Gui. Cloten, thou double villain, be thy name,
I cannot tremble at it; were it toad, or adder, spider,
'Twould move me sooner.
   Clo.   To thy further fear,

Nay, to thy mere confusion, thou shalt know
I'm son to the queen.
  Gui.   I'm sorry for't; not seeming
So worthy as thy birth.
  Clo.   Art not afeard?
  Gui. Those that I reverence, those I fear,—the wise:
At fools I laugh, not fear them.
  Clo.   Die the death:
When I have slain thee with my proper hand,
I'll follow those that even now fled hence,
And on the gates of Lud's town set your heads:
Yield, rustic mountaineer.   [*Exeunt fighting.*

Re-enter BELARIUS *and* ARVIRAGUS.

  Bel. No company's abroad.
  Arv. None in the world: you did mistake him, sure.
  Bel. I cannot tell: long is it since I saw him,
But time hath nothing blurr'd those lines of favour
Which then he wore; the snatches in his voice,
And burst of speaking, were as his: I am absolute
'Twas very Cloten.
  Arv.   In this place we left them:
I wish my brother make good time with him,
You say he is so fell.
  Bel.   Being scarce made up,
I mean to man, he had not apprehension
Of roaring terrors; for defect of judgment
Is oft the cure of fear.—But, see, thy brother.

Re-enter GUIDERIUS *with* CLOTEN'S *head.*

  Gui. This Cloten was a fool, an empty purse,—
There was no money in't: not Hercules
Could have knock'd out his brains, for he had none:
Yet I not doing this, the fool had borne
My head as I do his.
  Bel.   What hast thou done?
  Gui. I am perfect what: cut off one Cloten's head,
Son to the queen, after his own report;
Who call'd me traitor, mountaineer; and swore,
With his own single hand he'd take us in,
Displace our heads where,—thank the gods!—they grow,
And set them on Lud's town.
  Bel.   We are all undone.
  Gui. Why, worthy father, what have we to lose
But that he swore to take, our lives? The law
Protects not us: then why should we be tender,

To let an arrogant piece of flesh threat us;
Play judge and executioner all himself,
For we do fear the law? What company
Discover you abroad?
    Bel.   No single soul
Can we set eye on, but in all safe reason
He must have some attendants.   Though his humour
Was nothing but mutation,—ay, and that
From one bad thing to worse; not frenzy, not
Absolute madness could so far have rav'd,
To bring him here alone: although perhaps
It may be heard at court that such as we
Cave here, hunt here, are outlaws, and in time
May make some stronger head: the which he hearing,—
As it is like him,—might break out, and swear
He'd fetch us in; yet is't not probable
To come alone, either he so undertaking
Or they so suffering: then on good ground we fear,
If we do fear this body hath a tail
More perilous than the head.
    Arv.   Let ordinance
Come as the gods foresay it: howsoe'er,
My brother hath done well.
    Bel.   I had no mind
To hunt this day: the boy Fidele's sickness
Did make my way long forth.
    Gui.   With his own sword,
Which he did wave against my throat, I have ta'en
His head from him: I'll throw't into the creek
Behind our rock; and let it to the sea,
And tell the fishes he's the queen's son, Cloten:
That's all I reck.   [*Exit.*
    Bel. I fear 'twill be reveng'd:
'Would, Polydore, thou hadst not done't! though valour
Becomes thee well enough.
    Arv.   Would I had done't,
So the revenge alone pursu'd me!—Polydore,
I love thee brotherly; but envy much
Thou hast robb'd me of this deed: I would revenges,
That   possible strength might meet, would seek   us
          through,
And put us to our answer.
    Bel.   Well, 'tis done:—
We'll hunt no more to-day, nor seek for danger
Where there's no profit.   I pr'ythee, to our rock;
You and Fidele play the cooks: I'll stay

Till hasty Polydore return, and bring him
To dinner presently.
   Arv.   Poor sick Fidele!
I'll willingly to him: to gain his colour
I'd let a parish of such Clotens' blood,
And praise myself for charity.   [*Exit.*
   Bel.   O thou goddess,
Thou divine nature, how thyself thou blazon'st
In these two princely boys!   They are as gentle
As zephyrs blowing below the violet,
Not wagging his sweet head; and yet as rough,
Their royal blood enchaf'd, as the rud'st wind
That by the top doth take the mountain pine,
And make him stoop to the vale.   'Tis wonder
That an invisible instinct should frame them
To royalty unlearn'd, honour untaught;
Civility not seen from other; valour
That wildly grows in them, but yields a crop
As if it had been sow'd.   Yet still it's strange
What Cloten's being here to us portends,
Or what his death will bring us.

inherent nature

        Re-enter GUIDERIUS.

   Gui.   Where's my brother?
I have sent Cloten's clotpoll down the stream,
In embassy to his mother: his body's hostage
For his return.   [*Solemn music.*
   Bel.   My ingenious instrument!
Hark, Polydore, it sounds!   But what occasion
Hath Cadwal now to give it motion?   Hark!
   Gui. Is he at home?
   Bel.   He went hence even now.
   Gui. What does he mean? since death of my dear'st
       mother
It did not speak before.   All solemn things
Should answer solemn accidents.   The matter?
Triumphs for nothing and lamenting toys
Is jollity for apes and grief for boys.
Is Cadwal mad?
   Bel.   Look, here he comes,
And brings the dire occasion in his arms
Of what we blame him for!

Re-enter ARVIRAGUS, *bearing* IMOGEN *as dead in his arms.*

   Arv.   The bird is dead
That we have made so much on.   I had rather

Have skipp'd from sixteen years of age to sixty,
To have turn'd my leaping time into a crutch,
Than have seen this.

   Gui.   O sweetest, fairest lily!
My brother wears thee not the one half so well
As when thou grew'st thyself.

   Bel.   O melancholy!
Who ever yet could sound thy bottom? find
The ooze to show what coast thy sluggish crare
Might easiliest harbour in?—Thou blessed thing!
Jove knows what man thou might'st have made; but I,
Thou diedst, a most rare boy, of melancholy!
How found you him?

   Arv.   Stark, as you see:
Thus smiling, as some fly had tickled slumber,
Not as death's dart, being laugh'd at: his right cheek
Reposing on a cushion.

   Gui.   Where?

   Arv.   O' the floor;
His arms thus leagu'd: I thought he slept; and put
My clouted brogues from off my feet, whose rudeness
Answer'd my steps too loud.

   Gui.   Why, he but sleeps:
If he be gone he'll make his grave a bed;
With female fairies will his tomb be haunted,
And worms will not come to thee.

   Arv.   With fairest flowers,
Whilst summer lasts and I live here, Fidele,
I'll sweeten thy sad grave: thou shalt not lack
The flower that's like thy face, pale primrose; nor
The azure hare-bell, like thy veins; no, nor
The leaf of eglantine, whom not to slander,
Out-sweeten'd not thy breath: the ruddock would,
With charitable bill,—O bill, sore shaming
Those rich-left heirs that let their fathers lie
Without a monument!—bring thee all this;
Yea, and furr'd moss besides, when flowers are none,
To winter-ground thy corse.

   Gui.   Pr'ythee, have done;
And do not play in wench-like words with that
Which is so serious. Let us bury him,
And not protract with admiration what
Is now due debt.—To the grave!

   Arv.   Say, where shall's lay him?

   Gui. By good Euriphile, our mother.

   Arv.   Be't so:

And let us, Polydore, though now our voices
Have got the mannish crack, sing him to the ground,
As once our mother; use like note and words,
Save that Euriphile must be Fidele.

Gui. Cadwal,
I cannot sing: I'll weep, and word it with thee;
For notes of sorrow out of tune are worse
Than priests and fanes that lie.

Arv.　　　　　　　　We'll speak it, then.

Bel. Great griefs, I see, medicine the less: for Cloten
Is quite forgot. He was a queen's son, boys:
And though he came our enemy, remember,
He was paid for that: though mean and mighty, rotting
Together, have one dust, yet reverence,—
That angel of the world,—doth make distinction
Of place 'tween high and low. Our foe was princely;
And though you took his life, as being our foe,
Yet bury him as a prince.

Gui.　　　　　　　Pray you, fetch him hither.
Thersites' body is as good as Ajax',
When neither are alive.

Arv.　　　　　　If you'll go fetch him,
We'll say our song the whilst.—Brother, begin.

　　　　　　　　　　　　[*Exit* BELARIUS.

Gui. Nay, Cadwal, we must lay his head to the east;
My father hath a reason for't.

Arv.　　　　　　　　'Tis true.

Gui. Come on, then, and remove him.

Arv.　　　　　　　　So.—Begin.

SONG.

Gui.	Fear no more the heat o' the sun,
	Nor the furious winter's rages;
	Thou thy worldly task hast done,
	Home art gone, and ta'en thy wages:
	Golden lads and girls all must,
	As chimney-sweepers, come to dust.
Arv.	Fear no more the frown o' the great;
	Thou art past the tyrant's stroke:
	Care no more to clothe and eat;
	To thee the reed is as the oak:
	The sceptre, learning, physic, must
	All follow this, and come to dust.
Gui.	Fear no more the lightning-flash,
Arv.	Nor the all-dreaded thunder-stone;
Gui.	Fear not slander, censure rash;
Arv.	Thou hast finish'd joy and moan:
Both.	All lovers young, all lovers must
	Consign to thee, and come to dust.

Gui.	No exorciser harm thee!
Arv.	Nor no witchcraft charm thee!
Gui.	Ghost unlaid forbear thee!
Arv.	Nothing ill come near thee!
Both.	Quiet consummation have;
	And renowned be thy grave!

Re-enter BELARIUS *with the body of* CLOTEN.

Gui. We have done our obsequies: come, lay him down.

Bel. Here's a few flowers; but 'bout midnight, more:
The herbs that have on them cold dew o' the night
Are strewings fitt'st for graves.—Upon their faces.—
You were as flowers, now wither'd: even so
These herblets shall, which we upon you strew.—
Come on, away: apart upon our knees.
The ground that gave them first has them again:
Their pleasures here are past, so is their pain.

[*Exeunt* BEL., GUI., *and* ARV.

Imo. [*awaking.*] Yes, sir, to Milford-Haven; which is the
        way?—
I thank you.—By yon bush?—Pray, how far thither?
'Ods pittikins! can it be six mile yet?—
I have gone all night. Faith, I'll lie down and sleep.
But, soft! no bedfellow:—O gods and goddesses!

[*Seeing the body.*

These flowers are like the pleasures of the world;
This bloody man, the care on't.—I hope I dream;
For so I thought I was a cave-keeper,
And cook to honest creatures: but 'tis not so;
'Twas but a bolt of nothing, shot at nothing,
Which the brain makes of fumes: our very eyes
Are sometimes, like our judgments, blind. Good faith,
I tremble still with fear: but if there be
Yet left in heaven as small a drop of pity
As a wren's eye, fear'd gods, a part of it!
The dream's here still: even when I wake it is
Without me, as within me; not imagin'd, felt.
A headless man!—The garments of Posthumus!
I know the shape of's leg: this is his hand;
His foot Mercurial; his Martial thigh;
The brawns of Hercules: but his Jovial face—
Murder in heaven?—How!—'Tis gone.—Pisanio,
All curses madded Hecuba gave the Greeks,
And mine to boot, be darted on thee! Thou,
Conspir'd with that irregulous devil, Cloten,
Hast here cut off my lord.—To write and read
Be henceforth treacherous!—Damn'd Pisanio

Hath with his forged letters,—damn'd Pisanio,—
From this most bravest vessel of the world
Struck the main-top!—O Posthumus! alas,
Where is thy head? where 's that?   Ay me! where 's that!
Pisanio might have kill'd thee at the heart,
And left thy head on.— How should this be? Pisanio?
'Tis he and Cloten : malice and lucre in them
Have laid this woe here.   O 'tis pregnant, pregnant!
The drug he gave me, which he said was precious
And cordial to me, have I not found it
Murderous to the senses?   That confirms it home
This is Pisanio's deed, and Cloten's : O!—
Give colour to my pale cheek with thy blood,
That we the horrider may seem to those
Which chance to find us : O, my lord, my lord!

> *Enter* LUCIUS, *a* Captain *and other* Officers, *and a*
> Soothsayer.

Cap. To them, the legions garrison'd in Gallia, .
After your will, have cross'd the sea; attending
You here at Milford-Haven with your ships :
They are in readiness.
   Luc.   But what from Rome?
Cap. The senate hath stirr'd up the confiners
And gentlemen of Italy; most willing spirits,
That promise noble service : and they come
Under the conduct of bold Iachimo,
Sienna's brother.
   Luc.   When expect you them?
Cap. With the next benefit o' the wind.
   Luc.   This forwardness
Makes our hopes fair.   Command our present numbers
Be muster'd ; bid the captains look to't.—Now, sir,
What have you dream'd of late of this war's purpose?
   Sooth. Last night the very gods show'd me a vision,—
I fast and pray'd for their intelligence,—thus :—
I saw Jove's bird, the Roman eagle, wing'd
From the spongy south to this part of the west,
There vanish'd in the sunbeams : which portends,—
Unless my sins abuse my divination,—
Success to the Roman host.
   Luc.   Dream often so,
And never false.—Soft, ho! what trunk is here
Without his top?—The ruin speaks that sometime
It was a worthy building.—How! a page!—
Or dead or sleeping on him? But dead, rather;

For nature doth abhor to make his bed
With the defunct, or sleep upon the dead.—
Let's see the boy's face.
  Cap.   He's alive, my lord.
  Luc. He'll, then, instruct us of this body.—Young one,
Inform us of thy fortunes; for it seems
They crave to be demanded. Who is this
Thou mak'st thy bloody pillow? or who was he,
That otherwise than noble nature did,
Hath alter'd that good picture? What's thy interest
In this sad wreck? How came it? Who is it?
What art thou?
  Imo.   I am nothing: or if not,
Nothing to be were better. This was my master,
A very valiant Briton and a good,
That here by mountaineers lies slain: alas!
There is no more such masters: I may wander
From east to occident, cry out for service,
Try many, all good, serve truly, never
Find such another master.
  Luc.   'Lack, good youth!
Thou mov'st no less with thy complaining than
Thy master in bleeding: say his name, good friend.
  Imo. Richard du Champ.—[*Aside.*] If I do lie, and do
No harm by it, though the gods hear, I hope
They'll pardon it.—Say you, sir?
  Luc.   Thy name?
  Imo.   Fidele.
  Luc. Thou dost approve thyself the very same:
Thy name well fits thy faith, thy faith thy name.
Wilt take thy chance with me? I will not say
Thou shalt be so well master'd; but, be sure,
No less belov'd. The Roman emperor's letters,
Sent by a consul to me, should not sooner
Than thine own worth prefer thee: go with me.
  Imo. I'll follow, sir. But first, an't please the gods,
I'll hide my master from the flies, as deep
As these poor pickaxes can dig: and when
With wild wood-leaves and weeds I ha' strew'd his grave,
And on it said a century of prayers,
Such as I can, twice o'er, I'll weep and sigh;
And leaving so his service, follow you,
So please you entertain me.
  Luc.   Ay, good youth;
And rather father thee than master thee.—
My friends,

The boy hath taught us manly duties: let us
Find out the prettiest daisied plot we can,
And make him with our pikes and partisans
A grave: come, arm him.—Boy, he is preferr'd
By thee to us; and he shall be interr'd
As soldiers can.   Be cheerful; wipe thine eyes:
Some falls are means the happier to arise.   [*Exeunt.*

SCENE III.—BRITAIN.   *A Room in* CYMBELINE'S *Palace.*

Enter CYMBELINE, Lords, PISANIO, *and* Attendants.

Cym. Again; and bring me word how 'tis with her.
A fever with the absence of her son;   [*Exit an* Attendant.
A madness, of which her life 's in danger,—Heavens,
How deeply you at once do touch me! Imogen,
The great part of my comfort, gone; my queen
Upon a desperate bed, and in a time
When fearful wars point at me; her son gone,
So needful for this present: it strikes me, past
The hope of comfort.—But for thee, fellow,
Who needs must know of her departure, and
Dost seem so ignorant, we'll enforce it from thee
By a sharp torture.
Pis.   Sir, my life is yours,
I humbly set it at your will: but, for my mistress,
I nothing know where she remains, why gone,
Nor when she purposes return.   Beseech your highness,
Hold me your loyal servant.
  1 Lord.   Good my liege,
The day that she was missing he was here:
I dare be bound he 's true, and shall perform
All parts of his subjection loyally.
For Cloten,—
There wants no diligence in seeking him,
And will no doubt be found.
  Cym.   The time is troublesome,—
We'll slip you for a season; but our jealousy [*To* PISANIO.
Does yet depend.
  1 Lord.   So please your majesty,
The Roman legions, all from Gallia drawn,
Are landed on your coast; with a supply
Of Roman gentlemen by the senate sent.
  Cym. Now for the counsel of my son and queen!—
I am amaz'd with matter.
  1 Lord.   Good my liege,

Your preparation can affront no less
Than what you hear of : come more, for more you're ready :
The want is but to put those powers in motion
That long to move.

Cym. I thank you. Let's withdraw,
And meet the time as it seeks us. We fear not
What can from Italy annoy us; but
We grieve at chances here.—Away!

[*Exeunt all but* PISANIO.

Pis. I heard no letter from my master since
I wrote him Imogen was slain : 'tis strange :
Nor hear I from my mistress, who did promise
To yield me often tidings : neither know I
What is betid to Cloten; but remain
Perplex'd in all : the heavens still must work.
Wherein I am false I am honest; not true to be true :
These present wars shall find I love my country,
Even to the note o' the king, or I'll fall in them.
All other doubts, by time let them be clear'd :
Fortune brings in some boats that are not steer'd. [*Exit.*

SCENE IV.—WALES. *Before the Cave.*

Enter BELARIUS, GUIDERIUS, *and* ARVIRAGUS.

Gui. The noise is round about us.
Bel. Let us from it.
Arv. What pleasure, sir, find we in life, to lock it
From action and adventure?
Gui. Nay, what hope
Have we in hiding us? this way the Romans
Must or for Britons slay us or receive us
For barbarous and unnatural revolts
During their use, and slay us after.
Bel. Sons,
We'll higher to the mountains; there secure us.
To the king's party there's no going : newness
Of Cloten's death,—we being not known, not muster'd
Among the bands,—may drive us to a render
Where we have liv'd; and so extort from 's
That which we've done, whose answer would be death,
Drawn on with torture.
Gui. This is, sir, a doubt
In such a time nothing becoming you
Nor satisfying us.
Arv. It is not likely

That when they hear the Roman horses neigh,
Behold their quarter'd fires, have both their eyes
And ears so cloy'd importantly as now,
That they will waste their time upon our note,
To know from whence we are.

    Bel.   O, I am known
Of many in the army: many years,
Though Cloten then but young, you see, not wore him
From my remembrance. And, besides, the king
Hath not deserv'd my service nor your loves;
Who find in my exile the want of breeding
The certainty of this hard life; aye hopeless
To have the courtesy your cradle promis'd,
But to be still hot summer's tanlings and
The shrinking slaves of winter.

    Gui.   Than be so,
Better to cease to be. Pray, sir, to the army:
I and my brother are not known; yourself
So out of thought, and thereto so o'ergrown,
Cannot be question'd.

    Arv.   By this sun that shines,
I'll thither: what thing is it that I never
Did see man die! scarce ever look'd on blood,
But that of coward hares, hot goats, and venison!
Never bestrid a horse, save one that had
A rider like myself, who ne'er wore rowel
Nor iron on his heel! I am asham'd
To look upon the holy sun, to have
The benefit of his blessed beams, remaining
So long a poor unknown.

    Gui.   By heavens, I'll go:
If you will bless me, sir, and give me leave,
I'll take the better care; but if you will not,
The hazard therefore due fall on me by
The hands of Romans!

    Arv.   So say I,—Amen.

    Bel. No reason I, since of your lives you set
So slight a valuation, should reserve
My crack'd one to more care. Have with you, boys!
If in your country wars you chance to die,
That is my bed too, lads, and there I'll lie:
Lead, lead.—[*Aside.*] The time seems long; their blood
        thinks scorn
Till it fly out, and show them princes born.   [*Exeunt.*

ACT V.

SCENE I.—BRITAIN.   *A Field between the British and Roman Camps.*

Enter POSTHUMUS *with a bloody handkerchief.*

Post. Yea, bloody cloth, I'll keep thee; for I wish'd
Thou shouldst be colour'd thus.   You married ones,
If each of you should take this course, how many
Must murder wives much better than themselves
For wrying but a little!   O Pisanio!
Every good servant does not all commands:
No bond but to do just ones.—Gods! if you
Should have ta'en vengeance on my faults, I never
Had liv'd to put on this: so had you sav'd
The noble Imogen to repent; and struck
Me, wretch more worth your vengeance.   But, alack,
You snatch some hence for little faults; that's love,
To have them fall no more: you some permit
To second ills with ills, each elder worse,
And make them dread it, to the doers' thrift.
But Imogen is your own: do your best wills,
And make me bless'd to obey!—I am brought hither
Among the Italian gentry, and to fight
Against my lady's kingdom: 'tis enough
That, Britain, I have kill'd thy mistress; peace!
I'll give no wound to thee.   Therefore, good heavens,
Hear patiently my purpose:—I'll disrobe me
Of these Italian weeds, and suit myself
As does a Briton peasant: so I'll fight
Against the part I come with; so I'll die
For thee, O Imogen, even for whom my life
Is every breath a death: and thus unknown,
Pitied nor hated, to the face of peril
Myself I'll dedicate.   Let me make men know
More valour in me than my habits show.
Gods, put the strength o' the Leonati in me!
To shame the guise o' the world, I will begin
The fashion,—less without and more within.   [*Exit.*

SCENE II.—Britain. *A Field between the Camps.*

Enter, at one side, Lucius, Iachimo, Imogen, *and the*
  Roman Army; *at the other side, the* British Army;
  Leonatus Posthumus *following it like a poor soldier.*
  They march over and go out. Alarums. Then enter again,
  in skirmish, Iachimo *and* Posthumus: *he vanquisheth*
  and disarmeth Iachimo, *and then leaves him.*

Iach. The heaviness and guilt within my bosom
Takes off my manhood: I have belied a lady,
The princess of this country, and the air on't
Revengingly enfeebles me; or could this carl,
A very drudge of nature's, have subdu'd me
In my profession? Knighthoods and honours borne
As I wear mine are titles but of scorn.
If that thy gentry, Britain, go before
This lout as he exceeds our lords, the odds
Is that we scarce are men, and you are gods.   [*Exit.*

The battle continues; the Britons fly; Cymbeline *is taken:*
  then enter to his rescue Belarius, Guiderius, *and*
  Arviragus.

Bel. Stand, stand! We have the advantage of the ground;
The lane is guarded: nothing routs us but
The villany of our fears.
  Gui. and Arv.   Stand, stand, and fight!

Re-enter Posthumus, *and seconds the Britons: they rescue*
  Cymbeline, *and exeunt. Then re-enter* Lucius, Iachimo,
  and Imogen.

Luc. Away, boy, from the troops, and save thyself;
For friends kill friends, and the disorder's such
As war were hoodwink'd.
  Iach.   'Tis their fresh supplies.
  Luc. It is a day turn'd strangely: or betimes
Let 's re-enforce or fly.   [*Exeunt*

SCENE III.—Britain. *Another part of the Field.*

Enter Posthumus *and a* British Lord.

Lord. Cam'st thou from where they made the stand?
  Post.   I did:
Though you, it seems, come from the fliers.
  Lord.   I did.

Post. No blame be to you, sir; for all was lost,
But that the heavens fought: the king himself
Of his wings destitute, the army broken,
And but the backs of Britons seen, all flying
Through a strait lane; the enemy full-hearted,
Lolling the tongue with slaughtering, having work
More plentiful than tools to do't, struck down
Some mortally, some slightly touch'd, some falling
Merely through fear; that the strait pass was damm'd
With dead men hurt behind, and cowards living,
To die with lengthen'd shame.
　　　Lord.　　　　　　　Where was this lane?
　　　Post. Close by the battle, ditch'd, and wall'd with turf,
Which gave advantage to an ancient soldier,—
An honest one, I warrant; who deserv'd
So long a breeding as his white beard came to,
In doing this for 's country:—athwart the lane
He, with two striplings,—lads more like to run
The country base than to commit such slaughter;
With faces fit for masks, or rather fairer
Than those for preservation cas'd, or shame,—
Made good the passage; cried to those that fled,
Our Britain's harts die flying, not our men:
To darkness fleet, souls that fly backwards! Stand;
Or we are Romans, and will give you that
Like beasts which you shun beastly, and may save,
But to look back in frown: stand, stand!—These three,
Three thousand confident, in act as many,—
For three performers are the file when all
The rest do nothing,—with this word, *Stand, stand!*
Accommodated by the place, more charming
With their own nobleness,—which could have turn'd
A distaff to a lance,—gilded pale looks,
Part shame, part spirit renew'd; that some, turn'd coward
But by example,—O, a sin in war
Damn'd in the first beginners!—'gan to look
The way that they did, and to grin like lions
Upon the pikes o' the hunters. Then began
A stop i' the chaser, a retire; anon
A rout, confusion thick: forthwith they fly,
Chickens, the way which they stoop'd eagles; slaves,
The strides they victors made: and now our cowards,—
Like fragments in hard voyages,—became
The life o' the need; having found the back-door open
Of the unguarded hearts, heavens, how they wound!
Some slain before; some dying; some their friends

O'erborne i' the former wave: ten chas'd by one
Are now each one the slaughter-man of twenty:
Those that would die or ere resist are grown
The mortal bugs o' the field.
　　Lord.　　　　　　　　　This was strange chance,—
A narrow lane, an old man, and two boys!
　　Post. Nay, do not wonder at it: you are made
Rather to wonder at the things you hear
Than to work any. Will you rhyme upon't,
And vent it for a mockery? Here is one:
Two boys, an old man twice a boy, a lane,
Preserv'd the Britons, was the Romans' bane.
　　Lord. Nay, be not angry, sir.
　　Post.　　　　　　　　'Lack, to what end?
Who dares not stand his foe I'll be his friend;
For if he'll do as he is made to do
I know he'll quickly fly my friendship too.
You have put me into rhyme.
　　Lord.　　　　　　　　Farewell; you're angry. [*Exit.*
　　Post. Still going?—This is a lord! O noble misery,—
To be i' the field and ask what news of me!
To-day how many would have given their honours
To have sav'd their carcasses! took heel to do't,
And yet died too! I, in mine own woe charm'd,
Could not find death where I did hear him groan,
Nor feel him where he struck: being an ugly monster,
'Tis strange he hides him in fresh cups, soft beds,
Sweet words; or hath more ministers than we
That draw his knives i' the war.—Well, I will find
　　　him:
For being now a favourer to the Briton,
No more a Briton, I have resum'd again
The part I came in: fight I will no more,
But yield me to the veriest hind that shall
Once touch my shoulder. Great the slaughter is
Here made by the Roman; great the answer be
Briton's must take: for me, my ransom 's death;
On either side I come to spend my breath;
Which neither here I'll keep nor bear again,
But end it by some means for Imogen.

　　　　　Enter two British Captains *and* Soldiers.

　　1 *Cap.* Great Jupiter be prais'd! Lucius is taken:
'Tis thought the old man and his sons were angels.
　　2 *Cap.* There was a fourth man, in a silly habit,
That gave the affront with them.

1 *Cap.*   So 'tis reported:
But none of 'em can be found.—Stand! who's there?
   Post. A Roman;
Who had not now been drooping here if seconds
Had answer'd him.
   2 *Cap.*   Lay hands on him; a dog!—
A leg of Rome shall not return to tell
What crows have peck'd them here:—he brags his service,
As if he were of note: bring him to the king.

Enter CYMBELINE *attended;* BELARIUS, GUIDERIUS, ARVI-
   RAGUS, PISANIO, *and* Roman Captives. *The* Captains
   present POSTHUMUS *to* CYMBELINE, *who delivers him over
   to a Gaoler: after which all go out.*

SCENE IV.—BRITAIN. *A Prison.*

Enter POSTHUMUS *and two* Gaolers.

1 *Gaol.* You shall not now be stolen, you have locks upon
    you;
So, graze as you find pasture.
   2 *Gaol.* Ay, or a stomach.   [*Exeunt* Gaolers.
   Post. Most welcome, bondage! for thou art a way,
I think, to liberty: yet am I better
Than one that's sick o' the gout; since he had rather
Groan so in perpetuity than be cur'd
By the sure physician death, who is the key
To unbar these locks. My conscience, thou art fetter'd
More than my shanks and wrists: you good gods, give me
The penitent instrument to pick that bolt,
Then free for ever! Is't enough I am sorry?
So children temporal fathers do appease:
Gods are more full of mercy. Must I repent?
I cannot do it better than in gyves,
Desir'd more than constrain'd: to satisfy,
If of my freedom 'tis the main part, take
No stricter render of me than my all.
I know you are more clement than vile men,
Who of their broken debtors take a third,
A sixth, a tenth, letting them thrive again
On their abatement: that's not my desire:
For Imogen's dear life take mine; and though
'Tis not so dear, yet 'tis a life; you coin'd it:
'Tween man and man they weigh not every stamp;
Though light, take pieces for the figure's sake:

You rather mine, being yours: and so, great powers,
If you will take this audit, take this life,
And cancel these cold bonds.—O Imogen!
I'll speak to thee in silence.   [*Sleeps.*

Solemn Music. Enter, as in an apparition, SICILIUS LEO-
NATUS, *father to* POSTHUMUS, *an old man attired like a
warrior, leading in his hand an ancient matron, his wife
and mother to* POSTHUMUS, *with music before them:
then, after other music, follow the two young* LEONATI,
brothers to POSTHUMUS, *with wounds, as they died in the
wars. They circle* POSTHUMUS *round as he lies sleeping.*

Sici. No more, thou thunder-master, show
        Thy spite on mortal flies:
    With Mars fall out, with Juno chide,
        That thy adulteries
            Rates and revenges.
    Hath my poor boy done aught but well,
        Whose face I never saw?
    I died whilst in the womb he stay'd
        Attending nature's law:
    Whose father then,—as men report
        Thou orphans' father art,—
    Thou shouldst have been, and shielded him
        From this earth-vexing smart.

Moth. Lucina lent not me her aid,
        But took me in my throes;
    That from me was Posthumus ripp'd,
        Came crying 'mongst his foes,
            A thing of pity!

Sici. Great nature, like his ancestry,
        Moulded the stuff so fair
    That he deserv'd the praise o' the world
        As great Sicilius' heir.

1 Bro. When once he was mature for man,
        In Britain where was he
    That could stand up his parallel;
        Or fruitful object be
    In eye of Imogen, that best
        Could deem his dignity?

Moth. With marriage wherefore was he mock'd,
        To be exil'd, and thrown
    From Leonati' seat, and cast
        From her his dearest one,
            Sweet Imogen?

Sici. Why did you suffer Iachimo,
    Slight thing of Italy,
To taint his nobler heart and brain
    With needless jealousy;
And to become the geck and scorn
    O' the other's villany?

2 *Bro.* For this from stiller seats we came,
    Our parents and us twain,
That, striking in our country's cause,
    Fell bravely and were slain;
Our fealty and Tenantius' right
    With honour to maintain.

1 *Bro.* Like hardiment Posthumus hath
    To Cymbeline perform'd:
Then, Jupiter, thou king of gods,
    Why hast thou thus adjourn'd
The graces for his merits due,
    Being all to dolours turn'd?

Sici. Thy crystal window ope; look out;
    No longer exercise
Upon a valiant race thy harsh
    And potent injuries.

Moth. Since, Jupiter, our son is good,
    Take off his miseries.

Sici. Peep through thy marble mansion; help;
    Or we poor ghosts will cry
To the shining synod of the rest
    Against thy deity.

Both Bro. Help, Jupiter; or we appeal,
    And from thy justice fly.

JUPITER *descends in thunder and lightning, sitting upon an
eagle: he throws a thunderbolt. The* Ghosts *fall on their
knees.*

Jup. No more, you petty spirits of region low,
  Offend our hearing; hush!—How dare you ghosts
Accuse the thunderer, whose bolt, you know,
  Sky-planted, batters all rebelling coasts?
Poor shadows of Elysium, hence; and rest
  Upon your never-withering banks of flowers:
Be not with mortal accidents oppress'd;
  No care of yours it is; you know 'tis ours.
Whom best I love I cross; to make my gift,
  The more delay'd, delighted. Be content;

Your low-laid son our godhead will uplift:
  His comforts thrive, his trials well are spent.
Our Jovial star reign'd at his birth, and in
  Our temple was he married.—Rise, and fade!—
He shall be lord of Lady Imogen,
  And happier much by his affliction made.
This tablet lay upon his breast, wherein
  Our pleasure his full fortune doth confine:
And so away: no further with your din
  Express impatience, lest you stir up mine.—
  Mount, eagle, to my palace crystalline.   [*Ascends.*
    Sici. He came in thunder; his celestial breath
Was sulphurous to smell: the holy eagle
Stoop'd, as to foot us: his ascension is
More sweet than our bless'd fields: his royal bird
Prunes the immortal wing, and cloys his beak,
As when his god is pleas'd.
    All.   Thanks, Jupiter!
    Sici. The marble pavement closes, he is enter'd
His radiant roof.—Away! and, to be blest,
Let us with care perform his great behest. [*Ghosts vanish.*
    Post. [*waking.*] Sleep, thou hast been a grandsire, and
        begot
A father to me; and thou hast created
A mother and two brothers: but, O scorn!
Gone! they went hence so soon as they were born.
And so I am awake.—Poor wretches that depend
On greatness' favour dream as I have done,
Wake and find nothing.—But, alas, I swerve:
Many dream not to find, neither deserve,
And yet are steep'd in favours; so am I,
That have this golden chance, and know not why.
What fairies haunt this ground? A book? O rare one!
Be not, as is our fangled world, a garment
Nobler than that it covers: let thy effects
So follow, to be most unlike our courtiers,
As good as promise.

    [Reads.] *Whenas a lion's whelp shall, to himself unknown,*
without seeking find, and be embraced by a piece of tender
air; and when from a stately cedar shall be lopped branches
which, being dead many years, shall after revive, be jointed
to the old stock, and freshly grow; then shall Posthumus
end his miseries, Britain be fortunate, and flourish in peace
and plenty.

"Tis still a dream; or else such stuff as madmen

Tongue, and brain not: either both or nothing:
Or senseless speaking, or a speaking such
As sense cannot untie. Be what it is,
The action of my life is like it, which
I'll keep, if but for sympathy.

Re-enter Gaoler.

Gaol. Come, sir, are you ready for death?

Post. Over-roasted rather; ready long ago.

Gaol. Hanging is the word, sir: if you be ready for that,
you are well cooked.

Post. So, if I prove a good repast to the spectators, the
dish pays the shot.

Gaol. A heavy reckoning for you, sir. But the comfort
is, you shall be called to no more payments, fear no more
tavern bills; which are often the sadness of parting, as the
procuring of mirth: you come in faint for want of meat,
depart reeling with too much drink; sorry that you have
paid too much, and sorry that you are paid too much; purse
and brain both empty,—the brain the heavier for being too
light, the purse too light, being drawn of heaviness: O, of
this contradiction you shall now be quit.—O, the charity
of a penny cord! it sums up thousands in a trice: you have
no true debitor and creditor but it; of what's past, is, and
to come, the discharge:—your neck, sir, is pen, book, and
counters; so the acquittance follows.

Post. I am merrier to die than thou art to live.

Gaol. Indeed, sir, he that sleeps feels not the toothache:
but a man that were to sleep your sleep, and a hangman
to help him to bed, I think he would change places with
his officer; for, look you, sir, you know not which way
you shall go.

Post. Yes, indeed do I, fellow.

Gaol. Your death has eyes in 's head, then; I have not
seen him so pictured: you must either be directed by some
that take upon them to know, or take upon yourself that
which I am sure you do not know; or jump the after-
inquiry on your own peril: and how you shall speed in
your journey's end I think you'll never return to tell
one.

Post. I tell thee, fellow, there are none want eyes to
direct them the way I am going, but such as wink and
will not use them.

Gaol. What an infinite mock is this, that a man should
have the best use of eyes to see the way of blindness! I
am sure hanging's the way of winking.

Enter a Messenger.

Mess. Knock off his manacles; bring your prisoner to the king.

Post. Thou bringest good news,—I am called to be made free.

Gaol. I'll be hanged, then.

Post. Thou shalt be then freer than a gaoler; no bolts for the dead. [*Exeunt* POST. *and* Messenger.

Gaol. Unless a man would marry a gallows and beget young gibbets I never saw one so prone. Yet, on my conscience, there are verier knaves desire to live, for all he be a Roman: and there be some of them too that die against their wills; so should I if I were one. I would we were all of one mind, and one mind good; O, there were desolation of gaolers and gallowses! I speak against my present profit; but my wish hath a preferment in't. [*Exit.*

SCENE V.—BRITAIN. CYMBELINE'S *Tent.*

Enter CYMBELINE, BELARIUS, GUIDERIUS, ARVIRAGUS, PISANIO, Lords, Officers, *and* Attendants.

Cym. Stand by my side, you whom the gods have made
Preservers of my throne. Woe is my heart
That the poor soldier that so richly fought,
Whose rags sham'd gilded arms, whose naked breast
Stepp'd before targes of proof, cannot be found:
He shall be happy that can find him, if
Our grace can make him so.
Bel.   I never saw
Such noble fury in so poor a thing;
Such precious deeds in one that promis'd naught
But beggary and poor looks.
Cym.   No tidings of him?
Pis. He hath been search'd among the dead and living,
But no trace of him.
Cym.   To my grief, I am
The heir of his reward, which I will add
To you, the liver, heart, and brain of Britain,
                          [*To* BEL., GUI., *and* ARV.
By whom I grant she lives. 'Tis now the time
To ask of whence you are:—report it.
Bel.   Sir,
In Cambria are we born, and gentlemen:

Further to boast were neither true nor modest,
Unless I add we are honest.

Cym.   Bow your knees.
Arise my knights o' the battle : I create you
Companions to our person, and will fit you
With dignities becoming your estates.

Enter CORNELIUS *and* Ladies.

There 's business in these faces.—Why so sadly
Greet you our victory? you look like Romans,
And not o' the court of Britain.

Cor.   Hail, great king!
To sour your happiness, I must report
The queen is dead.

Cym.   Who worse than a physician
Would this report become? Bi t I consider
By medicine life may be prolong'd, yet death
Will seize the doctor too.—How ended she?

Cor. With horror, madly dying, like her life;
Which, being cruel to the world, concluded
Most cruel to herself.   What she confess'd
I will report, so please you : these her women
Can trip me if I err; who with wet cheeks
Were present when she finish'd.

Cym.   Pr'ythee, say.
Cor. First, she confess'd she never lov'd you ; only
Affected greatness got by you, not you :
Married your royalty, was wife to your place ;
Abhorr'd your person.

Cym.   She alone knew this ;
And but she spoke it dying, I would not
Believe her lips in opening it.   Proceed.

Cor. Your daughter, whom she bore in hand to love
With such integrity, she did confess
Was as a scorpion to her sight; whose life,
But that her flight prevented it, she had
Ta'en off by poison.

Cym.   O most delicate fiend!
Who is't can read a woman?—Is there more?

Cor. More, sir, and worse.   She did confess she had
For you a mortal mineral ; which, being took,
Should by the minute feed on life, and, lingering,
By inches waste you : in which time she purpos'd,
By watching, weeping, tendance, kissing, to
O'ercome you with her show ; and in time,
When she had fitted you with her craft, to work

Her son into the adoption of the crown :
But, failing of her end by his strange absence,
Grew shameless-desperate ; open'd, in despite
Of heaven and men, her purposes ; repented
The evils she hatch'd were not effected ; so,
Despairing, died.

   Cym.   Heard you all this, her women?

   1 *Lady.* We did, so please your highness.

   Cym.   Mine eyes
Were not in fault, for she was beautiful ;
Mine ears, that heard her flattery ; nor my heart,
That thought her like her seeming ; it had been vicious
To have mistrusted her : yet, O my daughter!
That it was folly in me thou mayst say,
And prove it in thy feeling. Heaven mend all !

Enter LUCIUS, IACHIMO, *the* Soothsayer, *and other* Roman
   Prisoners, *guarded ;* POSTHUMUS *behind, and* IMOGEN.

Thou com'st not, Caius, now for tribute ; that
The Britons have raz'd out, though with the loss
Of many a bold one, whose kinsmen have made suit
That their good souls may be appeas'd with slaughter
Of you their captives, which ourself have granted:
So, think of your estate.

   Luc. Consider, sir, the chance of war : the day
Was yours by accident ; had it gone with us
We should not, when the blood was cool, have threaten'd
Our prisoners with the sword. But since the gods
Will have it thus, that nothing but our lives
May be call'd ransom, let it come : sufficeth
A Roman with a Roman's heart can suffer :
Augustus lives to think on't : and so much
For my peculiar care. This one thing only
I will entreat ; my boy, a Briton born,
Let him be ransom'd : never master had
A page so kind, so duteous, diligent,
So tender over his occasions, true,
So feat, so nurse-like : let his virtue join
With my request, which I'll make bold your highness
Cannot deny ; he hath done no Briton harm
Though he have serv'd a Roman : save him, sir,
And spare no blood beside.

   Cym.   I have surely seen him :
His favour is familiar to me.—
Boy, thou hast look'd thyself into my grace,
And art mine own.— I know not why nor wherefore

To say live, boy: ne'er thank thy master; live:
And ask of Cymbeline what boon thou wilt,
Fitting my bounty and thy state, I'll give it;
Yea, though thou do demand a prisoner,
The noblest ta'en.

Imo.   I humbly thank your highness.

Luc. I do not bid thee beg my life, good lad;
And yet I know thou wilt.

Imo.   No, no: alack,
There's other work in hand: I see a thing
Bitter to me as death: your life, good master,
Must shuffle for itself.

Luc.   The boy disdains me,
He leaves me, scorns me: briefly die their joys
That place them on the truth of girls and boys.—
Why stands he so perplex'd?

Cym.   What wouldst thou, boy?
I love thee more and more: think more and more
What's best to ask. Know'st him thou look'st on? speak,
Wilt have him live? Is he thy kin? thy friend?

Imo. He is a Roman; no more kin to me
Than I to your highness; who, being born your vassal,
Am something nearer.

Cym.   Wherefore ey'st him so?

Imo. I'll tell you, sir, in private, if you please
To give me hearing.

Cym.   Ay, with all my heart,
And lend my best attention. What's thy name?

Imo. Fidele, sir.

Cym.   Thou'rt my good youth, my page;
I'll be thy master: walk with me; speak freely.

                 [CYM. and IMO. *converse apart.*

Bel. Is not this boy reviv'd from death?

Arv.   One sand another
Not more resembles that sweet rosy lad
Who died, and was Fidele.—What think you?

Gui. The same dead thing alive.

Bel. Peace, peace! see further; he eyes us not; forbear;
Creatures may be alike: were't he, I am sure
He would have spoke to us.

Gui.   But we saw him dead.

Bel. Be silent; let's see further.

Pis. [*aside.*]   It is my mistress:
Since she is living, let the time run on
To good or bad.   [CYM. and IMO. *come forward.*

Cym.   Come, stand thou by our side;

Make thy demand aloud.—[*To* Iach.] Sir, step you forth;
Give answer to this boy, and do it freely;
Or, by our greatness and the grace of it,
Which is our honour, bitter torture shall
Winnow the truth from falsehood.—On, speak to him.
    Imo. My boon is that this gentleman may render
Of whom he had this ring.
    Post. [*aside.*]   What's that to him?
    Cym. That diamond upon your finger, say,
How came it yours?
    Iach. Thou'lt torture me to leave unspoken that
Which to be spoke would torture thee.
    Cym.   How! me?
    Iach. I am glad to be constrain'd to utter that which
Torments me to conceal. By villany
I got this ring: 'twas Leonatus' jewel,
Whom thou didst banish; and,—which more may grieve
        thee,
As it doth me,—a nobler sir ne'er liv'd
'Twixt sky and ground. Wilt thou hear more, my lord?
    Cym. All that belongs to this.
    Iach.   That paragon, thy daughter,—
For whom my heart drops blood, and my false spirits
Quail to remember,—Give me leave; I faint.
    Cym. My daughter! what of her? Renew thy strength:
I had rather thou shouldst live while nature will
Than die ere I hear more: strive, man, and speak.
    Iach. Upon a time,—unhappy was the clock
That struck the hour!—it was in Rome,—accurs'd
The mansion where!—'twas at a feast,—O, would
Our viands had been poison'd, or at least
Those which I heav'd to head!—the good Posthumus,—
What should I say? he was too good to be
Where ill men were; and was the best of all
Amongst the rar'st of good ones,—sitting sadly,
Hearing us praise our loves of Italy
For beauty that made barren the swell'd boast
Of him that best could speak; for feature laming
The shrine of Venus, or straight-pight Minerva,
Postures beyond brief nature; for condition,
A shop of all the qualities that man
Loves woman for; besides that hook of wiving,
Fairness which strikes the eye,—
    Cym.   I stand on fire:
Come to the matter.
    Iach.   All too soon I shall,

Unless thou wouldst grieve quickly.—This Posthumus,—
Most like a noble lord in love, and one
That had a royal lover,—took his hint;
And not dispraising whom we prais'd,—therein
He was as calm as virtue,—he began
His mistress' picture; which by his tongue being made,
And then a mind put in't, either our brags
Were crack'd of kitchen trulls, or his description
Prov'd us unspeaking sots.

   Cym.   Nay, nay, to the purpose.
   Iach. Your daughter's chastity—there it begins.
He spake of her as Dian had hot dreams
And she alone were cold: whereat I, wretch,
Made scruple of his praise; and wager'd with him
Pieces of gold, 'gainst this, which then he wore
Upon his honour'd finger, to attain
In suit the place of's bed, and win this ring
By hers and mine adultery: he, true knight,
No lesser of her honour confident
Than I did truly find her, stakes this ring;
And would so, had it been a carbuncle
Of Phœbus' wheel; and might so safely, had it
Been all the worth of's car.   Away to Britain
Post I in this design.   Well may you, sir,
Remember me at court, where I was taught
Of your chaste daughter the wide difference
'Twixt amorous and villanous.   Being thus quench'd
Of hope, not longing, mine Italian brain
'Gan in your duller Britain operate
Most vilely,—for my vantage excellent;
And, to be brief, my practice so prevail'd
That I return'd with simular proof enough
To make the noble Leonatus mad,
By wounding his belief in her renown
With tokens thus and thus; averring notes
Of chamber-hanging, pictures, this her bracelet,—
O cunning how I got it!—nay, some marks
Of secret on her person, that he could not
But think her bond of chastity quite crack'd,
I having ta'en the forfeit.   Whereupon,—
Methinks I see him now,—
   Post. [*coming forward.*]   Ay, so thou dost,
Italian fiend!—Ah me, most credulous fool,
Egregious murderer, thief, anything
That's due to all the villains past, in being,
To come!—O, give me cord, or knife, or poison,

Some upright justicer!   Thou, king, send out
For torturers ingenious: it is I
That all the abhorred things o' the earth amend
By being worse than they.   I am Posthumus,
That kill'd thy daughter:—villain-like, I lie,—
That caus'd a lesser villain than myself,
A sacrilegious thief, to do't:—the temple
Of virtue was she; yea, and she herself.
Spit, and throw stones, cast mire upon me, set
The dogs o' the street to bay me: every villain
Be call'd Posthumus Leonatus; and
Be villany less than 'twas!—O Imogen!
My queen, my life, my wife!   O Imogen,
Imogen, Imogen!
   Imo.   Peace, my lord; hear, hear,—
   Post. Shall 's have a play of this?   Thou scornful page,
There lie thy part.   [*Striking her: she falls.*
   Pis.   O, gentlemen, help!
Mine and your mistress!—O, my lord Posthumus!
You ne'er kill'd Imogen till now.—Help, help!—
Mine honour'd lady!
   Cym.   Does the world go round?
   Post. How come these staggers on me?
   Pis.   Wake, my mistress!
   Cym. If this be so, the gods do mean to strike me
To death with mortal joy.
   Pis.   How fares my mistress?
   Imo. O, get thee from my sight;
Thou gav'st me poison: dangerous fellow, hence!
Breathe not where princes are.
   Cym.   The tune of Imogen.
   Pis. Lady,
The gods throw stones of sulphur on me if
That box I gave you was not thought by me
A precious thing: I had it from the queen.
   Cym. New matter still?
   Imo.   It poison'd me.
   Cor.   O gods!—
I left out one thing which the queen confess'd,
Which must approve thee honest: *If Pisanio
Have,* said she, *given his mistress that confection
Which I gave him for cordial, she is serv'd
As I would serve a rat.*
   Cym.   What 's this, Cornelius?
   Cor. The queen, sir, very oft importun'd me
To temper poisons for her; still pretending

The satisfaction of her knowledge only
In killing creatures vile, as cats and dogs,
Of no esteem: I, dreading that her purpose
Was of more danger, did compound for her
A certain stuff, which, being ta'en, would cease
The present power of life; but in short time
All offices of nature should again
Do their due functions.—Have you ta'en of it?
 Imo. Most like I did, for I was dead.
 Bel.   My boys,
There was our error.
 Gui.   This is sure Fidele.
 Imo. Why did you throw your wedded lady from
   you?
Think that you are upon a rock; and now
Throw me again.   [*Embracing him.*
 Post.   Hang there like fruit, my soul,
Till the tree die!
 Cym.   How now, my flesh, my child!
What, mak'st thou me a dullard in this act?
Wilt thou not speak to me?
 Imo.   Your blessing, sir. [*Kneeling.*
 Bel. Though you did love this youth, I blame ye not;
You had a motive for it. [*To* GUIDERIUS *and* ARVIRAGUS.
 Cym.   My tears that fall
Prove holy water on thee! Imogen,
Thy mother's dead.
 Imo.   I am sorry for't, my lord.
 Cym. O, she was naught; and long of her it was
That we meet here so strangely: but her son
Is gone, we know not how nor where.
 Pis.   My lord,
Now fear is from me, I'll speak troth. Lord Cloten,
Upon my lady's missing, came to me
With his sword drawn; foam'd at the mouth, and
   swore,
If I discover'd not which way she was gone,
It was my instant death. By accident
I had a feigned letter of my master's
Then in my pocket; which directed him
To seek her on the mountains near to Milford;
Where, in a frenzy, in my master's garments,
Which he enforc'd from me, away he posts
With unchaste purpose, and with oath to violate
My lady's honour: what became of him
I further know not.

Gui.   Let me end the story:
I slew him there.
    Cym.   Marry, the gods forfend!
I would not thy good deeds should from my lips
Pluck a hard sentence: pr'ythee, valiant youth,
Deny't again.
    Gui.   I have spoke it, and I did it.
    Cym. He was a prince.
    Gui. A most incivil one: the wrongs he did me
Were nothing prince-like; for he did provoke me
With language that would make me spurn the sea,
If it could so roar to me: I cut off's head;
And am right glad he is not standing here
To tell this tale of mine.
    Cym.   I am sorry for thee:
By thine own tongue thou art condemn'd, and must
Endure our law: thou'rt dead.
    Imo.   That headless man
I thought had been my lord.
    Cym.   Bind the offender,
And take him from our presence.
    Bel.   Stay, sir king:
This man is better than the man he slew,
As well descended as thyself; and hath
More of thee merited than a band of Clotens
Had ever scar for.—Let his arms alone;   [*To the* **Guard.**
They were not born for bondage.
    Cym.   Why, old soldier,
Wilt thou undo the worth thou art unpaid for
By tasting of our wrath? How of descent
As good as we?
    Arv.   In that he spake too far.
    Cym. And thou shalt die for't.
    Bel.   We will die all three:
But I will prove that two on's are as good
As I have given out him.—My sons, I must,
For mine own part, unfold a dangerous speech,
Though, haply, well for you.
    Arv.   Your danger's
Ours.
    Gui. And our good his.
    Bel.   Have at it, then!—
By leave,—thou hadst, great king, a subject who
Was call'd Belarius.
    Cym.   What of him? he is
A banish'd traitor.

Bel.   He it is that hath
Assum'd this age: indeed, a banish'd man;
I know not how a traitor.
  Cym.   Take him hence:
The whole world shall not save him.
  Bel.   Not too hot:
First pay me for the nursing of thy sons;
And let it be confiscate all so soon,
As I have receiv'd it.
  Cym.   Nursing of my sons!
  Bel. I am too blunt and saucy: here's my knee:
Ere I arise I will prefer my sons;
Then spare not the old father. Mighty sir,
These two young gentlemen, that call me father,
And think they are my sons, are none of mine;
They are the issue of your loins, my liege,
And blood of your begetting.
  Cym.   How! my issue!
  Bel. So sure as you your father's. I, old Morgan,
Am that Belarius whom you sometime banish'd:
Your pleasure was my mere offence, my punishment
Itself, and all my treason; that I suffer'd
Was all the harm I did. These gentle princes,—
For such and so they are,—these twenty years
Have I train'd up: those arts they have as I
Could put into them; my breeding was, sir, as
Your highness knows. Their nurse, Euriphile,
Whom for the theft I wedded, stole these children
Upon my banishment: I mov'd her to't;
Having receiv'd the punishment before
For that which I did then: beaten for loyalty
Excited me to treason: their dear loss,
The more of you 'twas felt, the more it shap'd
Unto my end of stealing them. But, gracious sir,
Here are your sons again; and I must lose
Two of the sweet'st companions in the world:—
The benediction of these covering heavens
Fall on their heads like dew! for they are worthy
To inlay heaven with stars.
  Cym.   Thou weep'st, and speak'st.
The service that you three have done is more
Unlike than this thou tell'st. I lost my children:
If these be they, I know not how to wish
A pair of worthier sons.
  Bel.   Be pleas'd awhile.—
This gentleman, whom I call Polydore,

Most worthy prince, as yours, is true Guiderius:
This gentleman, my Cadwal, Arviragus.
Your younger princely son; he, sir, was lapp'd
In a most curious mantle, wrought by the hand
Of his queen mother, which, for more probation,
I can with ease produce.

 Cym.   Guiderius had
Upon his neck a mole, a sanguine star;
It was a mark of wonder.

 Bel.   This is he;
Who hath upon him still that natural stamp:
It was wise nature's end in the donation,
To be his evidence now.

 Cym.   O, what, am I
A mother to the birth of three? Ne'er mother
Rejoic'd deliverance more.—Bless'd may you be,
That, after this strange starting from your orbs,
You may reign in them now!—O Imogen,
Thou hast lost by this a kingdom.

 Imo.   No, my lord;
I have got two worlds by't.—O my gentle brothers,
Have we thus met? O, never say hereafter
But I am truest speaker: you call'd me brother
When I was but your sister; I you brothers
When you were so indeed.

 Cym.   Did you e'er meet?

 Arv. Ay, my good lord.

 Gui.   And at first meeting lov'd;
Continued so until we thought he died.

 Cor. By the queen's dram she swallow'd.

 Cym.   O rare instinct!
When shall I hear all through? This fierce abridgment
Hath to it circumstantial branches, which
Distinction should be rich in.—Where? how liv'd you?
And when came you to serve our Roman captive?
How parted with your brothers? how first met them?
Why fled you from the court? and whither? These,
And your three motives to the battle, with
I know not how much more, should be demanded;
And all the other by-dependencies,
From chance to chance: but nor the time nor place
Will serve our long inter'gatories. See,
Posthumus anchors upon Imogen;
And she, like harmless lightning, throws her eye
On him, her brothers, me, her master; hitting
Each object with a joy: the counterchange

Is severally in all.—Let's quit this ground,
And smoke the temple with our sacrifices.—
Thou art my brother; so we'll hold thee ever.

[*To* BELARIUS.

Imo. You are my father too; and did relieve me,
To see this gracious season.
Cym.   All o'erjoy'd,
Save these in bonds: let them be joyful too,
For they shall taste our comfort.
Imo.   My good master,
I will yet do you service.
Luc.   Happy be you!
Cym. The forlorn soldier, that so nobly fought,
He would have well becom'd this place, and grac'd
The thankings of a king.
Post.   I am, sir,
The soldier that did company these three
In poor beseeming; 'twas a fitment for
The purpose I then follow'd.—That I was he,
Speak, Iachimo: I had you down, and might
Have made you finish.
Iach.   I am down again: [*Kneeling.*
But now my heavy conscience sinks my knee,
As then your force did. Take that life, beseech you,
Which I so often owe: but your ring first;
And here the bracelet of the truest princess
That ever swore her faith.
Post.   Kneel not to me:
The power that I have on you is to spare you;
The malice towards you to forgive you: live,
And deal with others better.
Cym.   Nobly doom'd!
We'll learn our freeness of a son-in-law;
Pardon 's the word to all.
Arv.   You holp us, sir,
As you did mean indeed to be our brother;
Joy'd are we that you are.
Post. Your servant, princes.—Good my lord of Rome,
Call forth your soothsayer: as I slept, methought
Great Jupiter, upon his eagle back,
Appear'd to me, with other spritely shows
Of mine own kindred: when I wak'd I found
This label on my bosom; whose containing
Is so from sense in hardness that I can
Make no collection of it: let him show
His skill in the construction.

Luc. Philarmonus,—
Sooth. Here, my good lord.
Luc. Read, and declare the meaning.
Sooth. [reads.] *Whenas a lion's whelp shall, to himself
unknown, without seeking find, and be embraced by a piece
of tender air; and when from a stately cedar shall be lopped
branches, which, being dead many years, shall after revive,
be jointed to the old stock, and freshly grow; then shall
Posthumus end his miseries, Britain be fortunate, and
flourish in peace and plenty.*
Thou, Leonatus, art the lion's whelp;
The fit and apt construction of thy name,
Being Leo-natus, doth import so much:
The piece of tender air, thy virtuous daughter,   [*To* Cym.
Which we call *mollis aer;* and *mollis aer*
We term it *mulier;* which *mulier* I divine
Is this most constant wife; who even now,
Answering the letter of the oracle,
Unknown to you, unsought, were clipp'd about
With this most tender air.
    Cym. This hath some seeming.
    Sooth. The lofty cedar, royal Cymbeline,
Personates thee: and thy lopp'd branches point
Thy two sons forth, who, by Belarius stol'n,
For many years thought dead, are now reviv'd,
To the majestic cedar join'd; whose issue
Promises Britain peace and plenty.
    Cym. Well,
By peace we will begin:—and, Caius Lucius,
Although the victor, we submit to Cæsar,
And to the Roman empire; promising
To pay our wonted tribute, from the which
We were dissuaded by our wicked queen;
Whom heavens, in justice both on her and hers,
Have laid most heavy hand.
    Sooth. The fingers of the powers above do tune
The harmony of this peace. The vision,
Which I made known to Lucius ere the stroke
Of this yet scarce-cold battle, at this instant
Is full accomplish'd; for the Roman eagle,
From south to west on wing soaring aloft,
Lessen'd herself, and in the beams o' the sun
So vanish'd: which foreshow'd our princely eagle,
The imperial Cæsar, should again unite
His favour with the radiant Cymbeline,
Which shines here in the west.

Cym.   Laud we the gods;
And let our crooked smokes climb to their nostrils
From our bless'd altars.   Publish we this peace
To all our subjects.   Set we forward: let
A Roman and a British ensign wave
Friendly together: so through Lud's town march:
And in the temple of great Jupiter
Our peace we'll ratify; seal it with feasts.—
Set on there!—Never was a war did cease,
Ere bloody hands were wash'd, with such a peace. [*Exeunt.*

TITUS ANDRONICUS.

PERSONS REPRESENTED.

SATURNINUS, *Son to the late Emperor of Rome, and after-wards declared Emperor.*

BASSIANUS, *Brother to* SATURNINUS, *in love with* LAVINIA.

TITUS ANDRONICUS, *a noble Roman, General against the Goths.*

MARCUS ANDRONICUS, *Tribune of the People, and Brother to* TITUS.

LUCIUS,
QUINTUS,
MARTIUS, } *Sons to* TITUS ANDRONICUS.
MUTIUS,

YOUNG LUCIUS, *a Boy, Son to* LUCIUS.

PUBLIUS, *Son to* MARCUS *the Tribune.*

ÆMILIUS, *a noble Roman.*

ALARBUS,
DEMETRIUS, } *Sons to* TAMORA.
CHIRON,

AARON, *a Moor, beloved by* TAMORA.

A Captain, Tribune, Messenger, *and* Clown,—*Romans.*

Goths *and* Romans.

TAMORA, *Queen of the Goths.*

LAVINIA, *Daughter to* TITUS ANDRONICUS.

A Nurse, *and a black* Child.

Kinsmen of TITUS, Senators, Tribunes, Officers, Soldiers, *and* Attendants.

SCENE,--ROME, *and the Country near it.*

TITUS ANDRONICUS.

ACT I.

SCENE I.—ROME. *Before the Capitol.*

The Tomb of the ANDRONICI *appearing; the* Tribunes *and* Senators *aloft. Enter, below,* SATURNINUS *and his* Followers *on one side, and* BASSIANUS *and his* Followers *on the other, with drums and colours.*

Sat. Noble patricians, patrons of my right,
Defend the justice of my cause with arms;
And, countrymen, my loving followers,
Plead my successive title with your swords:
I am his first-born son that was the last
That wore the imperial diadem of Rome:
Then let my father's honours live in me,
Nor wrong mine age with this indignity.

    Bas. Romans,—friends, followers, favourers of my right,—
If ever Bassianus, Cæsar's son,
Were gracious in the eyes of royal Rome,
Keep, then, this passage to the Capitol;
And suffer not dishonour to approach
The imperial seat, to virtue consecrate,
To justice, continence, and nobility:
But let desert in pure election shine;
And, Romans, fight for freedom in your choice.

    Enter MARCUS ANDRONICUS *aloft, with the crown.*

    Marc. Princes,—that strive by factions and by friends
Ambitiously for rule and empery,—
Know that the people of Rome, for whom we stand
A special party, have by common voice,
In election for the Roman empery,
Chosen Andronicus, surnamed Pius
For many good and great deserts to Rome:
A nobler man, a braver warrior,
Lives not this day within the city walls:

He by the senate is accited home
From weary wars against the barbarous Goths;
That, with his sons, a terror to our foes,
Hath yok'd a nation strong, train'd up in arms.
Ten years are spent since first he undertook
This cause of Rome, and chastised with arms
Our enemies' pride: five times he hath return'd
Bleeding to Rome, bearing his valiant sons
In coffins from the field;
And now at last, laden with honour's spoils,
Returns the good Andronicus to Rome,
Renowned Titus, flourishing in arms.
Let us entreat,—by honour of his name
Whom worthily you would have now succeed,
And in the Capitol and senate's right,
Whom you pretend to honour and adore,—
That you withdraw you, and abate your strength;
Dismiss your followers, and, as suitors should,
Plead your deserts in peace and humbleness.
　　Sat. How fair the tribune speaks to calm my thoughts!
　　Bas. Marcus Andronicus, so I do affy
In thy uprightness and integrity,
And so I love and honour thee and thine,
Thy noble brother Titus and his sons,
And her to whom my thoughts are humbled all,
Gracious Lavinia, Rome's rich ornament,
That I will here dismiss my loving friends;
And to my fortunes and the people's favour
Commit my cause in balance to be weigh'd.
　　　　　　　　[*Exeunt the* Followers *of* Bas.
　　Sat. Friends, that have been thus forward in my right,
I thank you all, and here dismiss you all;
And to the love and favour of my country
Commit myself, my person, and the cause.
　　　　　　　　[*Exeunt the* Followers *of* Sat.
Rome, be as just and gracious unto me
As I am confident and kind to thee.—
Open the gates, tribunes, and let me in.
　　Bas. Tribunes, and me, a poor competitor.
　[*Flourish. Exeunt;* Sat. *and* Bas. *go up into the Capitol.*

Enter a Captain.

　　Cap. Romans, make way. The good Andronicus,
Patron of virtue, Rome's best champion,
Successful in the battles that he fights,
With honour and with fortune is return'd

From where he circumscribed with his sword,
And brought to yoke, the enemies of Rome.

Flourish of trumpets, &c. Enter MARTIUS *and* MUTIUS;
after them two Men *bearing a coffin covered with black;
then* LUCIUS *and* QUINTUS. *After them* TITUS ANDRO-
NICUS; *and then* TAMORA, *with* ALARBUS, DEMETRIUS,
CHIRON, AARON, *and other* Goths, *prisoners;* Soldiers
and People *following. The bearers set down the coffin,
and* TITUS *speaks.*

Tit. Hail, Rome, victorious in thy mourning weeds!
Lo, as the bark that hath discharg'd her fraught
Returns with precious lading to the bay
From whence at first she weigh'd her anchorage,
Cometh Andronicus, bound with laurel boughs,
To re-salute his country with his tears,—
Tears of true joy for his return to Rome.—
Thou great defender of this Capitol,
Stand gracious to the rites that we intend!—
Romans, of five-and-twenty valiant sons,
Half of the number that King Priam had,
Behold the poor remains, alive and dead!
These that survive let Rome reward with love;
These that I bring unto their latest home,
With burial amongst their ancestors:
Here Goths have given me leave to sheathe my sword.
Titus, unkind, and careless of thine own,
Why suffer'st thou thy sons, unburied yet,
To hover on the dreadful shore of Styx?—
Make way to lay them by their brethren.—

                        [*The tomb is opened.*

There greet in silence, as the dead are wont,
And sleep in peace, slain in your country's wars!
O sacred receptacle of my joys,
Sweet cell of virtue and nobility,
How many sons of mine hast thou in store,
That thou wilt never render to me more!

Luc. Give us the proudest prisoner of the Goths,
That we may hew his limbs, and on a pile
Ad manes fratrum sacrifice his flesh
Before this earthly prison of their bones;
That so the shadows be not unappeas'd,
Nor we disturb'd with prodigies on earth.

Tit. I give him you,—the noblest that survives,
The eldest son of this distressed queen.

Tam. Stay, Roman brethren!—Gracious conqueror,

Victorious Titus, rue the tears I shed,
A mother's tears in passion for her son :
And if thy sons were ever dear to thee,
O, think my son to be as dear to me!
Sufficeth not that we are brought to Rome,
To beautify thy triumphs and return,
Captive to thee and to thy Roman yoke :
But must my sons be slaughter'd in the streets
For valiant doings in their country's cause?
O, if to fight for king and common weal
Were piety in thine, it is in these.
Andronicus, stain not thy tomb with blood :
Wilt thou draw near the nature of the gods?
Draw near them, then, in being merciful :
Sweet mercy is nobility's true badge :
Thrice-noble Titus, spare my first-born son.

   Tit. Patient yourself, madam, and pardon me.
These are their brethren, whom you Goths beheld
Alive and dead ; and for their brethren slain
Religiously they ask a sacrifice :
To this your son is mark'd ; and die he must,
To appease their groaning shadows that are gone.

   Luc. Away with him ! and make a fire straight;
And with our swords, upon a pile of wood,
Let 's hew his limbs till they be clean consum'd.

            [*Exeunt* LUC., QUIN., MARC., *and* MUT., *with*
             ALARBUS.

   Tam. O cruel, irreligious piety!
   Chi. Was ever Scythia half so barbarous?
   Dem. Oppose not Scythia to ambitious Rome.
Alarbus goes to rest ; and we survive
To tremble under Titus' threatening looks.
Then, madam, stand resolv'd ; but hope withal
The self-same gods that arm'd the Queen of Troy
With opportunity of sharp revenge
Upon the Thracian tyrant in his tent,
May favour Tamora, the queen of Goths,—
When Goths were Goths and Tamora was queen,—
To quit the bloody wrongs upon her foes.

   Re-enter LUCIUS, QUINTUS, MARTIUS, *and* MUTIUS, *with*
          their swords bloody.

   Luc. See, lord and father, how we have perform'd
Our Roman rites : Alarbus' limbs are lopp'd,
And entrails feed the sacrificing fire,
Whose smoke like incense doth perfume the sky

Remaineth naught but to inter our brethren,
And with loud 'larums welcome them to Rome.
 Tit. Let it be so, and let Andronicus
Make this his latest farewell to their souls.
          [*Trumpets sounded and the coffin laid in the tomb.*
In peace and honour rest you here, my sons;
Rome's readiest champions, repose you here in rest,
Secure from worldly chances and mishaps!
Here lurks no treason, here no envy swells,
Here grow no damned grudges; here are no storms,
No noise, but silence and eternal sleep:

                Enter LAVINIA.

In peace and honour rest you here, my sons!
 Lav. In peace and honour live Lord Titus long;
My noble lord and father, live in fame!
Lo, at this tomb my tributary tears
I render for my brethren's obsequies;
And at thy feet I kneel, with tears of joy
Shed on the earth for thy return to Rome:
O, bless me here with thy victorious hand,
Whose fortunes Rome's best citizens applaud!
 Tit. Kind Rome, that hast thus lovingly reserv'd
The cordial of mine age to glad my heart!—
Lavinia, live; outlive thy father's days,
And fame's eternal date, for virtue's praise!

Enter, below, MARCUS ANDRONICUS *and* Tribunes; *re-enter*
     SATURNINUS, BASSIANUS, *and* Attendants.

 Marc. Long live Lord Titus, my beloved brother,
Gracious triumpher in the eyes of Rome!
 Tit. Thanks, gentle tribune, noble brother Marcus.
 Marc. And welcome, nephews, from successful wars,
You that survive and you that sleep in fame!
Fair lords, your fortunes are alike in all,
That in your country's service drew your swords:
But safer triumph is this funeral pomp
That hath aspir'd to Solon's happiness,
And triumphs over chance in honour's bed.—
Titus Andronicus, the people of Rome,
Whose friend in justice thou hast ever been,
Send thee by me, their tribune and their trust,
This palliament of white and spotless hue;
And name thee in election for the empire
With these our late-deceased emperor's sons:

Be *candidatus*, then, and put it on,
And help to set a head on headless Rome.
  Tit. A better head her glorious body fits
Than his that shakes for age and feebleness:
What, should I don this robe and trouble you?
Be chosen with proclamations to-day,
To-morrow yield up rule, resign my life,
And set abroach new business for you all?
Rome, I have been thy soldier forty years,
And led my country's strength successfully,
And buried one-and-twenty valiant sons,
Knighted in field, slain manfully in arms,
In right and service of their noble country:
Give me a staff of honour for mine age,
But not a sceptre to control the world:
Upright he held it, lords, that held it last.
  Marc. Titus, thou shalt obtain and ask the empery.
  Sat. Proud and ambitious tribune, canst thou tell?
  Tit. Patience, Prince Saturninus.
  Sat.   Romans, do me right;—
Patricians, draw your swords, and sheathe them not
Till Saturninus be Rome's emperor.—
Andronicus, would thou wert shipp'd to hell
Rather than rob me of the people's hearts!
  Luc. Proud Saturnine, interrupter of the good
That noble-minded Titus means to thee!
  Tit. Content thee, prince; I will restore to thee
The people's hearts, and wean them from themselves.
  Bas. Andronicus, I do not flatter thee,
But honour thee, and will do till I die:
My faction if thou strengthen with thy friends,
I will most thankful be; and thanks to men
Of noble minds is honourable meed.
  Tit. People of Rome, and people's tribunes here,
I ask your voices and your suffrages:
Will you bestow them friendly on Andronicus?
  Trib. To gratify the good Andronicus,
And gratulate his safe return to Rome,
The people will accept whom he admits.
  Tit. Tribunes, I thank you: and this suit I make,
That you create your emperor's eldest son,
Lord Saturnine; whose virtues will, I hope,
Reflect on Rome as Titan's rays on earth,
And ripen justice in this commonweal:
Then, if you will elect by my advice,
Crown him, and say, *Long live our emperor!*

Marc. With voices and applause of every sort,
Patricians and plebeians, we create
Lord Saturninus Rome's great emperor;
And say, *Long live our emperor Saturnine!* [*A long flourish.*
Sat. Titus Andronicus, for thy favours done
To us in our election this day
I give thee thanks in part of thy deserts,
And will with deeds requite thy gentleness;
And for an onset, Titus, to advance
Thy name and honourable family,
Lavinia will I make my empress,
Rome's royal mistress, mistress of my heart,
And in the sacred Pantheon her espouse:
Tell me, Andronicus, doth this motion please thee?
Tit. It doth, my worthy lord; and in this match
I hold me highly honour'd of your grace:
And here, in sight of Rome, to Saturnine,—
King and commander of our commonweal,
The wide world's emperor,—do I consecrate
My sword, my chariot, and my prisoners;
Presents well worthy Rome's imperial lord:
Receive them, then, the tribute that I owe,
Mine honour's ensigns humbled at thy feet.
Sat. Thanks, noble Titus, father of my life!
How proud I am of thee and of thy gifts
Rome shall record; and when I do forget
The least of these unspeakable deserts,
Romans, forget your fealty to me.
Tit. [*to* TAMORA.] Now, madam, are you prisoner to an
emperor;
To him that for your honour and your state
Will use you nobly and your followers.
Sat. A goodly lady, trust me; of the hue
That I would choose were I to choose anew.—
Clear up, fair queen, that cloudy countenance:
Though chance of war hath wrought this change of
cheer,
Thou com'st not to be made a scorn in Rome:
Princely shall be thy usage every way.
Rest on my word, and let not discontent
Daunt all your hopes: madam, he comforts you
Can make you greater than the Queen of Goths.—
Lavinia, you are not displeas'd with this?
Lav. Not I, my lord; sith true nobility
Warrants these words in princely courtesy.
Sat. Thanks, sweet Lavinia.—Romans, let us go:

Ransomless here we set our prisoners free:
Proclaim our honours, lords, with trump and drum.

     [*Flourish.* SAT. *courts* TAMORA *in dumb show.*
 Bas. Lord Titus, by your leave, this maid is mine.

         [*Seizing* LAVINIA.
 Tit. How, sir! are you in earnest, then, my lord?
 Bas. Ay, noble Titus; and resolv'd withal
To do myself this reason and this right.
 Marc. Suum cuique is our Roman justice:
This prince in justice seizeth but his own.
 Luc. And that he will and shall, if Lucius live.
 Tit. Traitors, avaunt!—Where is the emperor's guard?—
Treason, my lord,—Lavinia is surpris'd!
 Sat. Surpris'd! by whom?
 Bas.   By him that justly may
Bear his betroth'd from all the world away.

     [*Exeunt* BAS. *and* MAR. *with* LAV.
 Mut. Brothers, help to convey her hence away,
And with my sword I'll keep this door safe.

     [*Exeunt* LUC., QUIN., *and* MAR.
 Tit. Follow, my lord, and I'll soon bring her back.
 Mut. My lord, you pass not here.
 Tit.   What, villain boy!
Barr'st me my way in Rome?   [*Stabbing* MUTIUS.
 Mut.   Help, Lucius, help! [*Dies.*

      Re-enter LUCIUS.

 Luc. My lord, you are unjust; and more than so,
In wrongful quarrel you have slain your son.
 Tit. Nor thou nor he are any sons of mine;
My sons would never so dishonour me:
Traitor, restore Lavinia to the emperor.
 Luc. Dead, if you will; but not to be his wife,
That is another's lawful promis'd love.   [*Exit.*
 Sat. No, Titus, no; the emperor needs her not,
Nor her, nor thee, nor any of thy stock:
I'll trust by leisure him that mocks me once;
Thee never, nor thy traitorous haughty sons,
Confederates all thus to dishonour me.
Was there none else in Rome to make a stale
But Saturnine? Full well, Andronicus,
Agree these deeds with that proud brag of thine,
That said'st I begg'd the empire at thy hands.
 Tit. O monstrous! what reproachful words are these?
 Sat. But go thy ways; go, give that changing piece
To him that flourish'd for her with his sword:

A valiant son-in-law thou shalt enjoy;
One fit to bandy with thy lawless sons,
To ruffle in the commonwealth of Rome.

Tit. These words are razors to my wounded heart.

Sat. And therefore, lovely Tamora, Queen of Goths,—
That, like the stately Phœbe 'mongst her nymphs,
Dost overshine the gallant'st dames of Rome,—
If thou be pleas'd with this my sudden choice,
Behold, I choose thee, Tamora, for my bride,
And will create thee empress of Rome.
Speak, Queen of Goths, dost thou applaud my choice?
And here I swear by all the Roman gods,—
Sith priest and holy water are so near,
And tapers burn so bright, and everything
In readiness for Hymenæus stand,—
I will not re-salute the streets of Rome,
Or climb my palace, till from forth this place
I lead espous'd my bride along with me.

Tam. And here, in sight of heaven, to Rome I swear,
If Saturnine advance the Queen of Goths,
She will a handmaid be to his desires,
A loving nurse, a mother to his youth.

Sat. Ascend, fair queen, Pantheon.—Lords, accompany
Your noble emperor and his lovely bride,
Sent by the heavens for Prince Saturnine,
Whose wisdom hath her fortune conquered:
There shall we consummate our spousal rites.

             [*Exeunt* SAT. *and his* Followers; TAM.
             and her sons; AARON *and* Goths.

Tit. I am not bid to wait upon this bride.—
Titus, when wert thou wont to walk alone,
Dishonour'd thus, and challenged of wrongs?

Re-enter MARCUS, LUCIUS, QUINTUS, *and* MARTIUS.

Marc. O Titus, see, O see what thou hast done!
In a bad quarrel slain a virtuous son.

Tit. No, foolish tribune, no; no son of mine,—
Nor thou, nor these, confederates in the deed
That hath dishonour'd all our family;
Unworthy brother and unworthy sons!

Luc. But let us give him burial, as becomes;
Give Mutius burial with our brethren.

Tit. Traitors, away! he rests not in this tomb:—
This monument five hundred years hath stood,
Which I have sumptuously re-edified:
Here none but soldiers and Rome's servitors

Repose in fame; none basely slain in brawls:—
Bury him where you can, he comes not here.
   Marc. My lord, this is impiety in you:
My nephew Mutius' deeds do plead for him;
He must be buried with his brethren.
   Quin. and Mart. And shall, or him we will accompany.
   Tit. And shall! What villain was it spake that word?
   Quin. He that would vouch it in any place but here.
   Tit. What, would you bury him in my despite?
   Marc. No, noble Titus; but entreat of thee
To pardon Mutius, and to bury him.
   Tit. Marcus, even thou hast struck upon my crest,
And with these boys mine honour thou hast wounded:
My foes I do repute you every one;
So trouble me no more, but get you gone.
   Mart. He is not with himself; let us withdraw.
   Quin. Not I, till Mutius' bones be buried.
                      [MARCUS *and the Sons of* TITUS *kneel.*
   Marc. Brother, for in that name doth nature plead,—
   Quin. Father, and in that name doth nature speak,—
   Tit. Speak thou no more, if all the rest will speed.
   Marc. Renowned Titus, more than half my soul,—
   Luc. Dear father, soul and substance of us all,—
   Marc. Suffer thy brother Marcus to inter
His noble nephew here in virtue's nest,
That died in honour and Lavinia's cause:
Thou art a Roman,—be not barbarous.
The Greeks upon advice did bury Ajax,
That slew himself; and wise Laertes' son
Did graciously plead for his funerals:
Let not young Mutius, then, that was thy joy,
Be barr'd his entrance here.
   Tit.   Rise, Marcus, rise:
The dismall'st day is this that e'er I saw,
To be dishonour'd by my sons in Rome!—
Well, bury him, and bury me the next.
                      [MUTIUS *is put into the tomb.*
   Luc. There lie thy bones, sweet Mutius, with thy friends,
Till we with trophies do adorn thy tomb.
   All. [*kneeling.*] No man shed tears for noble Mutius;
He lives in fame that died in virtue's cause.
   Marc. My lord,—to step out of these dreary dumps,—
How comes it that the subtle Queen of Goths
Is of a sudden thus advanc'd in Rome?
   Tit. I know not, Marcus; but I know it is,—
Whether by device or no, the heavens can tell:

Is she not, then, beholden to the man
That brought her for this high good turn so far?
Marc. Yes, and will nobly him remunerate.

Flourish. *Re-enter, at one side,* SATURNINUS *attended;*
    TAMORA, DEMETRIUS, CHIRON, *and* AARON: *at the other,*
    BASSIANUS, LAVINIA, *and others.*

Sat. So, Bassianus, you have play'd your prize:
God give you joy, sir, of your gallant bride!
Bas. And you of yours, my lord! I say no more,
Nor wish no less; and so I take my leave.
Sat. Traitor, if Rome have law or we have power,
Thou and thy faction shall repent this rape.
Bas. Rape, call you it, my lord, to seize my own,
My true-betrothed love, and now my wife?
But let the laws of Rome determine all;
Meanwhile I am possess'd of that is mine.
Sat. 'Tis good, sir: you are very short with us;
But if we live we'll be as sharp with you.
Bas. My lord, what I have done, as best I may,
Answer I must, and shall do with my life.
Only thus much I give your grace to know,—
By all the duties that I owe to Rome,
This noble gentleman, Lord Titus here,
Is in opinion and in honour wrong'd,
That, in the rescue of Lavinia,
With his own hand did slay his youngest son,
In zeal to you, and highly mov'd to wrath
To be controll'd in that he frankly gave:
Receive him, then, to favour, Saturnine,
That hath express'd himself, in all his deeds,
A father and a friend to thee and Rome.
Tit. Prince Bassianus, leave to plead my deeds:
'Tis thou and those that have dishonour'd me.
Rome and the righteous heavens be my judge
How I have lov'd and honour'd Saturnine!
Tam. My worthy lord, if ever Tamora
Were gracious in those princely eyes of thine,
Then hear me speak indifferently for all;
And at my suit, sweet, pardon what is past.
Sat. What, madam! be dishonour'd openly,
And basely put it up without revenge?
Tam. Not so, my lord; the gods of Rome forfend
I should be author to dishonour you!
But on mine honour dare I undertake
For good Lord Titus' innocence in all,

Whose fury not dissembled speaks his griefs:
Then at my suit look graciously on him;
Lose not so noble a friend on vain suppose,
Nor with sour looks afflict his gentle heart.—
My lord, be rul'd by me, be won at last;   [*Aside.*
Dissemble all your griefs and discontents:
You are but newly planted in your throne;
Lest, then, the people and patricians too,
Upon a just survey, take Titus' part,
And so supplant you for ingratitude,—
Which Rome reputes to be a heinous sin,—
Yield at entreats; and then let me alone:
I'll find a day to massacre them all,
And raze their faction and their family,
The cruel father and his traitorous sons,
To whom I sued for my dear son's life;
And make them know what 'tis to let a queen
Kneel in the streets and beg for grace in vain.—
Come, come, sweet emperor,—come, Andronicus,—
Take up this good old man, and cheer the heart
That dies in tempest of thy angry frown.

    Sat. Rise, Titus, rise; my empress hath prevail'd.

    Tit. I thank your majesty and her, my lord:
These words, these looks, infuse new life in me.

    Tam. Titus, I am incorporate in Rome,
A Roman now adopted happily,
And must advise the emperor for his good.
This day all quarrels die, Andronicus;—
And let it be mine honour, good my lord,
That I have reconcil'd your friends and you.—
For you, Prince Bassianus, I have pass'd
My word and promise to the emperor
That you will be more mild and tractable.—
And fear not, lords,—and you, Lavinia,—
By my advice, all humbled on your knees,
You shall ask pardon of his majesty.

    Luc. We do; and vow to heaven and to his highness
That what we did was mildly as we might,
Tendering our sister's honour and our own.

    Marc. That on mine honour here I do protest.

    Sat. Away, and talk not; trouble us no more.

    Tam. Nay, nay, sweet emperor, we must all be friends:
The tribune and his nephews kneel for grace;
I will not be denied: sweet heart, look back.

    Sat. Marcus, for thy sake and thy brother's here,
And at my lovely Tamora's entreats,

I do remit these young men's heinous faults:
Stand up.—
Lavinia, though you left me like a churl,
I found a friend; and sure as death I swore
I would not part a bachelor from the priest.
Come, if the emperor's court can feast two brides,
You are my guest, Lavinia, and your friends.
This day shall be a love-day, Tamora.

    Tit. To-morrow, an it please your majesty
To hunt the panther and the hart with me,
With horn and hound we'll give your grace *bonjour.*

    Sat. Be it so, Titus, and gramercy too.   [*Exeunt.*

ACT II.

SCENE I.—ROME. *Before the Palace.*

Enter AARON.

    Aar. Now climbeth Tamora Olympus' top,
Safe out of fortune's shot; and sits aloft,
Secure of thunder's crack or lightning's flash;
Advanc'd above pale envy's threatening reach.
As when the golden sun salutes the morn,
And, having gilt the ocean with his beams,
Gallops the zodiac in his glistering coach,
And overlooks the highest-peering hills;
So Tamora:
Upon her will doth earthly honour wait,
And virtue stoops and trembles at her frown.
Then, Aaron, arm thy heart and fit thy thoughts
To mount aloft with thy imperial mistress,
And mount her pitch, whom thou in triumph long
Hast prisoner held, fetter'd in amorous chains,
And faster bound to Aaron's charming eyes
Than is Prometheus tied to Caucasus.
Away with slavish weeds and servile thoughts!
I will be bright, and shine in pearl and gold,
To wait upon this new-made empress.
To wait, said I? to wanton with this queen,
This goddess, this Semiramis, this nymph,
This syren, that will charm Rome's Saturnine,
And see his shipwreck and his commonweal's.—
Holla! what storm is this?

Dem. Chiron, thy years want wit, thy wit wants edge
And manners, to intrude where I am grac'd;
And may, for aught thou know'st, affected be.

Chi. Demetrius, thou dost over-ween in all;
And so in this, to bear me down with braves.
'Tis not the difference of a year or two
Makes me less gracious or thee more fortunate:
I am as able and as fit as thou
To serve and to deserve my mistress' grace;
And that my sword upon thee shall approve,
And plead my passions for Lavinia's love.

Aar. [*aside.*] Clubs, clubs! these lovers will not keep the
        peace.

Dem. Why, boy, although our mother, unadvis'd,
Gave you a dancing-rapier by your side,
Are you so desperate grown to threat your friends?
Go to; have your lath glu'd within your sheath
Till you know better how to handle it.

Chi. Meanwhile, sir, with the little skill I have,
Full well shalt thou perceive how much I dare.

Dem. Ay, boy, grow ye so brave?   [*They draw.*

Aar. [*coming forward.*] Why, how now, lords!
So near the emperor's palace dare you draw,
And maintain such a quarrel openly?
Full well I wot the ground of all this grudge:
I would not for a million of gold
The cause were known to them it most concerns;
Nor would your noble mother for much more
Be so dishonour'd in the court of Rome.
For shame, put up.

Dem.   Not I, till I have sheath'd
My rapier in his bosom, and withal
Thrust these reproachful speeches down his throat
That he hath breath'd in my dishonour here.

Chi. For that I am prepar'd and full resolv'd,—
Foul-spoken coward, that thunder'st with thy tongue,
And with thy weapon nothing dar'st perform.

Aar. Away, I say!—
Now, by the gods that warlike Goths adore,
This petty brabble will undo us all.—
Why, lords, and think you not how dangerous
It is to jet upon a prince's right?
What, is Lavinia, then, become so loose,
Or Bassianus so degenerate.

That for her love such quarrels may be broach'd
Without controlment, justice, or revenge?
Young lords, beware! and should the empress know
This discord's ground, the music would not please.

Chi. I care not, I, knew she and all the world:
I love Lavinia more than all the world.

Dem. Youngling, learn thou to make some meaner choice:
Lavinia is thine elder brother's hope.

Aar. Why, are you mad? or know ye not in Rome
How furious and impatient they be,
And cannot brook competitors in love?
I tell you, lords, you do but plot your deaths
By this device.

Chi.   Aaron, a thousand deaths
Would I propose to achieve her whom I love.

Aar. To achieve her!—How?

Dem.   Why mak'st thou it so strange?
She is a woman, therefore may be woo'd;
She is a woman, therefore may be won;
She is Lavinia, therefore must be lov'd.
What, man! more water glideth by the mill
Than wots the miller of; and easy it is
Of a cut loaf to steal a shive, we know:
Though Bassianus be the emperor's brother,
Better than he have worn Vulcan's badge.

Aar. [*aside.*] Ay, and as good as Saturninus may.

Dem. Then why should he despair that knows to court it
With words, fair looks, and liberality?
What, hast not thou full often struck a doe,
And borne her cleanly by the keeper's nose?

Aar. Why, then, it seems some certain snatch or so
Would serve your turns.

Chi.   Ay, so the turn were serv'd.

Dem. Aaron, thou hast hit it.

Aar.   Would you had hit it too!
Then should not we be tir'd with this ado.
Why, hark ye, hark ye,—and are you such fools
To square for this? Would it offend you, then,
That both should speed?

Chi.   Faith, not me.

Dem. Nor me, so I were one.

Aar. For shame, be friends, and join for that you jar:
'Tis policy and stratagem must do
That you affect; and so must you resolve
That what you cannot as you would achieve,
You must perforce accomplish as you may.

Take this of me,—Lucrece was not more chaste
Than this Lavinia, Bassianus' love.
A speedier course than lingering languishment
Must we pursue, and I have found the path.
My lords, a solemn hunting is in hand;
There will the lovely Roman ladies troop:
The forest-walks are wide and spacious;
And many unfrequented plots there are
Fitted by kind for rape and villany:
Single you thither, then, this dainty doe,
And strike her home by force if not by words:
This way, or not at all, stand you in hope.
Come, come, our empress, with her sacred wit
To villany and vengeance consecrate,
Will we acquaint with all that we intend;
And she shall file our engines with advice
That will not suffer you to square yourselves,
But to your wishes' height advance you both.
The emperor's court is like the house of fame,
The palace full of tongues, of eyes, and ears:
The woods are ruthless, dreadful, deaf, and dull;
There speak and strike, brave boys, and take your turns;
There serve your lust, shadow'd from heaven's eye,
And revel in Lavinia's treasury.

　　Chi. Thy counsel, lad, smells of no cowardice.

　　Dem. Sit fas aut nefas, till I find the stream
To cool this heat, a charm to calm these fits,
Per Styga, per manes vehor.　　　　　　　[*Exeunt.*

SCENE II.—*A Forest near Rome: a Lodge seen at a distance.
Horns and cry of hounds heard.*

Enter Titus Andronicus, *with* Hunters, *&c.,* Marcus,
Lucius, Quintus, *and* Martius.

　　Tit. The hunt is up, the morn is bright and gay,
The fields are fragrant, and the woods are green.
Uncouple here, and let us make a bay,
And wake the emperor and his lovely bride,
And rouse the prince, and ring a hunter's peal,
That all the court may echo with the noise.
Sons, let it be your charge, as it is ours,
To attend the emperor's person carefully:
I have been troubled in my sleep this night,
But dawning day new comfort hath inspir'd.

Horns wind a peal.   Enter SATURNINUS, TAMORA, BASSIA-
   NUS, LAVINIA, DEMETRIUS, CHIRON, *and* Attendants.

Many good-morrows to your majesty:—
Madam, to you as many and as good:—
I promised your grace a hunter's peal.
   Sat. And you have rung it lustily, my lord;
Somewhat too early for new-married ladies.
   Bas. Lavinia, how say you?
   Lav.   I say no;
I have been broad awake two hours and more.
   Sat. Come on, then, horse and chariots let us have,
And to our sport.—[*To* TAMORA.] Madam, now shall ye see
Our Roman hunting.
   Marc.   I have dogs, my lord,
Will rouse the proudest panther in the chase,
And climb the highest promontory top.
   Tit. And I have horse will follow where the game
Makes way, and run like swallows o'er the plain.
   Dem. Chiron, we hunt not, we, with horse nor hound,
But hope to pluck a dainty doe to ground.   [*Exeunt.*

SCENE III.—*A lonely part of the Forest.*

Enter AARON *with a bag of gold.*

   Aar. He that had wit would think that I had none,
To bury so much gold under a tree,
And never after to inherit it.
Let him that thinks of me so abjectly
Know that this gold must coin a stratagem,
Which, cunningly effected, will beget
A very excellent piece of villany:
And so repose, sweet gold, for their unrest [*Hides the gold.*
That have their alms out of the empress' chest.

Enter TAMORA.

   Tam. My lovely Aaron, wherefore look'st thou sad
When everything doth make a gleeful boast?
The birds chant melody on every bush;
The snake lies rolled in the cheerful sun;
The green leaves quiver with the cooling wind,
And make a chequer'd shadow on the ground:
Under their sweet shade, Aaron, let us sit,
And, whilst the babbling echo mocks the hounds,
Replying shrilly to the well-tun'd horns,

As if a double hunt were heard at once,
Let us sit down and mark their yelping noise;
And,—after conflict such as was suppos'd
The wandering prince and Dido once enjoy'd,
When with a happy storm they were surpris'd,
And curtain'd with a counsel-keeping cave,—
We may, each wreathed in the other's arms,
Our pastimes done, possess a golden slumber;
Whiles hounds and horns and sweet melodious birds
Be unto us as is a nurse's song
Of lullaby to bring her babe asleep.

 Aar. Madam, though Venus govern your desires,
Saturn is dominator over mine:
What signifies my deadly-standing eye,
My silence and my cloudy melancholy,
My fleece of woolly hair that now uncurls
Even as an adder when she doth unroll
To do some fatal execution?
No, madam, these are no venereal signs,
Vengeance is in my heart, death in my hand,
Blood and revenge are hammering in my head.
Hark, Tamora,—the empress of my soul,
Which never hopes more heaven than rests in thee,—
This is the day of doom for Bassianus:
His Philomel must lose her tongue to-day;
Thy sons make pillage of her chastity,
And wash their hands in Bassianus' blood.
Seest thou this letter? take it up, I pray thee,
And give the king this fatal-plotted scroll.—
Now question me no more,—we are espied;
Here comes a parcel of our hopeful booty,
Which dreads not yet their lives' destruction.

 Tam. Ah, my sweet Moor, sweeter to me than life!

 Aar. No more, great empress, Bassianus comes:
Be cross with him; and I'll go fetch thy sons
To back thy quarrels, whatsoe'er they be. [*Exit.*

Enter BASSIANUS *and* LAVINIA.

 Bas. Who have we here? Rome's royal empress,
Unfurnish'd of her well-beseeming troop?
Or is it Dian, habited like her,
Who hath abandoned her holy groves
To see the general hunting in this forest?

 Tam. Saucy controller of our private steps!
Had I the power that some say Dian had,
Thy temples should be planted presently

With horns, as was Actæon's; and the hounds
Should drive upon thy new-transformed limbs,
Unmannerly intruder as thou art!

Lav. Under your patience, gentle empress,
'Tis thought you have a goodly gift in horning;
And to be doubted that your Moor and you
Are singled forth to try experiments:
Jove shield your husband from his hounds to-day!
'Tis pity they should take him for a stag.

Bas. Believe me, queen, your swarth Cimmerian
Doth make your honour of his body's hue,
Spotted, detested, and abominable.
Why are you sequester'd from all your train,
Dismounted from your snow-white goodly steed,
And wander'd hither to an obscure plot,
Accompanied but with a barbarous Moor,
If foul desire had not conducted you?

Lav. And, being intercepted in your sport,
Great reason that my noble lord be rated
For sauciness.—I pray you, let us hence,
And let her joy her raven-colour'd love;
This valley fits the purpose passing well.

Bas. The king my brother shall have note of this.

Lav. Ay, for these slips have made him noted long:
Good king, to be so mightily abus'd!

Tam. Why have I patience to endure all this?

Enter DEMETRIUS *and* CHIRON.

Dem. How now, dear sovereign, and our gracious mother!
Why doth your highness look so pale and wan?

Tam. Have I not reason, think you, to look pale?
These two have 'tic'd me hither to this place:—
A barren detested vale you see it is;
The trees, though summer, yet forlorn and lean,
O'ercome with moss and baleful mistletoe:
Here never shines the sun; here nothing breeds,
Unless the nightly owl or fatal raven:—
And when they show'd me this abhorred pit
They told me, here at dead time of the night
A thousand fiends, a thousand hissing snakes,
Ten thousand swelling toads, as many urchins,
Would make such fearful and confused cries
As any mortal body hearing it
Should straight fall mad or else die suddenly.
No sooner had they told this hellish tale
But straight they told me they would bind me here

Unto the body of a dismal yew,
And leave me to this miserable death:
And then they call'd me foul adulteress,
Lascivious Goth, and all the bitterest terms
That ever ear did hear to such effect:
And had you not by wondrous fortune come,
This vengeance on me had they executed.
Revenge it, as you love your mother's life,
Or be ye not henceforth call'd my children.

 Dem. This is a witness that I am thy son.
         [*Stabs* BASSIANUS.
 Chi. And this for me, struck home to show my strength.
       [*Also stabs* BAS., *who dies.*
 Lav. Ay, come, Semiramis,—nay, barbarous Tamora,
For no name fits thy nature but thy own!
 Tam. Give me thy poniard;—you shall know, my boys,
Your mother's hand shall right your mother's wrong.
 Dem. Stay, madam; here is more belongs to her;
First thrash the corn, then after burn the straw:
This minion stood upon her chastity,
Upon her nuptial vow, her loyalty,
And with that painted hope braves your **mightiness**:
And shall she carry this unto her grave?
 Chi. An if she do, I would I were an eunuch.
Drag hence her husband to some secret hole,
And make his dead trunk pillow to our lust.
 Tam. But when ye have the honey ye desire,
Let not this wasp outlive, us both to sting.
 Chi. I warrant you, madam, we will make that sure.—
Come, mistress, now perforce we will enjoy
That nice-preserved honesty of yours.
 Lav. O Tamora! thou bear'st a woman's face,—
 Tam. I will not hear her speak; away with her!
 Lav. Sweet lords, entreat her hear me but a word.
 Dem. Listen, fair madam: let it be your glory
To see her tears; but be your heart to them
As unrelenting flint to drops of rain.
 Lav. When did the tiger's young ones teach the dam?
O, do not learn her wrath,—she taught it thee;
The milk thou suck'dst from her did turn to marble;
Even at thy teat thou hadst thy tyranny.—
Yet every mother breeds not sons alike:
Do thou entreat her show a woman pity. [*To* CHIRON.
 Chi. What, wouldst thou have me prove myself a bastard?
 Lav. 'Tis true, the raven doth not hatch a lark:
Yet have I heard,—O, could I find it now!—

The lion, mov'd with pity, did endure
To have his princely paws par'd all away:
Some say that ravens foster forlorn children,
The whilst their own birds famish in their nests
O, be to me, though thy hard heart say no,
Nothing so kind, but something pitiful!

Tam. I know not what it means :—away with her!

Lav. O, let me teach thee! for my father's sake,
That gave thee life, when well he might have slain thee,
Be not obdurate, open thy deaf ears.

Tam. Hadst thou in person ne'er offended me,
Even for his sake am I pitiless.—
Remember, boys, I pour'd forth tears in vain
To save your brother from the sacrifice;
But fierce Andronicus would not relent:
Therefore away with her, and use her as you will;
The worse to her the better lov'd of me.

Lav. O Tamora, be call'd a gentle queen,
And with thine own hands kill me in this place!
For 'tis not life that I have begg'd so long;
Poor I was slain when Bassianus died.

Tam. What begg'st thou, then? fond woman, let me go.

Lav. 'Tis present death I beg; and one thing more,
That womanhood denies my tongue to tell:
O, keep me from their worse than killing lust,
And tumble me into some loathsome pit,
Where never man's eye may behold my body:
Do this, and be a charitable murderer.

Tam. So should I rob my sweet sons of their fee:
No, let them satisfy their lust on thee.

Dem. Away! for thou hast stay'd us here too long.

Lav. No grace? no womanhood? Ah, beastly creature!
The blot and enemy to our general name!
Confusion fall,—

Chi. Nay, then I'll stop your mouth :—bring thou her
This is the hole where Aaron bid us hide him.   [husband:
         [DEM. *throws* BAS.'s *body into the pit; then*
            exit with CHI., *dragging off* LAV.

Tam. Farewell, my sons: see that you make her sure :—
Ne'er let my heart know merry cheer indeed
Till all the Andronici be made away.
Now will I hence to seek my lovely Moor,
And let my spleenful sons this trull deflower.   [*Exit.*

Re-enter AARON, *with* QUINTUS *and* MARTIUS.

Aar. Come on, my lords, the better foot before:

Straight will I bring you to the loathsome pit
Where I espied the panther fast asleep.

Quin. My sight is very dull, whate'er it bodes.

Mart. And mine, I promise you; were't not for shame,
Well could I leave our sport to sleep awhile.

[*Falls into the pit.*

Quin. What, art thou fallen?—What subtle hole is this,
Whose mouth is cover'd with rude-growing briers,
Upon whose leaves are drops of new-shed blood
As fresh as morning's dew distill'd on flowers?
A very fatal place it seems to me.—
Speak, brother, hast thou hurt thee with the fall?

Mart. O brother, with the dismallest object hurt
That ever eye with sight made heart lament!

Aar. [*aside.*] Now will I fetch the king to find them
here,
That he thereby may give a likely guess
How these were they that made away his brother. [*Exit.*

Mart. Why dost not comfort me, and help me out
From this unhallow'd and blood-stained hole?

Quin. I am surprised with an uncouth fear;
A chilling sweat o'er-runs my trembling joints;
My heart suspects more than mine eye can see.

Mart. To prove thou hast a true-divining heart,
Aaron and thou look down into this den,
And see a fearful sight of blood and death.

Quin. Aaron is gone; and my compassionate heart
Will not permit mine eyes once to behold
The thing whereat it trembles by surmise:
O, tell me how it is; for ne'er till now
Was I a child to fear I know not what.

Mart. Lord Bassianus lies embrewed here,
All on a heap, like to a slaughter'd lamb,
In this detested, dark, blood-drinking pit.

Quin. If it be dark, how dost thou know 'tis he?

Mart. Upon his bloody finger he doth wear
A precious ring that lightens all the hole,
Which, like a taper in some monument,
Doth shine upon the dead man's earthy cheeks,
And shows the ragged entrails of the pit:
So pale did shine the moon on Pyramus
When he by night lay bath'd in maiden blood.
O brother, help me with thy fainting hand,—
If fear hath made thee faint, as me it hath,—
Out of this fell devouring receptacle,
As hateful as Cocytus' misty mouth.

Quin. Reach me thy hand, that I may help thee out;
Or, wanting strength to do thee so much good,
I may be pluck'd into the swallowing womb
Of this deep pit, poor Bassianus' grave.
I have no strength to pluck thee to the brink.

Mart. Nor I no strength to climb without thy help.

Quin. Thy hand once more; I will not lose again,
Till thou art here aloft or I below:
Thou canst not come to me,—I come to thee. *[Falls in.*

Enter SATURNINUS *with* AARON.

Sat. Along with me: I'll see what hole is here,
And what he is that now is leap'd into it.—
Say, who art thou that lately didst descend
Into this gaping hollow of the earth?

Mart. The unhappy son of old Andronicus,
Brought hither in a most unlucky hour,
To find thy brother Bassianus dead.

Sat. My brother dead! I know thou dost but jest:
He and his lady both are at the lodge
Upon the north side of this pleasant chase;
'Tis not an hour since I left him there.

Mart. We know not where you left him all alive;
But, out, alas! here have we found him dead.

Re-enter TAMORA, *with* Attendants; TITUS ANDRONICUS *and* LUCIUS.

Tam. Where is my lord the king?

Sat. Here, Tamora; though griev'd with killing grief.

Tam. Where is thy brother Bassianus?

Sat. Now to the bottom dost thou search my wound:
Poor Bassianus here lies murdered.

Tam. Then all too late I bring this fatal writ,
                                        [Giving a letter
The complot of this timeless tragedy;
And wonder greatly, that man's face can fold
In pleasing smiles such murderous tyranny.

Sat. [reads.] *An if we miss to meet him handsomely,*
Sweet huntsman, Bassianus 'tis we mean,—
Do thou so much as dig the grave for him:
Thou know'st our meaning. Look for thy reward
Among the nettles at the elder tree
Which overshades the mouth of that same pit
Where we decreed to bury Bassianus.
Do this, and purchase us thy lasting friends.
O Tamora! was ever heard the like?—

This is the pit and this the elder tree:—
Look, sirs, if you can find the huntsman out
That should have murder'd Bassianus here.

Aar. My gracious lord, here is the bag of gold.
                              [*Showing it.*

Sat. [*to* TITUS.] Two of thy whelps, fell curs of bloody
Have here bereft my brother of his life.—   [kind,
Sirs, drag them from the pit unto the prison:
There let them bide until we have devis'd
Some never-heard-of torturing pain for them.

Tam. What, are they in this pit?   O wondrous thing!
How easily murder is discovered!

Tit. High emperor, upon my feeble knee
I beg this boon, with tears not lightly shed,
That this fell fault of my accursed sons,—
Accursed if the fault be prov'd in them,—

Sat. If it be prov'd! you see it is apparent. —
Who found this letter?   Tamora, was it you?

Tam. Andronicus himself did take it up.

Tit. I did, my lord: yet let me be their bail;
For, by my father's reverend tomb, I vow
They shall be ready at your highness' will
To answer their suspicion with their lives.

Sat. Thou shalt not bail them: see thou follow me.—
Some bring the murder'd body, some the murderers:
Let them not speak a word,—the guilt is plain;
For, by my soul, were there worse end than death,
That end upon them should be executed.

Tam. Andronicus, I will entreat the king:
Fear not thy sons; they shall do well enough.

Tit. Come, Lucius, come; stay not to talk with them.
          [*Exeunt severally.*   Attendants *bearing the body.*

SCENE IV.—*Another part of the Forest.*

Enter DEMETRIUS *and* CHIRON, *with* LAVINIA *ravished; her
          hands cut off and her tongue cut out.*

Dem. So, now go tell, an if thy tongue can speak,
Who 'twas that cut thy tongue and ravish'd thee.

Chi. Write down thy mind, bewray thy meaning so,
An if thy stumps will let thee play the scribe.

Dem. See, how with signs and tokens she can scrowl.

Chi. Go home, call for sweet water, wash thy hands.

Dem. She hath no tongue to call, nor hands to wash;
And so let's leave her to her silent walks.

Chi An 'twere my case I should go hang myself.
Dem. If thou hadst hands to help thee knit the cord.
[*Exeunt* DEM. *and* CHI.

Enter MARCUS.

Marc. Who is this,—my niece,—that flies away so fast?—
Cousin, a word; where is your husband?—
If I do dream, would all my wealth would wake me!
If I do wake, some planet strike me down,
That I may slumber in eternal sleep!—
Speak, gentle niece,—what stern ungentle hands
Have lopp'd, and hew'd, and made thy body bare
Of her two branches,—those sweet ornaments
Whose circling shadows kings have sought to sleep in,
And might not gain so great a happiness
As have thy love? Why dost not speak to me?—
Alas, a crimson river of warm blood,
Like to a bubbling fountain stirr'd with wind,
Doth rise and fall between thy rosed lips,
Coming and going with thy honey breath.
But sure some Tereus hath deflowered thee,
And, lest thou shouldst detect him, cut thy tongue.
Ah, now thou turn'st away thy face for shame!
And, notwithstanding all this loss of blood,—
As from a conduit with three issuing spouts,—
Yet do thy cheeks look red as Titan's face
Blushing to be encounter'd with a cloud.
Shall I speak for thee? shall I say 'tis so?
O, that I knew thy heart, and knew the beast,
That I might rail at him, to ease my mind!
Sorrow concealed, like an oven stopp'd,
Doth burn the heart to cinders where it is.
Fair Philomela, she but lost her tongue,
And in a tedious sampler sew'd her mind:
But, lovely niece, that mean is cut from thee;
A craftier Tereus, cousin, hast thou met,
And he hath cut those pretty fingers off
That could have better sew'd than Philomel.
O, had the monster seen those lily hands
Tremble, like aspen leaves, upon a lute,
And make the silken strings delight to kiss them,
He would not then have touch'd them for his life!
Or had he heard the heavenly harmony
Which that sweet tongue hath made,
He would have dropp'd his knife, and fell asleep
As Cerberus at the Thracian poet's feet.

Come, let us go, and make thy father blind;
For such a sight will blind a father's eye:
One hour's storm will drown the fragrant meads;
What will whole months of tears thy father's eyes?
Do not draw back, for we will mourn with thee:
O, could our mourning ease thy misery!   [*Exeunt.*

ACT III.

SCENE I.—ROME.   *A Street.*

Enter Senators, Tribunes, *and* Officers of Justice, *with*
MARTIUS *and* QUINTUS *bound, passing on to the place of
execution;* TITUS *going before, pleading.*

Tit. Hear me, grave fathers! noble tribunes, stay!
For pity of mine age, whose youth was spent
In dangerous wars, whilst you securely slept;
For all my blood in Rome's great quarrel shed;
For all the frosty nights that I have watch'd;
And for these bitter tears, which now you see
Filling the aged wrinkles in my cheeks;
Be pitiful to my condemned sons,
Whose souls are not corrupted as 'tis thought.
For two-and-twenty sons I never wept,
Because they died in honour's lofty bed.
For these, good tribunes, in the dust I write
                [*Throwing himself on the ground.*
My heart's deep languor and my soul's sad tears:
Let my tears stanch the earth's dry appetite;
My sons' sweet blood will make it shame and blush.
            [*Exeunt* Sen., Trib., *&c., with the prisoners.*
O earth, I will befriend thee more with rain,
That shall distil from these two ancient ruins,
Than youthful April shall with all his showers:
In summer's drought I'll drop upon thee still;
In winter, with warm tears I'll melt the snow,
And keep eternal spring-time on thy face,
So thou refuse to drink my dear sons' blood.

Enter LUCIUS *with his sword drawn.*

O reverend tribunes! O gentle aged men!
Unbind my sons, reverse the doom of death;

And let me say, that never wept before,
My tears are now prevailing orators.

Luc. O noble father, you lament in vain:
The tribunes hear you not, no man is by;
And you recount your sorrows to a stone.

Tit. Ah, Lucius, for thy brothers let me plead.—
Grave tribunes, once more I entreat of you.

Luc. My gracious lord, no tribune hears you speak.

Tit. Why, 'tis no matter, man: if they did hear
They would not mark me; or if they did mark
They would not pity me; yet plead I must,
And bootless unto them.
Therefore I tell my sorrows to the stones;
Why, though they cannot answer my distress,
Yet in some sort they are better than the tribunes,
For that they will not intercept my tale:
When I do weep they humbly at my feet
Receive my tears, and seem to weep with me;
And were they but attired in grave weeds
Rome could afford no tribune like to these.
A stone is soft as wax, tribunes more hard than stones;
A stone is silent, and offel deth not,—
And tribunes with their tongues doom men to death. [*Rises.*
But wherefore stand'st thou with thy weapon drawn?

Luc. To rescue my two brothers from their death:
For which attempt the judges have pronounc'd
My everlasting doom of banishment.

Tit. O happy man! they have befriended thee.
Why, foolish Lucius, dost thou not perceive
That Rome is but a wilderness of tigers?
Tigers must prey; and Rome affords no prey
But me and mine: how happy art thou, then,
From these devourers to be banished!—
But who comes with our brother Marcus here?

Enter MARCUS *and* LAVINIA.

Marc. Titus, prepare thy aged eyes to weep;
Or, if not so, thy noble heart to break:
I bring consuming sorrow to thine age.

Tit. Will it consume me? let me see it, then.

Marc This was thy daughter.

Tit. Why, Marcus, so she is.

Luc. Ay me! this object kills me!

Tit. Faint-hearted boy, arise, and look upon her.—
Speak, my Lavinia, what accursed hand
Hath made thee handless in thy father s sight!

What fool hath added water to the sea,
Or brought a fagot to bright-burning Troy?
My grief was at the height before thou cam'st;
And now, like Nilus, it disdaineth bounds.
Give me a sword, I'll chop off my hands too;
For they have fought for Rome, and all in vain;
And they have nurs'd this woe in feeding life;
In bootless prayer have they been held up,
And they have serv'd me to effectless use:
Now all the service I require of them
Is, that the one will help to cut the other. —
'Tis well, Lavinia, that thou hast no hands;
For hands, to do Rome service, are but vain.

    Luc. Speak, gentle sister, who hath martyr'd thee?
    Marc. O, that delightful engine of her thoughts,
That blabb'd them with such pleasing eloquence,
Is torn from forth that pretty hollow cage,
Where, like a sweet melodious bird, it sung
Sweet varied notes, enchanting every ear!
    Luc. O, say thou for her, who hath done this deed?
    Marc. O, thus I found her, straying in the park,
Seeking to hide herself, as doth the deer
That hath receiv'd some unrecuring wound.
    Tit. It was my deer; and he that wounded her
Hath hurt me more than had he kill'd me dead:
For now I stand as one upon a rock,
Environ'd with a wilderness of sea;
Who marks the waxing tide grow wave by wave,
Expecting ever when some envious surge
Will in his brinish bowels swallow him.
This way to death my wretched sons are gone;
Here stands my other son, a banish'd man;
And here my brother, weeping at my woes:
But that which gives my soul the greatest spurn
Is dear Lavinia, dearer than my soul. —
Had I but seen thy picture in this plight
It would have madded me: what shall I do
Now I behold thy lively body so?
Thou hast no hands to wipe away thy tears,
Nor tongue to tell me who hath martyr'd thee:
Thy husband he is dead; and for his death
Thy brothers are condemn'd, and dead by this. —
Look, Marcus!—ah, son Lucius, look on her!
When I did name her brothers, then fresh tears
Stood on her cheeks, as doth the honey dew
Upon a gather'd lily almost wither'd.

Marc. Perchance she weeps because they kill'd her
	husband:
Perchance because she knows them innocent.
	Tit. If they did kill thy husband, then be joyful,
Because the law hath ta'en revenge on them.—
No, no, they would not do so foul a deed;
Witness the sorrow that their sister makes.—
Gentle Lavinia, let me kiss thy lips;
Or make some sign how I may do thee ease:
Shall thy good uncle, and thy brother Lucius,
And thou, and I, sit round about some fountain,
Looking all downwards, to behold our cheeks
How they are stain'd, as meadows, yet not dry,
With miry slime left on them by a flood?
And in the fountain shall we gaze so long,
Till the fresh taste be taken from that clearness,
And made a brine-pit with our bitter tears?
Or shall we cut away our hands like thine?
Or shall we bite our tongues, and in dumb shows
Pass the remainder of our hateful days?
What shall we do? let us, that have our tongues,
Plot some device of further misery,
To make us wonder'd at in time to come.
	Luc. Sweet father, cease your tears; for at your grief
See how my wretched sister sobs and weeps.
	Marc. Patience, dear niece.—Good Titus, dry thine eyes.
	Tit. Ah, Marcus, Marcus! brother, well I wot
Thy napkin cannot drink a tear of mine,
For thou, poor man, hast drown'd it with thine own.
	Luc. Ah, my Lavinia, I will wipe thy cheeks.
	Tit. Mark, Marcus, mark! I understand her signs:
Had she a tongue to speak, now would she say
That to her brother which I said to thee:
His napkin, with his true tears all bewet,
Can do no service on her sorrowful cheeks.
O, what a sympathy of woe is this,—
As far from help as limbo is from bliss!

Enter AARON.

	Aar. Titus Andronicus, my lord the emperor
Sends thee this word,—that if thou love thy sons,
Let Marcus, Lucius, or thyself, old Titus,
Or any one of you, chop off your hand
And send it to the king: he for the same
Will send thee hither both thy sons alive;
And that shall be the ransom for their fault.

Tit. O gracious emperor! O gentle Aaron!
Did ever raven sing so like a lark
That gives sweet tidings of the sun's uprise?
With all my heart I'll send the emperor
My hand: ·
Good Aaron, wilt thou help to chop it off?

Luc. Stay, father! for that noble hand of thine,
That hath thrown down so many enemies,
Shall not be sent: my hand will serve the turn:
My youth can better spare my blood than you;
And therefore mine shall save my brothers' lives.

Marc. Which of your hands hath not defended Rome,
And rear'd aloft the bloody battle-axe,
Writing destruction on the enemy's castle!
O, none of both but are of high desert:
My hand hath been but idle; let it serve
To ransom my two nephews from their death;
Then have I kept it to a worthy end.

Aar. Nay, come, agree whose hand shall go along,
For fear they die before their pardon come.

Marc. My hand shall go.

Luc.   By heaven, it shall not go!

Tit. Sirs, strive no more: such wither'd herbs as these
Are meet for plucking up, and therefore mine.

Luc. Sweet father, if I shall be thought thy son,
Let me redeem my brothers both from death.

Marc. And for our father's sake and mother's care,
Now let me show a brother's love to thee.

Tit. Agree between you; I will spare my hand.

Luc. Then I'll go fetch an axe.

Marc.   But I will use the axe.

[*Exeunt* LUCIUS *and* MARCUS.

Tit. Come hither, Aaron: I'll deceive them both:
Lend me thy hand, and I will give thee mine.

Aar. [*aside.*] If that be call'd deceit, I will be honest,
And never whilst I live deceive men so:—
But I'll deceive you in another sort,
And that you'll say ere half an hour pass.

[*He cuts off* TITUS's *hand.*

Re-enter LUCIUS *and* MARCUS.

Tit. Now stay your strife: what shall be is despatch'd.--
Good Aaron, give his majesty my hand:
Tell him it was a hand that warded him
From thousand dangers; bid him bury it;
More hath it merited,—that let it have.

As for my sons, say I account of them
As jewels purchas'd at an easy price;
And yet dear too, because I bought mine own.

Aar. I go, Andronicus: and for thy hand
Look by and by to have thy sons with thee:—
Their heads I mean.   O, how this villany   [*Aside.*
Doth fat me with the very thoughts of it!
Let fools do good, and fair men call for grace,
Aaron will have his soul black like his face.   [*Exit.*

Tit. O, here I lift this one hand up to heaven,
And bow this feeble ruin to the earth:
If any power pities wretched tears,   [me?
To that I call!—[*To* LAVINIA.] What, wilt thou kneel with
Do, then, dear heart; for heaven shall hear our prayers;
Or with our sighs we'll breathe the welkin dim,
And stain the sun with fog, as sometime clouds
When they do hug him in their melting bosoms.

Marc. O brother, speak with possibilities,
And do not break into these deep extremes.

Tit. Is not my sorrow deep, having no bottom?
Then be my passions bottomless with them.

Marc. But yet let reason govern thy lament.

Tit. If there were reason for these miseries,
Then into limits could I bind my woes:
When heaven doth weep, doth not the earth o'erflow?
If the winds rage, doth not the sea wax mad,
Threatening the welkin with his big-swoln face?
And wilt thou have a reason for this coil?
I am the sea; hark, how her sighs do flow!
She is the weeping welkin, I the earth:
Then must my sea be moved with her sighs;
Then must my earth with her continual tears
Become a deluge, overflow'd and drown'd:
For why my bowels cannot hide her woes,
But like a drunkard must I vomit them.
Then give me leave; for losers will have leave
To ease their stomachs with their bitter tongues.

Enter a Messenger, *with two heads and a hand.*

Mess. Worthy Andronicus, ill art thou repaid
For that good hand thou sent'st the emperor.
Here are the heads of thy two noble sons;
And here's thy hand, in scorn to thee sent back,—
Thy griefs their sports, thy resolution mock'd:
That woe is me to think upon thy woes,
More than remembrance of my father's death.   [*Exit.*

VOL. V.   2 F

Marc. Now let hot Ætna cool in Sicily,
And be my heart an ever-burning hell!
These miseries are more than may be borne.
To weep with them that weep doth ease some deal;
But sorrow flouted at is double death.

Luc. Ah, that this sight should make so deep a wound,
And yet detested life not shrink thereat!
That ever death should let life bear his name,
Where life hath no more interest but to breathe!

[LAVINIA *kisses him.*

Marc. Alas, poor heart, that kiss is comfortless
As frozen water to a starved snake.

Tit. When will this fearful slumber have an end?

Marc. Now, farewell, flattery : die, Andronicus;
Thou dost not slumber : see thy two sons' heads,
Thy warlike hand, thy mangled daughter here;
Thy other banish'd son, with this dear sight
Struck pale and bloodless; and thy brother, I,
Even like a stony image, cold and numb.
Ah! now no more will I control thy griefs :
Rent off thy silver hair, thy other hand
Gnawing with thy teeth; and be this dismal sight
The closing up of our most wretched eyes :
Now is a time to storm; why art thou still?

Tit. Ha, ha, ha!

Marc. Why dost thou laugh? it fits not with this hour.

Tit. Why, I have not another tear to shed :
Besides, this sorrow is an enemy,
And would usurp upon my watery eyes,
And make them blind with tributary tears :
Then which way shall I find revenge's cave?
For these two heads do seem to speak to me,
And threat me I shall never come to bliss
Till all these mischiefs be return'd again
Even in their throats that have committed them.
Come, let me see what task I have to do. —
You heavy people circle me about,
That I may turn me to each one of you,
And swear unto my soul to right your wrongs. —
The vow is made. — Come, brother, take a head;
And in this hand the ot! er will I bear.
Lavinia, thou shalt be employ'd in these things;
Bear thou my hand, sweet wench, between thy teeth.
As for thee, boy, go, get thee from my sight;
Thou art an exile, and thou must not stay :
Hie to the Goths, and raise an army there :

And if you love me, as I think you do,
Let's kiss and part, for we have much to do.
[*Exeunt* TITUS, MARCUS, *and* LAVINIA.

Luc. Farewell, Andronicus, my noble father,—
The woefull'st man that ever liv'd in Rome:
Farewell, proud Rome; till Lucius come again,
He leaves his pledges dearer than his life:
Farewell, Lavinia, my noble sister;
O, would thou wert as thou 'tofore hast been!
But now nor Lucius nor Lavinia lives
But in oblivion and hateful griefs.
If Lucius live, he will requite your wrongs,
And make proud Saturnine and his empress
Beg at the gates, like Tarquin and his queen.
Now will I to the Goths, and raise a power
To be reveng'd on Rome and Saturnine. [*Exit.*

SCENE II.—ROME. *A Room in* TITUS'S *House.*
A Banquet set out.

Enter TITUS, MARCUS, LAVINIA, *and* YOUNG
LUCIUS, *a boy.*

Tit. So, so; now sit: and look you eat no more
Than will preserve just so much strength in us
As will revenge these bitter woes of ours.
Marcus, unknit that sorrow-wreathen knot:
Thy niece and I, poor creatures, want our hands,
And cannot passionate our tenfold grief
With folded arms. This poor right hand of mine
Is left to tyrannize upon my breast;
And when my heart, all mad with misery,
Beats in this hollow prison of my flesh,
Then thus I thump it down.—
Thou map of woe, that thus dost talk in signs!
[*To* LAVINIA.
When thy poor heart beats with outrageous beating,
Thou canst not strike it thus to make it still.
Wound it with sighing, girl, kill it with groans;
Or get some little knife between thy teeth,
And just against thy heart make thou a hole,
That all the tears that thy poor eyes let fall
May run into that sink, and, soaking in,
Drown the lamenting fool in sea-salt tears.

Marc. Fie, brother, fie! teach her not thus to lay
Such violent hands upon her tender life.

Tit. How now! has sorrow made thee dote already?
Why, Marcus, no man should be mad but I.
What violent hands can she lay on her life?
Ah, wherefore dost thou urge the name of hands;—
To bid Æneas tell the tale twice o'er
How Troy was burnt and he made miserable?
O, handle not the theme, to talk of hands,
Lest we remember still that we have none.—
Fie, fie, how frantically I square my talk,—
As if we should forget we had no hands,
If Marcus did not name the word of hands!—
Come, let's fall to; and, gentle girl, eat this.—
Here is no drink!—Hark, Marcus, what she says;—
I can interpret all her martyr'd signs;—
She says she drinks no other drink but tears,
Brew'd with her sorrow, mesh'd upon her cheeks:—
Speechless complainer, I will learn thy thought;
In thy dumb action will I be as perfect
As begging hermits in their holy prayers:
Thou shalt not sigh, nor hold thy stumps to heaven,
Nor wink, nor nod, nor kneel, nor make a sign,
But I of these will wrest an alphabet,
And by still practice learn to know thy meaning.

    Y. Luc. Good grandsire, leave these bitter deep laments:
Make my aunt merry with some pleasing tale.

    Marc. Alas, the tender boy, in passion mov'd,
Doth weep to see his grandsire's heaviness.

    Tit. Peace, tender sapling; thou art made of tears,
And tears will quickly melt thy life away.—

                [MARCUS *strikes the dish with a knife.*
What dost thou strike at, Marcus, with thy knife?

    Marc. At that that I have kill'd, my lord,—a fly.

    Tit. Out on thee, murderer! thou kill'st my heart;
Mine eyes are cloy'd with view of tyranny:
A deed of death done on the innocent
Becomes not Titus' brother: get thee gone;
I see thou art not for my company.

    Marc. Alas, my lord, I have but kill'd a fly

    Tit. But how if that fly had a father and mother?
How would he hang his slender gilded wings,
And buzz lamenting doings in the air!
Poor harmless fly,
That with his pretty buzzing melody
Came here to make us merry! and thou hast kill'd him.

    Marc. Pardon me, sir; 'twas a black ill-favour'd fly,
Like to the empress' Moor: therefore I kill'd him.

Tit. O, O, O,
Then pardon me for reprehending thee,
For thou hast done a charitable deed.
Give me thy knife, I will insult on him;
Flattering myself as if it were the Moor
Come hither purposely to poison me.—
There's for thyself, and that's for Tamora.—
Ah, sirrah!
Yet I do think we are not brought so low
But that between us we can kill a fly
That comes in likeness of a coal-black Moor.
　　Marc. Alas, poor man! grief has so wrought on him,
He takes false shadows for true substances.
　　Tit. Come, take away.—Lavinia, go with me:
I'll to thy closet; and go read with thee
Sad stories chanced in the times of old.—
Come, boy, and go with me: thy sight is young,
And thou shalt read when mine begins to dazzle. [*Exeunt.*

ACT IV.

SCENE I.—ROME. *Before* TITUS's *House.*

Enter TITUS *and* MARCUS. *Then enter* YOUNG LUCIUS *running, with books under his arm, and* LAVINIA *running after him.*

　Y. Luc. Help, grandsire, help! my aunt Lavinia
Follows me everywhere, I know not why.—
Good uncle Marcus, see how swift she comes!
Alas, sweet aunt, I know not what you mean.
　　Marc. Stand by me, Lucius: do not fear thine aunt.
　　Tit. She loves thee, boy, too well to do thee harm.
　　Y. Luc. Ay, when my father was in Rome she did.
　　Marc. What means my niece Lavinia by these signs?
　　Tit. Fear her not, Lucius: somewhat doth she mean:—
See, Lucius, see how much she makes of thee:
Somewhither would she have thee go with her.
Ah, boy, Cornelia never with more care
Read to her sons than she hath read to thee
Sweet poetry and Tully's Orator.
　　Marc. Canst thou not guess wherefore she plies thee thus?
　　Y. Luc. My lord, I know not, I, nor can I guess,
Unless some fit or frenzy do possess her:
For I have heard my grandsire say full oft

Extremity of griefs would make men mad;
And I have read that Hecuba of Troy
Ran mad through sorrow: that made me to fear;
Although, my lord, I know my noble aunt
Loves me as dear as e'er my mother did,
And would not, but in fury, fright my youth:
Which made me down to throw my books, and fly,—
Causeless, perhaps: but pardon me, sweet aunt:
And, madam, if my uncle Marcus go,
I will most willingly attend your ladyship.

   Marc. Lucius, I will.

              [LAVINIA *turns over with her stumps the*
              books which LUCIUS *has let fall.*

   Tit. How now, Lavinia!—Marcus, what means this?
Some book there is that she desires to see.
Which is it, girl, of these?—Open them, boy.—
But thou art deeper read and better skill'd:
Come, and take choice of all my library,
And so beguile thy sorrow, till the heavens
Reveal the damn'd contriver of this deed.—
Why lifts she up her arms in sequence thus?

   Marc. I think she means that there was more than one
Confederate in the fact;—ay, more there was,
Or else to heaven she heaves them for revenge.

   Tit. Lucius, what book is that she tosseth so?

   Y. Luc. Grandsire, 'tis Ovid's Metamorphosis;
My mother gave it me.

   Marc.   For love of her that's gone,
Perhaps she cull'd it from among the rest.

   Tit. Soft! see how busily she turns the leaves!
Help her:
What would she find?—Lavinia, shall I read?
This is the tragic tale of Philomel,
And treats of Tereus' treason and his rape;
And rape, I fear, was root of thine annoy.

   Marc. See, brother, see; note how she quotes the leaves.

   Tit. Lavinia, wert thou thus surpris'd, sweet girl,
Ravish'd, and wrong'd, as Philomela was,
Forc'd in the ruthless, vast, and gloomy woods?—
See, see!—
Ay, such a place there is where we did hunt,—
O, had we never, never hunted there!—
Pattern'd by that the poet here describes,
By nature made for murders and for rapes.

   Marc. O, why should nature build so foul **a den,**
Unless the gods delight in tragedies?

Tit. Give signs, sweet girl,—for here are none but friends,—
What Roman lord it was durst do the deed:
Or slunk not Saturnine, as Tarquin erst,
That left the camp to sin in Lucrece' bed?

Marc. Sit down, sweet niece:—brother, sit down by me.—
Apollo, Pallas, Jove, or Mercury,
Inspire me, that I may this treason find!—
My lord, look here:—look here, Lavinia:
This sandy plot is plain; guide, if thou canst,
This after me, when I have writ my name
Without the help of any hand at all.

> [*He writes his name with his staff, guiding it with his feet and mouth.*

Curs'd be that heart that forc'd us to this shift!—
Write thou, good niece; and here display at last
What God will have discover'd for revenge:
Heaven guide thy pen to print thy sorrows plain,
That we may know the traitors and the truth!

> [*She takes the staff in her mouth, guides it with her stumps, and writes.*

Tit. O, do ye read, my lord, what she hath writ?
Stuprum—Chiron—Demetrius.

Marc. What, what!—the lustful sons of Tamora
Performers of this heinous, bloody deed?

Tit. Magni Dominator poli,
Tam lentus audis scelera? tam lentus vides?

Marc. O, calm thee, gentle lord; although I know
There is enough written upon this earth
To stir a mutiny in the mildest thoughts,
And arm the minds of infants to exclaims,
My lord, kneel down with me; Lavinia, kneel;
And kneel, sweet boy, the Roman Hector's hope;
And swear with me,—as, with the woeful fere
And father of that chaste dishonour'd dame,
Lord Junius Brutus sware for Lucrece' rape,—
That we will prosecute, by good advice,
Mortal revenge upon these traitorous Goths,
And see their blood, or die with this reproach.

Tit. 'Tis sure enough, an you knew how.
But if you hunt these bear-whelps, then beware:
The dam will wake; and if she wind you once,
She's with the lion deeply still in league,
And lulls him whilst she playeth on her back,
And when he sleeps will she do what she list.
You are a young huntsman, Marcus; let it alone;
And, come, I will go get a leaf of brass,

And with a gad of steel will write these words,
And lay it by: the angry northern wind
Will blow these sands, like Sybil s leaves, abroad,
And where's your lesson then?—Boy, what say you?

Y. Luc. I say, my lord, that if I were a man,
Their mother's bedchamber should not be safe
For these bad-bondmen to the yoke of Rome.

Marc. Ay, that's my boy! thy father hath full oft
For his ungrateful country done the like.

Y. Luc. And, uncle, so will I, an if I live.

Tit. Come, go with me into mine armoury;
Lucius, I'll fit thee; and withal, my boy,
Shalt carry from me to the empress' sons
Presents that I intend to send them both:
Come, come; thou'lt do thy message, wilt thou not?

Y. Luc. Ay, with my dagger in their bosoms, grandsire.

Tit. No, boy, not so; I'll teach thee another course.—
Lavinia, come.—Marcus, look to my house:
Lucius and I'll go brave it at the court;
Ay, marry, will we, sir; and we'll be waited on.
                 [*Exeunt* TIT., LAV., *and* Y. LUC.

Marc. O heavens, can you hear a good man groan,
And not relent, or not compassion him?
Marcus, attend him in his ecstasy,
That hath more scars of sorrow in his heart
Than foemen's marks upon his batter'd shield;
But yet so just that he will not revenge:—
Revenge, ye heavens, for old Andronicus!   [*Exit.*

SCENE II.—ROME.   *A Room in the Palace.*

Enter AARON, DEMETRIUS, *and* CHIRON, *at one door; at
another door,* YOUNG LUCIUS *and an* Attendant, *with a
bundle of weapons, and verses writ upon them.*

Chi. Demetrius, here's the son of Lucius;
He hath some message to deliver us.

Aar. Ay, some mad message from his mad grandfather.

Y. Luc. My lords, with all the humbleness I may,
I greet your honours from Andronicus,—
And pray the Roman gods confound you both !   [*Aside.*

Dem. Gramercy, lovely Lucius: what's the news?

Boy. [*aside.*] That you are both decipher'd, that's the
news,

For villains mark'd with rape.—May it please you,
My grandsire, well-advis'd, hath sent by me
The goodliest weapons of his armoury
To gratify your honourable youth,
The hope of Rome ; for so he bade me say ;
And so I do, and with his gifts present
Your lordships, that whenever you have need,
You may be armed and appointed well :
And so I leave you both,—[*aside*] like bloody villains.
                    [*Exeunt* Y. Luc. *and* Attendant.

Dem. What's here? A scroll ; and written round about ?
Let's see :—
[*Reads.*]   *Integer vitæ, scelerisque purus,*
            Non eget Mauri jaculis, nec arcu.

Chi. O, 'tis a verse in Horace ; I know it well :
I read it in the grammar long ago.

Aar. Ay, just,—a verse in Horace ;—right, you have it.—
Now, what a thing it is to be an ass!   [*Aside.*
Here's no sound jest! the old man hath found their
        guilt ;
And sends them weapons wrapp'd about with lines,
That wound, beyond their feeling, to the quick.
But were our witty empress well a-foot,
She would applaud Andronicus' conceit.
But let her rest in her unrest awhile —
And now, young lords, was't not a happy star
Led us to Rome, strangers, and more than so,
Captives, to be advanced to this height?
It did me good before the palace gate
To brave the tribune in his brother's hearing.

Dem. But me more good to see so great a lord
Basely insinuate and send us gifts.

Aar. Had he not reason, Lord Demetrius?
Did you not use his daughter very friendly?

Dem. I would we had a thousand Roman dames
At such a bay, by turn to serve our lust.

Chi. A charitable wish, and full of love.

Aar. Here lacks but your mother for to say amen.

Chi. And that would she for twenty thousand more.

Dem. Come, let us go ; and pray to all the gods
For our beloved mother in her pains.

Aar. [*aside.*] Pray to the devils ; the gods have given us
        over.   [*Flourish within.*

Dem. Why do the emperor's trumpets flourish thus?

Chi. Belike, for joy the emperor hath a son.

Dem. Soft! who comes here?

Enter a Nurse, *with a blackamoor* Child *in her arms.*

Nur.   Good-morrow, lords:
O, tell me, did you see Aaron the Moor?

Aar. Well, more or less, or ne'er a whit at all,
Here Aaron is; and what with Aaron now?

Nur. O gentle Aaron, we are all undone!
Now help, or woe betide thee evermore!

Aar. Why, what a caterwauling dost thou keep!
What dost thou wrap and fumble in thine arms?

Nur. O, that which I would hide from heaven's eye,
Our empress' shame and stately Rome's disgrace!—
She is deliver'd, lords,—she is deliver'd.

Aar. To whom?

Nur.   I mean, she's brought a-bed.

Aar. Well, God give her good rest! What hath he sent
          her?

Nur. A devil.

Aar. Why, then she is the devil's dam; a joyful issue.

Nur. A joyless, dismal, black, and sorrowful issue:
Here is the babe, as loathsome as a toad
Amongst the fairest breeders of our clime:
The empress sends it thee, thy stamp, thy seal,
And bids thee christen it with thy dagger's point.

Aar. Zounds, ye whore! is black so base a hue?—
Sweet blowse, you are a beauteous blossom, sure.

Dem. Villain, what hast thou done?

Aar. That which thou canst not undo.

Chi. Thou hast undone our mother.

Aar. Villain, I have done thy mother.

Dem. And therein, hellish dog, thou hast undone.
Woe to her chance, and damn'd her loathed choice!
Accurs'd the offspring of so foul a fiend!

Chi. It shall not live.

Aar. It shall not die.

Nur. Aaron, it must; the mother wills it so.

Aar. What, must it, nurse? then let no man but I
Do execution on my flesh and blood.

Dem. I'll broach the tadpole on my rapier's point:—
Nurse, give it me; my sword shall soon despatch it.

Aar. Sooner this sword shall plough thy bowels up.
                    [*Takes the* Child *from the* Nurse, *and draws.*
Stay, murderous villains! will you kill your brother?
Now, by the burning tapers of the sky,
That shone so brightly when this boy was got,
He dies upon my scimitar's sharp point

FAC-SIMILE

IRA ALDRIDGE AS AARON

Titus Andronicus, Act IV, Scene II.

That touches this my first-born son and heir!
I tell you, younglings, not Enceladus,
With all his threatening band of Typhon's brood,
Nor great Alcides, nor the god of war,
Shall seize this prey out of his father's hands.
What, what, ye sanguine, shallow-hearted boys!
Ye white-lim'd walls! ye alehouse-painted signs!
Coal-black is better than another hue,
In that it scorns to bear another hue;
For all the water in the ocean
Can never turn a swan's black legs to white,
Although she lave them hourly in the flood.
Tell the empress from me, I am of age
To keep mine own,—excuse it how she can.
  Dem. Wilt thou betray thy noble mistress thus?
  Aar. My mistress is my mistress; this, myself,—
The vigour and the picture of my youth:
This before all the world do I prefer;
This maugre all the world will I keep safe,
Or some of you shall smoke for it in Rome.
  Dem. By this our mother is for ever sham'd.
  Chi. Rome will despise her for this foul escape.
  Nur. The emperor, in his rage, will doom her death.
  Chi. I blush to think upon this ignomy.
  Aar. Why, there's the privilege your beauty bears:
Fie, treacherous hue, that will betray with blushing
The close enacts and counsels of the heart!
Here's a young lad fram'd of another leer:
Look how the black slave smiles upon the father,
As who should say, *Old lad, I am thine own.*
He is your brother, lords; sensibly fed
Of that self-blood that first gave life to you;
And from that womb where you imprison'd were
He is enfranchised and come to light:
Nay, he is your brother by the surer side,
Although my seal be stamped in his face.
  Nur. Aaron, what shall I say unto the empress?
  Dem. Advise thee, Aaron, what is to be done,
And we will all subscribe to thy advice:
Save thou the child, so we may all be safe.
  Aar. Then sit we down, and let us all consult.
My son and I will have the wind of you:
Keep there: now talk at pleasure of your safety. [*They sit.*
  Dem. How many women saw this child of his?
  Aar. Why, so, brave lords! when we join in league
I am a lamb: but if you brave the Moor,

The chafed boar, the mountain lioness,
The ocean swells not so as Aaron storms. --
But say, again, how many saw the child?

   Nur. Cornelia the midwife and myself;
And no one else but the deliver'd empress.

   Aar. The empress, the midwife, and yourself:
Two may keep counsel when the third's away:
Go to the empress, tell her this I said :—
                         [Stabs her, and she dies.
Weke, weke!—so cries a pig prepar'd to the spit.

   Dem. What mean'st thou, Aaron?   Wherefore didst thou
     this?

   Aar. O Lord, sir, 'tis a deed of policy :
Shall she live to betray this guilt of ours,—
A long-tongu'd babbling gossip? no, lords, no :
And now be it known to you my full intent.
Not far, one Muliteus lives, my countryman;
His wife but yesternight was brought to bed;
His child is like to her, fair as you are:
Go pack with him, and give the mother gold,
And tell them both the circumstance of all ;
And how by this their child shall be advanc'd,
And be received for the emperor's heir,
And substituted in the place of mine,
To calm this tempest whirling in the court ;
And let the emperor dandle him for his own.
Hark ye, lords; ye see I have given her physic,
                    [Pointing to the Nurse.
And you must needs bestow her funeral ;
The fields are near, and you are gallant grooms :
This done, see that you take no longer days,
But send the midwife presently to me.
The midwife and the nurse well made away,
Then let the ladies tattle what they please.

   Chi. Aaron, I see thou wilt not trust the air
With secrets.

   Dem.   For this care of Tamora,
Herself and hers are highly bound to thee.
     [Exeunt DEM. *and* CHI., *bearing off the dead* Nurse.

   Aar. Now to the Goths, as swift as swallow flies;
There to dispose this treasure in mine arms,
And secretly to greet the empress' friends.—
Come on, you thick-lipp'd slave, I'll bear you hence;
For it is you that puts us to our shifts:
I'll make you feed on berries and on roots,
And feed on curds and whey, and suck the goat,

And cabin in a cave; and bring you up
To be a warrior and command a camp.   [*Exit.*

SCENE III.—ROME. *A public Place.*

Enter TITUS, *bearing arrows, with letters at the ends of them;
with him* MARCUS, YOUNG LUCIUS, *and other* Gentlemen,
with bows.

Tit. Come, Marcus, come:—kinsmen, this is the way.—
Sir boy, now let me see your archery;
Look ye draw home enough, and 'tis there straight.—
Terras Astræa reliquit:
Be you remember'd, Marcus, she's gone, she's fled.
Sirs, take you to your tools. You, cousins, shall
Go sound the ocean and cast your nets;
Happily you may catch her in the sea;
Yet there's as little justice as at land. —
No; Publius and Sempronius, you must do it:
'Tis you must dig with mattock and with spade,
And pierce the inmost centre of the earth:
Then, when you come to Pluto's region,
I pray you deliver him this petition;
Tell him it is for justice and for aid,
And that it comes from old Andronicus,
Shaken with sorrows in ungrateful Rome.—
Ah, Rome!—Well, well; I made thee miserable
What time I threw the people's suffrages
On him that thus doth tyrannize o'er me.—
Go, get you gone; and pray be careful all,
And leave you not a man-of-war unsearch'd:
This wicked emperor may have shipp'd her hence;
And, kinsmen, then we may go pipe for justice.
    Marc. O Publius, is not this a heavy case,
To see thy noble uncle thus distract?
    Pub. Therefore, my lord, it highly us concerns
By day and night to attend him carefully,
And feed his humour kindly as we may,
Till time beget some careful remedy.
    Marc. Kinsmen, his sorrows are past remedy.
Join with the Goths; and with revengeful war
Take wreak on Rome for this ingratitude,
And vengeance on the traitor Saturnine.
    Tit. Publius, how now! how now, my masters!
What, have you met with her?

Pub. No, my good lord; but Pluto sends you word,
If you will have Revenge from hell, you shall:
Marry, for Justice, she is so employ'd,
He thinks, with Jove in heaven, or somewhere else,
So that perforce you must needs stay a time.

Tit. He doth me wrong to feed me with delays.
I'll dive into the burning lake below,
And pull her out of Acheron by the heels.—
Marcus, we are but shrubs, no cedars we,
No big-bon'd men, fram'd of the Cyclops' size;
But metal, Marcus, steel to the very back,
Yet wrung with wrongs more than our backs can bear:
And, sith there is no justice in earth nor hell,
We will solicit heaven, and move the gods
To send down Justice for to wreak our wrongs.—
Come, to this gear.—You are a good archer, Marcus.
　　　　　　　　　　　[*He gives them the arrows.*
Ad Jovem, that's for you:—here, *ad Apollinem:—*
Ad Martem, that's for myself:—
Here, boy, to Pallas:—here, to Mercury:—
To Saturn, Caius, not to Saturnine;
You were as good to shoot against the wind.—
To it, boy.—Marcus, loose when I bid.—
Of my word, I have written to effect;
There's not a god left unsolicited.

Marc. Kinsmen, shoot all your shafts into the court:
We will afflict the emperor in his pride.

Tit. Now, masters, draw. [*They shoot.*]　O, well said,
Good boy, in Virgo's lap; give it Pallas.　　　　[Lucius!

Marc. My lord, I aim a mile beyond the moon:
Your letter is with Jupiter by this.

Tit. Ha! ha!
Publius, Publius, what hast thou done?
See, see, thou hast shot off one of Taurus' horns.

Marc. This was the sport, my lord: when Publius shot,
The Bull, being gall'd, gave Aries such a knock
That down fell both the Ram's horns in the court;
And who should find them but the empress' villain?
She laugh'd, and told the Moor he should not choose
But give them to his master for a present.

Tit. Why, there it goes: God give his lordship joy!

　　　Enter a Clown, *with a basket and two pigeons in it.*

News, news from heaven! Marcus, the post is come.
Sirrah, what tidings? have you any letters?
Shall I have justice? what says Jupiter?

Clo. Ho, the gibbet-maker? he says that he hath taken them down again, for the man must not be hanged till the next week.

Tit. But what says Jupiter, I ask thee?

Clo. Alas, sir, I know not Jupiter; I never drank with him in all my life.

Tit. Why, villain, art not thou the carrier?

Clo. Ay, of my pigeons, sir; nothing else.

Tit. Why, didst thou not come from heaven?

Clo. From heaven! alas, sir, I never came there: God forbid I should be so bold to press to heaven in my young days. Why, I am going with my pigeons to the tribunal plebs, to take up a matter of brawl betwixt my uncle and one of the imperial's men.

Marc. Why, sir, that is as fit as can be to serve for your oration; and let him deliver the pigeons to the emperor from you.

Tit. Tell me, can you deliver an oration to the emperor with a grace?

Clo. Nay, truly, sir, I could never say grace in all my life.

Tit. Sirrah, come hither: make no more ado,
But give your pigeons to the emperor:
By me thou shalt have justice at his hands.
Hold, hold; meanwhile here's money for thy charges.—
Give me pen and ink.—
Sirrah, can you with a grace deliver a supplication?

Clo. Ay, sir.

Tit. Then here is a supplication for you. And when you come to him, at the first approach you must kneel; then kiss his foot; then deliver up your pigeons; and then look for your reward. I'll be at hand, sir; see you do it bravely.

Clo. I warrant you, sir, let me alone.

Tit. Sirrah, hast thou a knife? Come, let me see it.
Here, Marcus, fold it in the oration;
For thou hast made it like an humble suppliant:—
And when thou hast given it to the emperor,
Knock at my door, and tell me what he says.

Clo. God be with you, sir; I will

Tit. Come, Marcus, let us go.—Publius, follow me.

[*Exeunt.*

SCENE IV.—ROME.   *Before the Palace.*

Enter SATURNINUS, TAMORA, DEMETRIUS, CHIRON, Lords, *and others;* SATURNINUS *with the arrows in his hand that* TITUS *shot.*

Sat. Why, lords, what wrongs are these! was ever seen

An emperor in Rome thus overborne,
Troubled, confronted thus; and, for the extent
Of legal justice, us'd in such contempt?
My lords, you know, as do the mightful gods,
However these disturbers of our peace
Buzz in the people's ears, there naught hath pass'd,
But even with law, against the wilful sons
Of old Andronicus.   And what an if
His sorrows have so overwhelm'd his wits,
Shall we be thus afflicted in his freaks,
His fits, his frenzy, and his bitterness?
And now he writes to heaven for his redress:
See, here's to Jove, and this to Mercury;
This to Apollo; this to the god of war;—
Sweet scrolls to fly about the streets of Rome!
What's this but libelling against the senate,
And blazoning our injustice everywhere?
A goodly humour, is it not, my lords?
As who would say, in Rome no justice were.
But if I live, his feigned ecstasies
Shall be no shelter to these outrages:
But he and his shall know that justice lives
In Saturninus' health; whom, if she sleep,
He'll so awake as she in fury shall
Cut off the proud'st conspirator that lives.
   Tam. My gracious lord, my lovely Saturnine,
Lord of my life, commander of my thoughts,
Calm thee, and bear the faults of Titus' age,
The effects of sorrow for his valiant sons,
Whose loss hath pierc'd him deep, and scarr'd his heart;
And rather comfort his distressed plight
Than prosecute the meanest or the best
For these contempts.—[*Aside.*]   Why, thus it shall become
High-witted Tamora to gloze with all:
But, Titus, I have touch'd thee to the quick,
Thy life-blood on't: if Aaron now be wise,
Then is all safe, the anchor's in the port.—

Enter Clown.

How now, good fellow! wouldst thou speak with us?
   Clo. Yes, forsooth, an your mistership be imperial.
   Tam. Empress I am, but yonder sits the emperor.
   Clo. 'Tis he. — God and Saint Stephen give you good-
den: I have brought you a letter and a couple of pigeons
here.   [Saturninus *reads the letter.*
   Sat. Go, take him away, and hang him presently.

Clo. How much money must I have?

Tam. Come, sirrah, you must be hang'd.

Clo. Hang'd! By'r lady, then I have brought up a neck to a fair end.   [*Exit guarded.*

Sat. Despiteful and intolerable wrongs!
Shall I endure this monstrous villany?
I know from whence this same device proceeds:
May this be borne,—as if his traitorous sons,
That died by law for murder of our brother,
Have by my means been butcher'd wrongfully?—
Go, drag the villain hither by the hair;
Nor age nor honour shall shape privilege.—
For this proud mock I'll be thy slaughter-man;
Sly frantic wretch, that holp'st to make me great,
In hope thyself should govern Rome and me.

Enter ÆMILIUS.

What news with thee, Æmilius?

Æmil. Arm, my lord! Rome never had more cause!
The Goths have gather'd head; and with a power
Of high-resolved men, bent to the spoil,
They hither march amain, under conduct
Of Lucius, son to old Andronicus;
Who threats, in course of this revenge, to do
As much as ever Coriolanus did.

Sat. Is warlike Lucius general of the Goths?
These tidings nip me; and I hang the head
As flowers with frost, or grass beat down with storms:
Ay, now begin our sorrows to approach:
'Tis he the common people love so much;
Myself hath often overheard them say,—
When I have walked like a private man,—
That Lucius' banishment was wrongfully,
And they have wish'd that Lucius were their emperor.

Tam. Why should you fear? is not your city strong?

Sat. Ay, but the citizens favour Lucius,
And will revolt from me to succour him.

Tam. King, be thy thoughts imperious, like thy name.
Is the sun dimm'd, that gnats do fly in it?
The eagle suffers little birds to sing,
And is not careful what they mean thereby,
Knowing that with the shadow of his wing
He can at pleasure stint their melody:
Even so mayst thou the giddy men of Rome.
Then cheer thy spirit: for know, thou emperor,
I will enchant the old Andronicus

With words more sweet, and yet more dangerous,
Than baits to fish or honey-stalks to sheep,
Whenas the one is wounded with the bait,
The other rotted with delicious feed.

Sat. But he will not entreat his son for us.

Tam. If Tamora entreat him, then he will:
For I can smooth and fill his aged ear
With golden promises that, were his heart
Almost impregnable, his old ears deaf,
Yet should both ear and heart obey my tongue.—
Go thou before [*to* ÆMILIUS]; be our ambassador:
Say that the emperor requests a parley
Of warlike Lucius, and appoint the meeting
Even at his father's house, the old Andronicus.

Sat. Æmilius, do this message honourably:
And if he stand on hostage for his safety,
Bid him demand what pledge will please him best.

Æmil. Your bidding shall I do effectually.   [*Exit.*

Tam. Now will I to that old Andronicus,
And temper him, with all the art I have,
To pluck proud Lucius from the warlike Goths.
And now, sweet emperor, be blithe again,
And bury all thy fear in my devices.

Sat. Then go successfully, and plead to him.   [*Exeunt.*

ACT V.

SCENE I.—*Plains near Rome.*

Enter LUCIUS *and* Goths, *with drum and colours.*

Luc. Approved warriors and my faithful friends,
I have received letters from great Rome,
Which signify what hate they bear their emperor,
And how desirous of our sight they are.
Therefore, great lords, be as your titles witness,
Imperious and impatient of your wrongs:
And wherein Rome hath done you any scath
Let him make treble satisfaction.

1 *Goth.* Brave slip, sprung from the great Andronicus,
Whose name was once our terror, now our comfort;
Whose high exploits and honourable deeds
Ingrateful Rome requites with foul contempt,
Be bold in us: we'll follow where thou lead'st,—
Like stinging bees in hottest summer's day,

Led by their master to the flowered fields,—
And be aveng'd on cursed Tamora.
 Goths. And as he saith, so say we all with him.
 Luc. I humbly thank him, and I thank you all.
But who comes here, led by a lusty Goth?

 Enter a Goth, *leading* AARON *with his* Child *in his arms.*

 2 *Goth.* Renowned Lucius, from our troops I stray'd
To gaze upon a ruinous monastery;
And as I earnestly did fix mine eye
Upon the wasted building, suddenly
I heard a child cry underneath a wall.
I made unto the noise; when soon I heard
The crying babe coutroll'd with this discourse:—
Peace, tawny slave, half me and half thy dam!
Did not thy hue bewray whose brat thou art,
Had nature lent thee but thy mother's look,
Villain, thou mightst have been an emperor:
But where the bull and cow are both milk-white
They never do beget a coal-black calf.
Peace, villain, peace!—even thus he rates the babe,—
For I must bear thee to a trusty Goth;
Who, when he knows thou art the empress' babe,
Will hold thee dearly for thy mother's sake.
With this, my weapon drawn, I rush'd upon him,
Surpris'd him suddenly, and brought him hither,
To use as you think needful of the man.
 Luc. O worthy Goth, this is the incarnate devil
That robb'd Andronicus of his good hand;
This is the pearl that pleas'd your empress' eye;
And here's the base fruit of his burning lust.—
Say, wall-ey'd slave, whither wouldst thou convey
This growing image of thy fiend-like face?
Why dost not speak? what, deaf? No; not a word?—
A halter, soldiers; hang him on this tree,
And by his side his fruit of bastardy.
 Aar. Touch not the boy,—he is of royal blood.
 Luc. Too like the sire for ever being good.—
First hang the child, that he may see it sprawl,—
A sight to vex the father's soul withal.
Get me a ladder. [*A ladder brought, which* AARON *is*
     obliged to ascend.
 Aar.   Lucius, save the child,
And bear it from me to the empress.
If thou do this, I'll show thee wondrous things
That highly may advantage thee to hear:

If thou wilt not, befall what may befall,
I'll speak no more,—but vengeance rot you all!

   Luc. Say on: an if it please me which thou speak'st,
Thy child shall live, and I will see it nourish'd.

   Aar. An if it please thee! why, assure thee, Lucius,
'Twill vex thy soul to hear what I shall speak;
For I must talk of murders, rapes, and massacres,
Acts of black night, abominable deeds,
Complots of mischief, treason, villanies
Ruthful to hear, yet piteously perform'd:
And this shall all be buried by my death,
Unless thou swear to me my child shall live.

   Luc. Tell on thy mind; I say thy child shall live.

   Aar. Swear that he shall, and then I will begin.

   Luc. Who should I swear by? thou believ'st no god:
That granted, how canst thou believe an oath?

   Aar. What if I do not? as, indeed, I do not;
Yet, for I know thou art religious,
And hast a thing within thee called conscience,
With twenty popish tricks and ceremonies
Which I have seen thee careful to observe,
Therefore I urge thy oath;—for that I know
An idiot holds his bauble for a god,
And keeps the oath which by that god he swears;
To that I'll urge him:—therefore thou shalt vow
By that same god,—what god soe'er it be
That thou ador'st and hast in reverence,—
To save my boy, to nourish and bring him up;
Or else I will discover naught to thee.

   Luc. Even by my god I swear to thee I will.

   Aar. First know thou, I begot him on the empress.

   Luc. O most insatiate luxurious woman!

   Aar. Tut, Lucius, this was but a deed of charity
To that which thou shalt hear of me anon.
'Twas her two sons that murder'd Bassianus;
They cut thy sister's tongue, and ravish'd her,
And cut her hands, and trimm'd her as thou saw'st.

   Luc. O détestable villain! call'st thou that trimming?

   Aar. Why, she was wash'd, and cut, and trimm'd; and
      'twas
Trim sport for them that had the doing of it.

   Luc. O barbarous, beastly villains, like thyself!

   Aar. Indeed, I was their tutor to instruct them:
That codding spirit had they from their mother,
As sure a card as ever won the set;
That bloody mind, I think, they learn'd of me,

As true a dog as ever fought at head.
Well, let my deeds be witness of my wort'h.
I train'd thy brethren to that guileful hole
Where the dead corpse of Bassianus lay :
I wrote the letter that thy father found,
And hid the gold within the letter mention'd,
Confederate with the queen and her two sons
And what not done, that thou hast cause to rue,
Wherein I had no stroke of mischief in't ?
I play'd the cheater for thy father's hand ;
And when I had it, drew myself apart,
And almost broke my heart with extreme laughter :
I pry'd me through the crevice of a wall
When, for his hand, he had his two sons' heads ;
Beheld his tears, and laugh'd so heartily
That both mine eyes were rainy like to his :
And when I told the empress of this sport,
She swooned almost at my pleasing tale,
And for my tidings gave me twenty kisses.
   1 *Goth.* What, canst thou say all this, and never blush
   Aar. Ay, like a black dog, as the saying is.
   Luc. Art thou not sorry for these heinous deeds?
   Aar. Ay, that I had not done a thousand more.
Even now I curse the day,—and yet, I think,
Few come within the compass of my curse,—
Wherein I did not some notorious ill :
As, kill a man, or else devise his death ;
Ravish a maid, or plot the way to do it ;
Accuse some innocent, and forswear myself ;
Set deadly enmity between two friends ;
Make poor men's cattle stray and break their necks ;
Set fire on barns and hay-stacks in the night,
And bid the owners quench them with their tears.
Oft have I digg'd up dead men from their graves,
And set them upright at their dear friends' doors,
Even when their sorrows almost were forgot ;
And on their skins, as on the bark of trees,
Have with my knife carved in Roman letters,
Let not your sorrow die, though I am dead.
Tut, I have done a thousand dreadful things
As willingly as one would kill a fly ;
And nothing grieves me heartily indeed
But that I cannot do ten thousand more.
   Luc. Bring down the devil ; for he must not die
So sweet a death as hanging presently.
   Aar. If there be devils, would I were a devil,

To live and burn in everlasting fire,
So I might have your company in hell,
But to torment you with my bitter tongue!
 Luc. Sirs, stop his mouth, and let him speak no more.

Enter a Goth.

3 *Goth.* My lord, there is a messenger from Rome
Desires to be admitted to your presence.
 Luc. Let him come near.

Enter ÆMILIUS.

Welcome, Æmilius: what's the news from Rome?
 Æmil. Lord Lucius, and you princes of the Goths,
The Roman emperor greets you all by me;
And, for he understands you are in arms,
He craves a parley at your father's house,
Willing you to demand your hostages,
And they shall be immediately deliver'd.
 1 *Goth.* What says our general?
 Luc. Æmilius, let the emperor give his pledges
Unto my father and my uncle Marcus,
And we will come.—March away.   [*Exeunt.*

SCENE II.—ROME. *Before* TITUS'S *House.*

Enter TAMORA, DEMETRIUS, *and* CHIRON, *disguised.*

 Tam. Thus, in this strange and sad habiliment
I will encounter with Andronicus,
And say I am Revenge, sent from below
To join with him and right his heinous wrongs.
Knock at his study, where they say he keeps
To ruminate strange plots of dire revenge;
Tell him Revenge is come to join with him,
And work confusion on his enemies.   [*They knock.*

Enter TITUS, *above.*

 Tit. Who doth molest my contemplation?
Is it your trick to make me ope the door,
That so my sad decrees may fly away,
And all my study be to no effect?
You are deceiv'd: for what I mean to do
See here in bloody lines I have set down;
And what is written shall be executed.
 Tam. Titus, I am come to talk with thee.
 Tit. No, not a word: how can I grace my talk,

Wanting a hand to give it action?
Thou hast the odds of me; therefore no more.

Tam. If thou didst know me, thou wouldst talk with me.

Tit. I am not mad; I know thee well enough:
Witness this wretched stump, witness these crimson lines;
Witness these trenches made by grief and care;
Witness the tiring day and heavy night;
Witness all sorrow, that I know thee well
For our proud empress, mighty Tamora:
Is not thy coming for my other hand?

Tam. Know thou, sad man, I am not Tamora;
She is thy enemy and I thy friend:
I am Revenge; sent from the infernal kingdom
To ease the gnawing vulture of thy mind
By working wreakful vengeance on thy foes.
Come down and welcome me to this world's light;
Confer with me of murder and of death:
There's not a hollow cave or lurking-place,
No vast obscurity or misty vale,
Where bloody murder or detested rape
Can couch for fear, but I will find them out;
And in their ears tell them my dreadful name,—
Revenge, which makes the foul offenders quake.

Tit. Art thou Revenge? and art thou sent to me
To be a torment to mine enemies?

Tam. I am; therefore come down and welcome me.

Tit. Do me some service ere I come to thee.
Lo, by thy side where Rape and Murder stands;
Now give some 'surance that thou art Revenge,—
Stab them, or tear them on thy chariot wheels;
And then I'll come and be thy waggoner,
And whirl along with thee about the globe.
Provide thee two proper palfreys, black as jet,
To hale thy vengeful waggon swift away,
And find out murderers in their guilty caves:
And when thy ear is loaden with their heads
I will dismount, and by the waggon-wheel
Trot, like a servile footman, all day long,
Even from Hyperion's rising in the east
Until his very downfall in the sea:
And day by day I'll do this heavy task,
So thou destroy Rapine and Murder there.

Tam. These are my ministers, and come with me.

Tit. Are these thy ministers? what are they call'd?

Tam. Rapine and Murder; therefore called so
Cause they take vengeance of such kind of men.

Tit. Good lord, how like the empress' sons they are !
And you the empress! But we worldly men
Have miserable, mad, mistaking eyes.
O sweet Revenge, now do I come to thee ;
And, if one arm's embracement will content thee,
I will embrace thee in it by and by.   [*Exit from above.*

Tam. This closing with him fits his lunacy:
Whate'er I forge to feed his brain-sick fits,
Do you uphold and maintain in your speeches,
For now he firmly takes me for Revenge ;
And, being credulous in this mad thought,
I'll make him send for Lucius his son ;
And, whilst I at a banquet hold him sure,
I'll find some cunning practice out of hand
To scatter and disperse the giddy Goths,
Or, at the least, make them his enemies.
See, here he comes, and I must ply my theme.

Enter TITUS.

Tit. Long have I been forlorn, and all for thee:
Welcome, dread fury, to my woeful house ;—
Rapine and Murder, you are welcome too :—
How like the empress and her sons you are!
Well are you fitted, had you but a Moor:
Could not all hell afford you such a devil?—
For well I wot the empress never wags
But in her company there is a Moor ;
And, would you represent our queen aright,
It were convenient you had such a devil:
But welcome as you are. What shall we do?

Tam. What wouldst thou have us do, Andronicus?

Dem. Show me a murderer, I'll deal with him.

Chi. Show me a villain that hath done a rape,
And I am sent to be reveng'd on him.

Tam. Show me a thousand that have done thee wrong,
And I will be revenged on them all.

Tit. Look round about the wicked streets of Rome,
And when thou find'st a man that 's like thyself,
Good Murder, stab him ; he 's a murderer.—
Go thou with him ; and when it is thy hap
To find another that is like to thee,
Good Rapine, stab him ; he 's a ravisher.—
Go thou with them ; and in the emperor's court
There is a queen, attended by a Moor ;
Well mayst thou know her by thy own proportion,
For up and down she doth resemble thee ;

I pray thee, do on them some violent death;
They have been violent to me and mine.
Tam. Well hast thou lesson'd us; this shall we do.
But would it please thee, good Andronicus,
To send for Lucius, thy thrice-valiant son,
Who leads towards Rome a band of warlike Goths,
And bid him come and banquet at thy house;
When he is here, even at thy solemn feast,
I will bring in the empress and her sons,
The emperor himself, and all thy foes;
And at thy mercy shall they stoop and kneel,
And on them shalt thou ease thy angry heart.
What says Andronicus to this device?
Tit. Marcus, my brother!—'tis sad Titus calls.

Enter MARCUS.

Go, gentle Marcus, to thy nephew Lucius;
Thou shalt inquire him out among the Goths:
Bid him repair to me, and bring with him
Some of the chiefest princes of the Goths;
Bid him encamp his soldiers where they are:
Tell him the emperor and the empress too
Feast at my house, and he shall feast with them.
This do thou for my love; and so let him
As he regards his aged father's life.
Marc. This will I do, and soon return again. [*Exit.*
Tam. Now will I hence about thy business,
And take my ministers along with me.
Tit. Nay, nay, let Rape and Murder stay with me,
Or else I'll call my brother back again,
And cleave to no revenge but Lucius.
Tam. [*aside to them.*] What say you, boys? will you abide
            with him,
Whiles I go tell my lord the emperor
How I have govern'd our determin'd jest?
Yield to his humour, smooth and speak him fair,
And tarry with him till I come again.
Tit. [*aside.*] I know them all, though they suppose me mad,
And will o'er-reach them in their own devices,—
A pair of cursed hell-hounds and their dam.
Dem. Madam, depart at pleasure; leave us here.
Tam. Farewell, Andronicus: Revenge now goes
To lay a complot to betray thy foes.
Tit. I know thou dost; and, sweet Revenge, farewell!
                                        [*Exit* TAMORA.
Chi. Tell us, old man, how shall we be employ'd?

Tit. Tut, I have work enough for you to do.—
Publius, come hither, Caius, and Valentine!

Enter PUBLIUS *and others.*

Pub. What is your will?
Tit. Know you these two?
Pub. The empress' sons,
I take them, Chiron and Demetrius.

Tit. Fie, Publius, fie! thou art too much deceiv'd, --
The one is Murder, Rape is the other's name;
And therefore bind them, gentle Publius:—
Caius and Valentine, lay hands on them:—
Oft have you heard me wish for such an hour,
And now I find it; therefore bind them sure;
And stop their mouths if they begin to cry.
     [*Exit.* PUBLIUS, *&c., lay hold on* CHIRON *and*
          DEMETRIUS.

Chi. Villains, forbear! we are the empress' sons.
Pub. And therefore do we what we are commanded.—
Stop close their mouths, let them not speak a word.
Is he sure bound? look that you bind them fast.

Re-enter TITUS ANDRONICUS, *with* LAVINIA; *he bearing*
a knife and she a basin.

Tit. Come, come, Lavinia; look, thy foes are bound.—
Sirs, stop their mouths, let them not speak to me;
But let them hear what fearful words I utter.—
O villains, Chiron and Demetrius!
Here stands the spring whom you have stain'd with mud;
This goodly summer with your winter mix'd.
You kill'd her husband; and for that vile fault
Two of her brothers were condemn'd to death,
My hand cut off and made a merry jest;
Both her sweet hands, her tongue, and that, more dear
Than hands or tongue, her spotless chastity,
Inhuman traitors, you constrain'd and forc'd.
What would you say, if I should let you speak?
Villains, for shame you could not beg for grace.
Hark, wretches! how I mean to martyr you.
This one hand yet is left to cut your throats,
Whilst that Lavinia 'tween her stumps doth hold
The basin that receives your guilty blood.
You know your mother means to feast with me,
And calls herself Revenge, and thinks me mad:—
Hark, villains! I will grind your bones to dust,
And with your blood and it I'll make a paste;

And of the paste a coffin I will rear,
And make two pasties of your shameful heads;
And bid that strumpet, your unhallow'd dam,
Like to the earth, swallow her own increase.
This is the feast that I have bid her to,
And this the banquet she shall surfeit on;
For worse than Philomel you us'd my daughter,
And worse than Progne I will be reveng'd:
And now prepare your throats.—Lavinia, come,
                    [*He cuts their throats.*
Receive the blood: and when that they are dead,
Let me go grind their bones to powder small,
And with this hateful liquor temper it;
And in that paste let their vile heads be baked.
Come, come, be every one officious
To make this banquet; which I wish may prove
More stern and bloody than the Centaurs' feast.
So, now bring them in, for I will play the cook,
And see them ready 'gainst their mother comes.
                    [*Exeunt, bearing the dead bodies.*

SCENE III.—ROME.   *A Pavilion in* TITUS's *Gardens,
with tables, &c.*

Enter LUCIUS, MARCUS, *and* Goths, *with* AARON
prisoner.

Luc. Uncle Marcus, since 'tis my father's mind
That I repair to Rome, I am content.

1 *Goth.* And ours with thine, befall what fortune
will.

Luc. Good uncle, take you in this barbarous Moor,
This ravenous tiger, this accursed devil;
Let him receive no sustenance, fetter him,
Till he be brought unto the empress' face,
For testimony of her foul proceedings:
And see the ambush of our friends be strong;
I fear the emperor means no good to us.

Aar. Some devil whisper curses in mine ear,
And prompt me, that my tongue may utter forth
The venomous malice of my swelling heart!

Luc. Away, inhuman dog! unhallow'd slave!—
Sirs, help our uncle to convey him in.—
                [*Exeunt* Goths *with* AAR.   *Flourish within.*
The trumpets show the emperor is at hand.

Enter SATURNINUS *and* TAMORA, *with* ÆMILIUS, Tribunes,
          Senators. *and others.*

Sat. What, hath the firmament more suns than one?
Luc. What boots it thee to call thyself a sun?
Marc. Rome's emperor, and nephew, break the parle;
These quarrels must be quietly debated.
The feast is ready, which the careful Titus
Hath ordain'd to an honourable end,
For peace, for love, for league, and good to Rome:
Please you, therefore, draw nigh, and take your places.
          Sat. Marcus, we will.
                    [*Hautboys sound.   The company sit at table.*

Enter TITUS, *dressed like a cook,* LAVINIA, *vailed,* YOUNG
     LUCIUS, *and others.   Titus* places the dishes on the table.

Tit. Welcome, my gracious lord; welcome, dread queen;
Welcome, ye warlike Goths; welcome, Lucius;
And welcome all: although the cheer be poor,
'Twill fill your stomachs; please you eat of it.
Sat. Why art thou thus attir'd, Andronicus?
Tit. Because I would be sure to have all well,
To entertain your highness and your empress.
Tam. We are beholden to you, good Andronicus.
Tit. And if your highness knew my heart, you were.
My lord the emperor, resolve me this:
Was it well done of rash Virginius
To slay his daughter with his own right hand,
Because she was enforc'd, stain'd, and deflower'd?
Sat. It was, Andronicus.
Tit. Your reason, mighty lord.
Sat. Because the girl should not survive her shame,
And by her presence still renew his sorrows.
Tit. A reason mighty, strong, and effectual;
A pattern, precedent, and lively warrant
For me, most wretched, to perform the like:—
Die, die, Lavinia, and thy shame with thee;
                    [*Kills* LAVINIA.
And with thy shame thy father's sorrow die!
Sat. What hast thou done, unnatural and unkind?
Tit. Kill'd her for whom my tears have made me blind.
I am as woeful as Virginius was,
And have a thousand times more cause than he
To do this outrage;—and it is now done.
Sat. What, was she ravish'd? tell who did the deed.
Tit. Will't please you eat? will't please your highness feed?

Tam. Why hast thou slain thine only daughter thus?

Tit. Not I; 'twas Chiron and Demetrius:
They ravish'd her, and cut away her tongue;
And they, 'twas they that did her all this wrong.

Sat. Go, fetch them hither to us presently.

Tit. Why, there they are both, baked in that pie,
Whereof their mother daintily hath fed,
Eating the flesh that she herself hath bred.
'Tis true, 'tis true; witness my knife's sharp point.

[*Kills* TAMORA.

Sat. Die, frantic wretch, for this accursed deed!

[*Kills* TITUS.

Luc. Can the son's eye behold his father bleed?
There's meed for meed, death for a deadly deed.

[*Kills* SATURNINUS. *A great tumult.* LUCIUS, MARCUS,
and their partisans ascend the steps before TITUS'S
house.

Marc. You sad-fac'd men, people and sons of Rome,
By uproar sever'd, like a flight of fowl
Scatter'd by winds and high tempestuous gusts.
O, let me teach you how to knit again
This scatter'd corn into one mutual sheaf,
These broken limbs again into one body;
Lest Rome herself be bane unto herself,
And she whom mighty kingdoms court'sy to,
Like a forlorn and desperate castaway,
Do shameful execution on herself.
But if my frosty signs and chaps of age,
Grave witnesses of true experience,
Cannot induce you to attend my words,—
Speak, Rome's dear friend [*to* LUCIUS]: as erst our ancestor,
When with his solemn tongue he did discourse
To love-sick Dido's sad attending ear
The story of that baleful burning night
When subtle Greeks surpris'd King Priam's Troy,—
Tell us what Sinon hath bewitch'd our ears,
Or who hath brought the fatal engine in
That gives our Troy, our Rome, the civil wound.
My heart is not compact of flint nor steel;
Nor can I utter all our bitter grief,
But floods of tears will drown my oratory
And break my very utterance, even in the time
When it should move you to attend me most,
Lending your kind commiseration.
Here is a captain, let him tell the tale;
Your hearts will throb and weep to hear him speak.

Luc. Then, noble auditory, be it known to you
That cursed Chiron and Demetrius
Were they that murdered our emperor's brother;
And they it were that ravished our sister:
For their fell faults our brothers were beheaded;
Our father's tears despis'd, and basely cozen'd
Of that true hand that fought Rome's quarrel out
And sent her enemies unto the grave.
Lastly, myself unkindly banished,
The gates shut on me, and turn'd weeping out,
To beg relief among Rome's enemies;
Who drown'd their enmity in my true tears,
And op'd their arms to embrace me as a friend:
And I am the turn'd-forth, be it known to you,
That have preserv'd her welfare in my blood;
And from her bosom took the enemy's point,
Sheathing the steel in my adventurous body.
Alas! you know I am no vaunter, I;
My scars can witness, dumb although they are,
That my report is just and full of truth.
But, soft! methinks I do digress too much,
Citing my worthless praise: O, pardon me;
For when no friends are by, men praise themselves.

Marc. Now is my turn to speak. Behold this child.
　　　　[Pointing to the Child *in an* Attendant's *arms.*
Of this was Tamora delivered;
The issue of an irreligious Moor,
Chief architect and plotter of these woes:
The villain is alive in Titus' house,
Damn'd as he is, to witness this is true.
Now judge what cause had Titus to revenge
These wrongs unspeakable, past patience,
Or more than any living man could bear.
Now you have heard the truth, what say you, Romans?
Have we done aught amiss,—show us wherein,
And, from the place where you behold us now,
The poor remainder of Andronici
Will, hand in hand, all headlong cast us down,
And on the ragged stones beat forth our brains,
And make a mutual closure of our house.
Speak, Romans, speak; and if you say we shall,
Lo, hand in hand, Lucius and I will fall.

Æmil. Come, come, thou reverend man of Rome,
And bring our emperor gently in thy hand,
Lucius our emperor; for well I know
The common voice do cry it shall be so.

Romans. [*several speak.*] Lucius, all hail, Rome's royal
 emperor!
Marc. Go, go into old Titus' sorrowful house,
     [*To Attendants, who go into the house.*
And hither hale that misbelieving Moor,
To be adjudg'd some direful slaughtering death,
As punishment for his most wicked life.
     [LUCIUS, MARCUS, &c., *descend.*
Romans. [*several speak*] Lucius, all hail, Rome's gracious
 governor!
Luc. Thanks, gentle Romans: may I govern so
To heal Rome's harms and wipe away her woe!
But, gentle people, give me aim awhile,—
For nature puts me to a heavy task:—
Stand all aloof;—but, uncle, draw you near,
To shed obsequious tears upon this trunk.—
O, take this warm kiss on thy pale cold lips, [*Kisses* TITUS.
These sorrowful drops upon thy blood-stain'd face,
The last true duties of thy noble son!
Marc. Tear for tear and loving kiss for kiss
Thy brother Marcus tenders on thy lips:
O, were the sum of these that I should pay
Countless and infinite, yet would I pay them!
Luc. Come hither, boy; come, come, and learn of us
To melt in showers: thy grandsire lov'd thee well:
Many a time he danc'd thee on his knee,
Sung thee asleep, his loving breast thy pillow;
Many a matter hath he told to thee,
Meet and agreeing with thine infancy;
In that respect, then, like a loving child,
Shed yet some small drops from thy tender spring,
Because kind nature doth require it so:
Friends should associate friends in grief and woe:
Bid him farewell; commit him to the grave;
Do him that kindness, and take leave of him.
Y. Luc. O grandsire, grandsire! even with all my heart
Would I were dead, so you did live again!—
O Lord, I cannot speak to him for weeping;
My tears will choke me if I ope my mouth.

   Re-enter Attendants *with* AARON.

Æmil. You sad Andronici, have done with woes:
Give sentence on this execrable wretch,
That hath been breeder of these dire events.
Luc. Set him breast-deep in earth, and famish him;
There let him stand, and rave, and cry for food:

If any one relieves or pities him,
For the offence he dies.   This is our doom :
Some stay to see him fasten'd in the earth.

  Aar. O, why should wrath be mute and fury dumb?
I am no baby, I, that with base prayers
I should repent the evils I have done :
Ten thousand worse than ever yet I did
Would I perform, if I might have my will :
If one good deed in all my life I did,
I do repent it from my very soul.

  Luc. Some loving friends convey the emperor hence,
And give him burial in his father's grave :
My father and Lavinia shall forthwith
Be closed in our household's monument.
As for that heinous tiger, Tamora,
No funeral rite, nor man in mournful weeds,
No mournful bell shall ring her burial ;
But throw her forth to beasts and birds of prey :
Her life was beast-like and devoid of pity ;
And, being so, shall have like want of pity.
See justice done on Aaron, that damn'd Moor,
By whom our heavy haps had their beginning :
Then, afterwards, to order well the state,
That like events may ne'er it ruinate.   [*Exeunt.*

www.ingramcontent.com/pod-product-compliance
Lightning Source LLC
Chambersburg PA
CBHW032018110726
47901CB00004B/1126